BLUEBLOODS, PASSION
AND A NEWPORT SUMMER

They danced, Clemmie's eyes on a level with Whit's mouth. That afternoon, when they had met on the train to Newport, she had been intrigued by those eyes, dark and liquid under thick lashes, but now she couldn't help noticing his mouth. The sardonic smile did not hide a deep sensuality.

"And what is your idea of excitement, Miss Wilder?" Whit asked.

"Anything fast—automobiles . . . airplanes . . . speedboats. And anything dangerous. Dares . . . challenges." Clemmie looked up and saw the dark eyes watching her closely. "You don't believe me?"

"Oh, I believe you all right, Clemmie Wilder. I'm just wondering what I'm going to do about you."

"You mean because I'm your fiancee's guest and you'll have to entertain me?"

"I mean because I hate to see a fast horse—or woman—go unproven."

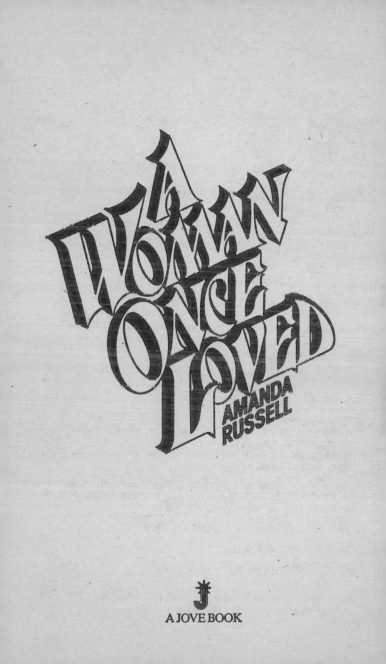

A WOMAN ONCE LOVED

AMANDA RUSSELL

A JOVE BOOK

Jove books are published by Jove Publications, Inc., 200 Madi-
son Avenue, New York, NY 10016

In memory of Dougie

and for W.C.B.

BOOK
ONE

Chapter 1

THE FIRST TIME Clemmie Wilder saw Whit Morris she was breaking one of her mother's cardinal rules, but there was scarcely a time during that roller-coaster summer of 1921 when Clemmie wasn't breaking one rule or another. It was one of the things that fascinated Whit about Clemmie. It was also one of the things that frightened him about her.

"Don't you ever get tired of doing what people don't want you to?" Whit asked her once.

"I never get tired," Clemmie said, "of doing what *I* want to."

Years later Whit remembered the conversation and decided Clemmie's answer had been characteristic, but that was years later. At the time he was sure there was another side to Clemmie, a softer, more vulnerable side, and he had a summer full of memories to prove it. For the rest of his life, at odd times when he was doing something that had no connection with Clemmie Wilder, an image would flash through Whit's mind—her childish excitement the first time he'd taken her to see Lancelot work out, the way she always smiled up at him for a silent moment after he'd cut in for a dance, how her eyes had looked that night at his Uncle Quentin's beach

9

house—and the image would tell him that indeed there had once been another side to Clemmie Wilder.

But even the images did not yet exist on that summer afternoon when Clemmie sat bored and impatient in the private railroad car that had been added to the Central's New York–Wickford run. On that sultry day Clemmie had not even heard of Whit Morris although she felt certain, as certain as she was of her own ideas and her right to live by them, that someone like Whit Morris existed.

The only problem, she thought, staring with unseeing eyes at the Connecticut shoreline as it raced past the windows, was finding him. According to her brothers, the sort of man Clemmie was interested in was unlikely to turn up in Newport.

"Unless it's race week or tennis tournament," Adam had said. "For the rest of the season it's an old-age colony."

"Adam's right," George added. "Anyone who's interested in a good time goes to Long Island. That's where the best house parties are. Newport's dead as a doornail and twice as stuffy."

"If you find anyone under sixty," Adam warned, "he's bound to be looking for an heiress."

"I must say you both paint a devastating picture," Clemmie said.

"Cheer up," George laughed. "After all, it's only for a month or two."

"Easy for you to say. You'll be cutting a swath through Long Island."

"And thinking of you every minute, kid."

Clemmie made a face at her brother.

"That," Adam said, "is exactly the sort of behavior we will not tolerate in Newport. Miss Wilder, you are banned from Bailey's Beach."

Remembering the conversation now, Clemmie made the same face at the unseeing countryside. It wasn't fair. Even if Adam or George chose to go to Newport, they wouldn't have to go in their father's private railroad car. Oh no, Adam and George could go anywhere and do anything, but for Clemmie it was a different story. The VanNests had invited her to Newport and, her mother said, she would go to Newport. Dolly Wilder had pointed out to her daughter that she and Grace VanNest had been childhood friends and Clemmie and Alison had known each other for years, so they could scarcely refuse the invitation. But Clemmie knew the real reason for her mother's eagerness. In Newport, Clemmie would be likely to meet the sort of man she would never find in Scranton, the sort of man Dolly was hoping her daughter would marry. Dolly was not a bad or unfeeling mother. Unlike many of her friends she had not set her heart on a spectacular social match for her daughter, to be gained at any cost to her daughter's happiness or her husband's pocketbook. She hadn't set her heart on it, but she couldn't help hoping it would happen, and it was more likely to happen in Newport than Scranton.

Dolly had even toyed with the idea of taking a house in Newport for the season. Elias could provide a perfectly satisfactory one. Then she remembered something she'd heard as a girl during her own summer in Newport. It was the advice of Harry Lehr, court jester to those within Newport's charmed circle, tyrant to those outside it. If you wanted to storm the citadel of Newport society, he'd warned, never take a house the first season. Arrange to be invited as someone's guest. Then if your assault failed, you could retreat quietly and simply say the climate didn't agree with you.

Strictly speaking, Dolly was not storming the citadel of Newport society. Back when Newport stood for more than mere money, when the *palazzi* and *châteaux* and castles were still in Italy and France and Scotland rather than on Bellevue Avenue, when people of means came to Newport to enjoy the cool breezes and plunge into the invigorating sea rather than the social swim, Dolly's own father had occupied a certain position in the summer colony. But that was before Newport had grown richer and her father poorer, before she'd married Elias Wilder whose fortune was secure but whose social position was still open to question. It took three generations to make a gentleman—such had been the decree of Ward McAlister, Harry Lehr's predecessor, and of Mrs. Astor, and Elias was still one generation short. So Dolly had decided to approach cautiously. She and Clemmie would pay a visit to her old friend Grace VanNest. If Clemmie made a spectacular match this summer, so much the better. If she showed signs of doing so in the future, perhaps they'd take a cottage of their own next summer. Dolly was hopeful, but not especially optimistic. She knew her daughter well enough to realize that the sort of men Clemmie would meet in Newport were more to her own taste than her daughter's. Clemmie's behavior at several coming-out balls in Philadelphia had left no doubt of that.

There was the time Clemmie had convinced the scions of three old Philadelphia families to arrive at one of those proper balls dressed as jewel thieves. Unfortunately their disguises had been too convincing, and all three men had been barred from at least a dozen parties that season. Perfect gentlemen all, they hadn't mentioned that the escapade had been Clemmie's idea, but she had refused to relinquish her share of the limelight and when the story got out that Clemmie Wilder had been behind the whole thing, she found that her name too had been crossed off the list for the better parties. Clemmie said she didn't care, the prank was worth a dozen dull parties, but Dolly couldn't help noticing a certain restiveness in her daughter as the balls she was not invited to approached. Clemmie could be hurt a good deal more easily than she liked to pretend.

Neither mother nor daughter, however, was thinking of Clemmie's vulnerability that afternoon on the way to Newport. Dolly, hoping to arrive as fresh as possible, had retreated to one of the staterooms of the private car for a nap.

Clemmie was becoming dangerously bored. From

the small alcove off the main saloon came the sound of quiet snoring. Ellen, her mother's maid, dozed fitfully. She reminded Clemmie of a sleepy Cerberus guarding the gates leading out of Hades, a gilt-edged Hades, but a Hades just the same.

Clemmie looked around the private car. The heavy, tasseled draperies that framed the windows muffled the sounds without obscuring the view. The cushiony chairs invited sleep. The heavy silver tea service stood ready on the mahogany sideboard. They had just finished lunch, but the steward was always one step ahead of them.

Everything in the car was solid and comfortable and designed to cushion the rigors and dangers of travel, and Clemmie would have traded them all to sit in the public parlor car and look at the other passengers rather than the monotonous countryside. She decided she'd probably die of boredom before she even reached Newport. She yawned and stretched again and admired her long legs. A walk was what she needed, a walk to the dining car. She'd have a lemonade and be back before her mother or Ellen noticed she was gone.

Clemmie carefully opened the heavy door with the polished brass fittings and closed it quietly behind her. It was cooler on the platform, and the wind whipped the thin material of her dress about her legs. When the workers had hooked the car on in New York this morning, Clemmie hadn't realized there was another private car between them and the public cars. Well, she'd simply ask if she might go through. Her mother would be appalled if she knew, but her mother was not going to know. Clemmie crossed the platform unsteadily and opened the door to the next car. In a small sitting room a man sat reading. When he looked up she realized he had the darkest eyes she had ever seen. They traveled over her with curiosity.

"I was just on my way through to the dining car," Clemmie said.

The man unfolded himself from the chair. He was

tall and slender and moved gracefully. "I'm afraid I can't let you do that, Miss Wilder."

"How do you know who I am?" she demanded.

"That's *Aries,* the number-one car of the Allegheny and Western Railroad behind us," he said, nodding in the direction she'd come. "The private car of Elias Wilder, the owner of the A&W." The dark eyes combed her again and she wondered what the verdict was.

Clemmie's brothers delighted in teasing her. "You're too thin," said George, whose taste ran to more voluptuous women. "And your legs are too long."

"And your coloring," Adam would add. "George, what are we going to do about her coloring? The hair's all right. Black hair isn't as good as blond, but at least it's not a mousy brown. But gray eyes, Clemmie—what a pity the baby blues were wasted on George."

Clemmie knew they were only teasing her, and one of the three notorious young men from Philadelphia had told her last winter, when they'd stolen a moment from a dance and gone out onto the country-club terrace, that he'd never seen eyes like hers in his life. "One minute they're slate gray and the next they're so soft you could swear they're velvet."

Clemmie pulled herself up. What was she doing worrying about whether some stranger—some rude stranger by all appearances—liked her eyes or found her legs too long?

"I doubt that you're Mrs. Elias Wilder," the man continued, "though I admit it's a possibility. And ladies' maids aren't usually so fashionably dressed."

Clemmie felt herself color under his scrutiny, and cursed herself. Why was she thrown off balance by him? "Now that you've proved your detective skills, Mr. Holmes, I'd like to get by." She took a step forward but he reached an arm across the door to block her path.

"I'm afraid I can't let you do that," he repeated.

"But that's ridiculous."

"Not ridiculous, just dangerous. There's a very high-strung two-year-old in there. I can't take the chance."

14

"I'm not afraid of your horse."

"I wasn't worried about you, Miss Wilder, I was worried about Lancelot. I don't want him upset."

There was an insolent edge to his voice. Clemmie began to piece together the clues. He wore flannel trousers and a tweed jacket. When the train had lurched a moment ago she had been thrown against the arm that blocked the door to the horse stall, and the tweed felt soft against her bare arm. There was no doubt that his clothes were good, but they were wrinkled as if he hadn't bothered to dress for the journey. And the way his eyes had traveled over her reminded Clemmie of the way the workmen in her father's yards looked at her when she drove down to see him—except that there was nothing surreptitious in this man's gaze. She looked at the book he'd put aside when she'd entered. It was a stud book. He was clearly one of those trainers whose success with horses had made him forget his place with people.

"I won't upset your precious Lancelot," she insisted. She'd had enough of this sparring. At first she'd found him attractive, but now his obstinacy annoyed her.

"I know you won't upset him, Miss Wilder, because you're not going through there."

"See here, I don't know whom you work for or whose horse that is, but if you know who my father is then I'm sure you know that I'm not accustomed to being insulted on a New York Central train. Or anywhere else."

His voice, when he spoke, was soft and ironic. It held none of Clemmie's impatient anger. "I didn't mean to insult you, Miss Wilder, but I do have my orders, and they're to make sure that no one goes through that car. So now if you'll just go back to your own . . ."

"I'll do nothing of the kind. I started out for the dining car, and I'm going to the dining car."

"Well, Miss Wilder, you're perfectly welcome to stay here with me. I don't have anything to offer you to eat, but I do have a bottle of whiskey. Not that bootleg stuff, but some real English whiskey." He was still leaning against the door to the other compartment, and still smiling as if he found Clemmie and the whole incident vastly amusing.

For a moment she wondered what it would be like to sit alone with him in the vestibule of the trailer, drinking English whiskey and talking of . . . Then she caught herself.

"You can keep your whiskey and your precious two-year-old," she said, turning and starting back toward her own car. "But I warn you, the people at the Central home office will hear about this."

"I'll tell them myself, Miss Wilder."

The last thing Clemmie heard before she slammed the door was his laughter. He sounded as if he'd had a very good time.

When the train arrived at Wickford Junction the Van-Nests' Dusenberg was waiting to take them to Newport. On her way to the car Clemmie passed the trainer. He turned from supervising the detraining of the horse just in time to see her.

"Miss Wilder," he said with a nod of his head.

"Who is that?" Dolly Wilder asked her daughter.

"I haven't the faintest idea," Clemmie said, and kept her eyes straight ahead.

It was not, Dolly thought as the Dusenberg headed toward the Wickford ferry that would carry them across Narragansett Bay to the island of Newport, an auspicious beginning. Earlier that afternoon Dolly had been awakened by the sounds of Clemmie returning to their private car. Clemmie had said she'd only gone out on the observation platform for a breath of air, but now Dolly wondered—wondered, and thought again of the suitable men Clemmie would meet in Newport and of Clemmie's annoying habit of finding the most unsuitable men attractive. She remembered those three young men from Philadelphia Clemmie had convinced to dress up as jewel thieves. Two of them had been half in love with Clemmie, one boasting a name almost as legendary in Philadelphia as that of Ben Franklin, and a fortune to match. But Clemmie had insisted on disappearing from country-club dances with the less-pedigreed suitor, the son of a man who'd made his fortune in, of all things, vacuum cleaners. To be sure, he was the more handsome of the two, but in Dolly's eyes at least, a strong jaw and a head of curly dark hair were no match for a three-hundred-year-old name and a vintage fortune. The only solace Dolly could find was that Clemmie had really cared very little for either young man. Clemmie was a mistress of flirtation, a dabbler in romance, and a stranger, Dolly was sure, to love. But she would not always be a stranger, Dolly knew, and thought of the man in the station. She wished Elias were along on the trip.

Dolly was no match for Clemmie, but Elias could be —when he made the effort. That he took the trouble less often than Dolly might have wished was a sign not of his lack of love for his daughter, but only of his obsessive concern for his railroad. Elias Wilder reflected the ambitions of his own father, a self-made man, and of the era in which he'd grown up, the era of America's expanding greatness. He inhabited a man's world, the world of business and money and power. Elias's success in that world had insured his family's security. He left the rest to his wife. And the rest meant, among other things, the children. To be sure, in moments of crisis, when special discipline was required, Elias was always prepared, especially when it involved the boys. And he had never really neglected Clemmie. But as Adam and George had grown older, he'd begun to take more of a hand in their affairs; not so with Clemmie. Dolly had called Elias's attention to the difference.

"That's as it should be, my dear," he'd said. "I can rely on you to teach Clemmie the sorts of things a girl ought to know, but the boys' futures, and their preparation for it, are my responsibility. Not that it's much of a burden when it comes to Adam, but George is another story."

"George is merely high-spirited," Dolly said with a quick maternal instinct for the runt of the litter, although in George's case he was clearly the moral rather than the physical runt.

"I could do with a little less spirit and a little more self-discipline."

"It's true that George cut up a bit at Yale...."

"Cut up," Elias observed, "and was thrown out."

"But he finished perfectly respectably at Lafayette, and you must admit he's worked hard since then. If you don't think so, it's only because you compare him to Adam. And to yourself. You're both so devoted to the railroad that you make George look uninterested by comparison."

"George *is* uninterested, my dear. George is more interested in having a good time than running the railroad."

"Perhaps he's interested in both," Dolly said.

"I hope you're right. For once in my life I fervently pray I'm wrong and you're right. I hope with time George will begin to settle down, that he'll find the right girl and give up all the parties and settle down to helping Adam run the railroad and producing another generation of Wilders to carry it on. I hope so, Dolly, but I don't count on it."

Elias might not count on it, Dolly thought, but he continued to work for it. He watched George carefully and oversaw his every move. If he hadn't things might have been better. Perhaps if Elias held the reins less tightly, the horse might not champ at the bit so fiercely.

At the moment, however, George and his wildness were far away, and Clemmie was the problem at hand. Dolly knew her daughter's spirit, just as she knew Grace VanNest's sense of propriety. She only hoped the two would not clash. Dolly thought again of the strange

18

young man who'd nodded to Clemmie as they'd left the train. Grace would have been horrified.

The VanNest house was one of those vast, airy "Palladian" edifices that Newport in her perversity insisted on calling a cottage. Grace VanNest and her daughter Alison were waiting for their guests on the west veranda, overlooking the bay.

"Clemmie," Alison said, jumping up and kissing her on the cheek. "I'm so glad you could come."

Clemmie forced herself not to pull away. She had few girl friends and recoiled from the little intimacies other girls regarded as natural. The fact that Alison was small and fair and looked as fragile as a china doll only made it worse. And the long blond hair that she continued to wear down during the day increased the impression of delicacy. For some reason Clemmie never understood, she had always felt a kind of rangy awkwardness around Alison, as if she were a frisky colt and Alison a startled fawn. One thing was certain, Clemmie thought, looking down at Alison, all pink blushes and innocent blue eyes. Any man who was attracted to Alison VanNest was unlikely to look twice at Clemmie Wilder. Clemmie wondered about the other side of the coin. Was it possible, despite her brothers' taunts, that any man who responded to Clemmie's less conventional appearance would find Alison a little bland by comparison? She told herself so when she was alone, but confronted with Alison's delicate loveliness, she wondered.

Several hours later, when Alison entered Clemmie's room looking like a portrait in a Victorian locket, her thick blond hair piled elaborately on her head, Clemmie was struck by the same thought.

"Let me sit with you while you finish dressing," Alison said. Though they were to leave in a few minutes, Clemmie was still in her chemise. She was as habitually late as Alison was prompt.

"Tell me what kind of a party it's going to be,"

19

Clemmie said, turning back to the mirror and brushing her hair with vigorous strokes.

"Grand, terribly grand." Alison was watching Clemmie's preparations carefully. "I wish I had the nerve to bob my hair."

"But your hair is beautiful, Alison. Anyway, you're not the type for bobbed hair. Grand. That means stuffy."

"You mean I'm not daring enough. Not really stuffy, but it *is* at The Breakers, and Mrs. Vanderbilt does have her standards."

"Adam and George say Newport's become dull," Clemmie quoted her brothers. "They say all the interesting men go elsewhere."

"Well, a lot of them don't stay the season, but there are quite a few here now."

"But are any of them interesting?" Clemmie demanded, slipping the gray chiffon over her head. She looked at her reflection in the mirror and again remembered the Philadelphian's comment about her eyes.

"The Goelets have the Earl of Weston up. Sebastion's rather nice."

"Lord, Alison, spare me the 'rather nice' ones. In fact, I think I'd prefer the *not* so nice ones."

"You know you don't mean that, Clemmie."

"Don't I though! I guess Adam and George were right after all. Stuffy."

"I'll introduce you to Whit Morris. He isn't stuffy."

Clemmie heard the change in Alison's tone, and knew that for Alison, at least, Whit Morris was special. "Who's Whit Morris?"

"Whitmore Vanderbilt Morris. The name speaks for itself, though not really for Whit. He's with the railroad, of course—his father's one of the directors and he's a vice president."

"I'm not interested in his family tree or a financial report, Alison. I asked what he was like."

"It's hard to describe Whit," Alison said, the pink rising in her cheeks.

"You mean he's too wonderful for words." Clemmie could picture the kind of man Alison would find irresistible. Beautiful manners and dull as dishwater.

"I didn't say that," Alison said quickly.

"You didn't have to. Come on," Clemmie said, taking the silver evening cape that had been laid out for her and starting for the door, "we might as well find out just how wonderful Whit Morris is."

Clemmie had heard stories of The Breakers. Her mother told her that years ago, when the old house burned down, Mrs. Vanderbilt had set out to build a new one that would outdo every other Newport house—especially Marble House, which had just been built by her sister-in-law. And she had succeeded. Clemmie had heard of the seventy rooms, the baths that ran hot and cold, fresh and salt water, the marble and alabaster billiards room with the English weighing chair that gave your weight in stones. She'd heard of it all, but she still hadn't been prepared for the reality of The Breakers. It made the VanNest house look almost like the "cottage" its owners pretended it was. Clemmie stood now in the vast enclosed center courtyard looking up at the ceiling painted cerulean blue and dotted with clouds. "I'm surprised they haven't worked out a way of making the clouds move," Clemmie whispered, and her mother shot her a disapproving glance. Clemmie didn't mind. She was sure she saw a flicker of amusement in the eyes of one of the footmen standing nearby. There were dozens of them stationed about the great hall, each resplendent in the maroon livery of the Vanderbilts.

"There he is," Alison murmured. "That's Whit Morris." Clemmie followed Alison's gaze to the landing halfway down the great staircase, and there, with the man who was supposed to be Whit Morris, stood the trainer who had been so rude that afternoon. He was dark and sleek in well-cut dinner clothes, and now Clemmie realized why she'd been so disconcerted earlier. It wasn't only his looks, though there was no disputing the fact he was outrageously handsome. But there was something about his manner, his ease of movement and self-assurance, that threw Clemmie off guard. She found him absolutely devastating, and was a little frightened by the fact.

"Does he always bring his trainer along to parties?" Clemmie asked.

"What do you mean?"

"The man with your Mr. Morris. I met him on the train this afternoon. He may be good with horses but he's a perfect boor with people."

"I don't understand what you're talking about, Clemmie. That's Sebastion Anvers, the Earl of Weston, with Whit."

The two men had descended the stairs and now Clemmie was standing face to face with the trainer who of course couldn't be a trainer after all, but was Clemmie's beau.

He interrupted Alison's introduction. "Miss Wilder and I have met. In fact, you might say we made the trip up together."

"You mean you thought Whit was a trainer?" Alison laughed.

"You have to admit you were acting like one, Mr. Morris," Clemmie said.

"Just because I was worried about your disturbing Lancelot? He's a high-strung animal, Miss Wilder. Especially when he's cooped up on a train. I'm sure *you* can understand that." His tone was polite, but there was a wicked light in the dark eyes.

Whatever else you might say about Whit Morris, Clemmie thought, he did not have beautiful manners and he was not dull as dishwater. But Sebastion Anvers had no intention of giving her time to contemplate the fact. Sebastion was tall and gaunt with pale eyes that looked bored and a little arrogant. They gave the lie to his polite, almost gallant words as he asked Clemmie to dance. Clemmie noticed her mother's pleasure as she let the Earl lead her out to the lower loggia where the younger guests were dancing, and Whit Morris's air of superior amusement, and she hated both.

"I hope you're going to be staying with us for a time, Miss Wilder," Lord Anvers said. Again she noticed that the unfailingly polite words were at variance with the coldness of the eyes. Those eyes dared her to be amusing and at the same time denied that she could be.

"I should think *you* wouldn't be staying for long, Lord Anvers. From what I hear it's deadly dull. If I were a man I'd escape in a flash." For a moment the arrogance gave way to interest, and Clemmie laughed. "Don't most of the girls tell you that?"

"No, they usually rave about Newport."

"That's only because they want you to stay."

"Don't you want me to stay, Miss Wilder?"

"That depends on whether you make Newport more exciting or," she tossed over her shoulder as she danced off in the arms of another man who had just cut in, "merely more stuffy."

Sebastion Anvers cut in regularly during the next few hours, but Clemmie did not dance more than a few steps—or a few sentences with any one man that night. Neither, however, did she dance with Whit Morris, at least not until after midnight. Twice before that Clemmie, looking idly over the shoulder of some less desirable dancing partner, had seen him start toward her, but the first time he had stopped short and cut in on Alison, and the second he had walked beyond her to dance with a pretty red-haired girl. Finally, when Clemmie had stopped expecting Whit Morris to cut in on her, she saw him standing behind Sebastion Anvers.

"Sorry, old man," Whit murmured to Sebastion without the least note of apology in his voice.

Clemmie's eyes were on a level with Whit's mouth. That afternoon she had been struck by his eyes, dark and liquid under thick lashes, but now she couldn't help noticing his mouth. The sardonic smile did not hide a deep sensuality.

"On behalf of the New York Central, Miss Wilder, I would like to apologize for the rude treatment you suffered this afternoon at the hands of one of our employees. I hope you won't demand we sack the fellow. He's a good worker, I hear—when he's on the job."

"I find that hard to believe."

"Ah, the lady has a hard heart. Actually, you ought to be grateful to me. There's no telling what kind of trouble you might have got into, wandering alone through the public cars. But of course that's what you had in mind, wasn't it?"

"All I had in mind, Mr. Morris, was a lemonade."

"You mean there were no lemons in Mr. Wilder's private car? And no steward to squeeze them."

"And a change of scene."

"So I was right. You were looking for a little adventure."

"There was precious little of it on today's trip, thanks to you."

"You mean you didn't find our encounter fascinating?"

"Why, it took my breath away."

"I invited you to stay. Things might have got more exciting if you had."

"Just you, me, and Lancelot . . ."

"Lancelot wouldn't have bothered us at all."

"Thank you, but that isn't my idea of excitement."

"What is your idea of excitement, Miss Wilder?"

"Anything fast—automobiles . . . airplanes . . . speedboats. And anything dangerous. Dares . . . Challenges." Clemmie looked up and saw the dark eyes watching her carefully. "You don't believe me?"

"Oh, I believe you, all right, Clemmie Wilder. I'm just wondering what I'm going to do about you."

"You mean because I'm Alison's guest and you're going to have to entertain me?"

"I mean because I hate to see a fast horse—or woman—" he said, relinquishing her to the man who had just cut in, "go unproven."

The VanNest "cottage" was not on Bellevue Avenue, but overlooked Narragansett Bay. The VanNest pedigree more than compensated for the lack of a Bellevue Avenue address, and the commanding view of the bay and the fleet of the Ida Lewis Yacht Club—not an ostentatious fleet, Stephen VanNest often said, but an interesting one—was as good if not better than the view from Bellevue Avenue. Dolly Wilder observed as much the morning after the ball at The Breakers, her first morning in Newport.

"There isn't a view like yours anywhere on the island," she told Grace.

Grace agreed. The bay below was a dazzling blue in the early-morning sunlight, the lawn a lush green carpet that sloped down to the water. At the rear of the house, white and spacious and symmetrical, open to the sea and its breezes, a striped awning shaded the terrace where they sat for breakfast, the two women erect and lovely in their morning silks, the two girls graceful and virginal in their white dresses. The glass-topped table was set with brightly flowered china and a gleaming silver coffee urn. Grace saw it all as if on a canvas by Sargent, precise, polite, a world of perfection and beauty. Even the faint sound of the telephone was appropriate, a promise of some future pleasure rather than an intrusion on the present one.

"That will be Sebastion again," Alison said. "You made quite a conquest last night, Clemmie. He's already called twice this morning, but I refused to wake you. I told him we'd be at Bailey's Beach this afternoon, but I guess he just can't wait."

"Oh, Sebastion Anvers." Clemmie's tone was deprecating. "I'm sure he's more interested in Father's money than in me."

The words and the way she tossed them out shattered Grace's image of harmonious perfection. She had the uncomfortable feeling Clemmie was going to prove difficult.

"That's a vulgar thing to say, Clemmie," Dolly reprimanded her.

"Vulgar, perhaps, but true."

"Well, it is true," Alison said, "that Sebastion has to marry an heiress. Everyone knows that if he doesn't, he'll never be able to hold on to the castle. But Sebastion won't settle for just anyone. Why, he's never looked at me twice."

"If Lord Anvers hasn't looked at you twice, as you put it," Grace VanNest said, "it's because he understands about you and Whit. He may be a fortune-hunter but he's a gentleman as well."

Clemmie saw the color rise in Alison's cheeks and, to hide the flush in her own face, looked down at the coffee that had just been set before her.

"There's nothing to understand, Mother. Except that Whit and I have known each other forever and we're good friends."

"In places like Newport, Alison, these things are understood, and a man of the world like Lord Anvers understands them perfectly." Grace VanNest's tone was final. Whit Morris might need another season or two to sow his wild oats—he was like his uncle Quentin rather than his father in that respect—but ultimately he would marry Alison. Everyone in Newport knew that, including Whit himself.

When they arrived at Bailey's Beach, Clemmie wondered whether Whit Morris would be there too, but she didn't ask. She was not going to question Alison about Whit, though she was dying to. There were a great many things she wanted to know about Whit Morris, including whether Mrs. VanNest were right. Was he in love with Alison? If so, Clemmie envied her, and felt a little sorry for her as well. It seemed to Clemmie, even from the brief dance they'd had last night, that he was much too attentive to other women. If Clemmie were Alison, she'd be furious. And darn lucky, Clemmie thought as she saw Whit emerging from one of the weathered wooden dressing cabañas. It was strange to see him in the dark woolen bathing trunks with the black-and-white-striped top. The third Whit, Clemmie thought. Yesterday afternoon he'd been casual and surly, last night elegant and superior. Now he looked simply boyish.

"There's Whit," Alison said, as if Clemmie had not noticed him.

By the time the two girls emerged from the VanNests' changing cabaña, Whit had joined a group of ten or a dozen young people lounging at the far end of the beach. As the two girls crossed the crescent of sand toward them, Alison was aware of the stares of certain of the matrons. Clemmie's bathing suit was red wool with a snug tank top and brief shorts that stopped well above the knee. She looked smashing in it, Alison had to admit, but also a little shocking, or so it seemed on a beach where most of the women still sported black silk bathing stockings.

When they reached the group at the end of the beach Alison noticed that Whit looked at Clemmie for what seemed like a long time. She noticed too that Clemmie dropped to the sand at the other side of the group from him.

I won't go out of my way to sit near him, Clemmie thought. It's probably exactly what he expects. She had seen the way Whit looked at her as she and Alison joined the group, and for a moment she wasn't sure whether she was glad she'd worn the red bathing suit or regretted it. She was certain, however, of one thing. Remembering the way his eyes had taken her in without haste or embarrassment, she knew Whit Morris was accustomed to conquests.

Sebastion Anvers was saying something to Clemmie about tides. Whatever the words, his voice seemed to imply, "Yes, I know one has to make conversation in company, but it would be so much better if one didn't."

"I've never understood," Clemmie answered him, digging her toes into the warm sand and striking a rock, "why everyone insists on coming to this beach. The sand's covered with rocks, the water's absolutely clogged with seaweed, and there's no surf at all. Might as well swim in a bathtub."

"Surely you don't want to go to the public beach?" a girl in pink beach pajamas said.

"Is it better?" Clemmie asked.

Whit laughed. "No one knows. No one's ever been there. But gossip has it that the surf's rougher."

Laurie Sedgewick, a red-haired girl Clemmie remembered from the night before, rolled over on the sand and looked at Clemmie coolly. "If you're looking for some excitement in the water, why don't you try the surfboard? I'm sure Sebastion will drive the speedboat for you."

"I don't think Clemmie ought to try that," Alison said quickly. "It's too dangerous. Especially if you've never done it before."

Clemmie was on her feet. "Will you drive the speedboat for me, Sebastion?"

"Alison's right," Sebastion said. He looked unhappy at the prospect of moving. "Unless you've done it before, it can be frightfully dangerous. Chap broke his leg that way last week."

"Will *anyone* drive the speedboat for me?" Clemmie looked at Whit. Her eyes flashed a challenge.

"Have you ever tried it?" Whit asked.

"No, but I've seen it done. All you have to do is get your balance on the surfboard."

"It looks easier than it is," Whit said.

"You worry about the speedboat, and I'll worry about my balance. I've never lost it yet."

"I'll bet you haven't," Whit said as they started off toward the dock.

"Please be careful, Clemmie," Alison's voice called after them, but neither Clemmie nor Whit was listening.

"It's wonderful," Clemmie called above the roar of the engine. "Absolutely wonderful." She loved the way her body cut through the water and the spray cascaded over her.

Driving the speedboat with one hand, Whit sat half-turned in the seat to watch her.

"Faster," Clemmie shouted. "Can't you go any faster?"

He pressed the accelerator down and the figure behind him disappeared in an explosion of spray. Clemmie was nothing but a fountain of silver droplets. Whit made an arc with the boat. The fountain curved to one side but did not fall. She'd boasted that she never lost her balance, and this time, at least, she'd been right.

Whit watched Clemmie as he helped her back into the boat. Her dark bob was slicked against her head like a sleek little cap and her skin, tawny and smooth in bright sunshine, was covered with droplets of water. She tugged a little at the brief woolen shorts, sat next to him, and stretched her legs before her.

"I told you I never lose my balance," she laughed.

"One swallow does not a summer make."

"Is that a dare, Mr. Morris? Because I can go around again."

"I think you'd better start calling me Whit. And it wasn't a dare. Merely a caution, Clemmie. What does Clemmie stand for anyway?"

She looked at him out of the corner of her eyes. "Why, Clementine, of course. Like in the song." She assumed a Western twang. "I'm just a little country girl from Scranton, Pennsylvania, out in the big wide world for the first time."

He looked at her for a moment, then started the engine. "I'll bet you are, Clemency Wilder. I'll just bet you are," he repeated above the roar of the motor.

*   *   *

There was a ball or a party almost every night, and within a week they began to take on a certain sameness for Clemmie. She could even predict the order in which various men would cut in on her and the frequency of Sebastion Anvers' dances. There he stood now, his long white fingers poised above her current partner's shoulder.

"Why, Sebastion," Clemmie said as he drew her to him. "I do believe you've been drinking whiskey."

The party at Mrs. Sherman's villa was in honor of her daughter, and Mrs. Sherman was a firm upholder of both Prohibition and her daughter's virtue. Clemmie adored champagne and found the absence of it tonight reprehensible on Mrs. Sherman's part. It served her right having a daughter as plain as Pamela, Clemmie thought.

"Sorry, Clemmie," Sebastion said. "Only a nip." He had the British aristocrat's habit of expressing himself with the fewest words possible.

"Don't be sorry, Sebastion. Just tell me where I can get some. Do you have a flask?" Clemmie usually refused Sebastion's suggestions that they get a breath of air on this or that terrace, but now she was willing to make an exception.

"I don't. Morris does."

Clemmie began to calculate. Unlike other men, Whit followed no pattern in his dances with Clemmie. Sometimes he cut in on her several times in an hour, others he danced with her only once or twice in an evening. He hadn't danced with her yet tonight, and she guessed he would soon. He had never gone for an entire evening without doing so.

Five minutes later Whit cut in. "I hear you're the bootlegger tonight. What does a girl have to do to get a drink?"

He looked down at her. "It's neat whiskey, you know. No champagne or orange blossoms."

"I'm familiar with flasks and their contents. Now do

30

you want to dance me toward the terrace or shall we walk?"

Once outside, he took her hand and began to lead her away from the house.

Where are we going?" Clemmie asked.

"I didn't want to scandalize Mr. Sherman. He was standing on the terrace. There's a gazebo at the end of this path."

"Do you know all the houses in Newport this well?"

"Some of them. I spent most of my summers here, at least until after the war. Since then I've only come up for a few weeks now and then."

"Where do you go for the rest of the time?"

"Bar Harbor when I want to get away. Long Island when I don't. Last summer I didn't get up at all. Father took a boat to the South Seas for six months on a scientific expedition."

"Did you discover anything?"

"A newt."

"It hardly seems worth it—six months at sea for a newt."

"It was a pleasant six months."

"Did Alison find it pleasant—six months of waiting?"

"Alison is a very patient girl."

"But I'm not," Clemmie said, sitting on the circular bench in the gazebo and looking up at him. "You promised me a drink."

Whit produced a slender silver flask from his breast pocket. He handed it to Clemmie and she took a long swallow.

"You're pretty accomplished at that."

"I told you I'm just a country girl. Not much to do in the backwoods of Pennsylvania except sit behind the barn and drink moonshine."

"Is that what they taught you at Miss Plymouth's?"

"That's why I was fired from Miss Plymouth's."

"You don't seem particularly embarrassed by the fact."

"Anybody who doesn't get fired from a school like

31

Miss Plymouth's must be so dull I don't want to know her."

They both remembered that Alison had been at Miss Plymouth's with her, but neither mentioned the fact.

"Tell me what else you do with your time besides discover newts and race Lancelot," Clemmie said.

"That's only a small part of it. I'm really a very serious fellow. Labor from eight-thirty to six, half-day on Saturdays, in the office of the Central."

"Ah, yes, the esteemed vice president. Something to do with finance, isn't it? Alison told me that's what you did, but I don't believe it. You see, I know about vice presidents in charge of finance, Whit. They lunch with gray-looking bankers and play golf with fat businessmen and sit in their offices arranging mergers and expansions. They do not spend their days sailing and playing with fast racehorses or tooling around the countryside in a Stutz or their nights drinking and dancing. In fact, in view of everything I doubt you even have an office."

"I have a perfectly respectable office. Entirely somber except for the view of Park Avenue."

Clemmie laughed. "I can just picture it. Filled with sailboat models and pictures of horses and . . . and stuffed newts."

"No stuffed newts."

"But I was right about the rest."

"A man has to relax every now and then. Besides, what's this sudden interest in how hard-working I am? Surely you, of all people, don't count that a virtue."

"Are you suggesting we're two of a kind?" she asked.

He had remained standing and now he leaned over until his face was only inches from hers. "What do you think?"

"I think you ought to give me another drink."

He handed her the flask again, and she took another swallow and stood.

"We could dance out here," Whit said. "You can still hear the music."

"Aren't you afraid of being missed?"

"About as much as you are." He reached a hand around her waist and began moving in time to the music.

He held her closer than he did on the dance floor, and she leaned her head against his cheek. She could feel the whiskey surging through her, and hear, over the music that floated down from the house, the sound of the waves crashing on the beach below. Through the thin material of her dress, his hand felt warm against her back.

He moved well. She had never realized how well when the proprieties of the ballroom kept an inch of air between them, but now she could feel the lean length of his body against hers, his chest hard beneath the stiff front of his dinner shirt, his legs graceful in movement, the long arms that held her to him as if they had no intention of relinquishing her.

She leaned her head against his again and felt his breath warm against her ear. Disconcertingly, maddeningly, she kept thinking what it would be like to turn her face so that his mouth was against hers, so that the warm breath became her breath.

The music ended, but Whit did not let her go, and she made no attempt to pull away from him. "We don't have to go back," he whispered into her hair. The arms were still around her, a prison of pure pleasure, and as if reading her mind, his mouth began to trace a line from her ear to her lips. Then there was a sound of footsteps on the gravel path and Whit stepped away quickly.

"Been looking all over for you, Clemmie," Sebastion said. If he was aware he'd surprised them, he did not seem to care. "You promised to have supper with me. Everyone's gone in." He turned to Whit. "Except Alison. She's waiting for you on the terrace."

The fortunate thing about having Sebastion as a supper partner, Clemmie thought as he took his seat beside her, was that you were free to pursue your own thoughts. Since Sebastion had no real interest in what he was saying, he never noticed that others were equally uninterested in the conversation. For a moment she wondered what life with Sebastion would be like. She'd be a brood mare, a lavishly doweried brood mare. Her father would provide the money to install central heating in the castle, she'd supply the son and heir—sons and heirs, she imagined, just to be on the safe side —and Sebastion would go his own way, drinking and hunting, enjoying his own friends and abusing her by his neglect. It was an old story that Clemmie had thought had been rewritten since the war, but she watched Sebastion pretending to be attentive and knew nothing had changed.

She glanced down the table to Whit and Alison. Whit was talking quietly, and, though Alison's eyes were lowered, her head was bent to him as if she were afraid of missing a single word. Clemmie wondered what Whit was saying. His eyes looked serious. No, not serious. They looked tender, and when Alison raised her face to his, her cheeks were flushed. Those moments in the gazebo seemed impossible now, or worse than that, shabby. He'd been flirting with her, aimlessly, boldly flirting, and she'd been taken in by him. He was probably laughing at her right now. But that was ridiculous. He wasn't laughing at her. He wasn't even thinking of her. He was thinking only of Alison.

"And it's driving Uncle Quentin wild," Whit was saying to Alison. "He has a syndicate for the America's Cup put together, but there are no challengers. He just can't understand it. Keeps trying to stir up his English friends, but there are no takers. So there he sits with his syndicate, his plans for the perfect racer, and no challengers."

Whit heard his own voice easily embracing the familiar topic, felt Alison listening to him as if he were saying something original and exciting, and all the time he was thinking of Clemmie. Whenever he looked at her —and it seemed to him he'd been doing nothing but looking at her for the past week—she seemed slender and almost rangy, but when he'd held her moments ago in the gazebo her body had been soft and yielding against his.

"Perhaps you ought to put Sebastion to work on it," Whit heard Alison say, and they both turned just in time to see Clemmie look up at Sebastion, say something in an undertone, and laugh. The laugh was quiet but the gray eyes were bright. Whit could see that even at a distance.

Clemmie felt Whit's eyes on her and was glad. A moment ago he would have found her watching him, and she would have been humiliated, but he had turned just in time to see her flirting with Sebastion. It didn't matter that she didn't mean it, just so long as Whit thought she did.

Whit wondered if Clemmie had been taken in by Sebastion. He didn't think so, despite what he'd just seen. Most girls would be. They'd pretend to be sophisticated or disdainful of the well-known fact that Sebastion was desperate for an heircss, but all he'd have to do was snap his fingers, and they'd think of the title and the castle and the chance to be presented at Court, and all the sophistication and disdain would disappear. Other girls would react that way, Whit thought, but not Clemmie. It was not that Clemmie was too serious —he'd have hated that—rather that she was too frivolous. She'd be more interested in the way he danced than the titles he held, care more about the speed of Sebastion's car than the size of his castle, prefer sneaking away from the party to being presented at Court.

"You know," Whit heard Alison saying, and realized that he was still watching Clemmie. "I think Clemmie's really beginning to like Sebastion. Wouldn't that be wonderful?"

Wonderful, Whit thought. Wonderful to trade her father's money for a title, to have her shipped off to England as a brood mare for some damn nobleman, to lock her up in a drafty castle till she lost all her fire.

Girls never saw that side of it, and he supposed it was lucky for fellows like Sebastion that they didn't, or at least they didn't until it was too late. Certainly Whit couldn't imagine painting such a picture for Alison. The colors were too harsh, the lines too cruelly drawn, and yet Whit had the feeling Clemmie would recognize the accuracy of such a landscape.

"I'm not sure it would be so wonderful," Whit said, and told himself he was thinking objectively, not of Clemmie, but of any girl, and certainly he was not considering himself. "I've never thought much of those marriages of convenience. They tend to be convenient for everyone but the poor girl."

Just as there was a sameness to the nights, a similarity to the balls and dances and dinners, so there was a regularity to the days. The Casino at eleven, lunch at one, Bailey's Beach at three, tea at five, the dressing gong at seven. Each golden day passed exactly as the one before it and Clemmie began to see Newport as an elegant, carefully run prison. Of course she would have to rattle her chains.

She was in the dressing room of the Casino, that long, handsome, half-timbered building at the beginning of Bellevue Avenue where Newport met each morning as much to see and be seen as to play tennis. Clemmie was an exception to that rule. She played often and well, and had just beaten Sebastion on one of the carefully manicured lawn courts. She'd beaten him roundly and was proud of the fact, though she knew Alison and the other girls were scandalized.

"Well, I don't think there's anything wrong with letting a man win at certain games," Laurie Sedgewick said, tossing her thick red bob.

"You mean as long as we win at the big game, Laurie? As long as we snare a husband?" Clemmie asked.

"I can't imagine any man worth his salt wanting to

marry a girl he couldn't even beat at tennis," Laurie countered.

"I can't imagine a man worth his salt who didn't want a girl to give him a run for his money. Besides, it isn't a question of letting a man win or not letting him win. I play tennis because I like it, not because I'm trying to flatter some great big male and his tiny little vanity. Why should we have to do everything to please them?"

"That's just the way things are, Clemmie, and you better get used to the fact," Pamela Sherman said. It was clear from the way she said it that poor plain Pamela had gotten used to the fact a long time ago.

"It may have been that way when our mothers were girls," Clemmie said, "but it doesn't have to be that way anymore. It seems to me if women can vote, they can do a lot of other things men can."

"Clemmie, I never knew you were a suffragette," Alison said.

"Any girl with half a brain in her head is a suffragette. Why should men have all the rights? And all the freedom."

"Oh, freedom," Laurie scoffed. "They'll always have more freedom than we do."

"You mean because we can have babies and they can't?" Clemmie demanded. She saw Alison's eyes pleading with her to stop, but she wouldn't. "Well, I don't think it's fair. It seems to me we ought to be able to do anything they can."

"Now you sound like a bohemian," Laurie said. "My brother's been to parties in Greenwich Village, and he said they all believe in free love." She dropped her voice a little on the last two words.

"I'm not talking about bohemians," Clemmie said. "I don't want to live in a garret or wear awful clothes. I just want to be free to do whatever I please. My brothers can go wherever they want and do anything they like, but with me it's always, 'Ladies don't do that, Clemmie.' "

"But they have to work too," Pamela said. "At least we don't have to worry about that."

"Well, I wouldn't mind running a railroad if it meant I could run it the way I wanted. It would be better than sitting around like a china doll all day, waiting for some man to come home and tell me what I could or couldn't do."

"Oh, you're wrong there, Clemmie," Pamela said. "I can't think of anything more wonderful."

Clemmie looked at Alison and Laurie. It was clear from the wistful expression on both faces that they agreed with Pamela. They were simps, Clemmie thought, silly, mindless simps. But Clemmie couldn't help thinking, too, as she watched Alison braiding her long blond hair, that waiting for Whit Morris to come home would be different from waiting for just any man.

That afternoon Alison reopened the subject. She and Clemmie had gone for a stroll along the Cliff Walk after lunch. Clemmie loved the long path that wound along the ocean. It appealed to her sense of contradiction. On one side stood the great mansions of Newport, huge, ornate, imposing behind their vast lawns and gardens that were more art than nature. On the other was the vast expanse of ocean, unending, unfathomable, occasionally smooth, but more often rough, uncontrollable, as frightening as it was beautiful when the wind whipped up the surf and sent waves crashing against the carefully maintained bulkheads of the great estates.

The Cliff Walk was an anachronism as well. It was public, virtually the only structure in Newport that was. It cut across miles and miles of private property, sliced through the lawns and gardens and rocky cliffs of the great private houses, and still anyone could walk on it. The right of access to the walk had been secured by local fishermen in a legendary legal battle of the last century, and it was jealously guarded. Decade after decade, the natives of Newport were free to stroll over Mrs. Astor's property, gawk at Mrs. Vanderbilt's garden parties, and enjoy the same view as Mrs. Goelet. It was outrageous, most of the summer residents agreed, but it was a fact of life.

It was not, however, the fact of life that was troubling Alison this afternoon. She was still thinking of what Clemmie had said that morning in the Casino.

"You really ought to be more careful, Clemmie. I know you didn't mean all those things you said this morning, but the others aren't so sure. Someone like Laurie Sedgewick just might take you seriously and then it will be all over Newport."

"But I was serious, Alison."

"Well, about the vote maybe, but—"

"About all of it." There was a silence. "Look, Alison, do you expect to be pure when you get married?"

Alison turned away and looked out to sea. "Of course," she said quietly.

"Then why shouldn't your husband be?"

"Well, men are different. For one thing my husband will probably be older."

"Then if you didn't marry until you were thirty you wouldn't expect to be pure? Is that what you're saying?"

"You know that isn't what I meant, Clemmie. Anyway, I hate to talk about these things."

"Well, I admit they probably aren't as much fun to talk about as they are to do . . ."

"Clemency Wilder!"

"Alison VanNest! All right, Ali dear, I'll behave. No more scandalous talk. At least, not in front of your friends."

The best lunches in Newport, Clemmie soon discovered, were the picnic lunches. They were less formal and stuffy than the "little" parties with a dozen footmen and as many courses, though they were still hardly what Clemmie would call a picnic. At home picnics meant a few straw hampers filled with cold chicken and ham and potato salad. If there were no older people present a flask or two might make an appearance. Newport picnics, on the other hand, involved servants carrying ice-cream chests and coolers of champagne. There were linen cloths to spread on the lawn and specially designed hampers equipped with crystal and china and silver. To be sure it wasn't the best crystal or china or silver, but it was quite good enough. One could hardly imagine eating such homey fare as roast chicken or baked ham or cold potato salad with such accoutrements, so of course there was caviar and duck or veal in aspic and cold poached fish with delicately herbed sauces. If it were a picnic arranged by as well as for the young people, it might be a little simpler, but not much. Alison and her friends, it seemed to Clemmie, were made very much in their mothers' molds. Still a picnic was preferable to a formal lunch, or so Clemmie was thinking that afternoon as the cars began to draw up behind the Casino. Whit's red Stutz was clearly the swankiest among them. Swanky. Clemmie had begun to use the word because it was such an obvious and offensive travesty of the place. Clemmie couldn't help envying Alison as she climbed into the Stutz, and the feeling was only accentuated when she compared Whit to Sebastion, who was struggling to get the picnic basket into the rumble seat of his Morris Cowley. Though no one could call Sebastion unattractive, the impassive face under the sandy-colored hair, the stiff manner, and those haughty, slightly bored eyes did not excite Clemmie. Occasionally, when she compared them to Whit's features, they even annoyed her.

"Let me drive, Sebastion." Clemmie could see him struggling between the desire to accommodate her, if only out of ultimate self-interest, and the feeling that things should be done a certain way. The lady did not drive.

"If you'd really like to," he said.

It was not far to Breton's Point, but there was a stretch of road that was flat and straight and ran for several miles.

"You're really quite good at this," Sebastion said as

Clemmie turned on to the flat stretch behind Whit's Stutz and two other cars from their party.

"Thank you, Sebastion. I guess I'm not bad for someone who's never driven before." Clemmie laughed, pressed her foot down on the accelerator, and swerved out past the Stutz. She overtook it quickly, then the car in front, and finally the first one. They were racing along now, and Clemmie loved the feeling of wind against her face and the way the trees that lined both sides of the road raced past. She turned to Sebastion and laughed again, but his face was pale and his eyes, no longer bored, were glued to the speedometer.

When they reached Breton's Point she made a final circle of the field, came to an abrupt halt, and turned to Sebastion. There was a thin but unmistakable film of perspiration on his upper lip. "You weren't frightened, were you?" Clemmie asked.

"Of course not." He smoothed his fair hair. "Just worried about you. If you haven't driven before, it's easy to lose control."

"Honestly, Sebastion," Clemmie said, jumping from the car. "You mustn't believe everything I tell you. Father bought me a Marmon for my birthday. I drive all the time."

The other cars were beginning to arrive now, and Clemmie, her hands plunged deep in the pockets of her white linen dress, strode across the field toward them. Whit could not help noticing the way her body moved beneath the soft fabric, though he tried not to look as he helped Alison from the Stutz.

"Are you all right?" Alison asked. "Really, Sebastion, you oughtn't to drive that fast."

"I was driving," Clemmie laughed.

"I might have guessed," Whit murmured.

"You ought to try it sometime, Whit. It's glorious, simply glorious," Clemmie said. "It would be even better in a Stutz. I bet you could get it up to ninety or even a hundred."

"Not with me in it," Alison said.

Clemmie looked at Whit and smiled.

On the Wednesday morning of her third week in Newport, Dolly Wilder sat alone in the Casino gallery watching her daughter and Whit Morris. Whit was a superb
tennis player but Clemmie kept him up to the mark.
They made a handsome sight. Whit tall and lean, in
white flannel trousers and a soft white shirt, Clemmie
looking slender and sleekly sporty in a pleated white
linen skirt and middy, her dark bob held back by a
white silk ribbon. They were like elegant colts racing
back and forth across the court in long easy strides.
Both had that innate coordination that makes every
movement graceful. Alison VanNest was almost as
good a player as Clemmie, but she was small and gave
the appearance of working hard on the court. Alison
was at her best in repose. Clemmie—well, Clemmie was
never in repose, but fortunately she had a grace as well
as vitality that made her attractive in movement.

Dolly watched them change sides, saw Whit say
something in passing, saw her daughter look up at him
as she answered. Clemmie was smiling in an offhand,
teasing way, but even at this distance Dolly could see
the fire in the gray eyes.

"She kept you on your toes, didn't she, Mr. Morris?"
Dolly said as they approached.

"That she did, Mrs. Wilder. For a while there I was
afraid she was going to win."

"And I would have if the sun hadn't been in my eyes
for that one shot."

"A very unsporting excuse," Whit said. "Why don't
you admit it, Clemmie? You're good, but not that
good."

"I've beaten every girl in the Casino. And half the
men."

"Which reminds me, Mr. Morris," Dolly said. "Alison
asked me to tell you that she was going back with Mrs.
VanNest. She said they were expecting you tonight."

42

"I'm looking forward to it, Mrs. Wilder," Whit said, and executed a little bow to Dolly.

"Beautiful manners," Dolly said when Whit was out of hearing. Clemmie did not answer. "So you've set your cap for Whit Morris."

"I didn't say that."

"You didn't have to."

"I suppose you're like Mrs. VanNest and think Whit is practically engaged to Alison."

"What I think doesn't matter, Clemmie. It's what Whit thinks that's important, and I don't think he's nearly so set on the match as Grace VanNest is."

"And therefore it's even more scandalous of me to interfere."

Dolly looked around to make sure there was no one within hearing distance. "Don't be silly, Clemmie. Grace VanNast is a very old friend, and I'm fond of Alison, but you're my daughter. I'd be very much the fool if I didn't prefer that Whit marry you rather than another girl."

"You mean when it comes to snaring a husband, it's every girl for herself?"

"You can be as sarcastic as you like, Clemmie, but Whit is a splendid match, and you know it as well as I do, though I doubt the attributes that recommend him to me are the ones that attract you. All the same, Whit's advantages aren't to be dismissed. The Morrises go back to old New York and the Vanderbilts have enough money not to have to worry how far back they go. In fact, on the Vanderbilt side of it, the future counts more than the past." Dolly remembered a conversation she'd had with Elias about the New York Central less than a year ago.

"It's not run as well as it used to be," Elias had observed. "That's because one man is no longer in control. The Vanderbilts have been dividing up the management of the roalroad for too long. Same as they've been dividing up the fortune. Do you know, when the old Commodore died back in '77, his personal fortune equalled the cash in the U.S. Treasury? His instructions were to keep it intact, but his sons didn't listen. Any more than they listened about the railroad. So now the pie's been divided into too many slices and the railroad doesn't have a real head. They'll have to find one if they want to keep up with the rest of us," Elias had added with some satisfaction.

According to Grace VanNest, Whit was the man for the job. Before Clemmie had become a threat to Alison's monopoly, Grace had observed smugly that Whit was sure to be running the Central some day. "He's terribly competent in business," Grace had said. "Not that one would guess as much meeting him socially. Beautiful manners. Say what you will about Whit, he's a gentleman above all else. Not like so many men who work." If any reference to Elias was intended, Dolly was careful not to notice. "Still," Grace had finished, "Whit has a spectacular career ahead of him."

And a considerable fortune, Dolly added to herself, knowing Grace was too fastidious to say it.

"There's no doubt about it," Dolly said to her daughter now, "Whit has everything to recommend him. If you can bring it off, I'd be delighted. But be careful. It may be easy to take him from Alison for the moment, but it won't be easy to hold him. You're a fascinating girl, Clemmie, but sometimes a man wants a little more peace and a little less excitement."

"Peace. I can't think of anything more boring."

"No, I don't suppose you can, but then everyone isn't like you."

"Well, if Whit wants peace he can have Alison."

"That, my dear, is exactly my point."

Clemmie had found her mother's words more distressing than she was willing to admit. It was not only that she'd warned Clemmie she might lose Whit, but the fact that Dolly had recognized how much she wanted him in the first place. It was a frightening experience, wanting someone this way, and it was alarming to

44

think other people might be aware of her feelings. She wondered if Whit discerned them as clearly as her mother did. Whit did not know her as well, but then the feelings were directed at him. It seemed impossible that he didn't know and terrifying that he did. She didn't want to stay away from him, couldn't stay away from him, but she swore she'd put on a better masquerade.

It was not an easy task. It took every effort to pretend she cared little for Whit when she cared for nothing and no one else. But, Clemmie told herself as sternly as she could when she saw him standing there next to Alison in the ballroom of Fair Isles that night, she'd reveal none of her own feelings until Whit had shown his. For the moment flirtation was acceptable, but feeling must be kept at bay.

Clemmie smiled up at him now, brightly, carelessly, as if he were merely one of the dozens of stags in the ballroom. But of course he wasn't a stag at all because he had come with Alison and would leave with her.

"Sebastion's being a perfect stuffed shirt," Clemmie said to Whit and Alison. She was standing with Anvers in one of the French doors that led from the large ballroom of Fair Isles to the terrace overlooking the vast expanse of lawn that stopped just short of the ocean. The strip of property between the water and Fair Isles was one of Mrs. Bentwin's greatest disappointments. She did, however, have her compensations. Tonight's ball was one of them. The walls of the ballroom were hung with silver and gold brocade and the banks of white orchids and roses and calla lilies were dusted with gold and silver particles. Like many of the more opulent parties in Newport, Mrs. Bentwin's always had a theme. This was her Gold and Silver Ball. Everyone murmured how spectacular the decor was, but Clemmie couldn't help thinking one precious metal would have sufficed. She'd said as much to Whit when they'd danced earlier in the evening, and he'd laughed, but he hadn't said whether he agreed with her or not.

"All I asked him to do," Clemmie went on as if Sebastion's behavior really interested her, "was sneak me into the billiards room of The Breakers. When there's a ball there, it's off limits to ladies, but there's no ball tonight, and I want to see that famous weighing chair. In fact, I want to try it out."

"Sebastion's right," Alison said. "Even if you could get past the servants, I'm sure Mrs. Vanderbilt would be furious. I doubt she welcomes uninvited guests."

"Mrs. Vanderbilt doesn't have to know."

"But what if you get caught?" Alison asked.

"I'll worry about that then." Clemmie turned to Whit. "Come on, Whit. She's your aunt."

"Married to my mother's cousin."

"Well, whatever the relationship," Clemmie persisted, "surely you can sneak me into her house. All I want to see is how many stone I weigh. That's little enough to ask."

Whit stood. "All right, Clemmie, we'll put you in the famous weighing chair. Do you want to come along, Alison?" he added, knowing perfectly well it was the last thing Alison wanted.

Fair Isles bordered The Breakers, but it was a good ten-minute walk from one house to the next. They started off across the broad expanse of lawn that lay like a dark carpet in the moonlight.

"Cowards," Clemmie pronounced.

"As I understand it," Whit said, "Sebastion has a rather spectacular war record. Won a chest full of medals at Passchendale alone. And Alison is a lady."

"I suppose that means I'm not," Clemmie laughed, but she was not as amused as she pretended to be.

He stopped and turned to her. "I haven't figured out what you are yet." They stood looking at each other for a moment, two small figures on the vast plain between the two great houses. "Come on," Whit said, abruptly taking her hand. "I thought you wanted to weigh yourself."

Whit switched on a light and Clemmie was blinded

by the alabaster and marble shimmering in the brightness.

"Aren't you afraid that will attract attention?" Clemmie asked.

"We can't tell how many stone in the dark. Besides," he laughed, "Mrs. Vanderbilt is out for the evening and the servants are accustomed to me."

"So it wasn't so terribly dangerous after all?"

"That remains to be seen."

In the center of the room stood a mahogany billiards table. It was covered with a beautiful old tapestry. Mahogany furniture lined the room and formed a dark contrast to the grays and whites and yellows of the marble and alabaster walls and the mosaic ceiling. In a corner was the wood-and-leather weighing chair.

"It's so small," Clemmie said. She had expected something larger.

Whit laughed. "Just because it's talked about a great deal doesn't mean it *is* a great deal. Don't forget jockeys are small. Well, I thought you wanted to weigh yourself."

Clemmie sat in the chair and Whit fiddled with the contraption beside it.

"Almost eight stone," Whit pronounced. "Too heavy for a good jockey."

"Now you try it." Clemmie stood and let Whit try the chair. "Almost thirteen stone."

"Don't you want to know what we weigh together?" he asked, putting his arm around her waist and drawing her down on his lap.

She liked being so close to him, but was a little afraid of how much she liked it, there in the deserted house. "I'm very good at addition," Clemmie said, taking his hand from her waist and standing.

Whit shrugged and stood. "Well, what would you like to do now?"

"I suppose we ought to go back to the party."

"I thought Clemmie Wilder never did anything she ought to do."

She knew he was making fun of her. When he had pulled her down on his lap, it had been a dare, and she had not taken it. "Then why don't you take me for a drive?" she said. "I'd much rather do that than go back to the party."

"Not very dangerous," he said.

"That remains to be seen," she repeated his words of a few moments ago.

The red Stutz was parked at the edge of a sea of cars, far from the party. Whit held the door open for her.

"I'd rather drive," Clemmie said.

"I'm not Sebastion. I don't have to prove that I'm not afraid. I am. I'm petrified you'll hurt the car, and I'm very fond of this little baby."

"Where are we going? Breton's Point?"

"I have a better spot. Perfect view of the water. And more private." His tone hadn't changed at the last words, and Clemmie turned to look at his profile in the moonlight. He wasn't smiling.

Whit stopped the car on a cliff overlooking the water. Below them in the dark bay the lights of several yachts glittered like the jewels of a Newport matron in black satin.

"Tony Bayliss is having another party," Whit said.

"Which boat is his?"

Whit pointed to the largest yacht. Strings of multi-colored lights ran from each of her three masts to the deck, and every porthole blazed against the dark hull. There was an orchestra on deck and strains of music floated faintly over the water.

"It looks livelier than the party at Fair Isles," Clemmie said.

"Tony Bayliss's parties are always lively. That's why sweet young things like you aren't invited."

"In that case I want to go."

"I thought you might. Perhaps I'll take you some other time, but not tonight."

48

Clemmie didn't mind. She preferred being here alone with Whit, but was determined not to let him know it.

"That's what's so terrible about being a girl. You have to wait for people to take you places."

"You'd rather have been born a man?"

"No, I like being a girl. I just don't like the restrictions that go along with it."

"I thought," he said, reaching an arm around her shoulders, "Clemmie Wilder didn't care about restrictions."

Clemmie pulled away and was out of the car in a minute. "The view is even better from here," she said, leaning against the hood of the Stutz.

Whit got out of the car and walked around to where she stood. His hands on her arms were strong as he turned her to him. Even in the dim moonlight she could see that his eyes were dark with anger. "Why is it, Clemmie, that you'll risk almost anything—speed, danger, even Mrs. Vanderbilt's wrath—anything but me?" Suddenly, almost harshly, his arms were around her and his mouth was on hers, hungry and demanding. It was not the hesitant first kiss she'd expected, like that of the beaux who had adored her and, in their adoration, been a little afraid of her. She could smell that special fragrance she recognized every time she danced with him and had come to think of as Whit, and feel the roughness of his beard against her face, not rough really, but again just Whit, and taste the champagne on his tongue. Her hands were on his shoulders and through the soft fabric of his dinner coat she could feel the lean hard muscles, tensed to hold her, tensed because he wanted her. She sensed it all and realized with a shock the force of his passion. That and one other thing. In the warmth of his body pressed to hers and the heat of his mouth on hers and his hands rough and exciting against her skin, she knew the depth of her own desire as well. And she realized with a new force why she was a little afraid of Whit Morris.

* * *

The VanNest house was entirely dark by the time the Stutz crept up the circular drive.

"Would you like to drive over to see Lancelot work out tomorrow morning?" Whit asked.

"Is that what you do every morning?"

"Most of them."

"Then I'd like to go."

"You'll have to get up early. The crack of dawn."

"In that case I don't think I'll bother going to sleep. I think," Clemmie said, putting her arms around his neck and raising her face to his, "I'll just stay here with you until dawn."

"You'd be compromised," he said his mouth on hers.

"Irretrievably," she murmured, moving closer.

"I think," Whit said, removing her arms from his neck and getting out of the car, "I'd better see you in."

"Now who's afraid?" she taunted.

"Clemmie, my darling," he said, bending to kiss her lightly, "there are times when discretion is the better part of valor." His laughter was soft, but it carried up to the darkened window where Alison VanNest sat alone, staring down at her friend and the man she was supposed, according to all of Newport, to marry.

Chapter 2

ON FAIR MORNINGS the VanNests always breakfasted on the terrace. So pleasant, Grace VanNest always said, still painting pictures in her imagination, to watch the sun climbing up out of the bay, the flowers opening to the sun, the robins and bluejays dipping at the marble birdbath. This morning, however, a light rain had driven them inside. Still a pleasant room for breakfast, Grace always observed on inclement mornings. It was a formal dining room, but not too formal for breakfast, she insisted. Especially when the table was set with the linen place mats and the morning china. Grace knew for a fact that there were certain matrons in Newport who used gold plate or vermeil even for breakfast, but then what could one expect from *arrivistes*?

By the time Clemmie came down, however, most of the informal flower-strewn Lenox morning china had been removed. There was a single place left for her, and at another far down the long Chippendale table, her brother Adam sat finishing his breakfast. Clemmie was surprised to see him, but Adam wore his customary air, suggesting everything he did was carefully thought out. He might have driven all night to turn up at the VanNest breakfast table without warning, but he sat there eating ham and eggs as if breakfasting at the

51

VanNest table were something he did every morning. Everything about Adam was sturdy and reassuring. The calm gray eyes, the high intelligent forehead, the well-kept body of medium frame that wore clothes well, but not too well. The uniform of the day, dark blue blazer and white flannel trousers, made him look comfortable rather than dashing. It was hard to believe that Adam had been an aviator in the war. He presented an appearance of great determination, but there was nothing of the daredevil about him.

"What on earth brings you here?" Clemmie asked, returning his hug and presenting a cheek to be kissed. "I thought you and George had sworn off Newport forever. Too dull."

"You don't seem to find it that way. I talked to mother this morning—before Mrs. VanNest was down."

"Incidentally, where *are* Mother and Madame Malevolence?" Clemmie dropped her voice so the servants would not hear her description of their employer.

"You can't really blame her, Clemmie. She had the catch of Newport sewn up and then you came along."

"Then she didn't have him exactly sewn up, did she?"

"Well, I felt rather sorry for Alison. They all went off to some charity meeting and Alison looked pretty grim."

"Good Lord," Clemmie said, fingering the delicate George II spoon and thinking idly of monograms. CWM. "Why is everyone always feeling sorry for Alison. It isn't as if she's an ugly duckling. If she wants Whit Morris or anyone else she ought to fight for him."

"You've got a point there, only I'll tell you something, Clemmie. If I were a girl I wouldn't want to be up against you."

"Is that a compliment or an insult?"

"Merely an observation."

"You still haven't told me what brings you to Newport. Are you staying here?"

"No. Mrs. VanNest asked me to—I had the feeling

she'd be only too glad to trade your presence for mine at this point—but I'm staying with Tony Bayliss."

"Now I know what brings you here."

"What's that supposed to mean?"

"I hear he gives the wildest parties in Newport. Or rather offshore Newport. That's the funny thing about this place. It's so totally a woman's town. Women build the houses and furnish them and give the parties and run everything. And the men let them do it. They encourage them to do it. They hand over the money, and stay as far away from Newport as possible. When they do turn up, they keep to their yachts or hide out in the Reading Room drinking and telling off-color stories."

"How do you know about the Reading Room?"

"Honestly, Adam. It may be a private club, but it isn't exactly a private secret."

"I mean how do you know what goes on there?"

Clemmie smiled. "I'm not like the rest of the girls in this town. I've seen the parties and balls, and for the most part they're deadly dull. So I decided to find out about the rest. It's not too difficult. All you have to do is keep your eyes and ears open. I've heard about what goes on in the Reading Room and about the wild parties offshore. Will you take me to one of Tony Bayliss's?"

"I'll do better than that. There's some talk of cruising for a week or so on his boat. Would you like to come?"

"You know Mother wouldn't let me."

"All Mother knows about Tony Bayliss is that he's worth about five million and he's not married. Besides, you'll be well chaperoned. I'll be there. And Samantha Weymouth-Baldwin and her mother are going along."

"How do you know Samantha Weymouth-Baldwin?" Clemmie asked.

"Do you?"

"I've seen her at the Casino and at one or two parties. I was introduced to her at Fair Isles, but that's about all. Mother doesn't approve of her. Mother

53

doesn't approve of any divorcee, but she especially doesn't approve of her."

"Why her especially?" Adam asked quickly.

"Oh, you know, the usual talk."

"No, I don't know the usual talk."

"Don't jump at me, Adam. I'm not the one who disapproves of her." Clemmie looked across the table at her brother. "So we can thank Mrs. Weymouth-Baldwin for your sudden appearance. Mother isn't going to like that. And I shudder to think what Father would say if he knew."

"Well, neither of them knows, so I wish you'd keep it to yourself for a while."

"She must be years older than you, Adam."

"That's a rotten thing to say."

"Oh, my darling chivalrous brother, you are in bad shape, aren't you?"

"I'm not in bad shape, as you put it, Clemmie, but I don't see why everyone makes such a fuss about four years."

"And the fact that she's divorced."

"That was Baldwin's fault. She sued him for divorce—and won."

"Everything but a decent settlement. And everyone knows what that means. Baldwin let her sue, but the blame wasn't nearly so one-sided."

"Clemmie, this isn't like you."

"Adam, darling, I'm only playing the devil's advocate. I don't care if the beautiful Mrs. Weymouth-Baldwin—and she is beautiful, I'll give you that—is twenty years older than you and notorious on five continents." Clemmie saw the look on her brother's face. "I'm not saying she is, I'm just saying I wouldn't care if she were, but you might as well get used to the argument, because the family's bound to use it."

"Darn it, Clemmie, I'm a grown man. . . ."

"Would you like to hear the other side of the argument?" Clemmie began to imitate his voice. "Old enough to do as I please . . . served in the war . . .

proved myself in the railroad." She lapsed back into her own voice. "It isn't going to do a bit of good, and you know it. Father will put up with all sorts of scrapes—look at the way he forgives George again and again. Though I can't really blame George for that last thing. It's silly of him to go around proposing to every girl he wants to seduce, but any girl who would sue for breach of promise! She must be awfully plain or awfully stupid. Well, George and that lawsuit are beside the point. What I was saying is that Father will forgive a lot, but when it comes to marriage—not the promise of marriage, but marriage—that's something else. He's going to bring out the big guns for this one."

Adam said nothing, merely sat staring grimly down at his plate. He knew the truth of Clemmie's words, had known it for months now, know it and struggled against it ever since he'd fallen in love with Samantha Weymouth-Baldwin.

It was less than a year ago, but it seemed longer to Adam. It seemed impossible that only months ago he'd been reasonably happy, reasonably contented, involved in his work, pleasantly entertained by the company of two or three girls. Then he'd met Samantha.

He was in New York on business that week. Adam was not usually much affected by places or seasons, but that week in early October he'd felt the city coming alive. People walked more quickly down Fifth Avenue or darted through the traffic. The doorman at the hotel hailed cabs more briskly. Even the street noises did not grate on his nerves as they did during the heat of summer, and the lights of Broadway looked sharper and brighter. It was a wonderful time to be in town, and Adam felt himself keenly alive to every aspect of the city. Still, he didn't fool himself that the change in his attitude toward the city implied a similar change in New York's regard for him or the place he occupied in its social life, and he was surprised when the phone in his room at the Waldorf rang one morning and Polly Atherton invited him to dine that night. Or rather he was surprised at first by the fact that Polly Atherton should telephone him, and then it all fell into place. Someone had dropped out at the last minute and Polly was short a man for dinner. For Polly an unbalanced dinner table was a crisis that outstripped anything going on at the League of Nations, a crisis so serious that she would even telephone Adam Wilder and ask him to dine.

Polly had never liked Adam or, more to the point, approved of him. Not that she was stuffy. Far from it. Since her marriage to Tim Atherton right after the war she'd embraced the role of the modern woman, the sophisticated young matron, with a vengeance. Polly and Tim both came from old New York families, but she was determined to dominate new New York. She wore the latest fashions, read the newest books, or at least reviews of them, attended every opening night, quoted the latest witticism of the current social lion, and was determined to be shocked by nothing. It was for all these reasons, Adam supposed, that Polly Atherton disapproved of him. He was simply too unfashionable. She had only disdain for the fact that he'd chosen to transfer to Sheffield, the engineering school of Yale. She was impatient with him when he didn't recognize the names she dropped. He was not *au courant*. Her eyes became steely when he injected a word about someone as irrelevant as Mark Twain into her discussion of the latest best-seller. Before the war, when Adam and Tim were at Yale together, Polly had worked to sever the ties of friendship between them. Time had done a more effective job. But on that cool October day Polly Atherton needed an extra man for dinner and Adam Wilder was in town. It would be so wonderful to see him again, she cooed. So nice to reminisce about old times, she said. "Black tie, not white," she added crisply as she hung up.

The Athertons had the penthouse of one of those new skyscrapers that were springing up along Park Avenue. The first thing Adam noticed as he entered the large living room was not the striking view from the windows that ran the length of two walls, not the sleek black and white Art Moderne elegance achieved by Polly's "interior decorator," not the hearty greeting of Tim who seemed genuinely pleased to see him. All he could see in that crowded living room alive with the hum of well-modulated voices, was a young woman standing before the windows. She had dark gold hair and a delicately molded face, and when she turned, Adam saw her eyes. They were dark but full of lights. It seemed to Adam they glittered more brightly than the shimmering New York skyline behind her. There was something a little wild about the eyes, he thought.

Tim introduced her as Mrs. Weymouth-Baldwin. Was her husband one of those hyphenated Englishmen or was she divorced? Adam did not have time to find out before they went in to dinner.

He was not seated next to Mrs. Weymouth-Baldwin at dinner. Polly must have thought him too dull for the lively beauty who fenced wittily with the men on both sides of her. It was only after Adam had sat through the obligatory brandy and cigars, listening distractedly to talk of investments, the postwar slump, and the future of the economy, thinking all the time of the wild eyes and the way the candlelight had shone on the dark gold hair, that he found his way to Samantha's side. When they'd been introduced before dinner, he'd had time for no more than the customary greeting. Now he found that she and Polly were the dearest of friends, that she considered *The Emperor Jones* the best thing she'd seen on Broadway in ages, that she'd just returned from a summer in Montreux, and that the hyphenated name indicated a divorce somewhere in the recent past. Adam found the idea at once encouraging, disappointing, infuriating, and erotic. He envied the man who had possessed her. He marveled at the man who could have let her go.

Adam asked if he could see her home, but she said really, that was impossible. Her manner turned prim when she said it, but Adam thought of the divorce and looked into the eyes with the lights that no amount of propriety could dim, and felt confused. It was, he thought later in his hotel room, the first time a woman had made him feel that way.

He telephoned her the next morning at ten—he was sure his flowers had arrived by then—and asked her to dine. She said she had an engagement. He suggested she break it. He'd never done that before, either. She finally agreed to have tea with him.

The following day, the second after Polly's dinner party, Tim Atherton phoned and asked Adam to meet him for a drink. There was an empty cocktail glass in front of Tim when Adam joined him in the bar of the Yale Club that evening.

"Glad you started without me," Adam said. "I don't have much time."

"I know," Tim answered. "You're dining with Samantha and going on to see *Tip Top*. You must have had the devil's own time getting tickets at the last minute."

"I can see the girls have been talking." Adam was pleased. It must mean something that Samantha thought enough of their engagement to mention it to Polly.

Tim asked what he was drinking and ordered for both of them. Adam couldn't help noticing there was something distinctly uncomfortable about Tim's manner. He wondered if Atherton had a problem and had invited him for a drink to talk about it. Adam was willing to bet the trouble had to do with Polly. It must be impossible being married to a woman like that.

"About Mrs. Weymouth-Baldwin," Tim said, and Adam noticed the change. He'd called her Samantha before.

"What about her?"

"I know this isn't the place to discuss it. To this day my father won't mention a woman's name in a club . . ."

Ordinarily Adam would have been amused—he could picture Tim's old-fashioned propriety doing battle regularly with Polly's violent modernism—but at the moment he was too concerned about what Tim wanted to say about Samantha to be amused.

"But, hell, I can't see where else we can have a quiet drink and a few words after a long day. At any rate, it isn't as if it's the Knickerbocker or the Century. It's only a university club."

Adam was not sure what logic made the rules of behavior observed in a club proportionate to its exclusivity, but the question was not what concerned him at the moment. "A few words about what?" he asked impatiently.

"About Mrs. Weymouth-Baldwin. I've been thinking about this all day, thinking about it and wondering what was the right thing to do. Look, you know me, old man. I'm not one to carry stories, especially when they're probably only stories, but damn it, you and I go back a long way together. I like Samantha—Mrs. Weymouth-Baldwin," he corrected himself, "but you're one of my oldest friends."

"And as one of your oldest friends, as an old Grottie as well as an old Yalie, you're about to save me from something," Adam offered.

"As far as I can see, you've fallen for her pretty hard. If anyone had told me this would happen, I wouldn't have believed it. You weren't exactly the great lover back in New Haven. Oh, you had enough girls, all right, but you never went overboard about them. But the other night at our place I had the feeling Samantha could have asked you to jump off the terrace, and you'd have done it."

"That's going a bit far."

"Maybe, but you should have seen your face when I first mentioned her tonight. Lit up like a damn light bulb."

"Light bulbs burn out," Adam said, sure that what he felt for this woman never would.

"But some of them last for quite a while. Look, Adam, it isn't that I want to bring you down off that cloud and it certainly isn't that I want to gossip, but if you start seeing Samantha, you're going to hear stories, and I'd rather you heard them from me. At least that way, they won't be exaggerated."

"You mean she's a fallen woman because she's been divorced."

"It's a little more than that. There was a lot of talk during the divorce. A hell of a lot of talk."

"What kind of talk?"

Tim proceeded to tell everything he knew about the young tennis instructor at the Newport Casino and the divorce in which the husband rather than the wife was rumored to be the wronged party. The paucity of the settlement was reported to be Weymouth's price for playing the gentleman. When he finished, Adam was silent. He motioned to the waiter for another round of drinks, then turned back to Tim.

"You've told me all the rumors. Now tell me one more thing. Do you believe them?"

"Hell, no," Tim said immediately. "Sam's a great girl. She and Polly are like sisters," he added, a little irrationally.

The answer had come too quickly and too heartily, and Tim knew it. But his story had come too late for Adam.

He began going up to New York to see Samantha as often as possible. When he arrived without warning, as he occasionally did since the demands of the A&W did not always permit him to plan ahead, Samantha never broke an appointment for him, but she always found time to see him.

It was Samantha who brought up the specter of her scandalous past. Adam had, of course, never questioned her about it, but neither had he stopped thinking of it.

They were in Samantha's apartment on Sixty-ninth Street just off Fifth Avenue. It was common gossip that she'd got little from Baldwin and that her own family had no fortune, but nothing about the apartment or the way she lived in it suggested that Samantha worried about money. She and her mother—they shared the apartment, though Mrs. Weymouth had a habit of disappearing at all the right times—kept a maid, a cook, and a driver for the Brewster town car Samantha had won in the settlement. She didn't entertain often, but when she did have fifty for cocktails or a dozen in to dine, she did it with opulence as well as style. Samantha did not live extravagantly by the standards of the time or the expectations of her set, but she did live well. Adam recognized the fact and admired her for her skillful management. It never occurred to him that she might be managing on borrowed money. Love had not made him blind—he still worried about the gossip that surrounded her divorce—but it had made him slightly myopic.

That December afternoon when Samantha decided it was time to tell Adam about her past—her checkered past, she said jokingly—they had just come back from walking in Central Park. Mrs. Weymouth was conveniently out, as usual, and the apartment felt warm and intimate after their walk. Samantha struck a match to the logs in the hearth, and Adam felt so peaceful and perfectly happy that he was almost sorry when she said she wanted to tell him what had really happened. He regretted the intrusion of the unpleasant subject, but he was too interested not to listen.

"Do you want tea or a drink?" she asked. "Maybe we'd both better have a drink if I'm going to tell you about it."

He mixed two Manhattans at the cocktail wagon, carried them carefully across the room, and handed one to Samantha as he sat beside her on the sofa.

"I know you've heard stories," she began, and Adam tried to look innocent. "Please, Adam, don't pretend you haven't. I'm going to be honest about this, and I'd like you to be the same. I know people talk. There was a great deal of gossip during the divorce. It died down as those things always do, but it will never be entirely forgotten. You know how it is. We begin to be seen together and some altruistic soul decides he, or perhaps she, ought to warn you off."

Adam thought of that afternoon with Tim Atherton, and of the other men who'd told him the same story since then, told him less discreetly than Tim had.

"They say that Baldwin wouldn't give me a decent settlement because I was the guilty one. They say I was having an affair with the tennis instructor at the Casino. Isn't that what they've told you?"

He looked away from Samantha to the portrait of her over the mantel. Baldwin had commissioned it during their marriage, Samantha had told him. Obviously it was a part of their community property that Baldwin had no desire to hold on to. It was a formal portrait of a wistful-looking Samantha in a blue velvet gown slashed to a deep décolletage. The artist was good with color, especially skin tones, and the white throat and smooth shoulders were magnificent against the deep blue. Adam's eyes moved from the portrait back to its subject.

"Isn't that what they've told you?" she repeated.

"Something like that," he admitted.

"People can be so filthy," she said as much to herself as to him. "I'll tell you about the tennis instructor, Adam. I want to tell you the whole thing. Harry—his name was Harry Courtland—was the sweetest boy. From a very good family, really. Boston. But there was no money, so he coached tennis during the summer to pay his way through Harvard. Still, you're probably thinking that no matter how sweet he was, it were peculiar—and foolish—of me to befriend him. Well, it was, but that's how little I knew at the time. I knew almost nothing about people then, and less about men. My father had died when I was three and there was just Mother and I roaming around Europe trying to be frugal but cultured in little *pensions*. Mother had the idea—and I'm not sure she was wrong—that a European upbringing would be an asset to me. To be crude about it—and women always are about these things,

Adam—without money I'd need a drawing card in the marriage game."

"I shouldn't think you'd need any drawing card at all," he said. "It seems to me just being you and looking like you would be enough."

Samantha blushed, but she was not to be deflected from her story. "Actually, that was part of the problem. When we came back to New York—because after all, the only American girls who stand a chance with Europeans, at least Europeans of any standing, are heiresses—there were plenty of beaux. But at that age, at that particular game, beaux aren't exactly friends. You see, Adam, I'd never had a man as a friend. I didn't even think it was possible. I was suspicious of men because they always seemed to want something of me." She looked down at her hands folded demurely in her lap. "Perhaps it's indelicate of me to say it, but even my husband, even Baldwin, seemed that way. And then I met Harry. Harry was the only man—the only boy I should say, because he was really only a child—who didn't seem to want anything from me. Except perhaps a little understanding. All he really wanted was someone to talk to. He was terribly lonely in Newport. You can't imagine how hard it was on the poor boy, being treated half like a servant, half like a pet. He was in an impossible position. As good if not better than most of those people, but since they had money and he didn't, they thought they could patronize him. I imagine I was the only one who didn't patronize him. And he was terribly grateful for it. That's all there was, Adam. Harry's gratitude and my kindness. It was the simplest of friendships, but of course, Newport had to turn it into more. Especially after that night Mrs. Bentwin saw us on the last ferry. It was only the purest coincidence that Harry and I had run into each other, but no one would ever believe that. They were enjoying themselves too much to be bothered by the truth.

"Then why did I divorce Baldwin? That's what you're wondering, isn't it? If Harry and I were no more than friends and if the rest was merely vicious gossip, why did I divorce Baldwin?"

It was exactly what he'd been wondering. Adam wasn't surprised. He'd discovered Samantha often knew what he was thinking.

"Because Baldwin believed the gossip, and I couldn't go on living with a man who didn't trust me, a man who'd believe other people's rumors over my word," Samantha finished quietly. Her eyes holding Adam's were bright, but steady. The implication was clear, the challenge direct. If Adam did not believe her, he might as well say so and be on his way. But he did believe her. The simple, straightforward tone in which she'd told the story, the earnestness of her expression, even the way she held herself a little away from him as if she were afraid of being hurt again convinced him, and he told her as much.

When she walked him to the door a little later and bid him good-bye, Adam took her in his arms and kissed her, and she returned his kiss with an ardor and a promise that were all he'd hoped for.

Back at the hotel Adam thought of her story. He hated Baldwin and all the gossiping old women for doubting her. He remembered the way she'd looked as she'd told him the story and the way her mouth had felt on his and her body against his own and wondered how they could have doubted her. But the next day in the cold gray light of a December morning, he remembered the uncomfortable speed of Tim Atherton's reassurance after he'd told him the terrible story, and the sneers he'd seen on the faces of other men who'd repeated the gossip, and he wasn't so confident. And when the telephone rang and he heard Elias's voice running on about business, Adam thought of what his father would say to the stories and to Samantha.

That was the first time he'd tried to stay away from her. He didn't return to New York for a month, but at the end of that month Adam found the flame she had

ignited burned no less brightly. But the doubts still
flickered in his mind as well.

Adam turned from his own memories of Samantha
back to Clemmie's talk of her. "Well, for what it's
worth, Adam, I'm on your side. What does it matter
what people say about her if you two love each other?
Of course, I don't suppose Mother and Daddy will take
the same attitude. You're in for a devil of a fight, and
we both know it."

"Will you be nice to Samantha at least? She knows
it isn't going to be easy, but I think it would help if she
felt someone in the family weren't against her."

Clemmie looked at her brother skeptically. From
what she'd seen of Samantha Weymouth-Baldwin, the
woman wasn't such a fragile flower. Clemmie remembered a story she'd overheard Mrs. Sherman telling her
mother. It concerned Samantha and, of all people, the
late J. P. Morgan.

It seemed that Samantha's childhood abroad wasn't
quite so bleak after all. One summer before the war
Mrs. Weymouth had been a member of a party Morgan
had taken to Egypt. Little Samantha had gone along,
although Mrs. Sherman suggested that Samantha hadn't
been quite so little as she liked to suggest. "She was
eighteen if she was a day," Mrs. Sherman had hissed.

One morning in Cairo, Morgan had gone to the
gold bazaar and returned to the hotel laden with neck-
laces and bracelets and an assortment of fabulous orna-
ments which he'd spread on a table in the sitting room
of his suite. The party had gathered there before lunch,
and Morgan insisted that the ladies take their choice.
The women hung back despite his urgings that he'd
bought the trinkets with them in mind, but then "little
Samantha" had sprung forward and chosen a handsome
gold choker from the table. After that the women in
the party showed no reluctance about dividing the
spoils. Clemmie remembered the story now, but she
wasn't going to report it to Adam. He looked unhappy
enough as it was.

"Of course I'll be nice to her, Adam. Who knows when I'll want you to return the favor?"

It took little effort for Clemmie to be nice to Samantha. At her best Samantha was a very likable woman, and she was going out of her way to be at her best for Adam's family. Marriage to Adam Wilder wasn't Samantha's last hope, but it was her last spectacular chance.

"After all, you're not getting any younger," Samantha's mother had an unpleasant habit of pointing out.

"Twenty-nine is not exactly over the hill, Mother, Samantha would answer, rubbing cream carefully into her skin and trying to overlook the delicate lines that were beginning to gather at the corner of each eye.

"We wouldn't have had this problem if you'd had the sense to hold on to Graham Baldwin. Or at least if you'd had the sense not to put yourself in a compromising position. When I think of the fortune you threw away for that, that—"

"Mother, we've been through this again and again. Anyway, things have turned out for the best. I love Adam and I never loved Graham."

Mrs. Weymouth looked at her daughter skeptically, and changed the subject. "Miss Spinner's sent another bill. I'm afraid you won't be able to buy your fall wardrobe there."

"Don't worry about Miss Spinner. I'm sure her bill will be paid in time for the new season."

"You're awfully sure of yourself," Mrs. Weymouth said.

Samantha looked at her reflection in the dressing-table mirror. She had removed the last traces of cream and her skin shone a warm pink beneath the dark gold hair. She looked all of twenty-one, she thought. "No, Mother, I'm awfully sure of Adam."

But when Adam had been in Newport for a week and they were no closer to marriage, Samantha began to fear that perhaps her mother was right. The idea infuriated her, and so when Adam suggested an afternoon sail with Clemmie and Whit Morris in Whit's small sloop, Samantha refused more sharply than she meant to.

"I don't blame her for being angry with you," Clemmie said as she tailed for Adam while he trimmed the jib. At the tiller Whit tried to look more interested in the set of the sails than Clemmie's words. It was like her to launch into the subject in front of him. He knew Adam Wilder, but not well enough to be privy to his personal problems.

"Either you're going to marry her or you're not," Clemmie continued.

Adam leaned back in the cockpit and looked at Whit helplessly.

"I'd offer to leave," Whit said, "but there doesn't seem to be any place to go."

"Stop being so polite, Whit. You know about Adam and Samantha, and there's no point in pretending you don't."

"All the same," Whit said, "Adam may not want to discuss it in front of me."

"All the same," Adam said, looking pointedly at Clemmie, "Adam may not want to discuss it at all. He may think it's none of his little sister's business."

"Then you should have said that in the first place," Clemmie answered. "But you came up here talking about it and asking me to be nice to her, and now I think you're the one who's not being nice, or at least fair, to Samantha. You can't keep her dangling while you try to get up the courage to tell Mother and Father." Clemmie moved to the low side of the boat and perched on the railing so her legs trailed in the water.

"You slow us down that way," Whit said.

"Are we in a hurry?" Clemmie asked.

"I thought you were the one concerned with speed."

Clemmie ignored the comment. "Why don't you simply elope and get it over with?"

Whit kept his eyes on the sails, but he was smiling. "That's the way Clemmie would do it."

"Well, I certainly wouldn't sit around all summer waiting for someone to get up the nerve to speak to his family. I'd hope the man I was going to marry would have more courage than that."

"Clemmie," Whit laughed, "the man who marries you has courage by definition."

"You're right," Adam said to Clemmie. He'd been telling himself the same thing all week. "I'll telephone Father tonight."

Clemmie swung her legs back into the boat and stretched, and Whit could not help noticing that they looked as sleek and brown as the teak deck he kept so carefully polished.

"And he'll be up on tomorrow's train," Clemmie pronounced.

She was right, of course. Elias Wilder did not take the time to have his private railroad car returned from Newport. He emerged from the public parlor car the following evening looking tired, disheveled, and ten years older than his sixty-one years. The gaunt face from behind which he could manipulate a million dollars' worth of stock without revealing a single emotion was taut with anger.

On the ride from Newport to Wickford Junction to meet his father's train, Adam had told himself there was nothing to fear. He was a grown man now, an equal of his father, but as he watched Elias's lean frame descend the three steps to the station platform, and saw the stern expression in the gray eyes that had never held anything but kindness for him, Adam was unmistakably frightened.

Elias started off down the platform at a clip, and Adam, who was a few inches shorter than his father, had to make an effort to keep up with him. Damn if he didn't make him feel like a child scampering to keep pace with an adult.

Elias was moving in that determined way of his, the

upper part of his body held a little forward as if ready for combat. Even the carefully custom-tailored English suit couldn't camouflage that aggressive aura.

"Since the Vanderbilts spend so much time in Newport, you'd think they'd build a decent branch straight through from New York." The gray mustache twitched angrily as he spoke. "Had to wait an hour in Westerly. And the windows in the car were filthy. If any man on the A&W sent a parlor car out in that condition I'd have his hide—and his job."

Adam knew his father's anger was meant for him rather than the New York Central, but he was willing to prolong the small talk as long as possible. "Most of the Vanderbilts and everyone else come up by private car. Or boat."

"Couldn't wait," Elias grumbled. "Wanted to get up here and get back."

"More trouble with the brotherhood?"

"It's the government's fault. Ever since they nationalized the lines for the war they're ready enough to tell us what we can buy, but ask them for a little help once we've bought a line and want to lay off a few men and they turn their back. When I think of the good a single National Guard unit would do . . ."

"Are you going to call in those men from Philadelphia again?"

"I don't think we'll have to resort to that. I left it in Hendreich's hands. George wanted to take care of things, but he'd only make them worse."

"I don't know . . . George gets along pretty well with the workmen."

"Your brother gets along well with the workmen when he walks through the yard saying hello, and he's good enough to buy drinks or pass his flask around when he runs into them in one of those disreputable roadhouses where he spends so much time. But he doesn't know the first thing about handling men."

"You're always too hard on George."

"So you and your mother say, but I don't think so.

I've been waiting a long time for him to settle down, and I'm getting a little impatient."

"He's settled down," Adam said. "More or less. Just because he shows an occasional weakness for a skirt. . . ."

"A skirt?" Elias growled. "Anything in a skirt is more like it."

The conversation had taken them out of the small station and across the street to Adam's car. The sleek Marmon, one of three Elias had bought for his children, suddenly seemed out of place to Adam. It was racy-looking, designed for a jaunt in the country or some speedy hijinks along a back road, but Adam knew there were no jaunts or hijinks in store for him tonight.

Elias folded himself into the car without pleasure. It was not built to his taste or frame. He preferred a higher touring car. "But it's not George and his women I'm concerned about now. It's you, Adam. Where on earth did you get this damn-fool notion? I would expect something like this from your brother but not from you. Well, we can't sit here in the street discussing it. Is there a decent restaurant in this town? I want to have this out right now. Stephen VanNest is a perfectly honorable man as far as I know, but I don't intend to conduct my family business under his roof."

There was a hotel a few blocks from the station. The simple brick façade and musty lobby furnished with a threadbare rug and a few worn leather chairs and chipped tables indicated that it was far from fashionable. The small dining room was almost empty except for the occasional traveling salesman who sat, straw hat on the chair by his side, newspaper on the table, trying to decide between Yankee pot roast and chicken pot pie. A large fan whirred overhead, but it did little to cool the room.

"Is it blackmail?" Elias asked as soon as they were seated. "Tell me right off if it is, and we'll take care of it. Lord knows we've taken care of worse for George."

Elias Wilder rarely misjudged a man, but he'd misjudged his son this time. There were any number of maneuvers that might have played on Adam's loyalty to his father, but insulting the woman Adam loved, insulting her as none of the gossips had, was not one of them. The fear he'd felt as he watched his father in the station evaporated in the heat of his anger.

"I'd like you to apologize for that, Father," Adam said.

"Apologize for what? Suggesting that you might have got yourself in a compromising situation?"

"For suggesting that Samantha might be the kind of woman who would do something like that."

"Do something like blackmailing you, or something like providing a cause for blackmail?" Elias asked calmly.

"Either one. Samantha is a lady."

"I daresay. Nevertheless I'm sure we both know that can mean a variety of things these days. What about that business with her divorce?"

"Divorce isn't a crime."

"Perhaps not, but it is a failure. But that's not what I meant. Why didn't she get a decent settlement? Baldwin's worth millions. She got a twenty-five-thousand-dollar settlement and no alimony."

"How do you know that?" Adam had heard all the stories, but he'd never got the actual figures.

"I take it that means you didn't know."

"I know Samantha has no money."

"It isn't the money I care about, Adam. It's the reason for not having it. There was talk Baldwin could have divorced her—without a cent." Elias looked thoughtful for a moment. "You weren't mixed up in that business, were you?"

"I was still in France when Samantha was divorced, Father."

"Well, that's a relief. It would be dishonorable enough to have broken up her marriage, but to break it up and then not marry her . . ."

"But I'm going to marry her," Adam said.

"I forbid it, Adam. I don't think I can make my feelings any clearer than that. I won't make threats. I won't talk about your inheritance or anything like that. I'll simply tell you I forbid it."

Both men were silent as the waiter arrived with the steaks they had ordered. Adam looked at the meat lying brown and unappetizing on the heavy white plate, and pushed it away. Elias, determined to show his son that the matter was solved and he was no longer troubled by it, cut into the unwanted dinner.

"But you haven't even let me tell you about her," Adam said.

Elias cut another piece of meat. "I know as much about Mrs. Weymouth-Baldwin as I want to. She's divorced. She's four years older than you. She hasn't a penny. And she has attracted more gossip than any woman in her position ought to."

"But it was just gossip. If you only knew her . . ."

"Where there's smoke there's fire." Elias looked up from his dinner, saw the pain in his son's eyes, and knew he'd struck something.

As much as Adam wanted to believe it was only gossip, he couldn't. The old images chased one another around in his imagination. He pictured Samantha as she'd looked that night when she'd first told him about Harry Courtland and her divorce. He saw her, lovely and cool and distant, being kind to a young man simply because no one else had taken the trouble to be kind to him and because Samantha knew what it was like to be poor and something of an outsider. But he remembered the way she'd kissed him that night and many nights since then, remembered the wild lights that danced in her eyes and the laugh that said she knew more than the prim divorcee ever admitted to knowing. He pictured Samantha in the arms of a strange man, not young and lonely and ostracized, but handsome and hungry and opportunistic. Scenes of passion rioted in his mind as they had for months now, and Elias saw the toll they took.

"Listen, my boy," Elias said, pushing the half-eaten steak away. The anger was gone now, and Elias felt only concern, concern for the son and heir who was the repository of all his hopes for the future. Elias loved all his children, but he counted on Adam.

"I know what it looks like to you. I come blustering up here, shouting about the woman you love, insulting her in your eyes, saying you mustn't marry her. I know what I look like to you—an unfeeling old bird—but that's not the whole story. I've given this a great deal of thought, Adam. A great deal." Elias looked up at the whirring fan thoughtfully, then back at his son. "Men like you, Adam, men like us," Elias spoke haltingly as if searching for the right words, "frequently go through life caring only about their work, only about the things they're building. Love, or what the poets call love, simply doesn't often happen to them. But if it does, it happens with a bang.

"Perhaps I'm not putting this very well," Elias continued. "What I'm trying to say is, I never wanted it not to happen to you. I never wanted you not to fall in love. It's a better thing for a man, especially a man like you, if he does. It's a sad thing if he doesn't."

Adam noticed the way his father slid from first person to third and back, and wondered for a moment about his parents' relationship.

"I wanted it to happen to you, but I always thought it would happen with a nice girl. . . ."

"Samantha is a nice girl."

"Mrs. Weymouth-Baldwin is a divorced woman, a divorced woman who's attracted quite a lot of talk. That's not my definition of a nice girl. Don't you see, Adam, it isn't only you I'm worried about. It isn't only this generation of Wilders I'm thinking of. It's the next and the one after that. You'll inherit the railroad. You know that. And I expect it to be passed on to your sons and grandsons. I don't see Mrs. Weymouth-Baldwin—less specifically, I don't see a divorced woman who's steeped in scandal—as the mother and grandmother of those future generations of Wilders." Elias stopped for a moment and looked gravely at his son. "What I've been trying to say, Adam, is that I don't dismiss the depth of your feeling for the woman, but more than your feelings are at stake. More than the passion of one man for one woman is at stake. An entire—well, the future of the railroad and our family is at stake."

Adam wondered what his father had been about to say. An entire dynasty?

"In the interest of the family and the future, I'm asking you to give up this woman. I know it won't be easy, Adam, but you're certainly old enough to know that many things in life aren't easy." Elias looked around the room, deserted now except for a single traveling salesman two tables away. "I have an idea. Why don't you go away for a while? We'll get along without you. Be good experience for George. Let him do some of the work for a change. Go to Europe. Or better yet, head west, all the way west. Go someplace new and different and away from this woman. I don't say it will be a cure, Adam, but it will be an antidote. I promise you that. As I said, I don't make light of your feelings, but neither do I believe that you're not man enough to overcome them and do the right thing. And the right thing is to get away from this woman and stay away."

"Don't you think I've tried? I've told myself all the things you have. I thought if I could just stay away from her for a month . . . but at the end of the month it wasn't any better than it was the day I left her. That's why I came up here. I had to see her. Don't you understand that?"

"Then, by God, make her your mistress, Adam, but don't marry her. You'll be ruining your life."

"She isn't like that." This time there was no anger in Adam's voice. "In spite of all the gossip, Samantha isn't like that."

"You mean she's holding out for the Wilder name," Elias said.

"Please don't talk that way about her," Adam said miserably. "I'm going to marry her and she's going to be your daughter-in-law, so I wish you wouldn't speak that way about her."

Elias wiped his mouth with his napkin, placed it beside his plate, and signaled the waiter. "Mrs. Weymouth-Baldwin may succeed in becoming your wife, Adam, but she will never be my daughter-in-law. And if you marry her, it will change things between us. I think you know what I mean. I'm not threatening you, but you must see just how serious I am about this business. I'm determined to keep you from marrying her. I'm determined to keep you from making a damn fool of yourself and ruining our family and your life in the bargain."

"It may be your family, but it's my life."

Compared to his father's words, Adam's sounded weak and childish in his ears. But for Elias they had a terrible force. "Adam," he said, and his eyes were more eloquent than any words. They were the eyes of a man who had been stabbed in the back and was shocked by the treachery.

"What I meant was that it's no good trying to tell people how to live their lives. Especially when it comes to something like this."

"And it's no good sitting by and watching your own son throw his life away. Don't marry her, Adam. I beg you not to marry her."

"I'm in love with her."

The simplicity of Adam's statement stopped him, but Elias told himself this was only the first skirmish. He was not finished yet. He took a gold pocket watch from his vest and opened it. "Well, I don't suppose we're going to settle anything this minute, and I told your mother we'd reach Newport by ten. In the meantime I want you to think about our conversation. You have a fine future, Adam. Don't throw it away on some fortune hunter with a past."

"Please, Father."

"There's a lot worse I could call her." And Elias was fairly sure he'd use all the names before the battle was over.

If Elias Wilder had been displeased with reports of his son's choice of a wife—he refused to meet Samantha so he could judge from no more than reports—he was delighted with the young man he met with his daughter the next afternoon. He and his host Stephen VanNest had returned from a round of golf to find Alison, Clemmie, and Whit on the terrace having tea. It was Alison who introduced Whit, and Stephen VanNest seemed to have a well-seasoned affection for the young man; but whatever Whit's relations with the VanNests, there was no mistaking, as far as Elias was concerned, Whit's interest in his daughter or hers in him.

Elias Wilder was as acute a judge of women as of men, and his daughter was no exception. The fact that she was in many ways made in his mold—certainly more so than George and perhaps even more than Adam— made him more fond of her, but no less aware of her wiles or her weaknesses. Over the past few years he'd watched her with dozens of young men. She viewed them, Elias knew, only as possible conquests, just as at a time in his life he had viewed every railroad as a possible acquisition. But this Whit Morris was something else. There was an attraction there that went beyond mere conquest. And Elias guessed, watching Whit's eyes as they followed Clemmie across the terrace, that the feeling was reciprocated.

The young man had what Dolly would call beautiful manners, but they were not so beautiful in regard to his daughter that they camouflaged all instinct and feeling. Elias saw the way Whit Morris inclined his body toward Clemmie when he spoke to her, saw the way he seemed to be listening for her voice even as he talked to someone else, saw the way the long slender hands touched Clemmie's as he took a cup of tea from her or passed a tray of cakes, touched hers as if they could not help doing so, and Elias knew that there was a powerful, almost palpable physical attraction between his daughter and Whit Morris.

"Nice young man," Elias said after Whit was gone. He'd said good-bye to both Clemmie and Alison with unfailing politeness, but there was no mistaking the look in his eyes as he'd stood over Clemmie uttering some parting joke. There was no mistaking it, and no one in the group had.

"Yes, we've known Whit for years," Stephen Van-Nest said pointedly. The thin aristocratic mouth smiled, but there was more warning than satisfaction in it. "And of course our families go back a long way together." The watery eyes narrowed a little as if they were gazing back over generations of Morrises and VanNests progressing hand in hand through history.

"Not like us newcomers, eh?" Elias had read his host correctly. Although Elias had inherited his coal mines, his own father had begun as a miner, and the real source of the Wilder wealth, the railroad, had been forged by Elias himself. The old VanNest land interests went back to colonial New York. But, Elias reasoned, thinking of Whitmore Vanderbilt Morris with some satisfaction, if the Morrises went back as far as the VanNests, the Vanderbilts clearly did not. Old Cornelius, the ferryboat captain, was barely a generation ahead of old Elias the miner.

"Now, that isn't what I meant, Eli," VanNest hastened to reassure his guest. "I was just reminiscing about how long we've known Whit—and his family. Why he and Alison practically grew up together. So did Whit's father Nicholas and I. I imagine the same thing's true in Pennsylvania," VanNest said, certain that nothing could be further from the truth, at least outside of Philadelphia. The idea of an old Scranton that might compare with an old New York was ludicrous to him. "Families just going on generation after generation, living the same kinds of lives, believing the same kinds of things, raising their children the same way, marrying each other."

"In that case," Elias said, "maybe it's time for some new blood. You don't want to get like those royal families in Europe, do you? All kinds of madness and infirmity there." Elias smiled to himself. He knew VanNest found him a little rough, but he knew too that VanNest did not underestimate his intelligence or his abilities. He had scored his point.

"He's a good catch, a darn good catch," Elias said to his daughter when they were alone.

"Aren't you jumping to conclusions, Daddy?"

"Don't play the demure little lady with me, Clemmie. I know you too well. I saw you with Morris—and him with you."

Clemmie did not say, and for once Elias did not see, that she was not being demure; she was sincerely worried. Everyone seemed to think she'd won Whit Morris. Mr. and Mrs. VanNest hated her for it. Alison reproached her with that sad, wounded manner for it. Her parents seemed pleased with her for it. But Clemmie was not nearly so sure of her triumph. She knew that Whit liked her, that, more important, he wanted her. But in what way. When they were alone together he made her feel there was nothing and no one in the world beyond the two of them. But then he'd say things, like that comment the other afternoon when they'd gone sailing—"the man who marries you has courage by definition"—and Clemmie wondered. And he was still scrupulously considerate of Alison. It was entirely possible that he was intrigued by Clemmie, attracted to Clemmie, but had every intention of marrying Alison.

Clemmie remembered an incident of several years ago. She hadn't thought of it in some time, but it had come back to her last night as she'd lain in bed watching the sliver of moon through the trees beyond the window. How long ago was it? Five years? Six? The end of her first year at Miss Plymouth's, and although the stigma of "new girl" had not yet vanished, it was definitely beginning to fade. That was one of the reasons she'd had the courage to hope. And as the week after tryouts passed, and one girl after another stopped her in the corridors to tell her how marvelous she'd been when she'd read for the part of Rosalind in the school production of *As You Like It,* hope had turned to certainty. The part was Clemmie's, and Alison, her only serious rival, didn't stand a chance, or so all the girls implied. Only something had gone wrong, and remembering it now, years later, Clemmie could still feel the hurt and shame she'd experienced when the cast was posted. Standing with a group of girls in the main hall of the classroom building, her eyes had fixed on the crucial line immediately: *Rosalind . . . Alison VanNest.*

"It's a shame," one girl had muttered, but Clemmie knew she didn't mean it. Alison was the winner and now all the girls who had sworn Clemmie was sure to get the part conveniently forgot their predictions.

"It doesn't matter," Clemmie had said casually and slipped away from the group. She was not going to permit anyone to see just how much it did matter.

Clemmie wished she hadn't remembered the incident just now. Losing the part to Alison had been bad enough at the time, but losing to her when Clemmie and everyone else had been so sure she'd win suddenly seemed ominous.

". . . but as much as I approve, Clemmie, I won't leave you a single A & W stock." Her father's voice called her back. "It's not that I disapprove of the match, you understand. Far from it. I don't see how you could do better. But I won't have A & W stock falling into Vanderbilt hands. The next thing I know my railroad will be owned by the New York Central. I've worked too long and hard to make the A & W what it is to have that happen. So you won't get any A & W stock, but there are still the mines. I don't think Mr. Morris will object to a few coal mines instead of the railroad. If I'm any judge of men, and I'll be darned if I'm not, it isn't your fortune he's marrying you for."

"But he isn't marrying me at all. He hasn't said a word about it."

"He will, Clemmie. Give him time. You know only one side of the young man. I'm sure it's a very charming side, but it's also a romantic side. Well, I'm accustomed to looking for something else in men, and I saw it in your Mr. Morris. He isn't quite as devil-may-care as he seems. Oh, he may be in some matters, I'll grant you that, but about something like marriage he'd be more deliberate. Especially in this situation." Elias raised his eyes to the windows above the terrace where Alison VanNest might be expected to be dressing for dinner. "Whit Morris isn't the sort to rush into marriage," Elias said quietly. "He may not even know that he's thinking of marriage, but I watched him with you this afternoon, Clemmie, and I can assure you he is. Give him time. He already knows he's in love with you. Now give him time to get used to the idea of marrying you and not—" Elias's voice dropped to a whisper "—Alison VanNest."

Just as Elias was sure Whit Morris would behave in one way, so Grace VanNest was certain he would do exactly the opposite—with a little help from her daughter. She had brought Alison up carefully and was pleased with the result. Alison was a good child and, more important, as far as Grace was concerned, a perfect lady. Which was more than could be said for Clemmie Wilder. Grace and Dolly had been friends since they were younger than their own daughters were now, but she couldn't help disapproving of Dolly's daughter—and regretting she'd ever invited her. It had been one thing when Clemmie was a child—a rather ill-mannered, spoiled child, Grace had always thought—and couldn't do much damage, but she had grown into a beautiful, headstrong woman and had shown that given the chance she'd do a good deal of damage. If Grace could have terminated the Wilders' visit, she would have, but that would have been not only rude, but stupid. Whit's infatuation with Clemmie must not be given such importance. Grace was fairly certain that it was no more than an infatuation. She'd known Whit all his life, watched him go from one girl to another, but always return to his firm affection for Alison. That was simply the way Whit was, perhaps the way he would always be, Grace thought, but there would be enough time to worry about that after the wedding. In that trait he took after his Uncle Quentin rather than his father.

Grace smiled for a moment, thinking of Quentin and wondering why Dolly hadn't the sense to see the connection herself and warn Clemmie that Whit might toy with her, but he'd come back to Alison in the end. Providing Alison gave him a little help, and that was precisely what worried Grace. The quiet, good-natured streak in her daughter that Grace had counted on to hold Whit in the long run was no match for Clemmie in close battle. Even Alison must see that she couldn't expect Whit to come back to her without some effort on her part, but she seemed resigned, almost willing, to hand Whit over to Clemmie without a struggle. Clearly Grace would have to speak to Alison at the first opportunity, and she found it on the way back from the Casino one afternoon when Clemmie had decided to stay on for another game of tennis with Adam and Samantha. They had coaxed Whit into being a fourth, although to be sure he'd needed little enough coaxing.

Grace had barely been able to conceal her anger as she'd led her daughter through the half-deserted gallery. When they reached the door of the rambling wooden building that served as the clubhouse, she'd stopped for a moment and taken a deep breath. There would be women inside, women who would notice the flush on Grace's usually pale cheeks. She squared her bony shoulders, as if challenging anyone to suggest that something was wrong, and lifted her sharp chin a few inches. The cold eyes stared straight ahead as she crossed the lounge with Alison at her side.

When she reached the safety of the familiar Dusenberg, Grace told the driver to take the long way home, rolled up the window between the front seat and back, and turned to her daughter. "You should have stayed, Alison."

"The five of us couldn't very well play," Alison said miserably. She'd been telling herself the same thing.

"Samantha said she'd played once today and would be happy to watch."

"Samantha was only being polite, Mother."

"Well, there was no reason you couldn't have taken advantage of her politeness. Or," Grace said, trying to hide the anger in her voice, "Clemmie could have watched."

Alison laughed, but there was no mirth to it. "Clemmie watch? You know better than that."

"Are you going to let that girl walk off with everything without even putting up a fight, Alison?"

"Everything?"

"You know exactly what I mean. Whit Morris."

"You talk as if Whit were a trophy that went to the girl who played the best game."

Grace's eyes held her daughter's for a moment. They were more expressive than words.

"Maybe you're right, Mother, but I'm simply no good at the game. And Clemmie's awfully good at it. She always has been."

"You don't even try."

"Try to be a carbon copy of Clemmie Wilder? Why would Whit want the copy if he can have the original?"

Grace looked at her daughter in surprise. She was more aware of the problem than Grace had thought. And perhaps wiser about it.

"We both know Whit, Mother. Clemmie isn't the first girl this has happened with." Unlike her mother, Alison did not add that she would probably not be the last. Marriage, she was certain, would change Whit. Surely that was what marriage was all about. "I can only pray it will turn out like all the others, and Whit will tire of her. If he does, he knows I'll be here waiting for him. It may not be the best way, but it's the way I am. And Whit knows it. I'm afraid Whit knows me as well as I know him."

"Perhaps you're right, dear. All the same, I can't help wishing you'd make a little more of an effort. Sometimes that girl makes me so angry. . . ."

"I know exactly what you mean, Mother. And who knows, maybe one of these days I'll get angry enough myself to do something. But I wouldn't count on it."

Elias stayed in Newport less than forty-eight hours. It was more than enough time, he reasoned. If he couldn't convince Adam in two days, he'd never convince him. But Elias felt certain he had convinced him. The defenses had begun to crumble. Adam had not said he wouldn't marry Mrs. Weymouth-Baldwin, but he no longer swore he would. And when Elias spoke of her in that deprecating way that implied misconduct and scandal beyond Adam's most horrible nightmares, he continued to protest, but without the old conviction.

Elias's last words to Adam were much the same as those he'd uttered at dinner two days earlier, and Elias felt sure as he boarded the New York train and waved good-bye to the unhappy-looking young man on the platform, that his words would be heeded.

Alone in a corner of the lower piazza that ran the length of the old frame building housing the exclusive Reading Room, Adam was not so sure. In fact, it seemed to him he was not sure of anything these days, or at least not for more than an hour or two at a time. Alone with Samantha, he was certain he would marry her, sure he could not go on living unless he did. In conversation with Elias, as he had been almost constantly for the past two days, he saw the folly of marrying Samantha. He loved her, wanted her, craved her with a force that was more instinct than emotion, but he didn't trust her. Sometimes he believed the story she'd told him of the incident with the tennis instructor, other times he knew it was only a story, knew it with a rage born of jealousy. He hated this Harry Courtland who tramped through his imagination, handsome in his tennis whites, lethally attractive to Samantha. And he hated the idea of future Harry Courtlands. That was the real obstacle to marrying Samantha. Not her past but their future. He'd always be expecting another Harry Courtland. Marriage to Samantha was, therefore, impossible. Separation from Samantha, however, was unimaginable. And so it went, round and round in Adam's mind, an exhausting treadmill. He'd gone walking alone above the ocean this afternoon, avoiding the Cliff Walk and Bailey's Beach for the more solitary rocks and cliffs near Breton's Point because he'd wanted to work things out, but he hadn't been able to. His indecision infuriated him. Adam had always admitted he lacked certain traits, but he'd never thought decisiveness was one of them. Until now.

Late in the afternoon, when it became apparent that no amount of climbing or hiking or staring off across Rhode Island Sound was going to put an end to his indecision, he'd repaired to the Reading Room. It was one place, probably the only place on the island of Newport, where one could enjoy a whiskey in solitude. The three older men at the end of the piazza had looked up and nodded at his arrival, but they had not intruded on his privacy. The Reading Room, like any decent men's club, provided companionship when it was sought and permitted antisocial behavior when it was desired.

The drink, however, did not settle his thoughts any more than the solitary walk had. Alternatives continued to go round and round and he kept remembering things Elias had said during his stay. "If you marry her, it will change things between us. I think you know what I mean." Adam could imagine what his father meant: the railroad would not be his after all. Adam told himself he didn't care, was not the kind of man who could be bought, even by Elias, even for so high a price as the A & W. There was some truth to the thought. Influenced by his desire to have the railroad, he would go out of his way to prove that he was not influenced by it. In fact, Elias's threat might have been a mistake. It was almost a challenge to Adam to prove that he was an honorable man.

From within the building he dimly heard Whit Morris's voice. Either he'd been upstairs all along or Adam had been so lost in his own thoughts he hadn't even noticed his arrival. Whit came striding out on the piazza now, and Adam was surprised at how glad he was to see him. He'd thought he wanted solitude, but he'd had enough of it for one day. He'd welcome Whit's company.

"Another fugitive from Newport's softer charms," Whit said and waited for Adam's invitation to take the wicker chair next to him. Although Whit was a member and Adam only a guest, the rule of privacy still applied. "Some days," Whit went on, stretching white-flanneled legs before him, "when there are too many lunch parties and too much tea offered by all those chirping voices, I can't wait to get away." He looked down the piazza to the three elderly men at the other end of it. Although one was speaking and the other two listening attentively, they all wore the same expression of sleepy self-satisfaction. It was impossible to tell whether the speaker was recounting a ribald story or sharing a tip on some current stock manipulation. All three expressions would have been the same in either case.

"And then when I get here," Whit went on, "I can't wait to get away. The old boys set this place up as a refuge from the ladies, but they've made it almost as dull as their wives have made Newport. A little more whiskey and a little less restraint with language, but that's about the only difference. Otherwise we might as well be in some dowager's drawing room. Sometimes," Whit said looking through half-closed eyes at the traffic that milled about the corner of Bellevue Avenue and Church Street, "I dream about doing something to shake them up. Like the time old James Gordon Bennett got that English captain to ride his horse onto the piazza and into the front room. Sometimes I dream about driving my Stutz right up the stairs and across," he dropped his voice, "old Mr. Finchot's toes. But the Stutz would only get scratched and I'd only end up feeling sorry for old man Finchot. So much for dreams of shaking things up."

Listening to Whit, Adam understood some of the attraction between him and Clemmie, only Clemmie, Adam knew, would have driven the Stutz up onto the porch and the consequences be damned. "The question is," Adam said, testing the waters, "why you stay?"

Whit looked at him closely, wondering if Adam really didn't know or only wanted him to admit the reason. He was thoughtful for a moment, then laughed. "I keep asking myself the same question. I hadn't planned to stay this long, and I really ought to get back to town." Whit thought of the New York Central takeover of the Dayton Southbound Railroad, but said nothing. He might consider Adam a friend, but he would always see the A & W as a competitor, albeit a minor one. "Every morning I tell myself I'll leave tomorrow. And every evening just being with your sister," Whit added silently, "convinces me I won't."

"I know exactly what you mean," Adam said.

"But I heard you were leaving."

Adam looked at Whit in surprise. He'd kept telling himself he'd leave Newport and Samantha, but he hadn't mentioned the fact to anyone. "Tony Bayliss said there's some talk of a cruise."

"Oh, that." To Adam a cruise on Bayliss's yacht wasn't leaving Newport, it was taking it along.

"Ought to have a good time. Say what you want about Bayliss"—and they both knew there was a good deal that could be and was said about him—"he throws a good party. I'd rather go off for a week or two on his boat than go back to town." It was what everyone, including Whit himself, expected him to say, but it was not entirely true. He enjoyed being a man of leisure, a sportsman, but he enjoyed his work at the Central more than the sportsman image—a very useful one in business—allowed him to admit.

"Well, if you'd like to join us . . . that is, if it comes off at all . . ." Samantha and Bayliss were making plans, but Adam was not at all sure he was willing to go along with them.

"Thanks, old man, but I'm afraid not this time." The idea of a cruise without Clemmie was not in the least attractive to him. Of course, the idea of a cruise with Clemmie and without the awkwardness of Alison's presence was something else entirely. Whit stood abruptly, as if to drive such disloyal thoughts from his mind, and looked at his watch. He knew the three men at the end of the piazza were watching him and disapproving.

"See young Morris with his wristwatch?" they'd say when he was gone. "Damn affected," they'd say. "He's not in the trenches now. Why doesn't he carry a pocket watch like a gentleman?"

"Back to the fray," Whit said to Adam. "Can you remember whose house it is tonight? I'll be damned if I can."

The party, Whit discovered when he consulted the creamy card with the engraved invitation that lay on the desk in his room, was at Mrs. McDermott Beesley's that evening. The theme was different—a carnival this time—but the people and the party were only too familiar.

As they had done at many of those other parties, he and Clemmie slipped away a little after midnight. Whit knew Alison hadn't seen them go, but would know without seeing or being told that they had gone. The knowledge plagued Whit, just as the desire to be alone with Clemmie overpowered him. Clemmie had no such compunctions. She knew she wanted Whit, just as he wanted her, and tonight, alone on the bluff overlooking the bay, far from the careful rules and wagging tongues of Newport, that was all that mattered.

His mouth was warm on hers, then like fire as it traced a line to where the dress had slipped from her shoulder. Through the thin chiffon she felt his hand against her breast, his fingers working at the small pearl disks that held the dress closed. His touch on her skin was maddening, and she clung to him wildly, unthinkingly. Her lips were at his ear. "Whit," she murmured. "Whit." Clemmie didn't know if she meant it as an endearment or a reproach. She didn't know anything except the taste of his mouth on hers, the warmth of his hands against her flesh, the hot desire they knidled as they moved. The night air was cool against her skin where the dress had fallen away, but she felt as if she were on fire, burning with the desire Whit had aroused, that raged uncontrolled within her. She felt his hand hot against her skin above the smooth silk of her stocking, felt it and wanted it to go on, yet fought the wanting. She forced herself to struggle against the desire, against the hand that she did not want to fight; but knew from somewhere outside herself that she should fight.

She pulled away abruptly. In the quiet darkness she could hear her own breathing as ragged and sharp as Whit's and sense his eyes on her, as demanding as his hands had been a moment before. She did not have the courage to meet them and busied herself with her clothing. When she finally dared look at him, he was no longer looking at her but staring straight ahead at the lights of the bay below.

Numbly, as if he didn't realize what he was doing, Whit took a gold case from his breast pocket and placed a cigarette between his lips. He raised the lighter to it, and Clemmie could see that his mouth was an angry line. When he finally turned to her, his eyes were dark, too dark to read.

"We'd better start back." He stubbed out the cigarette. Clemmie said nothing, and they were silent on the drive back, lost in their separate thoughts.

She felt shaken by the emotions Whit had aroused,

by the struggle against them, and by one more thing. He had never said he loved her. Through all that had happened and all that had almost happened, he'd never said he loved her.

Damn it, Whit swore to himself. He was furious at Clemmie for pulling away when she had—and grateful to her. If she hadn't, at that moment, he didn't know what would have happened. Or rather, he knew and the knowledge plagued him.

Clemmie looked at Whit out of the corner of her eye. He seemed miles away. Only minutes ago they had been so close, and now he was miles away. Perhaps that was why he'd never said he loved her. Because he didn't. Perhaps his attraction to her was simpler than that—and less binding.

And if she hadn't stopped him, Whit thought, and struggled to replace the physical images that rioted in his mind with more sober thoughts. The most sobering of all was Alison. He'd never actually said anything about marriage to Alison, but he knew what people thought and what Alison, although she had never uttered a word to indicate as much, had come to expect. Whit, who always produced the right words and the correct actions for any situation, suddenly found himself at a loss. Just how did one break an engagement that had been acknowledged but never established? He had no idea, but he was certain of one thing. He had to clear things up with Alison before he could even consider marrying Clemmie. And if he could not yet consider marriage to Clemmie, the last thing he could afford to think of was making love to her. And yet Whit knew, stealing a glance at her now, her head held high with pride, her profile sharp and taut in the moonlight, he thought of almost nothing else.

Whit had been so busy thinking of Clemmie and himself that he was barely paying attention to the road that wound back toward Bellevue Avenue. As they rounded a curve the headlights of the Stutz picked up a car turned on its side at the edge of the road. The man beside the car was hailing them.

"It's Sebastion!" Clemmie said, suddenly roused from her thoughts.

Whit pulled the car to a stop behind the overturned one.

"Glad it's you," Sebastion said when he recognized them. "Didn't want to leave her to go for help. Beginning to think no one would ever come along."

"Leave who?" Whit asked. "What happened?"

"Alison. Must have hit her head on the windshield when we turned over. Still hasn't come to. Seems perfectly all right, but I can't bring her to."

Whit had pulled open the door of the overturned car and was into it before Sebastion had finished speaking. Alison, propped up by the steering wheel, half sat, half lay across the inclined front seat. Except for a small patch of dried blood on her forehead, she looked as if she were sleeping peacefully.

"Didn't want to move her," Sebastion said.

"I'll stay with her," Whit snapped. "You get into town and bring back an ambulance. And Dr. Verney. Tell him it's Alison. He'll come." Whit looked from Alison to the two of them standing beside the car. "You go with him, Clemmie. Take my car." Sebastion thought he hadn't heard orders barked so sharply since the war, but Clemmie was thinking simply that she'd never been spoken to that way in her life.

By the time Clemmie and Sebastion returned with the doctor and ambulance, Alison had come to. Whit had spread a lap robe on the grass beside the road, and Alison, looking white in the faint moonlight, was stretched out on it.

"I didn't mean to put everyone to so much trouble," she said when she saw Dr. Verney. "I'm all right, really I am."

"You let me decide that," the doctor said, kneeling beside her. He looked her over quickly in the dim light from the lantern one of the ambulance men held. Yes, you look well enough to take home. Get the stretcher, boys," he said to the driver and his aide.

"I can walk," Alison insisted.

"I'm sure you can, Alison," Dr. Verney said, "but for the moment I don't want you to."

"I feel so foolish," Alison murmured as they lifted her gently onto the stretcher. "And your car, Sebastion. I'm so sorry about your lovely car."

"Don't give it a thought," Sebastion said.

"But it was my fault." It was the last thing Alison said as Dr. Verney climbed into the ambulance after her and closed the doors.

The three of them stood for a moment looking after the vehicle. When Whit spoke his voice sounded strained. "I'll take you back to Alison's, Clemmie. We can see how she is then. You might as well come along, Anvers," Whit added as he started toward his own car. "You can't do anything about that," he nodded toward the overturned Morris-Cowley, "till tomorrow."

"What I don't understand," Whit said when they were all in his car, "is why Alison insisted it was her fault."

"It wasn't Alison's fault," Sebastion said. His tone was chivalrous, but unconvincing.

Whit turned to look at him. "Then why did she insist it was?"

"Alison was driving. Said she wanted to see what it felt like. Driving fast, that is. She said," Sebastion added, looking from one to the other, "if Clemmie could do it, she could."

On the way back to the house the words echoed in Whit's head like an accusation, but to Clemmie the words meant less than Whit's actions. When they arrived at the house he went straight to Mr. VanNest.

"How is she, sir?" Whit asked.

"Mrs. VanNest and Dr. Verney are with her now. He thinks she'll be all right. Just shaken up, he said. Though of course we can't really be sure yet. How did it happen?"

"My fault, sir," Sebastion said, stepping forward as if he were volunteering for a dangerous assignment.

Clemmie listened to the three men talking in hushed tones. Whit's face was half turned from her, but she could still read the anxiety in it and hear the concern in his voice. Even the way he stood leaning over Mr. VanNest seemed to imply protectiveness. Nothing must be allowed to happen to Alison. For the moment at least, Whit seemed to have forgotten Clemmie's existence.

By the next morning it was clear that except for the small bruise on her high pale forehead, Alison had not been injured. A week later, however, Clemmie still carried her own wounds. She could not forget how Whit had barked orders at her, then ignored her. And his coolness since then didn't help. There was a certain preoccupation on Whit's part that Clemmie found more painful than any real rupture between them might be. If they'd quarreled, she'd be angry at him, and the anger would cut the edge of her desire for him. But there was no anger on her part, only the realization, stronger than ever since the night of Alison's accident, that she felt something for Whit she'd never experienced in her life. She supposed people would say she was in love, but what she felt for Whit seemed too strong, too turbulent for such a simple, hackneyed word that could be, and continually was, applied to other people's emotions. Whatever the word, Clemmie knew one thing. She had to have Whit. And yet in the days after Alison's accident, she seemed to have less of him than ever. Even when he was with her, he seemed not to be there. Something, Clemmie decided, had to be done.

They had planned to go sailing that afternoon. Just the two of them, Whit had said. "No Adam, no Samantha, no one but us," he'd murmured, and for a moment Clemmie had been able to forget his reserve of the past few days, but the moment had passed and Whit's aloofness had returned and with it Clemmie's resolve. She would break through the barriers he'd erected.

Whit was early, but not early enough. "Miss Wilder is out," Haxton the butler told him.

"Out?" Whit repeated as if a mistake had been made.

"Out, sir," Haxton repeated. He wanted to add that Miss Alison was upstairs, but it was not the place of a butler, even a butler who'd been with the family for twenty-five years, to volunteer such information.

"Is there any message, Mr. Morris?" he added when Whit continued to stand there staring off across the green carpet of grass that ran down to the wall of hedges, wondering what Clemmie was up to now.

"What?" Whit said. "Oh, no. No message, Haxton." Whatever words he had for Clemmie he'd have to deliver himself.

Whit had his chance that night. There was another ball and Clemmie had taken special care dressing for it. She chose a gown Whit had never seen before, a pale chiffon so delicately hued that it seemed to be nothing more than a blush. Her skin glowed a tawny gold against it, and her hair looked black in the shimmering candlelight of the foyer. For a moment, when Whit first saw her, he forgot how angry he was. Then the sight of her laughing up at Sebastion Anvers reminded him.

Whit walked to where they stood and without a word held out his hand to Clemmie. She hesitated for only a moment before she took it and let him lead her into the ballroom. They had circled the dance floor once and Whit still had not spoken. When Clemmie looked up at him she saw that he was watching her closely. The dark eyes were black with anger.

Clemmie smiled up at him brightly. "I suppose you're annoyed."

"Shouldn't I be?"

"Well, I did leave word with Haxton. It couldn't be helped, Whit. Sebastion said he simply had to talk to me. He was desperate."

93

So she had gone off with Sebastion Anvers. "And what was Sebastion so desperate about?"

She dropped her eyes for a moment. "I really don't think I ought to say."

Whit wondered if Anvers really had proposed to her. He thought it unlikely. Clemmie had spent too much time with him lately for Sebastion to be misled by a single afternoon. Whit recognized the ploy and his anger turned almost, but not quite, to amusement.

"You can do better than that, Clemmie."

"Better than the excuse or better than Sebastion?"

"Both."

"Better than an earl! Why that's heresy in Newport. What could be better than an earl?"

"Not what. Who?"

She looked up at him again. The dark eyes were laughing now. "All right, who could be better than an earl?"

Whit's smile was boyish and blatantly self-confident. "Me, of course."

Clemmie felt her heart pounding and struggled to make her voice light. "I should have seen that coming."

He was still smiling. "You did. That's why you asked. It was exactly what you wanted to hear."

Now the anger flashed in her eyes. "You're terribly smug."

Whit pulled her closer and she could feel the studs of his evening shirt hard against her skin. "Not so smug," he whispered in her ear, "that I don't get angry when you do something like you did this morning. Damn angry. Are you satisfied?"

Clemmie started to say something, but Whit saw Sebastion making his way toward them through the dancers. "Let's get out of here," he said, leading her off the dance floor and across the terrace.

"Where are we going?" she asked when they had left the lights of the terrace behind and the ball was no more than a distant sound of music.

"Anywhere. Just so long as it's away from everyone else."

She stopped walking and turned to him. "Let's go for a swim. I've been in Newport for more than a month and I've never gone for a midnight swim."

Whit was suddenly intensely aware of her standing there only inches from him. "It isn't midnight yet."

Her eyes held his. "We'll swim for a long time."

In the shadow of a willow tree he bent and kissed her. "You're like quicksilver, Clemmie."

She wanted to tell him that he was too, within her grasp one minute, out of reach the next, but she was determined to take a different tack. Her ploy that afternoon seemed to have worked. The reserve was gone. He said she was like quicksilver and he seemed to like her that way. She pulled away and started toward his car. "Does quicksilver dissolve in water?" she asked.

"Not if you hold on to it tightly," he said.

They had been driving for some time when Whit turned off the road into an estate Clemmie had never visited before. "It belongs to my Uncle Quentin," he explained. "They're away this week, but I'm sure they won't mind our using their beach. It's small, but at least it's private. Can't go for a midnight swim on Bailey's Beach. Especially when we don't have bathing suits." Whit looked at her out of the corner of his eye. "Or have you changed your mind?"

Clemmie raised her head a fraction. Whit had seen the gesture before. It meant she was having second thoughts but wouldn't give in to them. "I haven't changed my mind."

He turned the car on to a small path that led down to the beach. Set back from it, under a clump of trees, was a small bathhouse. Inside were comfortable rattan chairs and sofas covered in bright flowered prints, and there was a small bar in one corner.

"Do you want a drink?" Whit asked. "That water's going to be cold."

"Have you changed *your* mind?"

Whit shook his head. "Just fortifying myself for the ordeal." He poured whiskey into two glasses, handed her one, and took a long swallow from the other.

Clemmie followed his example. There was no ice and it tasted harsh, but she felt the warmth run through her and with it a certain courage. "Turn around," she said and began to unbutton her dress. Suddenly it seemed terribly important that she move quickly, that she not give herself a chance to think. She stripped down to her chemise and ran past Whit out the door and down the beach to the water. He watched her run, her long brown legs crossing the sand in easy leaps, the white satin chemise gleaming in the moonlight.

Whit's dark evening suit joined the pile of pale silk and chiffon on the floor of the bathhouse, and he was following her into the water. Clemmie floated on her back and watched Whit moving toward her with long, smooth strokes. She saw him raise his head once to determine her position, and his face was taut with concentration. When he had almost reached her she swam a few feet away and began treading water.

"You were right,'" she laughed. "It's freezing."

Before she could swim away again, he covered the distance between them and put his arms around her. She could feel his body through the thin material of her chemise and his legs, treading water, tangled with hers. His mouth tasted faintly of the whiskey and salt water, and as he kissed her again and again she felt as if she were drowning not in the sea but in Whit. She felt a shiver run through her body, and Whit must have felt it too, because he began swimming back toward the beach, carrying her gently along with him.

When they reached the ridge where the water shallowed out Clemmie stood. She could feel the wet chemise clinging to her as if it were another skin. She couldn't bring herself to look at Whit, but she knew he was watching her. She started to run to the bathhouse and he followed. Inside Whit found some towels and handed her one. Clemmie wrapped it around her shoulders and hugged it to her closely. She felt colder now than she had in the water.

"I think I need the other half of that drink," she said, taking the glass from the bar where she'd left it and downing the remaining whiskey. "I'm not sure I'd have suggested swimming if I'd known it was going to be that cold." She laughed, but Whit did not even smile. He walked to where she was standing and took the glass from her hand.

"It isn't a game anymore, Clemmie."

She started to answer but his mouth on hers silenced her. His skin was still damp, but warm, and through the wet satin she felt his hands pressing her to him. His fingers worked quickly at the small buttons that ran down one side of the chemise and then his hands felt like fire against her skin.

"Whit," she breathed.

"I love you, Clemmie." She could feel his mouth on hers forming the words. "I love you."

She heard herself repeating the words and then there were no words at all but only Whit beside her on the narrow sofa and his mouth avid on hers and his hands moving slowly but urgently over her body, warming it, caressing it, arousing it. She clung to him and felt the strength of his body above her in the half darkness, and tasted the words of love in his mouth. Her body was moving in rhythm with his now, as if it were a separate entity and not hers at all, but the small flash of pain was hers and then the pleasure that washed over her in wave after wave until she was drowning in Whit and he in her.

She felt his body relax, but he was still holding her to him and his breath against her ear was warm but uneven. They were silent for a moment, then Whit shifted position a little so he could see her face. "Are you all right?" he asked.

She nodded and he pulled her to him again. "I love you, Clemmie, and I'll never let you go. I couldn't. Not now. You belong to me now." The statement of ownership that might have rankled at another time, sounded wonderful now, as wonderful as his arms around her, his body against hers.

Suddenly he held her a little away again and looked into her eyes. His own were almost, but not quite, laughing. "Well, aren't you going to say anything?" he asked.

She brushed back a lock of hair that had fallen over his forehead. "I love you," she said quietly.

He pulled her to him and his words were soft but insistent at her ear. "Say it again."

"I love you, Whit." Then his mouth was on hers and his hands began to move again, awakening her body, bringing it to life, and she was responding to him, following him as if it were a familiar dance now, but one they'd never tire of.

Whit drove slowly on the way home. It was almost dawn but he was in no rush to leave Clemmie. Her head lay on his shoulder and the wind whipped her hair against his face. She smelled of a familiar perfume but Whit's senses told him there was nothing familiar about the fragrance on Clemmie. Everything about her was different. He'd thought he'd wanted her, but he hadn't known how much. It seemed to Whit now that he'd never stop wanting Clemmie—and he'd never again want anyone else.

Whit had never thought much about fidelity. It wasn't a problem for a single man, and when he married—well, he'd worry about that when it happened, he'd reasoned. But tonight had changed all that. Clemmie had changed all that. He remembered the way her body had looked in the dim light from the single lamp, the smooth white skin against the sunburned arms and legs. And then, for some reason Whit didn't understand, the thought of Clemmie's body, untouched by the sun, untouched by anyone but him, made him think of Alison.

He'd speak to her tomorrow, tell her he was in love

with Clemmie, was going to marry Clemmie. He'd let things drag on until everything had got out of hand. First Alison's crazy behavior that night when she'd almost killed herself, then Clemmie's running off with Sebastion this afternoon. Whit had procrastinated until he'd almost ruined everything, but all that was over. He was going to take things in hand.

"And one more thing," he whispered to the head that lay against his shoulder. "No more picnics with Sebastion Anvers."

"Aye, aye, sir."

"Or anyone else."

"Aye, aye, sir," Clemmie repeated, turning her face until her mouth lay against Whit's cheek.

Chapter 3

WHIT HAD NO opportunity to speak to Alison the next morning. He barely had time for a telephone call to Clemmie before he left Newport. He had never called Clemmie at the VanNest house, and when the maid came to her room to tell her Mr. Morris was on the phone, her tone was clearly disapproving. There was no doubt about it, Clemmie was in enemy territory, but after last night she could not have cared less. She had Whit, and nothing else mattered.

Clemmie had gone to sleep with that thought the night before and awakened with it this morning. She'd been afraid she might not. She'd been afraid that in the harsh morning light, with Whit gone and last night only a memory, she might feel some regret, but she felt nothing but an overwhelming desire to be with him. It was strange how all the rest had disappeared, all the games and the sparring and the terrible fears. They were all gone now, replaced by a kind of trust and belonging that were stronger than all the other emotions. She wasn't afraid of Whit or the power he had over her because you couldn't be afraid of part of yourself. She was sure she'd never have that frightened feeling of vulnerability again—until she heard Whit's voice say-

ing not the words she'd expected after last night but
that he was leaving for New York immediately.

"I don't see why you have to go," Clemmie said, but
what she meant was, *You can't go now, not after last
night.*

"Because someone has to, and I'm the financial vice
president. I know you think my office is only a place
to keep trophies, but I am expected to do something
occasionally."

"But surely it can wait." Clemmie tried to keep the
pleading tone from her voice.

Whit thought of the Dayton Southbound Railroad
stocks that were even now passing into the hands of the
Erie. The Dayton was one of the few profitable railroads that the government—so eager since the war to
have the solvent lines buy up those in trouble—would
permit the Central to buy. But the government would
also permit the Erie to take it over, and in twenty-four
hours the Erie seemed to have undone months of careful negotiation by Whit. Something had to be done
quickly. "No, Clemmie," Whit said evenly, "it can't
wait. You know I can't tell you the details, but you
must understand this kind of thing. At least, as Elias
Wilder's daughter you ought to."

All Clemmie understood, but could not bring herself
to say, was that last night Whit had said she belonged
to him, but apparently he did not belong to her. If he
did, he couldn't possibly pick up like this and leave her.
Not after last night. Clemmie didn't believe for a moment in the importance of Whit's mission. There were
scores of Vanderbilt underlings who could do the job
just as well.

"Now don't sound so glum, Clemmie." Whit tried
to make his voice bright. "I'll be back in no time, probably before the week is out."

His voice was casual, as if they were no more than
friends, acquaintances who could as easily see each
other as not. I'll be back in a week . . . we'll dine in a
month . . . perhaps we'll run into each other next sum-

mer. He might have been saying any of those things for all he seemed to care. And what of last night, what of trust and belonging, Clemmie asked herself, and knew the answer immediately. Last night had meant nothing to Whit. It had meant everything to her and nothing to him. He had probably arranged the trip to New York purposely to prove as much. She was no more than a casual affair to Whit, a *fling,* and his going away now was his way of telling her so, his way of preventing her from expecting anything binding or lasting.

She felt the tears welling up and swore she would not permit Whit to hear her cry. She thought of last night again. Clemmie had imagined she'd learned something about love and trust and herself, but now she knew she was being taught a different lesson.

"I'm sure to be back by Saturday at the latest," Whit continued.

And expect to find me here waiting, Clemmie thought. She wouldn't give him the satisfaction. She wouldn't sit home tending the fire in the hearth and burning the light in the window while he went off alone on business or pleasure or whatever he choose to call it. She wasn't Alison VanNest. She might be more foolish than Alison, since Alison in her propriety would never have behaved as Clemmie had last night, but she was prouder as well. She wouldn't spent six months waiting for Whit while he sailed the South Seas. She wouldn't spend a week waiting while he played with his railroad. She might love Whit, but she wouldn't let him take advantage of her. Two could play Whit's game—even if one of them ached doing it.

Clemmie's angry tone still echoed in Whit's head as he drove to the ferry. He was sorry. There was no doubt about it, the timing was terrible. He hadn't been near his office all summer, and now, after last night, he had to be called back. In a way he couldn't blame Clemmie. They hadn't had time to settle anything. He hadn't even mentioned marriage to her, he realized with

a start. *My God, that was stupid,* Whit swore to himself. *Especially after last night.*

But in Clemmie's eyes, Whit's omission was one not
of stupidity but of intention. And she had already set
in motion the wheels of retribution. When Whit returned to Newport—within the week, he'd said—he'd
find she hadn't sat waiting for him. She'd take Samantha and her brother up on their invitation. Clemmie
could just picture Whit's face when he discovered she'd
gone off for a cruise on Tony Bayliss's yacht.

Dolly did not object to Clemmie's plans. Tony Bayliss's reputation was a rarity in Newport—a source of
amusement and admiration to the men, a complete
secret from the women. There was no reason Clemmie,
well chaperoned by her brother and Samantha's mother,
should not go off on his boat, especially since Whit
had left Newport. Dolly would be glad to get away herself. Things were becoming entirely too uncomfortable
at the VanNest house. Dolly would go to New York
for a week of shopping. Then she and Clemmie—and
Adam, she hoped—would return to Scranton. And
there, Dolly hoped, Whit would follow.

Whit arrived in New York full of plans. He had
never thought seriously of marriage—or rather he had
tried not to think of it, for when he did, the restrictions
seemed to outweigh the advantages—but now that he
had Clemmie, all the details fell into place. He'd worried that marriage might be confining, but Clemmie
could never be confining. He was sure there was nothing she wouldn't want to try, no place she wouldn't dare
to go. It seemed to Whit that the entire world lay at his
feet and that Clemmie would always be at his side. It
took every ounce of concentration to keep his mind on
the business at hand during that endless day of meetings. Stock options swam before his eyes as the memory
of Clemmie, the way she'd clung to him in the water,
the way her voice had sounded in the half-darkness, the
way she'd looked after they'd made love, burned in his
brain. When he'd finally got to the Racquet and Tennis

that evening—his parents' house was closed for the summer—he'd put in a call to Newport immediately.

If Grace VanNest had spoken to Mrs. Sherman for a few minutes more, the operator would have told Whit that the Newport number was engaged. If she had spoken to Mrs. Sherman for a few minutes less, Grace would have left the small first-floor telephone closet, and Haxton would have answered Whit's call. As it was, Grace had just replaced the receiver when it rang again. She did not give Whit a chance to ask for Clemmie.

"Whit, dear"—her voice was almost a trill—"how nice of you to call. Alison isn't here just now. That party at The Elms, you know."

"Is Clemmie there . . . then?" Whit added the last word in embarrassment, then cursed himself for the hypocrisy.

Grace VanNest had not told a lie since she was eight years old and had broken the delicate porcelain face on her sister's doll, but Grace hadn't been faced with anything she wanted so much as that doll in a long time. Besides, it wasn't really a lie, or at least it would be true tomorrow morning. "Didn't you know, Whit? Clemmie left. She's off for a week or so on Tony Bayliss's yacht."

"Tony Bayliss," Whit repeated incredulously.

"That Weymouth-Baldwin woman was going, so of course Adam went along, and Clemmie decided to join them. As I understood it, Mr. Bayliss practically insisted that Clemmie go along." Grace wondered for a moment if she'd gone too far. There was no need for vulgar implications. It was better to let Whit piece things together himself. "Whit, are you still there?"

He was there, and wondering how on earth Mrs. Wilder had let Clemmie go for a week's cruise with Tony Bayliss. Everyone knew Bayliss's reputation.

After he'd hung up Whit sat for a long time staring at the telephone. Finally he went in to dinner.

Even at the busiest lunch or dinner hours the dining

room had a forbidding aura; the dark paneling with its massive carving, the huge scale of the furnishings—they were meant to lend an air of masculine comfort. Instead they tended to overpower. Now, when only a handful of diners sat scattered around the dimly lit room, Whit found the ambience depressing.

Two old classmates were lingering over coffee and brandy, but Whit refused an invitation to join them. He ordered a sandwich, but even that was more than he wanted. He left it untouched and downed one whiskey, then a second, finally a third. They did not brighten the picture. Surely if Mrs. Wilder had allowed Clemmie to go, she had been properly chaperoned. Mrs. VanNest had made it sound as if there were only the four of them, but that was impossible. Then Whit remembered the scores of carefully chaperoned parties he and Clemmie had slipped away from, and a wave of anger swept over him again. If the idea of Clemmie's recklessness with him excited Whit, the thought of similar behavior with Bayliss was torture.

Whit left the club and headed for a speakeasy on West Forty-fourth Street, but the image of Clemmie and Bayliss followed him. When he showed his membership card to the man at the door, Clemmie and Bayliss stood behind him. When he found a spot at the end of the long mahogany bar, they took their places at his side. Even in this dark, half-deserted speakeasy there was no escaping them. He pictured Clemmie taunting Bayliss, daring him, egging him on. This wasn't like that business with Sebastion Anvers. Bayliss wasn't a polite Englishman in search of an heiress. Whit pictured the tanned handsome face, the cold uncaring eyes, the knowing smile Bayliss flashed when the names of certain women were mentioned. Bayliss never said much. He didn't have to. He merely smiled that terrible, smug smile.

"Damn her," he swore, slamming the empty glass down on the bar. The bartender hadn't heard the words, but he looked at the empty glass and refilled it without question. *How could she,* Whit thought. *How could she after last night?* The question had been plaguing him ever since he'd spoken to Mrs. VanNest. Now, half drunk in a dismal West Side speakeasy, Whit found the answer unmistakably clear. She could because that was the way she was. He'd thought Clemmie loved him, but she'd only been toying with him, looking for a challenge, searching for a little excitement. That was all last night had meant to her. Not love, just adventure.

Whit looked at his reflection in the mirror behind the bar, and narrowed his eyes until the twin images merged into one. "She certainly turned the tables on you, pal," he murmured. "Certainly pulled the wool over your eyes," he added, trying to summon all the clichés that might turn last night into the joke Clemmie had made it, but he found nothing funny in the memory of those hours in the beach house, and nothing humorous in the irony of Whit Morris being taken in by a little girl from Scranton.

Clemmie had been directing her mother's maid Ellen as to what she wanted packed when the telephone rang. She stopped in mid-sentence and stood in the center of the room as if every fiber of her body were listening. It was Whit. She was sure of it. Clemmie had already begun to regret her intransigence and the plans she'd made and now she'd be able to tell him as much. They'd both be able to say all the things they hadn't said this morning, and Whit would tell her he'd be back tomorrow or the next day at the latest and everything would be all right.

"You won't want the blue chiffon, will you?" Ellen asked. "We can send that on to New York with your mother."

Clemmie did not answer. The packing was unnecessary. She wouldn't go off on Tony Bayliss's boat now. She didn't have to.

But the minutes passed, and Haxton did not come to call her to the telephone, and then she heard Mrs.

VanNest in the next room, her mother's, telling Dolly about a conversation with Mrs. Sherman. All the pain she'd felt this morning when Whit had said he was leaving flooded back, and with it the anger and the resolve. She'd given him everything, her love, her trust, herself, and he'd flung it all back. No, that wasn't entirely true. Not all. He'd taken *her,* but he'd made a joke of the love and the trust. How he'd laugh if he could see her, waiting, hoping, praying for a call from him. But she wouldn't give Whit Morris the chance to laugh at her. She'd never, she swore, give anyone the chance to laugh at her again.

"I'll take the blue chiffon, Ellen." Clemmie thought of Tony Bayliss. "It's too becoming to leave behind."

Tony Bayliss was delighted with the news that Adam Wilder's sister was to join them on the cruise. As a friend of Samantha's, he'd agreed to take a small party including her and Adam off for a week or ten days. It was, Samantha was convinced, the only way she could force Adam to action. She was counting on long lazy days and starry nights at sea, her constant proximity and the absence of any more rational or restraining souls, to push Adam over the precipice he'd been hovering at for the last month.

Tony Bayliss was aware of Samantha's plan and agreed with its wisdom—that was why he'd invited the small party for a cruise and given Adam the stateroom next to Sam's—but if he did not mind providing the means to Samantha's end, neither did he relish the prospect of ten days at sea with a pair of troubled lovers, Samantha's mother, the innocuous Mr. and Mrs. Colin Timball, and his old friend John Semple. Samantha had forbidden eligible young women of their own class as too much competition and enjoyable girls of another class as too distracting. Tony was therefore elated when Clemmie decided to join them.

He'd seen Clemmie Wilder at several balls and here and there at the golf club or a regatta or tennis match for the last month, and had been, if not intrigued, at leasted interested. Or at least he would have been if Clemmie hadn't been so young, and then so obviously caught up with Whit Morris. But Morris was out of the picture for the duration of the cruise, and if Clemmie was young, she immediately showed herself to be anything but one of those proper debutantes-in-search-of-a-husband that Tony Bayliss avoided as an endangered species avoids the hunter. The first day out Clemmie proved she wasn't afraid of baiting a hook, driving the small power launch as fast as it would go, or diving off a moving yacht at midnight—although Tony suspected the champagne had something to do with this last—and on the final night out she proved she wasn't afraid of Tony Bayliss, either.

They were at anchor in a small harbor on the Connecticut side of the Sound. Mrs. Weymouth had retired early and the Timballs had followed shortly after. Adam and Samantha were alone on an upper deck, and Clemmie sat with Tony and John Semple on the afterdeck. The night was warm and breezeless and the conversation had grown desultory. John finished off his highball and stood.

"What about taking the launch and going over to *Windsong* for a nightcap?" He referred to the sleek power yacht that had pulled in late that afternoon. It was owned by a friend of Tony's and an invitation had been sent over by a member of the crew, but from the way Tony and Adam had behaved, Clemmie suspected tonight's party was not one at which she or any of the women aboard would be welcome.

"You go ahead," Tony said. "I don't think I'm up to one of Morley's parties tonight."

Clemmie looked at her host. The tanned, unlined face radiated energy and good health and the gray temples, instead of underscoring his forty-some-odd years, only made Tony appear more youthful—and attractive. Clemmie hadn't stopped thinking of Whit for a moment, but she liked Tony. Moreover, she was intrigued by his reputation and she enjoyed his obvious admiration, enjoyed it almost as much as the knowledge that the whole incident was sure to get back to Whit. "You mean," she laughed, "that it would be rude to leave me, and you wouldn't dare take me along."

"I doubt you'd enjoy it," Tony said.

"I'm sure I'd enjoy it immensely."

"Then I doubt your brother or Mrs. Weymouth would approve."

"Adam is far too concerned with Samantha to notice where I am, and Mrs. Weymouth has been asleep for hours." She turned on him two eyes bright with challenge. "Please take me to Mr. Morley's party, Tony. It can't be so terribly dangerous, and even if it is, what can possibly happen with you and John to protect me?" Clemmie knew how preposterous the idea of either man as chaperone was, and the irony of the suggestion delighted her.

Tony laughed. "Oh, I wouldn't depend on John if I were you. Invariably drinks too much at these things and disappears—" Tony caught himself. He'd been about to say "disappears with some chorus girl."

"A clear case of the pot calling the kettle black," John said. He knew what Tony had been about to say. "Tony's merely describing his own behavior."

"Then I'll stay sober and take care of both of you," Clemmie said. "Only let's go. You know I'd never get to see anything like it in Newport. And certainly not in Scranton."

"Don't be so sure," Tony laughed.

"You know you'd take me if I were a man," Clemmie said.

"That, my child," Tony answered, feeling not in the least paternal toward her, "is precisely the point." He'd been watching Clemmie Wilder for a week now, watching her turning and stretching lazily in the afternoon sun, watching her dancing with the other men in the party in the light of the Japanese lanterns on the afterdeck, her thin dresses billowing about her like soft seductive veils, and he'd come to want Clemmie Wilder. He just didn't think it would be wise to have her. But wisdom was one trait Clemmie rarely aroused in men, and tonight Tony Bayliss was finding her especially provocative. "You are definitely and unmistakably not a man," he said.

John caught the provocative tone in his friend's voice and saw the way he was looking at Clemmie. Idly, vicariously, he wondered how the evening would end for them. "Well," John said, "I'll leave you two to settle the issue. I'm going over to Morley's."

Clemmie stood. "I'm going with you."

John looked suddenly uncomfortable, but Tony merely sat watching Clemmie move toward the gangway. When she had reached it, he stood. "All right, Clemmie. I never liked playing defender of the faith, anyway. We'll see," he said, putting an arm around her waist as he helped her into the launch, "how you fare in Sodom and Gomorrah."

There was something about his voice that made Clemmie vaguely uncomfortable, but she had no intention of turning back now.

As they drew closer to *Windsong* they could hear the sound of jazz over the noise of the motor launch. The strains of a saxophone and the brightly colored lights casting long shimmering reflections on the black water seemed strangely out of place in this quiet cove. Then they were walking up the small ladder to the deck and Clemmie could hear shouts and laughter and the sound of two dozen pairs of feet moving over the afterdeck in a double-shuffle. Most of the women seemed no older than Clemmie, but she knew none of them. And from the heavily painted faces and lacquered nails she knew why. All the same, unless a certain lack of taste was contagious, there seemed to be nothing especially dangerous about the party.

Tony was introducing her to their host, who was looking at her with mingled curiosity and admiration. "Miss Wilder insisted on coming," Tony explained.

"I'm delighted she did," Morley said. Although he must have been ten years younger than Bayliss, his heavy frame and round florid face made him look older. The appetites that seemed to have left little mark on Tony had scarred his friend.

When Semple led Clemmie away to dance, Tony apologized to his host. "Sorry about the girl." His eyes followed Clemmie around the dance floor. "I tried to keep her from coming. Wasn't even going to come myself. But she was hell-bent on it."

Morley, too, was watching Clemmie. "Well, Bayliss, old man, if she knew what kind of a party it was and still insisted on coming, she must have reasons. Girl probably wants a little fun. And if you won't oblige, I'd be happy to."

"That's kind of you, Morley," Tony said, taking a glass from the tray a waiter held before him, "but I never send a boy to do a man's job."

Clemmie danced with Tony, then with John again, then with several other men who never bothered to mention their last names and never asked hers. At one point when she was standing with Tony, a man who identified himself only as Pete, approached and asked if she were in the chorus of *Sally* too. Tony had laughed and told him he was on the wrong track.

"He thought I was a chorus girl, didn't he?" Clemmie asked when the other man had staggered off in the direction of a very pretty brunette.

"Are you insulted?"

"Not in the least. I'm flattered."

Tony looked at her closely. Ever since they'd arrived, he'd been wondering if Morley were right, if Clemmie really did want a little fun. Most girls like Clemmie would have been horrified at being mistaken for a chorus girl. The idea obviously delighted her.

Tony took the empty glass from her hand. "Let me get you more champagne."

Clemmie stood against the railing, watching the party. The dance floor was a bright circle of activity, but in dark corners around the deck shadows clutched at each other and whispered and giggled. Every so often one of the shadows split into two and one half followed the other down the passageway to the staterooms below.

In the center of the dancing area a small, pretty girl, all blond curls and flashing dimples, had drifted away from her partner and begun dancing alone. The other couples stopped dancing to watch and the orchestra began to urge her on musically. She kicked off her shoes, and then threw the long scarf she'd worn about her neck to Morley. There was a great deal of shouting and laughing, and without missing a beat the girl slipped out of her dress and threw that to Morley, too. She was dancing now in a chemise so sheer it was almost like dancing in nothing at all, and Clemmie felt the color rising in her own cheeks. Then a snatch of conversation caught her attention. Had they really mentioned Whit Morris's name?

Two men stood a few feet down the railing from her and were watching the girl with interest but without surprise. Their eyes never left her while they talked.

"As I heard the story it was Atlantic City. And Morris was fit to be tied. What can you do in a situation like that?"

"But didn't he know she was under age?"

"You look at her, old man. Can you guess her age? And that was less than a year ago. Though I'm sure Morley made sure she'd had a birthday since. The point is, when Morris ran into her—one of those stag things in town—I don't think he was worrying much about her age. But when they got to Atlantic City, he found out she was only seventeen. It would have been bad enough if it had been a hotel in New York, but he'd taken her across state lines. God knows why. Maybe he had a little midnight swimming in mind."

Clemmie felt as if a chill wind had suddenly come up off the water.

"You still haven't told me what he did once he found out," one of the men continued.

"As I heard the story, it was a little late to do anything about it, if you know what I mean. So the next morning he simply put her on a train to New York and drove back alone. Our little dancing girl was very put out about it. Called Morris every name in the book, even started to make a scene in the station."

"It must have cost him a pretty penny."

The man was still watching the girl and he narrowed his eyes. "I wonder if she was worth it?"

"I said," Tony repeated, "do you want me to take you back?"

Clemmie started. She realized she'd taken the drink from Tony without hearing his words. It seemed she could hear nothing but the echo of that terrible story and the laughter of the man who'd told it. *Maybe he had a little midnight swimming in mind*. The words beat in her head. "Take me back?" she repeated. "But the party's still going strong. Why would I want to leave?"

Tony Bayliss shrugged off the last vestiges of his reserve and laughed. "I can't imagine, Clemmie." Then he took her in his arms and they were moving slowly through the shadows in time to the music. He held her tightly and she did not resist. He wasn't as tall as Whit and she could feel his breath soft against her ear. She cared nothing about Tony Bayliss but his cheek was warm against hers and his arms strong around her. She leaned against him and let herself go and then she felt herself being carried along in rhythm with him.

When the music stopped Clemmie found herself standing only a few feet from the girl who had danced alone, the girl Whit had taken to Atlantic City, the girl Whit had made love to. Morley's arm was around the girl and his pudgy hand rested on her hip. Clemmie could see Whit's long, slender fingers in its place.

"I'd like some more champagne," Clemmie said. She downed the glass Tony handed her and reached for another, but he took her hand and turned her to him.

"Wouldn't you rather dance?" he said. His mouth

was against her ear and his arms were around her again and she let the words he was murmuring and the sound of the saxophone wailing in the night drive away the picture of Whit and the girl.

After that the evening passed in a confused kaleidoscope of music and champagne and Tony's face close to hers as they circled beneath the Japanese lanterns. Clemmie didn't remember leaving the party, but suddenly she found herself in the launch heading back to Tony's boat. Her foot slipped as she started up the ladder, but Tony caught her and lifted her aboard.

"Almost went swimming on that one," he said.

"No," she said sharply. "No more midnight swims."

Tony just laughed and with his arm still around her started down the companionway to her stateroom. She murmured good night, but he followed her in and closed the door behind him. Clemmie reached for the light but he caught her hand and pulled her to him. His mouth was harsh against hers and his hands worked quickly at the buttons of her dress. The clean-lined face that had been so handsome a few hours ago was a mask now, a mask of blind desire. Clemmie struggled against him, but her movements only aroused him more and then she felt his hands beneath her dress and she wanted to scream but it was like a terrible nightmare where she screamed and screamed and no sound came out. Then his voice, whispering words she'd never heard before, cut through the silence and she heard her own voice screaming at him to stop.

He clamped a hand over her mouth. "Be quiet! Do you want to wake everyone?"

They stood that way for what could not have been more than a few seconds but felt like hours to Clemmie. Then he let her go and she took a step back from him, holding her dress closed.

"Get out of here! Get out of here this minute." Her voice was quiet but sharp with anger.

He looked at her coolly. "You really mean it, don't you?"

"Get out!" she repeated.

"There are words for what you are, Clemmie. And they're not very nice words." He took a step toward the door, then turned back to her. "And I'd be careful if I were you. Someday you're going to go too far with someone who isn't a gentleman"—he smiled in a self-deprecating way—"and you're going to find yourself in trouble. You see, not everyone is going to stop just because you say so." He had regained his dignity and smiled at her as if she were a very foolish child. "Good night, Clemmie. I hope you sleep well."

The door closed behind Tony Bayliss, and Clemmie heard him singing quietly to himself as he made his way down the companionway to his own cabin. She sank down on the bed. Her heart was pounding and the room was spinning around her. The last sensation she had before she passed out was of Tony's hands, hot and searching, against her skin.

Clemmie awakened abruptly, but it took a few minutes for the furniture in the cabin to fall into place. Then she realized where she was and with that realization memories of the night before flooded back. She lay there staring at the ceiling, trying to piece together the disaster. She remembered the words Tony had spoken, first in passion, then in anger, and thought she'd never be able to face him again. Then the story of Whit and the girl in Atlantic City flashed through her mind, and the scene with Tony seemed unimportant. It was the story about Whit that had hurt, that had driven her to Tony Bayliss. It wasn't so much what had happened between Whit and that girl—Clemmie knew enough about her brothers' lives not to be shocked by that—but the horrible similarity between what had happened between Whit and that girl and what had happened between Whit and herself. The night that had seemed so rare and pure a week ago looked merely tawdry now. And that must have been the way Whit had seen it all along. Why else had he left so casually the next morning? She'd made a fool of herself and everyone must know it, just as they knew about that girl. She was sure that Tony knew it. That was why he'd behaved as he had last night.

Clemmie jumped out of bed, as if sudden movement could drive away the thoughts that haunted her. Beyond the porthole Long Island Sound glittered a bright blue in the morning sun. The light was harsh and unforgiving, and it seemed to Clemmie that if she went out into it, it would reveal her shame. She threw herself face down on the bed with a noise somewhere between a sob and a cry of anger, but the knock at the door silenced her immediately. What if it were Tony? She didn't think she could face him now.

"Clemmie," Adam called quietly, "are you up? I have good news."

It seemed impossible to Clemmie that anyone might have good news this morning. "I'm up," she said miserably.

The sight of Adam smiling and fit in his dark blazer and white trousers made Clemmie feel even worse. She realized with horror that she was still wearing last night's dress. It was wrinkled and open where Tony had undone the buttons, but Adam seemed not to notice. He sat on the end of the bed.

"How would you like to be maid of honor? In two hours. We're going to Samantha's uncle's house in Glen Cove. Judge Weymouth is going to marry us this afternoon."

Clemmie sat staring at her brother as if the words made no sense.

"Well, aren't you going to congratulate me?"

"I'm sorry, Adam. I mean, I'm not sorry. I'm very glad for you. Congratulations." Clemmie smiled and tried to straighten the dress that had slipped off one shoulder. As soon as she did, she cursed herself, for the gesture had only called Adam's attention to her appearance.

His eyes narrowed a little, as if he'd suddenly remem-

117

bered he was her brother. "Are you all right? Why are you still dressed? Were you up all night?"

"Not exactly. Just wasn't up to undressing. Too much champagne, I'm afraid." She tried to make her smile bright and innocent. She was not going to tell Adam about Tony. He'd only blame her for insisting on going to the party in the first place. And she certainly wasn't going to tell him about Whit and what really haunted her.

"I wasn't going to bring it up, but since you did, I might as well say it, Clemmie. You've been drinking entirely too much champagne every night."

Clemmie jumped up and walked to the porthole, but the brightness outside made her turn back to the room. "For Pete's sake, Adam, I've seen you tight more than once, so please, no lectures."

"I'm a man."

"And therefore allowed anything."

"Not anything, just more. And anyway, I can handle it."

"And you think I can't?"

He looked at her coolly. "Can you?"

Clemmie turned away from his gaze. "Well, you won't have to worry about me anymore. You're getting married this afternoon and I'll be back in New York with Mother tonight."

Adam sat staring in silence at the patterned carpet on the stateroom floor. He had been feeling wonderful this morning, and he wanted to go on feeling wonderful. Certainly he was entitled to it today. But Clemmie was clearly miserable, and much as he wanted to walk out and close the door on whatever was bothering her, he couldn't.

"Is it Whit Morris?" he asked. "Is that why you've been behaving the way you have?"

"How have I been behaving?" she demanded.

"Generally when people try that hard to have a good time, they're not having a good time at all, Clemmie.

118

Why did you decide to leave Newport so suddenly? Were you running away from Whit?"

"Whit left before I did."

"I see," Adam said.

"You may be my older brother, but that doesn't mean you know everything."

"Not everything, Clemmie, just a little about you. Whit left Newport, so you decided to show him and leave too."

"What if I did? I'm not going to sit around waiting for him to finish with his games."

"What kind of games?"

"How do I know? Something about some railroad stocks that couldn't wait. I could wait, but they couldn't."

"Good Lord, Clemmie, Whit left on business?"

"That's what he said."

"Do you believe him?"

She didn't answer.

"Do you?"

"I don't know. The timing was so bad . . ." She let her voice trail off.

"The timing was bad," he mimicked. "I can't believe this is you talking, Clemmie. You know there's no such thing as timing with something like this. You've seen Father drop everything and race halfway across the country to settle some problem or snatch another line for the A & W. I've done the same thing myself. You grew up in that world, Clemmie. I thought you understood it. I imagine Whit thought the same thing."

"Then he's going to be surprised, isn't he?" The uncertainty of her tone belied the challenge of her words.

"Surprised and disappointed. And probably hurt as well. I know I'd be."

"He could have telephoned," she shot back, remembering her last night at the VanNests'.

"Did you give him a chance, Clemmie? You ran away the next morning."

"He could have called me that evening."

119

"Clemmie, I've been in meetings that lasted till midnight. If you were in Whit's place, would you have called the VanNests in the middle of the night and asked for you?"

Clemmie felt her pride slipping away in the face of Adam's argument. She was suddenly too tired to keep up the façade. "Maybe he just doesn't care that much," she said miserably.

"Did Whit give you any reason to think he didn't care?"

She remembered the night before he'd left, remembered the way the words *I love you and I'll never let you go* had sounded in the dark privacy of the beach house.

"Any reason beyond going to New York on business for a few days?" Adam continued.

"No."

"Then you're a fool, and if I were you I'd call him as soon as we get in and tell him . . . well, I don't have to tell you what to say. Seems to me the two of you will come up with something. Now that we've solved your problems, we can get to work on mine. I need a couple of witnesses, so will you please get out of that darn dress and get into something appropriate for a wedding? We ought to be there in less than an hour and I will not have anyone, even you, holding up this wedding."

The simple ceremony in Judge Weymouth's study went off without a hitch. The bride was lovely in rose-colored lace, the bride's mother managed to summon a few tears, although nowhere near the copious flow she'd shed at Samantha's first wedding, and Tony Bayliss was quiet and dignified as the best man. From the moment they'd met on deck that morning until he'd headed back to his yacht after the ceremony, Tony had been unfailingly polite to Clemmie. If her own memory of the night before hadn't been so vivid, she would almost have been able to convince herself nothing had happened.

For a honeymoon, Adam had suggested a few weeks in Bar Harbor, but Samantha thought the South of France would be more amusing, so it was decided they would stay in New York for a week or two before sailing. That would give them a chance to see Dolly, and Elias if he chose to come up. Adam was sure that once his father met Samantha, once he saw how happy they were together, all opposition would evaporate. Perhaps it was the way Samantha had looked in the rose-colored lace and the fact that Adam had never been married before that gave rise to such optimism.

Adam called his mother from the Weymouths' guest house to tell her they would arrive in New York with Clemmie in tow the following afternoon. In the excitement of his own news and the distress of Dolly's reaction, he forgot that Clemmie had asked him to find out if her mother knew where Whit was. Well, Adam thought, as he stepped out onto the small terrace of the guest house where his wife sat staring serenely out at the Sound, there'll be plenty of time for Clemmie to find out about Whit tomorrow.

It was a sultry overcast day, the air so stifling it felt as if a lid had been clamped over Manhattan. The taxi inched its way through the crosstown traffic.

"I thought those traffic signals they installed after the war were supposed to move the traffic," Adam said. "If you ask me, they only slow it down." It was clear that the closer they got to the St. Regis and Dolly, the more nervous he became.

"We'll be there soon enough," Samantha said.

Clemmie barely heard them. She was thinking of Whit. Her mother was bound to have news of him. Clemmie had made up her mind to call him as soon as she found out where he was.

As the taxi pulled up to the wide awning, the doorman emerged from his little gilt booth. The small enclosure always looked so cozy in winter, but Clemmie wondered how the doorman could stand it in this heat.

She and Samantha left Adam to take care of the luggage and started up the thickly carpeted stairs to the lobby. It was cooler there. Huge fans whirred quietly in every corner, and the large palms gave the illusion of shaded glens.

"God, I could do with an orange blossom," Samantha murmured.

"But it isn't even eleven," Clemmie said, then realized that Samatha's thirst had nothing to do with the time or even the weather.

The concierge behind the gilt grille was solicitous, as always. Had Miss Wilder had a good trip? Mrs. Wilder was expecting them. The bellboy would take them right up to the suite.

The door was opened not by Dolly but by Elias. Inside, the draperies of the sitting-room windows were drawn back, and the light filtering from behind Elias made it difficult to see his face. Adam, however, knew its expression instinctively. He straightened his shoulders a little. Assuming Elias was still in Scranton, Adam had prepared for a minor skirmish. Instead he found himself confronting a major battle.

Elias brushed aside Adam's attempts at an introduction. "I'd like to speak to my son alone," he said to Samantha.

"Whatever you have to say to me, Father, you can say in front of my wife."

"You may regret that statement, Adam. I have some unpleasant things to say, and they concern your . . . Mrs. Weymouth-Baldwin."

"You mean Mrs. Wilder," Adam corrected.

"I won't spar with you, Adam," Elias said. He turned to Samantha. "You know I'm opposed to this marriage, Mrs. Weymouth-Baldwin, but perhaps you don't know how strongly. There are a good many factors that are not in your favor. Your age, for one. I believe you're considerably older than my son."

Clemmie, who sat forgotten in a corner, noticed

122

that the color had drained from Samantha's cheeks, but she appeared calm.

"The fact that I'm a few years older than your son, Mr. Wilder, doesn't mean that I don't love him. Or that he doesn't love me."

"Your previous marriage," Elias continued as if Samantha hadn't spoken. "I don't approve of divorce."

Samantha smiled. "I don't imagine anyone *approves* of divorce, Mr. Wilder. Nevertheless, it's sometimes necessary."

Elias looked at her with satisfaction. She'd walked right into the trap. "And that is my main objection to this marriage. The conditions that made your divorce necessary. There's been talk, entirely too much talk—"

"Father!" Adam cut in. Alone with Samantha day after day, night after night on Bayliss's yacht—or so it had seemed, for the others had left them mostly to themselves—Adam had managed to forget his doubts, and now he was furious with his father for reminding him of their existence.

"I told you this wouldn't be pleasant." Elias's face was impassive.

Adam stood. "Neither of us is going to listen to this sort of thing."

"Sit down." Elias said quietly. "I'm not finished."

Adam remained standing, but did not leave the room. Samantha sat opening and closing the clasp of her small handbag. It was the only movement that belied her air of calm.

"I don't suppose you'd consider an annulment, Adam. It's a little late for that," Elias said, looking pointedly at Samantha, "but I could arrange it."

"You know I wouldn't consider it," Adam said.

"No, I didn't think you would." Elias turned to Samantha. "But perhaps *you* might consider a settlement. I think you'd find me generous, more generous than your first husband."

"You're insulting," Adam broke in.

"Let the woman answer for herself," Elias said.

Samantha smiled again, but there was no conviction in it. "I agree with my husband, Mr. Wilder. You're insulting."

"Perhaps you'll both reconsider when you hear my plans," Elias said. "You knew my intentions, Adam. Perhaps your . . . your wife even guessed them. The railroad was to be yours. Oh, George and Clemmie would have their inheritance, but you were to have controlling interest in the A & W. You were going to run the A & W, Adam. Well, all that's over now. You're a hard worker, and more important, you're a good railroad man. I suspected as much when you decided to switch to Sheffield from Yale, and you've proven yourself half a dozen times since. You're the best Chief of Motive Power I've ever had, and you know finance as well. I'm not saying that because you're my son. In fact, as far as I'm concerned, you're no longer my son. But you're a good worker, and so long as you continue to be one"—Elias looked pointedly at Samantha— "there will always be a job for you with the A & W. But that's all there'll be, Adam. A job. I won't leave you a single share. In fact, I won't leave you anything. Or your children. From now on you're an employee, and nothing more."

Adam's face was now as white as Samantha's, and rigid with anger.

"I trust I've made my position clear," Elias said.

"Perfectly clear."

"Perhaps you'd like some time to think it over, Adam."

"I don't have to think it over. My wife and I are sailing for Europe next week. We expect to be away for six weeks or so. After that I accept your offer of . . . of a job."

"I'm afraid you didn't understand, after all, Adam. My employees receive two weeks' vacation a year. If you'd like to take your holiday now, you may. But I'll expect you in your office in two weeks. And as for sailing for Europe, it's none of my business how my employees spend their salaries, but I've closed out the accounts in your name. Those were for my son."

Adam walked to where Samantha was sitting and took her arm. "I think it's time we left, Samantha." He turned to Dolly. "Good-bye, Mother. If you want to reach us, we'll be in Bar Harbor."

Samantha preceded Adam out the door. She looked, if anything, even angrier than he did.

"How could you, Father?" Clemmie said when she heard the door to the suite close after them. "How could you be so mean?"

"Be quiet, Clemmie. You know nothing about it," he said.

"I know that you're being terribly unfair."

Dolly looked at her husband. The impassive mask he'd worn through the conversation had fallen away, and his face was naked with misery. "You heard your father, Clemmie. You'll understand when you're older," she said, in a tone that belied such perfect understanding on her own part.

"But you're stripping him of everything just to punish him."

"He married her against my wishes," Elias said.

"Against your wishes! Do you think you can tell people whom to love or not to love?"

"I expect my children to take my wishes into account in these matters. Now that's enough of this conversation, Clemmie. As I said, it has nothing to do with you."

"I just want you to know that in his place, I would have acted the same way Adam did," Clemmie said.

Elias looked at his daughter with tired amusement. "I expect you would, Clemmie. But fortunately, you're not in his place. How is Mr. Morris?" Elias had been so enraged at his son's behavior that he hadn't given a thought to Clemmie since he'd arrived. Now he saw Clemmie color and a look of discomfort pass across his wife's face. "A lovers' spat, eh? Well, I trust it's nothing that can't be patched up. Where is he now?"

Clemmie looked at her mother. It was exactly the question she'd been wanting to ask.

"Grace VanNest telephoned me last night," Dolly said. "Whit returned to Newport a few days ago. He and Alison are engaged to be married."

There was a terrible silence in the room, but for Clemmie it wasn't a silence at all. Her mother's words thundered in her head.

Finally Dolly spoke. "I'm sorry, Clemmie."

"There's no need to be sorry for me. It has nothing to do with me," she laughed. It was a sharp, unnatural sound. "You didn't think I really cared for Whit? I was just amusing myself and Newport was so dull and . . . excuse me. If I'm going to dress . . ." Her words drifted off, but her back was straight and her head high as she left the room.

"Clemmie," Dolly said. "Clemmie, wait . . ."

"Let her go," Elias said. "She's going to have to work this out, and if I know Clemmie, she's going to have to work it out alone. Rotten shame, though. And I was so sure he was going to marry Clemmie."

Dolly started to speak, then changed her mind.

"Well, he came close. Darn close. I'm sure of that."

"In matters like this, Elias, close scarcely counts."

Chapter 4

WHIT HAD RETURNED to Newport in four days. He'd asked himself why he was bothering to return at all. If Clemmie were cruising with Tony Bayliss, there was nothing in Newport to interest him. But something within Whit said that perhaps Clemmie had returned or, better yet, perhaps she'd changed her mind and never left. He told himself it was a foolish hope, but it continued to live in the face of every more realistic expectation.

Stephen VanNest was alone when Whit arrived that Saturday afternoon. It had rained earlier and the grass was still wet. Whit stopped at the edge of the terrace and brushed the damp blades of grass from the cuffs of his white flannel trousers.

"Sit down, my boy," Mr. VanNest said. "Would you like some tea or can I give you a drink? Alison should be back any moment," he went on quickly when Whit refused both.

"How is she?" Whit stalled for time, trying to think of how to ask about Clemmie.

"Fine, I'm happy to say. Very excited about going abroad." VanNest was watching Whit carefully, and he saw the look of surprise that crossed his face. "But of course, you didn't know. We decided only a day or two ago. Mrs. VanNest and Alison are going abroad for a few months. Alison hasn't been to Europe since that year she spent at school in Switzerland. And of course she only got around on holidays then. It's time she saw more of the Continent." VanNest's implication was clear, and Whit did not miss it. Alison was a grown woman, and if Whit couldn't see that fact and act upon it, they'd send her abroad. At best the move would force him to act. At worst it would preserve Alison's dignity.

"Will it be only the two of them?" Whit asked.

"I hope to join them later. You can keep the Continent as far as I'm concerned. Don't much like the food or the people, though they've got some good pictures, I'll give you that. But I think I might join up with them in England. Get in some shooting."

Whit tried to make his voice casual. "I thought perhaps Mrs. Wilder and Clemmie might be going with them."

VanNest held Whit's eyes with his own. It's time you straightened this thing out, they seemed to say. "No, no plans for that. Can't say we even discussed it. Of course, Clemmie didn't give us a chance. Dashed off on that cruise without a bit of warning. But that's Clemmie for you. Delightful child, but a little tiring to live with, I should think."

"Who's tiring to live with, Daddy?" Alison stood in the French doors that opened onto the terrace. She had not put her hair up that afternoon and it made a soft frame for her face. She looked very pretty, Whit thought, and he noticed with a stab of anxiety that her smooth pale skin was marred only by a faint line where she had cut her forehead weeks before.

"Certainly not you, my dear."

Alison smiled at Whit. "He makes me sound terribly boring, doesn't he? How was New York?"

"Hot, unbearably hot."

Stephen VanNest excused himself and left the two young people alone on the terrace. Unlike her father,

128

however, Alison made no pretense about Whit's reasons for coming.

"I suppose they told you Clemmie's not here. She left last week." Alison could not bring herself to add, "right after you did."

"I heard. On Tony Bayliss's yacht. Strange, I wasn't even aware she knew him."

Alison saw the look of pain mingled with anger that crossed Whit's face, but said nothing.

"She left so abruptly," Whit continued.

"You know Clemmie. She gets something into her head and that's it. No waiting around and no turning back."

"That's Clemmie all right," Whit said.

Alison couldn't tell if he were attracted by the idea or annoyed.

"Have you heard from her since she left?" What I mean, Whit thought but didn't say, is—did she leave a note for me.

What he really means, Alison thought, is—didn't she leave some word for him. She hesitated for a moment. She couldn't compete with Clemmie in hand-to-hand combat, but there was no reason to surrender when Clemmie wasn't even at the scene of the battle. "Not a word. But that's typically Clemmie. She's probably having such a marvelous time, she hasn't given a moment's thought to any of us. For Clemmie the only place that exists is the one she's at now and the only people are those she's with at the moment." The pain that flickered in Whit's eyes this time was so naked that Alison almost flinched. She didn't think she could fight for Whit if fighting meant hurting him so much.

Whit stood and paced across the terrace once, as if physical movement could drive away his thoughts.

"Well, so much for what Clemmie's been up to. What about you? Anything exciting happen while I was away?"

"The usual parties and things." Whit heard the message behind her words. How could anything exciting happen if you weren't here? It was a familiar message, but now with Clemmie gone, it seemed strangely touching.

"Your father says you're planning to go abroad."

Alison blushed. She knew Whit would understand why she was being sent to Europe. "Only for a few months," she said, and cursed herself. Why couldn't she make Europe sound like the challenge to Whit it was supposed to be? Why did she have to make it so obvious that no matter what she did or where she went she'd always wait for him?

Again, Whit heard the tone and was moved. He had remained standing, and now he walked to the edge of the terrace and stood looking across the lawn to the water. He could almost see his uncle's beach from here, and the memory of that night with Clemmie washed over him as it had a hundred times in the past week. But then the sight of a yawl beating into the wind made him think of Tony Bayliss's boat. Suddenly the memory of Clemmie's body in the half-darkness of the bathhouse was sullied by the vision of Tony Bayliss's hands on it.

He turned back to Alison. She had not taken her eyes from him and there was no mistaking the adoration in them. "I wish you wouldn't go away, Alison." She kept staring at him, but said nothing. "I wish you'd stay here and marry me."

"You know I will, Whit."

He took a step toward her. "You don't have to sound so glum about it." He laughed and put his arms around her. "It isn't the worst thing in the world."

"It's the most wonderful thing in the world, Whit. At least it is for me. You know that."

With one finger he raised her face to his. "Then the least you can do is smile about it."

Her mouth was warm and yielding, as yielding as Clemmie's, and he felt her arms about his neck and her small soft body pressed against him and knew that in her own quiet, diffident way Alison wanted him as much as Clemmie had ever pretended to. But even as he was kissing her, Whit cursed himself for thinking of Clemmie.

Elias's private car had passed through the tunnel on the Pennsylvania Railroad's tracks with the Pennsy's train number 23. In Jersey City it was uncoupled and added to the Allegheny & Western's all-Pullman number 18 to Scranton, and Elias's face brightened immediately. He hated to ride another man's railroad—unless he were about to buy it.

Clemmie's grim expression showed no such improvement. She had been sitting in the same position with the same look on her face for more than an hour now. She appeared equally immune to the world outside and the people within the car.

"I said," Dolly repeated, "would you like to go away for a while?" She had discussed the possibility with Elias, but waited until he'd left the car and she was alone wih Clemmie to broach the subject.

"Isn't that the usual remedy when a girl's been jilted?" Last night's façade had shattered before the second wave of pain, the assault that was not dulled by shock. "Send her off to Europe or California to stay with friends. That way she can recover and the family can save face."

"To begin with, Clemmie, we haven't lost face. And you weren't jilted. It's a vulgar word at best, but it simply doesn't apply in this case."

Clemmie looked at her mother and there was more anger than self-pity in her eyes. "What would you call it, Mother?"

"A case of bad judgment. On your part."

"You mean I should have known better in the first place?"

"I mean you shouldn't have run off with Adam and Samantha that way. I didn't entirely approve of your going, but I'd assumed you'd told Whit. I had no idea you thought you were going to teach him a lesson."

"I was the one who learned the lesson. I should have known it to begin with, but I'll never forget it now."

"If only you'd told me what you had in mind, Clemmie. You see, Whit's a Vanderbilt, but he's also a Morris. The Vanderbilts marry beautiful heiresses, but the Morrises marry even-tempered women who won't trouble them."

Clemmie thought she'd never heard a more apt description of Alison, but she found no satisfaction in the dismissal. "How do you know so much about it?" She asked, turning back to the window. If she had been looking at her mother instead of at the flat New Jersey countryside, she would have seen the peculiar expression that crossed Dolly's face. "You forget the summers I spent in Newport when I was your age." Several minutes passed before Dolly spoke again. "If you don't want to go away, Clemmie, what do you have in mind?"

"You mean what are my prospects, don't you, Mother? After all, I've been 'out' for two years, and I'm getting a little long in the tooth."

"I meant nothing of the sort, Clemmie. It's simply that I won't have you moping around the house as if your life were over." Dolly had never thought she'd say those words to her daughter. Clemmie was not the sort of girl to grieve over past defeats—not that she'd come across many till now. Clemmie had a passion as well as a flair for getting on with the business of living, or so Dolly had thought until yesterday.

"Don't worry, Mother, I have no intention of moping around the house or acting as if my life were over." I won't give Whit and Alison the satisfaction, she swore to herself.

Dolly heard the edge of determination in her daughter's voice. "Porter Lowry?" she asked. It wasn't a bad idea, Dolly thought. Porter wasn't the spectacular catch Whit was, but he'd make a good husband. If nothing else—and Dolly believed there was a good deal else to Porter—he seemed to be able to handle Clemmie. He liked her—that had been obvious since they were children together—but he wouldn't put up with all the little tricks the other young men did. Perhaps that was because they had been children together. Porter Lowry knew Clemmie almost as well as Dolly did.

"Not Porter, Mother. Never Porter."

"Why 'never Porter'? I can think of far worse catches. He's attractive, he has beautiful manners, and he comes from an old Philadelphia family—even if he did grow up in Scranton. Of course, he'll never make a fortune, but he'll inherit something and then there's all your money. The more I think of it, the more likely Porter seems."

"Likely! I don't want to marry someone who's likely. And I have no intention of spending the rest of my life as the wife of a country doctor."

"Have it your own way, Clemmie. You will anyway."

Clemmie remained staring out the window and said nothing. She'd told her mother the truth. The idea of marriage to Porter, whom she didn't love in the least, did not excite her. But there was another side to it she hadn't mentioned to Dolly. Everyone assumed because she and Porter were such old friends that Porter was in love with her, but Clemmie was fairly sure that wasn't the case. In fact, she suspected that it was because he knew her so well that Porter did not love her. The idea, if she allowed herself to dwell on it, was not particularly flattering, so Clemmie chose *not* to dwell on it.

Walter, the Wilders' driver, was waiting for them at the station. George Wilder, Elias's second son, stood leaning against the Crane-Simplex, chatting with Walter about the pros and cons of various engines. His hand moved absentmindedly over the sleek curves of the machine as he talked. It was an old automobile, but one that had been built to last. There was a dignity and style to its lines that impressed even George.

"You didn't have to come to the station, George." Elias cut short his son's welcome.

"Couldn't let your return go uncelebrated," George said, kissing his mother's cheek.

"It would have been celebration enough," Elias observed, "to find you at the office."

George had spent the day at the office and left only half an hour early to meet their train, but he knew the futility of arguing with his father. Besides, he hated to argue. "How are you, kid?" he asked, turning to Clemmie. "You look terrific. Did you knock 'em dead in Newport?"

Clemmie looked at her brother's face, at once so handsome and so vacant, and could not even be annoyed. The smile was so simple and meaningless, the jaw so straight and weak, there seemed to be nothing in the face to be annoyed at. George and Adam had the same coloring except for the eyes and similar features, although George was taller and more traditionally good-looking than his older brother. But despite the fact that they shared certain physical traits, they did not look alike. In a way Clemmie had always thought of George as a film negative of Adam. While Adam was a solid presence in the center of the photograph, George was a pale shadow in a more substantial world.

"No one to knock dead," Clemmie said lightly. "It was as dull as you predicted."

"Poor kid. Well, Porter's been around a couple of times. Wondering if you'd get back before he returned to school," George said.

"Good old Porter," Clemmie laughed.

"It seems," Dolly said, settling herself in the back of the car, "that Porter Lowry is in disfavor these days. And how are you, Walter?" she asked the driver. "I trust you've had a pleasant summer."

"Very pleasant, thank you, Mrs. Wilder." Walter permitted himself a glance in the rearview mirror. The mistress was looking a little tired, but still beautiful, he thought. He'd been driving for the Wilders for a dozen years, and he'd permitted himself more than one daydream in that time. The trouble was that his wife Hilda always guessed them. She could spot Walter's mental infidelities as surely as other women could recognize their husbands' actual strayings.

"You drove that woman somewhere today. Alone," Hilda would always say when he got home.

"Of course I drove Mrs. Wilder somewhere," Walter would answer. "It's part of my job." But the daydreams were not part of his job, and Hilda knew it.

"I hope you enjoyed your trip, Mrs. Wilder." Walter's voice could not have been more respectful.

Elias cut through the niceties. "What about that accident on 32?" he asked George. Have they found out what happened?"

"Hendreich just got back from Cleveland this afternoon. As a matter of fact he's waiting at the farm to talk to you about it."

Although nothing but flowers had been grown on the Wilder property outside of Scranton for more than a generation, it was still called the farm. Dolly especially liked the term. If you weren't going to have a house in town, that is, in New York or Philadelphia, then you lived a country life. It made no difference if railroads ran over your land and mines lay beneath it, you were still a country gentleman and a country gentleman lived on a farm.

It would have been clear to even the most casual observer, as soon as the car turned into the long curving drive that formed a crescent before the house, that the house and property were considerably more splendid than the term "farm" implied. The main part of the house, a simple two-story wood building, dated back almost a hundred years, but as Elias Wilder Senior's mines had flourished, so had the house he'd bought. Two long wings stretched out in symmetrical stateliness to give the house a definite Georgian flavor, and the present Elias had made his own additions and improvements that included two verandas that ran the length of the house in front and on one side, an enclosed porch behind the west wing, and several new rooms on the second floor.

He'd also added garage facilities for six cars to his father's stables and more modern servants' quarters. After the opulence of Newport, the house looked small and simple to Dolly, but the simplicity boasted a certain style, she thought, and if the house was not enormous, it was spacious.

To Thomas Hendreich, who had been waiting the last half-hour in the small study Elias used as an office, the house was more splendid than anything he'd ever imagined. Although he'd been inside it four or five times in the last two years, he never crossed the threshold without a certain shiver of emotion not unlike that of a believer entering a cathedral. Part of Tom Hendreich knew he'd have a house just like it someday, but another part of him knew he'd never belong in it.

Tom stood as soon as he saw Elias. "I hope you had a good trip, Mr. Wilder."

"I hope you had a productive trip, Hendreich," Elias answered as he lowered himself awkwardly into the large leather chair behind the mahogany desk. He'd slept little after his confrontation with Adam yesterday afternoon, and he felt stiff and out of sorts.

Tom watched the older man move and saw the look of discomfort that flickered across his face. He's getting old, he thought. The idea gave rise to a dozen now-familiar questions. How long does he have? Can Adam Wilder fill his shoes? Where do I stand with Adam in charge? Tom got on well with Adam, but it would be blind optimism to assume that a younger man would advance him as rapidly as Elias had, and there was no place for blind optimism in the uphill fight that had been Tom Hendreich's life. Tom was not the youngest chief engineer of a major railroad, but he was the youngest ever to have reached that position with neither family nor financial backing.

"Well, I think I have some answers for you about number 32, sir."

"The local brotherhood, right? Up to their old tricks again?"

136

"More likely the roadbed. That rainy spell last week did a lot of damage." Tom did not voice the sentence he knew should come next. It should have been reinforced a long time ago. The omission was intentional. Tom knew the answers he had were not the ones Elias wanted to hear, but he knew also that Elias was too intelligent not to listen to them. He would tell Elias the truth, but he would tell it as tactfully as possible.

"Damned government," Elias muttered. "They were right there when it came to nationalizing the railroads, but not when it came to keeping them up."

Both men knew the argument was only partly justified. The government had let the structures and the rolling stock deteriorate during the war, but it had been three years since the armistice and the A&W had done nothing to improve the branch where the accident had occurred. In fact, only months ago when Tom had warned Elias that branch was desperately in need of work, Elias had told him it would have to wait. There wasn't enough freight traffic on the branch to warrant major expenditures now. Not with all the labor problems peace had brought.

"It's a question of priorities," Elias had said. "First get the Water Gap route in shape so we can keep the coal moving and then we'll worry about the old Lock Haven branch."

Tom suspected Elias was remembering his words now.

"Exactly what kind of damage?" Elias asked, knowing he would not like the answer.

"The flooding weakened everything. When number 32 came down that stretch around the river, the right rail sank more than a foot. The engine went straight into the river and took four freight cars with it."

"Let's be thankful it didn't take any more." Elias looked at Tom coolly. "You going to say 'I told you so,' Hendreich?"

"But I didn't, sir. I told you that branch needed

attention, but an accident on one of the more heavily traveled lines could have been a lot worse."

"Try explaining that to the news boys when they start snooping around. How are those men in the hospital?"

"One of them died."

"Damn," Elias muttered. "That's two men dead."

"Do you want to look at the figures on the freight loss?" Tom asked.

"I'll look at them in the car. Come on, you can drive down to the yard with me. I want to check on a few things that won't wait until morning."

Tom followed Elias out of the study into the large entrance hall. Clemmie Wilder was standing at a small Sheraton table near the front door riffling through a pile of mail on a silver tray. Tom had known when he came out to the farm this afternoon that he might see her, yet he was never prepared for it. He could still remember the first time he'd seen Clemmie Wilder. He should have forgotten it by now, because it had happened a long time ago, when he'd been only a boy, but he hadn't forgotten.

Tom had been a caddy at the country club that summer. He'd hated the job, less for the back-breaking work of carrying bags full of heavy golf clubs up and down the rolling hills in the still heat of a Pennsylvania summer than for the way he was treated for such a service. It seemed to Tom that he was a non-presence that summer. Even when the players demanded a club or gave him a tip, they seemed not to see him. Some nights he'd arrive home exhausted and dispirited and stare at himself for a long time in the streaky parlor mirror to make certain he wasn't invisible.

To be sure he'd been invisible to Clemmie Wilder that first day he'd seen her. Clemmie had been too busy with her own disappointment to notice anyone else. He remembered an imperious little girl in a white dress who'd cried and shouted and threatened to strike the governess with a putter because the woman had said nine holes were enough for one afternoon. Tom had been horrified by the scene. And absolutely fascinated.

It was not the only time he'd responded so strongly to Clemmie. He remembered another afternoon at the country club. By then he was working for the A & W and had been sent to the club with some papers Elias had to see immediately. The steward, who remembered Tom from his caddying days with no particular fondness, told him to wait outside while he summoned Mr. Wilder, and Tom, feeling invisible again, had retired to the west lawn as instructed. He'd had to wait almost twenty minutes, but he hadn't minded. For the entire twenty minutes he'd been able to watch Clemmie Wilder on the terrace. She was in white again and the imperious little girl had grown into a self-confident and beautiful woman.

Clemmie was with two men that afternoon. Tom didn't know either of them, but he recognized their type from his college days. They were the kind of men who belonged to the best fraternities, drove the flashiest automobiles, always had plenty of pocket money, and, most painful of all, knew the prettiest girls to spend it on. All through college, through the long hours of study and the endless nights spent washing dishes and waiting tables and cleaning livery stables, he'd envied those men their comfortable fraternities and their fast cars, their easy spending money and, most of all, their girls, and now he envied those two men Clemmie Wilder. He envied them because she was the epitome of all those girls—and more. There was something in her, the way she moved when she crossed the terrace to talk to people at another table, the way she looked up at one of the men when she returned and they both stood for her, the way she placed a hand on the tennis-sweatered arm of the other man when he looked as if he'd been rebuffed, that stirred Tom Hendreich deeply. He looked at Clemmie, and all the lonely nights filled with aching desire and throbbing dreams washed back over him. He looked at Clemmie and he knew she could make up for the years of loneliness and longing, but he knew too that it was a futile thought because he could never have Clemmie Wilder.

He watched her now, standing at the hall table tossing the letters aside one after another. Clearly there was nothing in that tray full of invitations that interested her. She heard them approach and looked up. The eyes were flat. Tom had never seen them so flat, and he was an avid watcher of Clemmie Wilder's eyes. At least he was when he got the opportunity.

"Mr. Hendreich," she said. "Still keeping the trains on time?"

"To the minute. Welcome home, Miss Wilder. It's nice to have you back."

"It's nice to be back."

Had they been alone, Tom might have told her she didn't look as if it were nice to be back, but Elias was standing at the door, hat in hand. "Tell your mother I'll be back in time for dinner, Clemmie."

"You know you'll never make it, Father. It's almost six now."

"Then tell her I'll be a little late. I'll be back by eight. Or," he added, "a little after."

Clemmie looked at Tom. "That's the trouble with you railroad men. Everything has to wait—including dinner—while you take care of your trains." Clemmie had only meant to tease her father, but now the words were out, the memory of Whit and their last conversation rushed back, and she felt a flash of anger. Clemmie saw that Hendreich was watching her and wondered if he'd noticed anything. The eyes were canny, but not unkind, and though he was a big man, tall with a powerful chest and shoulders, there was something almost gentle about his movements. But Clemmie knew that was only part of Tom Hendreich, the part that came to the farm. Once when she'd gone to her father's office, she'd caught a glimpse of Hendreich talking to another man in the yard. He was speaking quietly and she couldn't hear what he was saying, but there was no mistaking the power, even the violence in him then. Though he was only a little taller than the other man, he seemed to tower over him, seething with barely suppressed rage. Clemmie had asked her father about the incident on the way home, and Elias had said that Tom Hendreich was as good with men as he was with machinery. "Only he can't tolerate incompetence."

"Was the other man incompetent?" she'd asked.

"If Hendreich was bawling him out, I'm willing to bet he was," Elias had answered.

Looking at him now, Clemmie wondered about the two sides of Tom Hendreich. She looked at his hands that were turning a straw hat around and around. They were large, but the fingers were strong and tapered.

"Why don't you come back for dinner too, Mr. Hendreich? Maybe you can keep Father on time—the way you do the trains."

Tom forced himself not to look at Elias. He refused to ask permission, even with his eyes, to dine at Elias Wilder's table. If Elias didn't want him there, he'd have to find a way to say so.

"Thank you, Miss Wilder, I'd like to very much."

"Then we'll see you both at eight," Clemmie said and started up the winding staircase. Without turning she knew that Tom Hendreich's eyes followed her until she was out of sight.

Tom would have liked to go back to the single room he rented to change his shirt before dinner, but Elias kept him busy the entire time they were in the A & W's central office. When they arrived back at the farm, Elias directed him to a small first-floor bathroom behind the stairs. Tom stood before the mirror straightening his stiff collar and tie. Suddenly a scene from a film he'd seen a month ago flashed through his mind. There had been a long comedy routine about dressing for dinner. With a sinking feeling he pictured Elias returning in a dinner suit. Well, he thought, smoothing the fair hair he kept properly short, if the Wilders dressed for dinner, they should have warned him. Not that the warning would have made the least difference. Tom did not own evening clothes.

When he entered the large front parlor, Tom was relieved to see Elias freshly washed and combed but in the same dark suit. Clemmie, however, had changed. She was wearing a violet dress of a soft silk that moved against her body as she crossed the room to him.

"I'm afraid your record with trains is better than with Father, Mr. Hendreich. Would you like a martini cocktail?"

"I recommend them highly," George said, without moving from the chair he was sprawled in. "I made them myself. In fact, I think I'll join you in another one."

"You've had enough, George," Dolly said meaningfully. "And I won't have dinner delayed. It's nice to see you, Mr. Hendreich." Dolly handed him a glass. "And you do have time for one before dinner."

Tom had been prepared for coolness on the part of Mrs. Wilder, but he found none in her words or her manner.

Dolly was determined to be perfectly polite to Tom Hendreich. She had been surprised and a little annoyed when Clemmie had invited him to dinner, but she had sufficient experience with her daughter to know that opposition to the man would only make Clemmie warmer to him.

On the way in to dinner Clemmie took Tom's arm. The casualness of the gesture annoyed as well as excited him. She seemed to be very sure of her power over him.

"Were you born in this area, Mr. Hendreich?" Dolly asked, noticing that Tom hesitated for only a moment before picking up the fish fork.

"Yes, my family still lives there," Tom answered, referring to a small mining town twelve miles west. What he did not add, though he knew Elias was aware of the fact, was that his father also still labored in one of

Elias's mines. Tom sent enough money home for Karl Hendreich to stop working—that was one of the reasons Tom lived so frugally himself—but his father said that as long as he could work, he would work.

"So you're a Pennsylvania boy at heart, Mr. Hendreich," Dolly said. "Even to your university. Mr. Wilder tells me you studied engineering at Lehigh. Adam considered Lehigh, but he decided on Yale instead. Though I know most Yale men don't consider Sheffield really Yale. And of course George was graduated from Lafayette. Practically your neighbor."

"After being booted out of dear old Yale," George added.

"That's nothing to be proud of," Elias snapped.

Clemmie turned to Tom. "But aren't you ever going to leave Pennsylvania, Mr. Hendreich?"

"Mr. Hendreich leaves Pennsylvania at least once a week," Elias said. "He just got back from Cleveland this morning."

"How terribly exciting," Clemmie said without taking her eyes from him.

"Not exciting," Tom said. "But productive."

"And where are you going next week, Mr. Hendreich?"

"Chicago."

"Chicago's not a bad town," George said, remembering a weekend that had stretched into a week last spring.

"The Paris of the Midwest, I'm sure," Clemmie said.

Tom looked across the table at her and for a moment he hated that beautiful mouth that was smiling at him with such self-confidence. "Not exactly, Miss Wilder, but it is a destination, isn't it?"

For a moment Clemmie looked decidedly off balance. Elias merely smiled down at his plate, while Dolly quickly changed the subject.

"Do you play bridge?" Clemmie asked Tom after dinner.

"Not very well, I'm afraid." In fact Tom had tried

to learn, but he was simply no good at cards or any other game. He supposed he didn't take them seriously enough.

"Well then, bridge is out. Why don't we go for a drive? You drive, don't you, Mr. Hendriech?"

"Whenever I get the chance."

"Can you drive a Marmon?"

"Tom drove everything from troop trucks to a general's staff car in the war," Elias said. "I think he can handle your Marmon, Clemmie."

Clemmie barely gave Tom a chance to thank Dolly for dinner. Once in the car, she watched as he backed out of the garage. Her father was right. He handled the car with complete confidence.

"Where to?" he asked when they'd reached the end of the driveway.

"You think of some place. You're the Pennsylvania boy."

"And you're darned rude some of the time, Miss Wilder." Tom hadn't meant to voice the words, but suddenly they were out.

"I'm sorry," she said quietly. "It doesn't matter where. I just want to drive around."

"Restless?" Tom asked more kindly.

Clemmie laughed. "If Mother's to be believed, I've been restless since I was born."

"And I guess coming home, coming back here, I mean, is something of a letdown. It can't be very exciting after Newport and New York."

"You know how people always talk about being lonely in the middle of a crowd? Well, it's the same with boredom. You can be just as bored in the middle of a big city as you can be lonely in a crowd. Right now it doesn't make much difference where I am."

Tom took his eyes from the road for a minute and looked at her. You mean you'll be bored no matter where you are and lonely no matter who you're with."

"I didn't say that," she answered quickly.

"But you meant it."

"What about you?" Clemmie asked. "What do you do here or in Cleveland or Chicago to keep from getting bored? Besides work?"

"There isn't much time for anything else."

"But some time, surely there's some time. Do you have a girl, Mr. Hendreich?"

"That's a pretty personal question."

"They're the only kind I like."

They had turned into a small dirt road and now Tom pulled the car onto the edge of a field and turned off the ignition. "Are you asking out of idle curiosity or interest?"

"That depends on the answer," Clemmie said.

"You know, with most girls I'd say if the answer were yes, it would be idle curiosity and if it were no, it would be interest, but with you I think it just might be the other way around."

Clemmie looked at him in surprise, then laughed. "Well, you're clever, Mr. Hendreich, I'll give you that."

"First of all, I think it's time you started calling me Tom. And second, your father could have told you I'm clever."

"I like to do my own research. And you still haven't answered my question."

"There's no girl," he said quietly.

It was only September, but a cool breeze had come up from the west and Clemmie shivered. Tom felt rather than saw the movement. He thought of offering her his jacket, but instead reached an arm around her shoulders. He was still staring straight ahead and she looked up at his profile. His jaw was sharp and he held it tensely as if he were ready for a fight. His face was stronger than Whit's, but not as handsome, Clemmie decided, then cursed herself for having thought of Whit. But why else was she bothering with Tom Hendreich if not because of Whit? Tom was nothing more than balm for her bruised feelings.

She moved a little closer and felt the muscles of his arm tighten around her shoulder. When she spoke her voice was light and teasing. "You can kiss me if you like."

Tom pulled his arm away with a sudden movement and turned on the ignition. "I'll kiss you when we both want to," he snapped above the noise of the engine, "not when you say it's time. I may be hired help in the A & W office, but this is after hours."

Clemmie was stung by his sudden movement and the anger in his voice, and turned away so he couldn't see the tears she was fighting back. They were both silent on the way home, but when he had pulled the car into the garage, they sat for a moment, each wanting to say something, but not knowing the right words.

Finally, without looking at him, Clemmie spoke. "It had nothing to do with the railroad or your job."

"Didn't it?"

"Well, maybe it did, but not in the way you think." She turned to him. "Maybe I thought you might be put off because of Father. Maybe I thought you needed encouragement. You wouldn't even have asked me to go for a drive tonight."

"Why didn't you wait and see?"

Clemmie got out of the car and stood with her hand on the door staring at him. "Well, I'm waiting."

"Darn it," Tom said. "You're right." He knew the social life of girls like Clemmie revolved around the country club and each other's houses. "There's no place I can ask you to go."

"Where do you take other girls?" She laughed. "I mean other nice girls."

His face darkened a little at the last words. "Moving pictures, things like that."

"I haven't seen Wallace Reid in *Nice People*."

He laughed. "Well, Clemmie, how would you like to go to the pictures tomorrow night?"

"I thought you'd never ask." But even as she spoke Clemmie wondered why she'd gone to the trouble. Twice today—when she'd asked him to dinner and when she'd told him he could kiss her—she'd gone out of her way to encourage Tom Hendreich, but she knew she didn't really want Tom. It was only that she couldn't stand not having Whit.

She looked at Tom now. It had been windy in the car and the fair hair falling over his forehead gave him a more rakish air than the proper façade he'd maintained before her parents. He was smiling up at her, not a self-satisfied smile like Whit's, but a deep smile that went right to his eyes and changed his whole face. For a moment Clemmie regretted the incident in the car, and wondered what it would be like to kiss Tom Hendreich.

BOOK
TWO

Chapter 5

In 1886 Elias Wilder was still a young man, but it was not his age that turned J. P. Morgan against Wilder's scheme. Elias had been running the Wilder mines for six years and running them more profitably, Morgan knew, than his late father had. Elias Wilder was a good risk, Morgan thought, looking at the lean young man sitting opposite him in the small saloon of the *Corsair*. Not much of a sailor, he suspected from Wilder's sallow face, but a good risk. Had he wanted financing for another scheme, Morgan would have considered it, but not for this one.

"Mr. Wilder," Morgan said, holding a gold humidor filled with fat black cigars toward Elias, "I expect you've heard of something I'm told has come to be called the Corsair Compact?"

"I've heard of it," Elias said, keeping his face impassive. He had not allowed himself to be intimidated by the legendary yacht, and he would not be cowed by the man who owned it. Elias had been careful to keep his eyes straight ahead when he boarded the boat. There'd be no mooning about eying the two towering masts, the long sleek lines that ran forward into a raffish bowsprit that seemed to Elias the physical incarnation of Morgan's own driving nature. And he'd been careful not to pay too much attention to the saloon when the steward showed him in. After all, he'd seen a Rubens and a Bruegel before, even if he'd never seen

151

them at sea. He was familiar with priceless Chinese carpets and good English antiques. And he was determined not to react to any of it, just as he refused to be intimidated by the dark eyes piercing him now like bullets or the bald dome of a head that housed the greatest financial brain in the world. And he kept his eyes from the bulbous red nose as well. Morgan's strange skin disease and his sensitivity about it were well known, although their notoriety had not kept Elias from being surprised at the effect. It was, on that particular day, grotesque. Apparently the laws of nature were more democratic than those of finance.

"The term refers to an agreement Mr. Roberts and Mr. Depew came to last summer aboard this boat," Morgan continued. "I find that a few hours on the water often help solve problems that sometimes seem insoluble on land. That's why I asked you aboard today, Mr. Wilder. It may interest you to know that we're following the same course Mr. Depew and Mr. Roberts did last summer—the same nautical course, that is. We'll go down the Hudson and into the harbor as far as Sandy Hook."

If Elias did not look forward to several hours at sea, he said nothing.

Morgan chewed thoughtfully on his cigar. "I mentioned my cruise with Mr. Roberts and Mr. Depew for a reason, Mr. Wilder. If I did not permit them to build new branches on the west bank of the Hudson, or in Pennsylvania, why would I allow you to construct a new New York–Chicago line?"

It was exactly the question Elias had been waiting for. "Because those lines were unnecessary, Mr. Morgan. The Central provides sufficient service for the Hudson River area and there's no need for a new line between Reading and Pittsburgh. In other words, each line was competing only to wreck the other. It was destructive competition."

"All competition is destructive, Mr. Wilder."

"Not if it provides better service, sir."

"And you intend to provide better service."

"Much better. I plan to build a direct line, as straight and flat as modern technology can make it, between New York and Chicago. No more of the Central's twists up through New York State and around the lakes, no more of the Pennsy's climbs over the mountains. My line will lie straight and flat between New York and Chicago."

"Permit me a personal question, Mr. Wilder. Why does a successful mining man want to get mixed up with railroads?"

"Because all the coal in the world—or any raw material or product you can name—won't do a bit of good unless it can be moved quickly and cheaply from one place to another. I'm tired of paying high rates for inferior service, and if I have to build my own line to remedy the situation, I will."

"Surely you don't intend to build an entire railroad just to carry Wilder coal?"

"There are hundreds of businessmen in Pennsylvania, and in Ohio and Indiana and anyplace else you can name, who will welcome faster, cheaper service. And it's not only freight I have in mind. The passengers want better service too."

"You're a young man with a big dream, Mr. Wilder, but I fear it's too costly a dream." Morgan saw Elias begin to speak, and went on quickly. "I don't mean costly in terms of the amount you're asking. I mean costly in terms of what it will do to the Pennsylvania and the Central, to the entire economy of this nation. You'll either do considerable damage to the other two lines or fail yourself. In either case I'll lose money, and so will a great many other investors. I'm afraid the country can't afford your dream, Mr. Wilder."

Elias went on to prove that it wasn't a dream but an eminently practical scheme to turn a profit and improve transportation between the East Coast and the Midwest, but the conversation was effectively over. Though Morgan talked and listened for another half-hour until the *Corsair* docked in Jersey City to put Elias ashore, there was little point to their words. Morgan had made up his mind. He had, Elias realized, made up his mind even before they'd met. That was why he'd chosen the *Corsair* for their meeting. It was a repeat performance of the Corsair Compact, but one of which few people would ever hear. The Pennsylvania and the Central had merely had a limb amputated; Elias's still unnamed railroad had been aborted.

Two years later, Elias bought his first railroad. It was a small line that ran from Scranton to Lock Haven. The old Lock Haven Line had overextended itself in an attempt to move south into Maryland and Elias had managed to get it for a fraction of what it was worth. Within five years he owned three railroads and by the time he married Dolly Lovington in the spring of 1895 he was preparing to take over his fourth and biggest line.

Elias had never talked much to Dolly about his business affairs. She learned from the Philadelphia aunt who introduced them that he had inherited several anthracite coal mines in the Scranton area and had recently taken to buying railroads. Dolly was the fourth daughter of a New York gentleman who had inherited a splendid pedigree but not the fortune befitting it. The idea that a man might begin collecting railroads as her father had once collected first editions was astonishing. The fact that the same man might be interested in Dolly Lovington, a pretty girl with no money and two still unmarried older sisters, was encouraging. But though Dolly was impressed by Elias Wilder's success, she was not much concerned with the details surrounding it. During their courtship Elias spoke little and Dolly asked nothing of his business affairs. So she was surprised when, a few weeks after they had returned from their wedding trip to Saratoga, Elias came home jubilant and eager to talk about his latest coup.

"It took ten months of some of the toughest negotiations I've ever seen, but I got it. I got the Toledo

Central. As long as they held out, there was no way I could join the Lock Haven and Oil City with the Michigan and Eastern Line. And it was no easy feat, I can tell you that. Those boys at the Central—the New York Central, I mean—gave me a run for my money."

Dolly was suddenly listening more carefully.

"Toledo's always been a New York Central town, and they must see what I have in mind. Right now I run from Scranton into Chicago, but before I'm finished the Allegheny & Western is going to run right from New York to Chicago. Incidentally, how do you like the name? Allegheny & Western."

"It sounds fine," Dolly said hesitantly, "unless of course you think it's a little provincial."

Elias laughed. "You're a real Easterner, Dolly. What's more provincial-sounding than the New York Central or the Pennsylvania? No, I like the sound of the Allegheny & Western. It's got sweep. Takes in the whole darn area. The Allegheny & Western," he repeated. "I think we'll drink to that. Don't we have any champagne in the house?"

Now Dolly knew it was a momentous occasion. Elias drank a little whiskey now and then, but wine rarely if at all. When she'd asked for champagne at the hotel where they'd stayed in Saratoga, Elias had, of course, ordered it for her, but he'd barely tasted it. Now he rang for the butler and told him to bring them a bottle of champagne. When it arrived, Elias insisted on opening it himself. He proposed a toast to the Allegheny & Western, and downed the glass in a single swallow.

"Straight from New York to Chicago," he took up the thread again. "Not Jersey City, but New York. No ferry service for the A & W. You'll be able to step aboard in New York and get off at the Illinois Central Station in Chicago. And the ride will be the fastest and smoothest in the East. It'll be more direct than the Central and with the improvements I'm going to make it'll be a smoother ride than the Pennsy." Elias thought of the years of battling with both lines over freight rates, the years of being at the mercy of the two railroad titans. "The A & W is going to outstrip them both. The A & W is going to be the greatest railroad in the country."

Elias's excitement was contagious, but even without it Dolly would have been thrilled by his plan. She had her own reason for wanting to outstrip the Central and it had to do with more than money. After a lifetime of genteel poverty, Dolly had welcomed the comfort and security of marriage to Elias, but she was not by nature an avaricious woman. She had every material comfort she wanted now, and five more railroads would not make her five times as happy. Outstripping the New York Central, however, would.

Since her marriage to Elias, Dolly had not allowed herself to think of Quentin Morris, and putting him out of her mind hadn't been as difficult as she'd expected. Elias was a considerate husband, especially for a man so caught up in his work, and Dolly found his determination strangely attractive. If she was not wildly in love with Elias, at least she no longer felt the same emotion for Quentin Morris. She felt nothing for Quentin Morris but hatred. As a Christian woman Dolly could not approve of the sentiment, but neither could she banish it; she would never have sought retribution, but if retribution were handed her, she would not refuse it.

That night as Elias talked of his plans for the railroad, Dolly found the memories of the summer before, the memories of Quentin Morris, returning with new force.

It seemed impossible that it had been only a year ago that she had planned marriage to Quentin. Surely the naive girl who had been Dolly Lovington had been dead for longer than that.

Dolly's Aunt Martha, her father's sister who'd had the good sense to marry down socially and up financially, had invited her to Newport for the season. Having no children of her own, Martha had given each of her brother's four daughters a summer in Newport. Ann, the oldest and the real beauty of the family, had been lucky enough to make a good match during her season. Lillian and Regina had not been so fortunate. Now it was Dolly's chance, and the moment she was introduced to Quentin Vanderbilt Morris at a small concert at the Morris home, she staked every hope on him.

Quentin, for his part, gave Dolly reason to hope. He had just emerged, unscathed as usual, from a rather unpleasant scrape with a Spanish dancer, and he found Dolly Lovington's simple manner and straightforward prettiness irresistible—for the moment. At every ball his name appeared again and again on her dance card. When she competed in the archery contest, he wore her colors. When his horse raced, he asked her to wear his. Every morning two dozen white roses arrived at Martha's door for Dolly. "Only white," Quentin had told the florist when placing the order. Since the Spanish dancer, he found he couldn't abide red roses.

Martha could not have been more pleased. She had never forgiven Lillian and Regina for throwing away the opportunity she had given them. Dolly was clearly making the most of it. Quentin Morris was one of Newport's most eligible bachelors. He had charm, wit, and good looks, and stood to inherit a large portion of Morris land and a huge chunk of the Central Railroad. As for his reputation—the scandal of the Spanish dancer had reached Newport—well, Quentin was still young and could be expected to outgrow that sort of thing. At any rate, there was no point in begrudging Quentin his effect on women. Dolly was clearly mad about him, and Martha had no objection to her niece marrying for love—as long as the money and position were there, too.

Both aunt and niece were so caught up in Quentin Morris and his imminent proposal that they barely noticed the fuss that accompanied the Duchesse de Saville's arrival in Newport. The duchess was a great beauty and had that special flair that is unique to French women, but the furor she caused in Newport was nothing compared to the havoc Quentin was wreaking in Dolly's trusting heart. Only the night before he'd danced with her more than a dozen times at the costume ball. While half the women there, as if in response to the Duchesse de Saville's presence, had come as Marie Antoinette or Madame de Pompadour, Dolly had heeded her aunt's advice and come in the simple, draped gown of a Grecian goddess. On someone more sophisticated than Dolly, the costume would have been almost suggestive, but Dolly carried it off splendidly. Quentin thought she had never looked more desirable. Later that night in a quiet corner, over the midnight "supper" that more closely resembled a fifteen-course dinner, he told her as much.

"But it's so simple," Dolly said. "And everyone else's costume is so splendid."

"But there's nothing more splendid than simplicity," Quentin said. "I'll admit the unusual, the sumptuous, is distracting for the moment, but it's simplicity that endures. And that's as true of people as it is of art." Quentin thought of the Spanish dancer, and Dolly, who by this time had heard the rumors, followed his mind. "A man may be intrigued by the artificial, the affected, but only intrigued. When it comes to love, when it comes to something more lasting—" Quentin was beginning to get as drunk on his own words and Dolly's radiant acceptance of them as on the champagne "—then it's artlessness he wants. The simple virtues. Honesty. Trust. Goodness," he finished lamely.

"And all this over my costume." Dolly tried to sound lighthearted, but she was almost breathless from Quentin's words and the implication they carried. "Love," he'd said. "Something more lasting." She was sure he was going to propose that night, and so when he suggested they get a breath of air, she agreed eagerly. Dolly was surprised when Quentin kept walking through the garden to the small tree-shaded area beyond, but decided that he wanted a more private setting. It wouldn't do to be interrupted by other strollers in the middle of a marriage proposal.

When they reached the privacy of the trees and Quentin put his arm around her waist and drew her close, she didn't stop him. And when he turned her to him and kissed her, at first gently, then with a mounting passion that excited as well as frightened her, she still did not pull away. She knew you did not kiss a man to whom you were not engaged, but after what Quentin had said earlier tonight, weren't they as good as engaged? And then with a shock she'd felt Quentin's hand beneath the white silk of the simple Grecian dress. Dolly knew she should stop him, but after all, they were engaged, and most terrible of all, she didn't want to stop him. Then they'd heard laughter in the darkness, and Quentin had released her suddenly and taken a step backward.

The next morning three dozen roses arrived. Quentin followed a few hours later. Dolly was sitting in the topiary garden, staring out over the water, and neither heard nor saw him approach from the house. Quentin was struck by the curve of her neck and, remembering the night before, he bent quickly and touched his lips to the soft pale skin. Dolly started and blushed deeply. The gesture was shockingly intimate and she felt as if Quentin had read her mind. She had, of course, been thinking of him.

"I didn't mean to startle you," he said.

"It's not that . . ." Dolly's voice trailed off, and her color deepened. Quentin wondered if he'd gone too far. It had been an unusual thing to do, but last night Dolly had shown an unexpected side to her nature.

"A good day for the regatta," Quentin said. He and his brother Nicholas were racing that afternoon. "It's a light breeze, but it seems to be building."

It seemed to Dolly that after the night before they ought to be talking about something more serious than the afternoon's sailboat race. "Father's coming up this weekend," she said.

"Perhaps he'd like to get in some sailing," Quentin offered. He'd never met Mr. Lovington, and couldn't imagine why Dolly had suddenly spoken of him.

"Father isn't much of a sportsman. He says it's the life of the mind that counts." She wondered how she'd got off on this tangent. Didn't Quentin see what she was getting at? "He'll be staying only till Monday, but I'm sure you'll be able to find a time to talk to him." Dolly swore to herself that if her father had to go sailing in order to bestow her hand in marriage to Quentin, he'd go.

"I'm looking forward to meeting him. He chose a good weekend. There's the ball at Beechwood Saturday and—"

"But surely you'll want to speak to him alone."

Quentin realized with a shock that she'd mistaken the meaning of his words the night before. But Dolly saw the embarrassed look on his face and knew only that he hadn't meant what he'd said at all. She'd made a fool of herself last night and a worse fool this morning. She turned away to hide her shame, and Quentin began talking rapidly, much too rapidly, about a game of lawn tennis he'd played that morning. He stayed for another ten minutes, but to Dolly it seemed like hours. She felt naked and exposed in the hot light of the midday sun and of Quentin's judgment. How he must be laughing at her, or worse than that. The memory of his hand beneath her dress flashed through her mind and she cringed in shame.

Dolly told herself she never wanted to see Quentin Morris again, but secretly she prayed he'd return and beg her to marry him. She could hear him explaining that it was what he'd had in mind all along, but he simply hadn't had the courage to ask.

Of course she did see Quentin again. The season was in full swing and everywhere she went, Quentin was likely to be, but he was distant now, as if realizing that her humiliation was his fault. And then little by little Dolly began to notice that the more Quentin avoided her, the more he sought out Gabrielle, the Duchesse de Saville. Now it was Gabrielle he danced with again and again, Gabrielle he took sailing, and most cruelly of all, Gabrielle with whom he slipped out for a breath of air.

When Dolly was not watching Quentin and Gabrielle, she was listening to gossip of them. It was rumored they'd marry before the year was out. A splendid match, everyone agreed; his millions, her title, and both of them so attractive. Dolly thought if she heard "what a handsome couple they make!" once more she'd throw herself off the Cliff Walk into the sea. But she did nothing so dramatic, not even when, alone at Bailey's Beach one day and all but invisible behind a large beach umbrella, she overheard two matrons discussing the match.

"I always knew he wouldn't marry the little Lovington girl."

"Now, Clara, you knew nothing of the sort," another voice sniffed. "Why, they were together constantly at the beginning of the season."

"But I wasn't taken in. I know Quentin Morris better than that. After all, his brother Nicholas is married to my niece. And that's precisely the point. Quentin is nothing like Nicholas."

"What is that supposed to mean?"

"Nicholas is pure Morris, but Quentin is all Vanderbilt, and everyone knows the Vanderbilts have a penchant for making spectacular marriages. No little Lovington churchmouse for Quentin—he needs a girl with more fire. And I'm sure the fact that she's French —one of France's oldest families, in fact—and a great beauty as well didn't hurt in the least."

The only thing that hurt was Dolly's heart. She was sure it would break in two right there on Bailey's Beach, but the human anatomy is not so fragile, and her heart remained intact even if her pride did not.

Dolly met Elias the following autumn and married him that spring. She never regretted the marriage. She was happy with her husband, happy in her new position as the mistress of a great house and one of the young leaders of local society, and delighted in the knowledge that she was going to be a mother. But sometimes at odd hours of the day, when she was arranging flowers or driving about, leaving her visiting cars, she'd remember that dark moment beneath the trees with Quentin Morris and that awful meeting the next day, and she would know that no one, not even Elias, who had done so much for her, could ever erase that awful shame. But it pleased her to think, as she sat listening to Elias's plans for the future, that he was going to take anything, even business, away from Quentin Morris.

When Clemmie was ten years old her father took her on a trip to New York. "Don't you think it's a little unusual?" Dolly asked, although she rarely disagreed with any of Elias's decisions.

"Don't care whether it's usual or not. I want to do it. I've taken the boys."

"But that's different. They're boys. They'll be running things one day. But a small girl on a business trip . . ."

"Clemmie may not be running things one day, but she'll be living off the railroad, and I like the idea of her seeing a bit of it. Besides, it will be a treat for her." And for me, he thought. Clemmie was an alert, inquisitive child, and he enjoyed showing her things.

Henry Ford had just announced that from now on he would manufacture only the Model T chassis, and predictions of an automobile in every American garage flew, but Elias, heading east with Clemmie in tow, was not worried. Could automobiles carry freight? Well, perhaps a small truckload, but not great cars full of coal and oil and the very raw materials that made America great. One couldn't board an automobile in New York in the evening, enjoy a superb dinner, get a good night's sleep, and wake up in Pittsburgh the next morning rested and ready for business. No, automobiles were fine for running about town or the local countryside—Elias enjoyed that himself—but they'd never take the place of railroads. Railroads kept the country running, and now Elias was going to keep his own slice of it on the move. He was on his way to New York to put the last piece in the puzzle of the A & W. Twenty-six years ago J. P. Morgan had refused to finance the line Elias had wanted to build. By doing so, he thought he'd put a stop to Elias's plans, but Morgan had discovered that Elias Wilder was not so easily thwarted. Piece by piece, line by line, Elias had put together a major railroad. By tomorrow at this time, it would run from Chicago to Hoboken. Only the ferry ride across the Hudson remained to be conquered.

Clemmie loved everything about the trip. From the first moment when she stood, her small hand tucked securely in her father's, watching the workmen coupling the private car to the end of the long train, she knew it was going to be a wonderful adventure. The car itself was like a little house with special rooms for sleeping and a funny little kitchen where everything was just as it was at home, only smaller. Best of all was the open observation platform at the rear. You could stand there and feel the wind racing past and see the tracks speeding back from under your feet.

After dinner in the long dining saloon her father took her for a walk through the other cars. When they reached the front of the next-to-first, there was a door with NO ADMITTANCE written in big red letters. Elias opened the door and walked in. Bags of letters were everywhere, and two men sat at a long table sorting. They stood when they saw her father.

"Keep working, men. Don't let us disturb you," Elias said, and moved on to the car ahead.

The engine was hot and noisy and very dirty. Clemmie loved it. It bucked along the tracks like a wild animal, and the feeling of speed and adventure was more exhilarating here than anywhere on the train.

"Watch this, Clemmie," her father said as a huge brawny man covered with perspiration and coal dust lifted a scoop of coal. With one foot he pressed a pedal on the floor, and a door flew open to reveal a raging fire. Clemmie jumped back, then giggled in embarrassment.

"This one steams like a beauty, Mr. Wilder," the engineer shouted above the noise. "Now fifty-two twenty-seven that we had on this run last week, couldn't keep a fire for anything, but this engine's a honey. I've never seen one steam so smooth."

"Glad to hear it, Travis."

"Perhaps the little girl would like to blow the whistle, Mr. Wilder," the engineer suggested.

"Could I, Daddy, could I?"

"I don't see why not."

Clemmie had to stand on her toes to reach the pull. When she yanked it, the whistle shrieked, and she jumped just as she had when the flames had darted out at her. Then she held one ear with her free hand and pulled again and again until her father said that was enough. She'd drive the passengers mad.

On the way back to their car Clemmie noticed a boy about her own age sitting with a woman in a green traveling suit. "Doesn't he want to blow the whistle?" she asked her father.

"I expect he does," Elias answered. They were back in the private car now.

"Then why doesn't the engineer let him?"

Her father seemed to be looking at her strangely. "Do you know why he let you blow the whistle, Clemmie?"

"Because of you?" she said.

"That's right. The engineer was being nice to you because I own this train."

"The whole train?" Clemmie asked solemnly. "Not just this car, but all of them that the other people are riding in?"

"That's right. And most of them you saw in the yard this morning too. As well as the tracks they run on."

In the face of this enormity, Clemmie was silent for a moment. She stared out the window at the scenery racing by. "What about the land the tracks are on?" she asked thoughtfully.

Elias laughed. "A good question, child. Most of that is only leased. That means I can use it. In this case, for 999 years."

Clemmie slept little that night. How could she be expected to sleep with so much going on just outside her window? She loved the way the lights of a town would race toward her, then she'd be in the middle of it, and just as suddenly it would be behind her and there'd be nothing but dark fields and a black sky for as far as she could see. She had turned around so her head lay at the foot of the bed, and raised the shade in order to watch it all. Finally, as she was beginning to doze off, she felt the rocking motion of the train gradually slow, and the lights of a town, larger than any they'd gone through since she'd been put to bed, drew near. Clemmie pulled the shade down, leaving only a few inches at the bottom to peer out. She saw a large station, much like the one at home, and then lots of people moving about on the platform and men in red uniforms carrying baggage. One of them stopped for a moment in front of her window. When he looked down and saw the two gray eyes peering out in wonder, he smiled broadly and waved. "You have a good trip now, missy," he called through the closed window, then picked up the baggage and followed a man quickly down the platform.

The next morning when they arrived in the station her father identified as Hoboken, a man with a brief-case entered their car. From the way he talked, stood around waiting until Elias had told him to sit down, even the way he greeted Clemmie, she knew the man was a little afraid of her father.

The man opened the leather case he carried, took some papers from it, and handed them to her father. They had obviously forgotten about Clemmie, and she retreated to a chair at the other end of the main saloon to wait for the boat ride her father had promised.

"Everything has gone according to plan, Mr. Wilder. All we need now is your signature, and I imagine they'll be happy to get it. I don't think they could have held out for another day. That last cut in our rates forced them down to a level they just couldn't afford. And then that accident in the yard . . ."

The look on Elias's face cut the man short. "That was an accident, Buchanan, and I don't want anyone thinking any different."

"Of course, sir. I didn't mean to imply—"

"I know exactly what you said, and what you meant to imply, and I'm going to tell you something. If you plan on staying with the A & W in any capacity, you'd better remember it. Some of our methods may not be nice, but I've never known a railroad or any other operation to make money by being nice. Rate wars aren't nice, but they don't hurt anyone. You might even say they help the fellows who are shipping. There are ways of buying stock in a railroad that may not be nice, but if a man can't hold on to his own stock, that's his problem. I've done a lot of things to put together the A & W, but I've never resorted to sabotage. I've never wrecked another man's train or set off an explosion in his yard or any of those practices I'm sure we both know about. And if I ever find one of my men doing any of that, he's out. Without explanation or reference. I'll do a lot for the A & W, but I will not murder and I will not destroy another man's property. Is that clear, Buchanan?"

"Absolutely, sir."

"Fine, then let's get on with these papers."

Clemmie didn't understand a word her father said, but she thought the man he called Buchanan looked as if he'd just been spanked. Clemmie had always taken her father's power over her and her brothers for granted, but she'd never imagined he had the same control over other adults. It was a sobering thought, especially when she remembered the long train and the miles and miles of tracks.

Chapter 6

CLEMMIE KNOCKED ON the door to Tom Hendreich's office and walked in without waiting for an answer. When she'd done the same thing several weeks before and interrupted a conference with Adam and the chief of freight operations, Tom had asked her to be more careful in the future. Clemmie had sworn she would—and gone on bypassing his secretary and bursting into his office.

He was on the telephone now and when he looked up and saw her, obvious pleasure at her presence mingled with annoyance at the manner of her arrival. She dropped into one of the two leather chairs in front of his desk, and looked around the familiar room. Every inch of wall space was covered with railroad maps, and in one corner stood a huge file filled, Clemmie knew, with more. A few were large scale, but most of them were so detailed that every foot of A & W tracks could be traced. Once or twice she'd seen Tom at these detailed maps. He knew them as intimately as she'd come in the past few months to know the lines in his face and the changing expression of his eyes. Sometimes she'd hear him talking to her father about a particular stretch of line and know he could conjure up every twist and turn from memory.

"I'm not interested in the weather, Novak. There was snow on the Central's lines too, but their trains weren't two hours late getting into Toledo."

Clemmie watched Tom's face as he listened to the man at the other end of the wire. Even if she hadn't heard the words and voice she would have known from the tautness of his jaw that he was angry. His long fingers held the telephone tightly, as if they wanted to strangle it.

"Damn it, Novak." Tom had been looking down at his desk, and now he lifted his eyes to her quickly as if in apology. "The switches wouldn't have frozen if you'd kept the fires going. Now I don't want any more excuses. If you can't keep to the schedule, we'll find someone who can."

"Poor Mr. Novak," Clemmie said when he'd hung up.

"I'm sorry about the language. . . ."

"Really, Tom, I've heard the word damn before."

"Well, you wouldn't have this time if you'd asked Miss Pollock whether I was busy," he added pointedly.

"I'd rather wait in here. Besides, it isn't nice to keep the boss's daughter waiting. Or have you forgotten? We're dining at the club with Adam and Samantha tonight. And you still have to go home and dress. That's why I came to get you. You can drop me at the farm, take the car, and come back to get me." Clemmie saw the look that crossed his face. "Now you're not going to start that again. Nobody minds your taking the car. If you don't take it, we'll never get to the club on time."

"And wouldn't that be terrible?"

"We've been through that before too, Tom. There's no place else to go."

"I have nothing against the country club—except that I can't take you there." Every time Tom signed Elias's name, he felt humiliated.

"Very well, I'll cancel dinner and we'll go to that roadhouse out on High Point Road." Clemmie knew it was the single suggestion that would put an end to the argument. If Tom was not entirely at ease at the club, he had been decidedly uncomfortable the night they'd gone to the roadhouse.

The place had been her suggestion. It was an Indian summer evening a few weeks after she'd first invited Tom to dinner, and they were sitting on the terrace of the farm.

"Where did you take other girls? Nice girls, I mean," she added as she had that first night. "I can imagine where you took the others."

"I wish you wouldn't say things like that, Clemmie."

"Now, Tom darling, you mustn't be bourgeois."

They had been sitting side by side on a wicker chaise and she felt him draw away from her.

"You're darn right I mustn't be bourgeois." His voice was quiet, but full of fury. "Because I'm not, Clemmie. I'm not at all middle class. My father's a miner, and I've been working since I was six years old. I'm a working man from a long line of working men. And you'd better not forget that."

Without saying a word she reached over and took his hand in both of hers. Gently she ran her fingers over his palm. He looked more surprised than angry. "I can't find the calluses," she said quietly.

"It's not a joke, Clemmie."

"It certainly isn't the serious matter you make it. Now if we can forget your father for a moment, you were going to take me out. What about that roadhouse out on High Point Road? Every time I pass it there are a dozen cars there."

"I don't think it's your kind of place."

"In that case I definitely want to go."

As soon as they entered the noisy smoke-filled room, Tom was sorry he'd agreed to come. The dance floor was mobbed and at a table a little way from the one they took he saw half a dozen men he knew slightly. They were good enough fellows, Tom supposed, but a little tough for his taste, or rather a little tough for his taste where Clemmie was concerned. One of them greeted Tom, then they all turned to stare at Clemmie. Finally one of the men made a circle with his thumb and forefinger and raised his hand in their direction. Tom wanted to hit him.

"Does that mean they approve of me?" Clemmie laughed.

"I'm sorry."

"Don't be. I'm flattered."

It was the first time they'd danced together. For all his size, Tom moved well, as well as Whit, Clemmie thought, then cursed herself for it. His hand at the small of her back was strong, and he was easy to follow, but he wasn't as smooth a dancer as Whit. He seemed too aware of his body, and of hers.

When they returned to the table, one of the men from the group approached them, and without waiting to be introduced, asked Clemmie to dance. Before Tom could say anything, Clemmie was moving off toward the dance floor. Tom saw the man put a hand familiarly around Clemmie's waist and felt the same surge of fury he had when the man made the sign with his thumb and forefinger. Tom watched the way he held Clemmie, the way he looked down at her when she spoke, and he could read the man's thoughts and hear his conversation when he returned to his friends. Once again Tom pictured his fist crashing into the tough, smiling face.

As soon as Clemmie returned to the table, he stood and held her coat for her.

"Where are we going?" she asked.

"Out of here."

"But we just got here."

"And now we're leaving."

Ordinarily Clemmie would have been annoyed, but Tom's determination and the way he practically dragged her across the parking lot and into the car were something she'd never seen before. She was fascinated.

"You can't possibly be jealous, Tom."

"It's not that." It was partly that, of course, but

170

there was more. "You don't belong in that place, Clemmie. You don't belong with fellows like that."

"I only danced with him."

"And I shouldn't have let you."

The words angered as well as excited Clemmie. Who was Tom Hendreich to let her dance or not dance with someone?

"I should never have taken you there in the first place."

"Well, you did, and I thank you for it. I enjoyed it, even if you didn't. But I think in view of your behavior I'll take you to the club next time. At least we'll get in more than one dance." They were still sitting in the parking lot and she lifted her face to his expectantly.

His mouth was soft on hers but she sensed the hunger behind it and was shocked at the similar response she felt rising within her. Clemmie had told herself after that night with Whit that she'd never love anyone else, and surely she didn't love Tom Hendreich. But she felt his mouth avid on hers and his hands crushing her to him, and desire stirred within her as if it had a will and a life of its own.

It was shortly after that night at the roadhouse that Clemmie decided she was going to marry Tom Hendreich though she swore it had less to do with the feelings he'd aroused in her than with a certain practical assessment of her life and her future. Her experience with Whit had convinced Clemmie that there were certain things she wanted, certain things she must have. No single word summed up what they were—not revenge nor retribution nor even triumph. Clemmie wanted not one of those things, but all of them. She wanted to rival Whit Morris, to hurt him, to be eternally and hopelessly loved by him. The means to all that was the railroad, and the means to the railroad was Tom. With help she could take on Whit Morris on every front and make him pay—for having made Clemmie love him, for having left her when he did.

They hadn't gone to the roadhouse again, and Clemmie, good as her word, had begun taking Tom to the club. Before the weather turned cold, she'd even convinced him to start golf lessons, although it was no easy task to drag him out of his office at noon on Saturday.

"Even Father takes a half-day on Saturday," Clemmie argued.

"Your father can afford to."

Clemmie gazed directly at him and there was a wicked light in her eyes. "Tom, darling, some day you're going to be dealing in men as well as trains, and for that you're going to have to know how to play golf."

Tom turned away and did not answer, but he began to take an interest in his handicap.

Clemmie had complained about Tom's tardiness that afternoon but when he arrived back at the farm she was still not ready. The only time Clemmie was ever ready was when Tom was inexcusably late.

Harry the butler told him everyone else was out, and Miss Clemmie had said she'd be down in a minute. "Can I get you a cocktail while you wait, Mr. Hendreich?" Harry's tone seemed to say that they both knew the duration of Clemmie's "minutes."

"Thank you, Harry," Tom said when the butler returned with a martini. Drink in hand, he began to pace the room. There was usually someone there while he waited for Clemmie, and Tom had always been too aware of being examined himself to be able to study the room carefully. Two large portraits hung on either side of the fireplace. The man bore a distinct resemblance to Elias. The woman was dark, very pretty, and at least twenty years younger than the man. The portraits could have been painted at different times, but Tom knew they had not been. Elias Wilder, Senior, had waited until he could afford to marry the sort of woman he

172

wanted. By that time he was almost fifty. The marriage, like many May–December unions had lasted only a few years, but not because of Elias Senior's advanced age. The tough old miner turned mine-owner had lived well into his eighties. His young wife had died giving birth to the present Elias Wilder. The story, like all stories pertaining to the Wilder family, was common knowledge in Scranton.

Tom sat in one of the comfortable English club chairs before the fireplace and surveyed the room. He could not tell Queen Anne from Duncan Phyfe, did not know if the rug were Bokhara or Samarkand, but he sensed that the furnishings were handsome. More than handsome, Tom thought. They were tasteful. There was no other word for the feeling of peace and comfort they gave him. Elias had told him once that the house was less splendid than many Tom would see in New York or Chicago, but it was that very lack of the obviously splendid that Tom liked. Any fool with enough money could buy expensive things, but it took more than money to put the right things together in the right way.

"I see you've started without me," Clemmie said, taking the drink from his hand and raising it to her mouth.

"Harry was afraid I'd die of thirst by the time you were ready."

"But," she said.

"But?" he asked.

"You're supposed to say, 'But you were worth waiting for.'"

"You generally are, Clemmie."

"Generally! I like that. Well, if you won't tell me how fetching I look, then I won't tell you how dashing you look." She reached up to straighten his tie. "Anyway, you're a washout with a black tie."

Shortly after he'd begun seeing Clemmie, Tom had taken an afternoon off during one of his business trips to New York and gone to Brooks Brothers. He still remembered the way the salesman had eyed him when he said he was looking for several suits and some evening clothes. The dark blue suit from Scranton's best store suddenly felt ill-fitting.

"I'm not sure we have your size," the salesman said. "Have you tried Macy's?"

Tom forgot the ill-fitting blue suit. He did not raise his voice, but his manner changed instantly. "I think you do have my size, and if you can't find it, I'm sure the manager will be able to."

"Of course, sir," the salesman mumbled quickly. "If you'll just follow me." Tom bought three suits—gray worsted and blue serge for winter and gray flannel for spring—a Norfolk jacket and pair of odd trousers, and what he still called, at that time, a tuxedo. Everything came off the rack and all together the purchases set him back three hundred twenty-eight dollars. For a little more he could have bought a Ford, but Tom didn't want a Ford. He'd rather wait a little and get something more than a Ford, nothing as flashy as a Marmon or a Stutz, but something a little more distinctive than a Ford.

Clemmie had told Tom the new wardrobe was a definite improvement, and for once had the sense not to mention that it would have been wiser to buy two custom-tailored suits rather than five ready-made costumes.

They arrived at the entrance to the club at the same moment as Adam and Samantha. "Clemmie," Samantha cried, "that cape, it's gorgeous. I didn't know you had a mink cape."

"I didn't until last week. Father was in Chicago when it started to snow and he said since he was bringing a blizzard with him, he might as well bring something to keep me warm."

The look Samantha shot her husband as she and Clemmie went off to the dressing room was one Adam had grown accustomed to in the months since their marriage. It seemed impossible that such a short time ago he'd thought he couldn't live without Samantha. But in those days it had seemed impossible she'd ever look at him that way. Marriage was, Adam thought, an instructive experience.

In the bar Adam made a point of telling the waiter to make the drinks with his bottle rather than Elias's. "Can't have the old man say I'm taking advantage of him," he said to Tom when the waiter had left. "All the same, it's damned expensive being disinherited. And it's worse for Sam than for me. She's accustomed to having a lot. And let's face it, my salary doesn't buy a lot."

Tom had heard Adam speak this way before. They'd always worked well together, and now that Tom was seeing so much of Clemmie, he'd found that Adam was eager to turn their professional friendship into a personal one. Tom suspected that these days Adam was desperate for someone to talk to. Most of the time, Tom was a willing listener, but tonight Adam's words had sent him off on his own train of thought. If Adam's salary as chief of motive power couldn't buy the things Samantha wanted then how could Tom's own salary keep Clemmie satisfied? Clemmie's car and Clemmie's club membership still rankled, but something more than the money worried Tom. Clemmie had a habit of demanding her own way—and getting it.

"I'll tell you, Tom," Adam said, staring moodily into his drink. "A man ought to be sure he can afford a girl before he marries her."

Tom watched Clemmie moving across the room toward him. She worked her way through the tables, greeting friends with that dismissive air he'd come to know well. I'll put up with you, she seemed to be saying, just as long as you amuse me.

There was no doubt about it, Tom thought. Clemmie was an expensive girl in more ways than one. And Adam was right. A man had to consider just how much he could afford. But sometimes, Tom thought as Clemmie leaned over to whisper something to him and he felt her body brush against his arm, the only things worth having were those you could least afford.

"I had lunch at the Century today," Elias said. He took little pleasure in clubs, but kept a membership in the more important ones in New York, Philadelphia, and Chicago. The men he wanted to see in those cities could often be found at their clubs when they were not available in their offices.

Dolly looked up expectantly from the tray of roast beef Harry was serving her. She enjoyed the gossip Elias brought back from his business trips. However, it was Clemmie that Elias was covertly watching.

"You remember Quentin Morris." Elias turned his attention to Dolly now. "I knew him from Central business, but I think you met him in Newport several times." Elias saw his wife's color rise. Clearly she was as nervous about Clemmie's reaction to the name Morris as he was. "I don't know whether you ran into him last summer, Clemmie."

Clemmie remembered a beach house, dark and private in the summer night, and struggled against the wave of memories that washed over her. "I never met him," she said evenly.

"Poor fellow died," Elias said. "Just last week. Terrible accident, but of course the fellows at the Century didn't see it that way. 'Died like a gentleman,' fellow who told me about it said. He was thrown from his horse in Central Park."

"I can't see that it makes much difference how the old boy went," George said. "Dead is dead."

Dolly and Clemmie said nothing, but Elias couldn't help noticing that his wife seemed almost more distressed than his daughter. He wondered if perhaps Clemmie's spectacular match hadn't meant more to Dolly than he'd imagined. For Elias's part, he didn't much care. He'd approved of Whit Morris but he approved of Tom Hendreich as well. The two men were as different as night and day, Elias thought, but each had a good deal to recommend him. Being a woman and an old New Yorker at heart, however, Dolly might not see things quite the same way.

Snow came early that year, and by the first week in December everyone was predicting it would be one of the worst winters ever. The countryside was buried beneath a thick white blanket, and just as its freshness started to turn gray each week, a fresh cover fell. Some mornings Clemmie would awaken early to the rasping sound of a shovel on the great circular drive in front of the house and the sight of fresh snow in the chestnut tree outside her window. She'd snuggle under the thick down comforter then, and think how warm it was here in her room with the radiator hissing quietly and the sun coming in through the south windows, and how cold it was outside. Briefly she'd feel sorry for old Joe the groundsman. When she'd finally get up and go down to breakfast, she'd remind Naomi the cook to send some hot coffee out to poor Joe, and Naomi would look annoyed at the idea that anyone might think she hadn't done her job properly and say Joe had already had two cups that morning and some fresh-baked biscuits, thank you very much.

Frequently Clemmie would go for a walk after breakfast. She enjoyed tramping through the fresh snow, liked the way her overshoes made great sloppy indentations in the pristine white surface. And she wasn't in the least cold; her new mink cape saw to that. The first morning Dolly had seen Clemmie returning from her walk in it, she'd pointed out that Clemmie really ought to save it for evening wear, but Clemmie said that was ridiculous. In the evening, stepping quickly from house to car to another house, she was never cold, but when she tramped in the woods behind the house she needed the fur's protection. Dolly had merely sighed at this further sign of her daughter's nonconformity, although she had to admit that there was logic if not convention behind Clemmie's argument.

Often on those walks Clemmie would make plans for the future. She saw herself married to Tom, saw Tom rising in the A & W, the two of them building it into the greatest line in the country. On some mornings she worked out a merger, and she could envision Tom taking over the Central's office, which was vivid in her imagination even though she'd never actually seen it. The idea was ambitious but not impossible. Smaller companies outstripped larger ones all the time. Nobody stayed on top forever. Occasionally on those icy walks a more romantic image of marriage to Tom interrupted her thoughts, but Clemmie never dwelled on it. She'd learned her lesson last summer; girlish dreams had died with the season.

Things were not as pleasant down at the A & W offices during those weeks. Snow was the enemy and there was a constant battle to keep the trains running on schedule. Tom was fighting valiantly, but the struggle was beginning to take its toll. He looked tired, Clemmie thought, when she opened the door for him that Wednesday evening. Harry was standing behind her, waiting to take Tom's things and looking a little disapproving. Clemmie ought to be waiting for Mr. Hendreich in the living room, not dashing around opening doors and behaving as if there weren't a proper butler in the house.

"It's begun to snow again." Tom looked bleak as he handed his hat and coat to Harry.

"I'll dry these out for you, sir," Harry said, and disappeared toward the back of the house.

Clemmie took Tom's hand to lead him into the living room. "You're freezing," she said. "Well, come in here and warm up. I had Harry build us a fire. It's just for us. Everyone else is gone. Mother's at the Meadows for bridge. And Father's off at some business dinner. He dragged poor George along, though George looked absolutely miserable at the prospect. I know he had one of his girls lined up, but Father was adamant. He has been ever since Adam's marriage. If George doesn't

178

make the grade, it certainly won't be Father's fault.
Though I doubt he will. Make the grade, I mean.
Locking up George night after night in a room filled
with cigar smoke and a bunch of stodgy old men isn't
going to change him. He'll just slip away to one of his
disreputable ladies afterward."

"Clemmie . . ."

"Oh, Tom. don't be such a stuffed shirt. You may
not like the fact that I know about these things, but I
do know about them."

"Well, you don't have to talk about them."

"Very well, no more talk of George." She crossed
the room to where Tom was standing and reached her
arms around his neck. Her mouth teased at his, and
she could feel his body tense against hers. "We'll talk
about you. I have a surprise for you." He was holding
her close and he seemed not to hear her words. His
mouth on hers, less tentatively than before, had a
language of its own. She pulled away from him and
turned quickly so he couldn't see her face. It seemed
important to Clemmie that Tom not know that she
wanted him as much as he wanted her, so important
that she wouldn't admit the fact even to herself.

When she turned back to Tom, he was no longer
looking at her, but staring somewhere in the middle
distance. At times like this Clemmie was an enigma to
him. Much as her taunts about "nice girls" annoyed
him, there was some truth to them. He'd had no money
for "nice girls" in college, little time for them since.
And now he wasn't sure what the lines of behavior
were. Sometimes Clemmie seemed to go too far; sometimes when she pulled away and left him almost angry
in his desire, he feared he had.

"Aren't you even interested in your surprise?" Clemmie asked.

"Desperately."

"Now you have to promise to act surprised when
Father tells you. He'd be furious if he knew I'd told
you first." Suddenly Tom was listening. "I thought that

might get your attention. Well, there'll be no Christmas bonus for Mr. Hendreich this year. Something much better than that. A big fat promotion and an even fatter raise. You're going to be a vice president, darling. Vice president in charge of passenger operations. I know you'd rather have freight, but Father said you'll have to work up to that. As for the raise, he wouldn't tell me how much. He said if you want me to know how much money you make, you'll tell me."

Tom had been anticipating the words for years, but he still couldn't believe them. Vice president in charge of passenger operations. He was moving in a rarefied atmosphere now. There were only a few steps between him and the very top.

"Do you realize that puts you above Adam, and as for George—well, whatever title Father gives George, it doesn't mean anything. George will never measure up." It was as if Clemmie were reading his mind, but Tom said nothing.

"Well, doesn't that suggest anything to you?" Clemmie continued. "Oh, Tom the whole railroad could be yours someday."

"I don't think your father would appreciate talk like that," he said evenly.

"But it's true. He's disinherited Adam, and George is hopeless. You're the logical choice, Tom. The only choice. And with my help—"

"Not that way!" he snapped. "Anything I do, I'll do on my own. When it comes to your father or the railroad or any of that, I don't want your help, Clemmie."

She caught herself. She'd remembered his ambition, but for a moment she'd forgotten his pride. Now she took it into account, and something else as well. Again she crossed the room to where he was standing, but this time she did not touch him. Clemmie stood there, only inches away, and the gray eyes looking up at him were wide with promise. "You don't want my help, Tom, but there have been times, even tonight, when I thought you did want me."

The arguments that raced through his mind were so familiar they'd become instincts rather than thoughts. He hadn't liked the way it looked, marrying the boss's daughter. As much as he wanted Clemmie, he'd always told himself he couldn't have her. Even lately, even since he'd begun to see so much of her, he'd gone on telling himself that, and secretly plotting to prove himself wrong. And now he'd reached a point where he could afford to risk proving himself wrong. He'd reached a point, Tom decided, as he drew Clemmie to him and felt her slender body against his, that he could afford anything. Even Clemmie Wilder.

On Christmas Day Elias Wilder opened his home to the men and women who worked for him. It was a tradition that went back to the later years of his father's life. As a rule only the people who worked in the offices of the mines and the railroad attended, but it was said, and had actually been proven once or twice, that any miner or gandy dancer who kept the rails in repair was welcome, providing he observed the amenities. It was during this traditional celebration that Elias planned to announce his daughter's engagement to Tom Hendreich.

"Don't you think it would be more fitting," Dolly asked "if we had a private party for the occasion?"

"We'll have that too," Elias said. "But these people are important to us. They have a responsibility to us and we have one to them. It's only when that's forgotten that those darn brotherhoods and outside agitators can move in. Besides, the fact that she's marrying Tom makes it especially appropriate."

Adam Wilder was expected to attend the party on Christmas Day. He hadn't wanted to go. Although he could not bring himself to break completely with his father or the railroad, he did not enjoy the idea of attending as an employee the reception he used to dominate as son and heir. Samantha, however, had her own ideas.

"We owe it to Clemmie," she pointed out, but Adam knew it was not Clemmie his wife had in mind. He watched her dressing for the party now in the small bedroom of the house they'd bought in one of the newer suburbs of the city. Although it was considerably more modest than the house Samantha had expected to occupy as Mrs. Adam Wilder, she'd never complained about it. She didn't have to. Without uttering a single complaint, Samantha was quite capable of making known her feelings about the cramped quarters and banal lines that detracted from the few good things she owned.

Adam watched her at the mirrored dressing table. Samantha hadn't said a word when the real estate agent had announced there were no dressing rooms off the master bedroom. She had merely looked surprised and a little offended. "I wish you wouldn't wear that necklace," he said. It was a heavy gold Egyptian choker. Samantha had told him the story of how J.P. Morgan had given it to her when she was a girl. She'd made the incident sound amusing, but Adam had not been amused. There was something unsavory about the unattractive old financier's buying baubles for pretty young girls.

Samantha turned to face him. "Don't you think it looks well with this dress?"

"It looks all right, but I still wish you wouldn't wear it."

"Oh, that." Samantha turned back to the mirror. "Well, I have to wear some jewelry, don't I?" The meaning behind her words was clear, and Adam understood it perfectly.

An hour later when they entered the large front hall of his former home, Adam inhaled the familiar smells of Christmas baking mingling with the fragrance of the tree that reached through the staircase to the second floor, and he felt the floodgates opening for a hundred memories. Every piece of furniture, each picture and object was a reminder of what he'd lost. Later, when he slipped out to the kitchen because Harry said Naomi, would be heartbroken if she didn't see him, he felt as if he were ten years old again. He had to promise to have a piece of her special brandied fruitcake before she'd allow him to leave the kitchen.

When Adam returned to the party, Elias was calling for quiet. He was standing in front of the fireplace with Clemmie and Tom on either side of him. George stood a little to one side and the twin portraits of Elias's parents looked down on the group as if they were standing guard.

"I have a special announcement to make," Elias boomed when the room had grown quiet. "An announcement that gives me great pleasure and I'm sure will please all of you. I'm happy," he hesitated for a moment and looked from Clemmie to Tom, "and very, very proud to announce my daughter Clemmie's engagement to Mr. Thomas Hendreich." There was a murmur of approval. "That's all," Elias added. "No speeches. Just good luck to them both and Merry Christmas to all of you."

The room erupted in noise as one after another of Elias's employees repeated the sentiment. "Good luck" and "Merry Christmas" echoed again and again, but in a far corner Adam Wilder stood alone and silent. He did not even see his wife, who was staring at him with that hard look he'd come to know so well. He only saw his father flanked by Clemmie and Tom Hendreich and George, and he knew finally that there would be no going back.

The wedding was planned for June, but the problems began almost immediately. One difficulty was avoided early when Adam refused Tom's request to serve as best man.

"It's nothing personal," Adam had explained. "In fact, I'd be delighted to stand up for you. But do yourself a favor. Ask someone else. It'll make the old man happier."

"It's not that I want to antagonize your father," Tom explained, "but, well, you know a little about my life. No old college ties, and I've been too busy working since then. You're the logical choice, Adam."

"The logical one, but not the right one. Ask George. That'll satisfy everyone."

And so George agreed to serve as best man, and two of the ushers, cousins of the bride, were detailed to see that George stayed sober, or at least relatively so, until after the ceremony.

Then a week before the wedding, when everything seemed in order, Clemmie awakened to find a very special gift among the dozens that arrived every morning. It wasn't the gift itself that was out of the ordinary. She'd already received five sets of silver candelabra, two from Tiffany's in New York, and three from Caldwells in Philadelphia, but it was the first time she'd heard from Alison since her marriage.

Clemmie sat cross-legged among the boxes and tissue paper from the gifts she and Dolly had been unwrapping and stared at the cream-colored card. *Mrs. Whitmore Vanderbilt Morris* was engraved in a simple script. *Mrs. Whitmore Vanderbilt Morris*. The name sounded like a taunt.

Clemmie tossed the card aside without reading the message inside and started out of the room.

"Where are you going?" Dolly called after her. "There are some gifts you haven't opened."

"I'll open them later," Clemmie tossed over her shoulder. "And you can put those with the things to be returned. I don't need six candelabra."

Dolly started to say that this set was the handsomest of all Clemmie had received, but when she picked up the card and saw the name, she said nothing at all.

Dolly was not so reticent when Clemmie agreed to permit *Town & Country* to send a reporter and a photographer to cover the wedding. "You can't let them, Clemmie. It's too vulgar."

184

"Why, Mother? I am getting married. Isn't that one of the three times? A lady appears in the newspapers only three times in her life. When she's born, when she marries, and when she dies," Clemmie quoted the law that Dolly and every other lady of her generation lived by.

"You know exactly what I mean, Clemmie. This won't be just a portrait of you and an announcement. This will be a *magazine article.*"

"That's right, Mother. Everyone, but simply everyone is going to know about my wedding."

And then all the preparations and the small arguments and the insurmountable problems of whether Jean Reynolds had to be a bridesmaid simply because Susan Beesley was and where to draw the line in inviting Elias's wide circle of associates were things of the past, and it was the morning of the wedding. The bridesmaids had assembled for the pictures, and Clemmie, looking beautiful in Dolly's simple white lace, was like a dove in the center of a dozen chattering blue jays.

"Aren't you nervous?" Susan Beesley asked as she helped adjust Clemmie's veil according to the photographer's directions.

"Why should I be nervous?" Clemmie said, and raised her chin a little to make sure the camera caught the line of her throat at its most flattering.

The ceremony proceeded more smoothly than Dolly had dared hope. George was sober enough to remember the ring and refrain from dropping it, and those awful people from the magazine had been barred until the reception. Tom's parents sat with quiet dignity in the first pew on the right side.

Mr. and Mrs. Karl Hendreich had given Dolly more than a few moments' worry. Aside from a handful of acquaintances, they were the only people Tom had invited. Dolly had debated how one entertained a miner and his wife or if one entertained them at all and finally decided that, regardless of their social standing, they were Tom's parents. She invited them for the weekend of the wedding. Mercifully they refused. Mrs. Hendreich wrote saying she appreciated the invitation, but she and her husband would arrive the morning of the wedding and would leave Scranton immediately afterward. No special arrangements need be made regarding their transportation or accommodations.

The Hendreichs had discussed the matter at length. They had worked hard for Tom and he'd worked hard for himself. Nothing must ruin it now. Not even them.

For Clemmie the reception passed in a haze of champagne and waltzes and hundreds of blurred faces telling her how beautiful she looked and how happy she was going to be. One minute she was dancing with her old friend Porter Lowry, who was telling her what a fine fellow Tom was, and then she was changing into the pale blue traveling suit and pushing through the crowd to the car where Walter sat waiting to drive them to the train and then suddenly she was alone with Tom in Elias's private railroad car. Elias had arranged to have the interior repainted and the master stateroom entirely redone for their wedding trip. It was a triumph of *style moderne,* all black basalt and white ivory, sleek sensuous lines and sophisticated simplicity. There wasn't a tassel or clawfoot in sight.

At first Tom had objected to Elias's arrangements and the gifts Clemmie reported he planned to give them. One night when Clemmie was upstairs dressing for another of the parties in their honor, he'd confronted Elias with the problem. He found Elias in the small study where they'd talked that first day Clemmie had asked Tom for dinner. Elias smiled when Tom entered.

"Can I give you a drink? I'm sure George offered you one of those fancy cocktails he's always mixing up, but personally I prefer my whiskey without a lot of embellishment. And I've got some prewar stuff here that can be drunk that way. The worst thing about Prohibition is the whiskey."

Tom took the glass from Elias. "I'd like to talk to you, sir."

Elias was not unprepared for what was coming. In the years Tom had worked for him, Elias had learned as much about the younger man's pride as he had about his abilities. He knew there would be problems when it came to the house and the expensive wedding trip and all the rest, but he was prepared for them.

"It's about the house," Tom began.

"If you're not satisfied, you'll have to talk to Clemmie. It's a bit modern for my taste, but she had her heart set on it."

"It's not that. The house is beautiful. . . ."

"But you don't want me to buy it for you?"

"Or the trip to Europe or the renovations to your private car . . ."

"Now hold on a minute, Tom. The car needed some refurbishing, so I'm having it done before your wedding, but I can assure you I'm not handing it over to you as a gift."

"You know what I mean, sir."

"Yes, I know what you mean. And I'm not surprised. I don't say I agree with the way you feel, but I'm not surprised by it."

"Then you'll see I can't possibly accept all that."

"I don't see anything of the sort. These gifts have nothing to do with your position at the railroad." Elias did not miss the glimmer of doubt in Tom's face. "And if you think that vice presidency had anything to do with Clemmie, you're wrong. You've won every promotion and every raise on your own, Tom. And you didn't win them till I thought you were ready for them. I'll do a lot for the man Clemmie marries, but I'll be darned if I'll let a man mess about with my railroad just because he's married to my daughter. The point is, Tom, there are things I would have given Clemmie if she had married a man with a fortune. Don't stop me from giving them to her because she married a man without one.

"Don't worry, you'll find plenty of ways to spend your own money on her. Buy her some clothes in Paris.

And a few jewels. That ought to put a dent in your new salary."

Elias stood and walked around his desk to where Tom was sitting. When he looked down at him his eyes were kind. "Be fair to Clemmie—and to yourself, Tom. You're making a good deal of money and you're going to make a good deal more before you're through. You're making it because you're the man you are, not because you're marrying Clemmie. Don't be foolish and keep yourself from enjoying it."

Tom had yielded as Elias had hoped he would, and now he found himself, six hours married, setting off in Elias Wilder's private car. He'd been in the business cars before, but never in Elias's own, and Tom had to admire its opulence. The master bedroom might have been redecorated in the current *style moderne,* but the rest of the car retained its old-world elegance, with fine wood paneling, brass fittings polished to a rich gleam, and deep upholstery and thick Oriental carpets to alleviate the noise and discomfort of high-speed travel. It was a new side of the railroad world Tom knew so well.

"At least that's over," Clemmie said, stretching out in one of the large club chairs next to the window and kicking off her shoes.

Tom laughed. "No one could accuse you of being a romantic." There was no rancor in his voice. It was exactly what he'd been thinking. Marriage to Clemmie was one thing, a wedding was something else. He'd thought they'd never get off by themselves.

"Don't tell me you wanted it to go on?"

"Of course not, but aren't girls supposed to?"

"The first thing you'd better learn about your wife, if you haven't learned it already, is that she's not like other girls."

Tom wanted to tell her that to him she was like no one else in the world, but he was not good with words like that. "I'll keep that in mind," he said.

"All the same, it was a splendid wedding."

"Is there any other kind?"

"Of course there is. When the champagne's warm or—" she made a face at him "—the bride ugly."

"And what about the groom?" he asked, thinking of the difference in their backgrounds; it had seemed so obvious to him in the face of all the Wilder guests.

"Oh, everyone thinks you're quite a catch. . . ."

"Certainly, you're lucky to get me."

"I mean it, Tom. Dear old Porter Lowry thinks," she lowered her voice to imitate Porter's, "you're a fine fellow." Tom said nothing. "You don't like Porter, do you?" she asked.

"It's not that. I'd like Porter a lot. . . ." He let the words drift off.

"If it weren't for me," she finished for him.

"All right, it's true. If it weren't for you."

"Well, there's no need to be jealous of old Porter. I've known him for ages, and there's never been a spark of romance between us, so you can stop worrying about him."

"Is there anyone I ought to start worrying about?"

Clemmie hesitated for only a moment before moving to the arm of Tom's chair and putting her arms around his neck. "I find that an extraordinary question to ask on your wedding night, darling."

She felt his arms tighten around her and leaned down till her mouth was touching his, but then there was a knock at the door and the special steward entered from the galley. Clemmie wasn't sure whether she was relieved or disappointed by the interruption.

As they sat and talked over the stew of terrapin that the steward assured them had come up from Baltimore on the afternoon train, the lights of the small towns of Pennsylvania and New Jersey raced by, and Clemmie was reminded of that night a decade ago when she'd taken her first overnight trip on the A & W.

"The first time I ever traveled in this car, Father took me to New York. I think I must have been about ten, and I was never so excited in my life. I stayed up half the night watching the countryside, and the hogger let me blow the whistle."

Tom laughed. "There's nothing as incongruous as railroad slang in your mouth, Clemmie. That fine finishing-schol accent and those awful-sounding words."

"I've been calling engineers hoggers ever since I can remember."

"A girl after my own heart."

"Anyway, it was a wonderful trip. I think it was the first time I realized what Father did. I mean how important he was. There was a little boy on the train, and I couldn't understand why he didn't get to blow the whistle too."

Tom said nothing. He was remembering the trains that had passed through his own childhood. He hadn't been allowed to blow the whistle. He hadn't even sat in a Pullman car wishing he could. He'd watched them race past the miniature plot that was the Hendreichs' yard, spewing cinders and filth on the laundry his mother had struggled to get clean. And later when he was older, he'd lie awake at night on the cot in the cold kitchen that was his bedroom, and listen to the trains. And like hundreds of other boys he'd swear that someday he'd take one of them away from the shabby house and the filthy yard and the meager life his parents eked out. He'd never taken the train away, but he'd gone those hundreds of boys one better. Now it was Tom who kept the trains racing through the night, inspiring another generation of dreams.

"What will you do with it when it's ours?" Clemmie's voice brought him back to the present.

"What do you mean?"

"The railroad, of course. The A & W. You must have some plans."

"I wish you wouldn't say things like that, Clemmie. You're bound to inherit part of it, and I'll go on working for it for as long as I can, but it's never going to be ours."

"Of course it is, darling. That's the whole plan."

190

"What about your brothers." Tom held her eyes with his own. It was an insane dream, he'd told himself over and over, as he'd fought to stifle it. It was too hopeless. And too unfair.

"Adam's been disinherited. And George . . . well, can you imagine letting George run anything more complex than a cocktail party?"

"George is young. He'll shape up."

"That's what Father says, but you know as well as I do George will never shape up. He may get older, but he won't grow up."

"Anyway, your father's bound to reconsider about Adam."

Clemmie remembered that day at the St. Regis. "I don't think so."

"Well, he ought to."

"Porter's right, darling, you really are a fine fellow. But you see, I'm not nearly so fine as you are, and I know exactly what I plan to do when it's ours. I'm going to do exactly what Father's been trying to do all his life. He hasn't had enough time, but we will. We can build the A & W into the best railroad in the country. A true competitor."

Tom looked across the table at his wife. Her eyes were wide with excitement, and her voice husky. Some women responded that way to jewels and furs, others to marriage or children. For Clemmie it was the railroad.

"A true competitor to what?"

"Why the Central . . . and the Pennsylvania, of course. We'll take them both on. And win."

Tom raised his wineglass toward her. "It's a peculiar wedding toast, but I'll drink to it."

"I knew you would, darling. I always knew you would."

The train had been pulled onto a siding for the night. In the morning it would move into the Hoboken station where carsfull of well-rested businessmen would pour onto the ferry and across the river into New York for a full day of work.

Clemmie was sitting alone in the darkened master stateroom, as sumptuous in its new decor as a bridal suite. She was staring out into the night, thinking of a beach house in Newport and trying desperately not to think of it. Then she heard a knock at the door and swore to herself she would banish Whit Morris from her mind.

When she opened the door the light from the main saloon filtered around Tom so that she could barely see his face. He was nothing but a dark silhouette. She felt his arms go around her, sensed the powerful shoulders beneath the smooth silk of his robe, tasted his mouth on hers, familiar yet strange in its unchecked hunger. His hands were gentle at the satin of her peignoir, then more urgent as they touched her skin, and without knowing it she forgot Whit or any fears that she might remember Whit. She forgot everything but the immediate sensation of Tom's mouth traveling over her body, his hands exploring as they had never dared to before, his own body moving against hers, leading her further and further away from herself or him, into some dark realm of pure abandon, of touch and taste and throbbing ecstasy that fed rather than fulfilled her desire, until she thought she'd scream with wanting him. Then he was inside her and the hunger mounted to a new pitch, pushing her, driving her, forcing her toward something unknown and inescapable, and she felt herself trembling with a pleasure so intense it was almost pain, a terrifying pleasure that seemed to go on and on echoing and re-echoing through her body with a fearful, overwhelming force. Then slowly, strangely, she felt herself coming back to herself and to Tom.

He was still holding her to him and his breathing was short and shallow. "I didn't know . . ." he whispered almost to himself.

"About nice girls, you mean?" She struggled to make her voice light. It seemed important that Tom not know how deeply he'd touched her. It seemed important that she protect herself.

"Don't, Clemmie."

She rested her head on his chest and said nothing.

"I love you, Clemmie." It was, Tom realized, the first time he'd said the words.

"Mmm . . ." It was her only answer, and after a few moments Tom thought she'd fallen asleep, but she was not asleep. She lay in the luxurious bed, feeling Tom's arms around her, still holding her to him, holding her even though he thought she was asleep, and wondered at what had just happened. In the last months she'd told herself that she was fond of Tom and wanted to marry him for a variety of practical reasons, but she didn't love him, not the way she'd loved Whit. That was true, but there was another truth as well, the truth of what had just happened. It was sex, Clemmie told herself, simply sex. That was what had just happened between them. That was the fierce bond holding her to Tom, a bond as strong as the railroad. Clemmie swore it was something she had not expected, but she knew she was lying. She'd suspected it all along but had been afraid to admit it to herself, even as she was afraid to confront it now. Tom must not have that great a hold over her. He must not have any hold over her. The scales of their marriage were intended to tip the other way.

Tom leaned against the railing of the *Majestic*'s A Deck and stared at the sea, blue-black in the late-afternoon sun. He was accustomed to trains that cut through the countryside, giving a sense of speed and substantial progress. The ship gave him a feeling of aimlessness. If he looked down at the hull cutting through the foam, he knew he was moving. If he looked off to the horizon, he felt as if he were adrift in a vast world without boundaries or destination.

He turned and put his back to the railing and the sea. From the private veranda that ran the width of the Royal Suite he could see into both the sitting room

and bedroom. Clemmie had just returned from a swim
—"ladies' hours at the baath," she'd imitated their
steward as she'd gone off—and was sitting at the dressing table brushing her hair. The satin of her peignoir
moved against her body with each stroke.

Tom walked to the table and stood behind her, watching her reflection in the mirror. Her face was pale
against the raven hair. Suddenly her reflection blurred
into another white face, ashen and exhausted. The black
hair was longer than Clemmie's but there was no lustre
to it, and the face was whimpering, whimpering in pain
as it had been for three days now.

"It hurts, Mama," the mouth in the white face muttered over and over in German.

And Tom's mother had held the face against the
rough cloth of her bosom and rocked the child back
and forth. "Shhh . . ." she'd repeated again and again
until the sound of his mother's voice comforting his
older sister had become as constant as the sound of the
ship, the cranking, wheezing, almost human-sounding
breathing of a ship's steerage. And through it all his
sister's cries persisted.

She was dead before they reached New York—they
never knew from what. In Germany the doctor for the
steamship line had pronounced her fit and taken the
money for her passage.

When the Statue of Liberty loomed into view, the
crowds pushed to one side to get a glimpse. "A long
journey," Karl Hendreich had pronounced. The endless days by foot and wagon from Silesia to Bremen and
the agonizing days aboard ship had given weight to
every word.

"A long journey," Tom's mother had repeated and
held him tightly to her. A long journey that had left
her with a single child.

"I said," Clemmie's voice brought her own face back
into focus, "why don't you ring for the steward and we
can have tea on the veranda."

*   *   *
194

"I told you I'd win today. I just knew it." Clemmie had taken the ship's daily pool, and she was terribly proud and none the worse for the second bottle of champagne she'd insisted they order in celebration. They were dancing now and when she looked up at him, her eyes were bright. "Tomorrow you must bet, Tom." He had refused to join the wagering on the number of miles the ship logged from noon one day to the next. Tom had never gambled in his life, except on his own future, and that, it seemed from this vantage point, had been a sure thing.

"Honestly, we're going to have to loosen you up a bit. I won't have a stuffed shirt for a husband." An image flashed through Clemmie's mind of Tom a few hours ago, his body naked and glistening with perspiration above her in the touseled bed of their stateroom. "Though you're not such a stuffed shirt as all that," she whispered against his ear."

She dropped her head back and looked up at him again. "I suspect you had a past, Thomas Hendreich." Then she leaned close and whispered, "Tell me about it. Tell me what it was like with other girls."

She felt him stiffen. "Don't talk that way, Clemmie. You know I hate it when you talk that way." It never occurred to him to ask the same question.

Clemmie insisted on a third bottle of champagne, to toast the stewards, she said, although the stewards, according to custom, had already received ten percent of her winnings. When they'd finished the last bottle, she said they needed a walk on the upper deck.

It was dark and deserted at this hour, and Clemmie began to hopscotch across one of the shuffleboard courts. As she reached the last number, the deck lurched a little, and Tom caught her just before she hit the railing.

"Easy," he said. "We don't want a woman overboard."

He was still holding her and she pressed her body against his. "Sturdy Tom."

"Absolutely," he answered, his mouth on hers.

"Reliable Tom."

"Without a doubt." He kissed her again.

"Doesn't gamble."

"Never."

She could taste the champagne on his tongue.

"Avoids danger."

"Whenever possible," he murmured against her mouth.

She pulled back a little. "Don't you ever want to do anything dangerous?"

"Such as?" His mouth was tracing the curve of her neck.

"Making love in a lifeboat?"

He straightened. "I'd rather go below."

"But I wouldn't, darling." Now she was the one holding tightly.

"Clemmie." It was a reproach.

Her hands were deft at the studs of his evening shirt, then cool and coaxing against his skin. They trailed down his trousers.

"Clemmie." It was a moan now.

She led him to one of the lifeboats. Then she felt his hands beneath the silk of her dress, beneath the chemise, felt the fire they flamed as they moved familiarly, fiercely against her skin, and she was no longer leading but following him. Her body moved in rhythm with his and she felt him inside her surging like the sea around them, explosive as the stars overhead.

"I think," Clemmie said, watching Tom's reflection in the mirror as he knotted his tie carefully, "when we get to London we'll have to get you a new wardrobe." She was sitting in bed with a breakfast tray on her lap.

Tom put on the Norfolk jacket he'd bought at Brooks Brothers. "I thought it was the bride who was supposed to go to Paris to do the shopping," he said.

"The bride will shop in Paris, but first the groom will get a new wardrobe in London."

Tom sat on the side of her bed. "I've got more than enough clothes, Clemmie. You don't want to make a lounge lizard out of me, do you?"

She laughed. "You've got more than enough ready-made suits. The vice president in charge of varnish"—she saw him smile at the railroad slang for passenger service—"wears custom-tailored clothes."

On their first afternoon in London they went straight to Savile Row. Clemmie insisted on a dozen suits, half a dozen odd jackets and trousers. The salesman opened bolt after bolt of fabrics for them. They had made almost all their choices when he flung a length of soft tweed across the table. It was the same fabric as the jacket Whit had been wearing the day she'd met him. Clemmie ran her fingers over it. She closed her eyes for a moment and could feel Whit's arm against hers as the train lurched.

"And this one too," Clemmie said. "You must have a jacket of this."

Tom laughed, and told the salesman to add it to his order.

Clemmie hadn't gone with Tom to the subsequent fittings, and she saw the jacket for the first time the day it was delivered to their hotel in Paris. She insisted Tom try it on for her.

"Don't be silly, Clemmie."

"It's not silly. You make me model everything I buy. Just that tweed jacket. I want to see if they got the fit right."

He slipped into the jacket reluctantly. Clemmie stood with her head tilted to one side, studying him. The tailoring was superb, too superb. Something was missing. "It doesn't look the same," she murmured.

"The same as what?"

Clemmie turned and began rifling through the rest of the clothes. "The same as I thought it would," she said quickly.

Chapter 7

TOM WAS GLAD to be home. Not since he was six years old had he gone for three months without working. But despite the souvenirs and a scrapbook full of photographs, the trip still had a curious unreality for him. To be sure, there were moments in those three months that lived in his memory with a special vividness: that night on the ship when Clemmie had won the pool; a morning in San Sebastián when he'd awakened in the huge room overlooking the sea and Clemmie, who'd been on the terrace, had come back to bed smelling of the morning and the salt breeze of the Atlantic; the way she'd looked coming out of the shadows of a Baroque church when the sunlight had suddenly flooded over them and she'd smiled as simply and openly as a child. A dozen different moments, perhaps a dozen different Clemmies. Tom didn't like all of them but he knew now with a fierce certainty that he loved and wanted all of them. And what about Clemmie? Tom had asked himself more than once in the months since they'd married. She wanted him. He knew that as certainly as he recognized his own desire. But love? It wasn't simply that she never said the words—he said them rarely enough himself. It was something more than that with Clemmie, something more elusive and maddening than the mere lack of words. He could possess her body, but he was unable to capture—capture what? Tom asked himself. Her soul? Her spirit? He wasn't sure, but he did know one thing for certain. That was the way Clemmie wanted it. And Tom knew something else as well. It would be dangerous for him if she ever realized how deeply he loved her. He could hold his own against Clemmie only as long as her desire equaled his and his aloofness matched her own.

Clemmie, for her part, gave less thought to her feelings or Tom's, and more to their future. She launched her attack as soon as they arrived home.

"Father," she began one Saturday afternoon when they were walking from the eighteenth hole to the clubhouse. "Don't you think Tom ought to be a member of the board?"

"Not yet," he answered as if he'd been expecting the question.

"But he's older than Adam, and Adam would have been by now if—"

"Adam is another matter entirely." He cut her short.

"Well, someone's going to have to take over."

Elias laughed but there was no mirth in it. He'd played badly today and at one point he'd felt almost too tired to shoot the last three holes. "Don't be in such a hurry to rush the old man out of the picture, Clemmie."

"You know I didn't mean that."

"Didn't you?" he asked, remembering his own guilty eagerness to have the mines in his hands.

Samantha was sitting alone at a table on the clubhouse terrace when they approached. "Clemmie, Mr. Wilder," she said. "How nice to see you."

Clemmie stopped, but Elias nodded curtly and kept walking. He could no longer call her Mrs. Weymouth-Baldwin and would not call her Samantha, or worse still Mrs. Wilder.

"Remember you and Mother are coming to dinner tonight," Clemmie called after her father, and dropped into a chair next to Samantha. "Tea or a cocktail?" Clemmie asked.

"He certainly doesn't give in easily."

"No, he doesn't," Clemmie said, thinking of her own conversation with Elias.

"He's making Adam miserable."

"Adam seems all right," Clemmie said, preoccupied with which tack to take with her father at dinner that night.

"He works twice as hard as he did before we were married. And he's become an absolute fanatic about money."

"That's funny," Clemmie said. "I always thought the money part of it bothered Adam less than the idea of the railroad itself."

"Oh, the money bothers Adam, all right. All he ever tells me anymore is that we can't afford this and we can't afford that. I can't imagine where it all goes. Sometimes I think that when Adam dies I'm going to find myself with hundreds of secret bank accounts all over the country." Samantha stopped abruptly and looked down at the drinks the waiter had set before them.

"What a peculiar thing to say," Clemmie said, and thought, but did not add, *especially since you're the older of the two.*

"The least you could do," Clemmie said to her father two weeks later, "is give him the title. He does all George's work so why can't he have the title too?"

Elias looked across the dinner table at his daughter. "You mean you think Tom ought to be vice president of finance as well as passenger operations?"

"If he does both jobs, he ought to have both titles."

"Please Clemmie, not at dinner," Dolly said.

"Someone has to defend Tom's interests," Clemmie continued, ignoring her mother's plea. "Right now Tom's in Chicago doing George's job while George— well, we can all guess where George is."

201

"It may interest you to know, Clemmie, that right now George is in Uniontown. I heard rumors the B & O was after some of our freight business, so I sent George down to sound out some of the coal men. I'm sure you'll be pleased to know your brother did a satisfactory job. The B & O won't make any inroads this year."

Clemmie was unimpressed. "It still can't compare to what Tom's done, to what he's doing for the railroad every day."

"Tom's doing a fine job," Elias said calmly. "You ought to be proud of him."

"I am proud, but you don't seem to be. That's why I'm trying to defend his interests."

"Are you sure it's Tom's interests that concern you?" Elias asked.

"Of course, they're mine too. After all, he is my husband."

"Then I'd appreciate it if you'd tell me exactly what it is you want," Elias said. "What is it you think you're lacking, Clemmie? It can't be money. With what I've given you, plus Tom's salary, you've plenty of that."

"It isn't the money."

"The railroad. That's it, isn't it? You want my railroad," Elias said evenly.

"I want Tom to be appreciated."

"I should think that would be your job."

"I mean, I want Tom's work to be appreciated," Clemmie explained.

"I do appreciate Tom's work. That's why he's gone as far as he has. Not because of you, Clemmie, but because of his ability. And it occurs to me that if Tom's dissatisfied, he ought to speak to me about it."

"Well, if you won't think about how unfair it is to Tom," Clemmie changed her tack, "then you ought to think about yourself and the railroad. Someone's going to have to take over—eventually."

"Clemmie!" Dolly broke in.

"And you think it ought to be Tom, with you behind him of course," Elias said.

"Why not? Tom's certainly a better choice than George. George doesn't know the first thing about the railroad. Tom knows everything there is to know. And he's made money for you. What's George ever done besides cost you money? One success in Uniontown doesn't undo all the rest. How much did it take to keep his name out of the paper after that incident in Youngstown?"

"That was almost a year ago," Elias said.

"Are you telling me George has reformed?"

"I'm telling you he's improved."

"And you think just because you haven't had to buy off a newspaper or an irate father or husband for almost a year that makes George better suited to take over the railroad than Tom!"

"Really, Clemmie," her mother interrupted. "You're making too much of a few boyish scrapes. George was never as bad as you make him out to be."

Elias's face gave no indication whether he agreed with his wife or not. He seemed to be thinking of something else as he folded his napkin and placed it next to his plate. "I told you once, Clemmie, not to rush me out of the picture, but for the moment we'll forget your eagerness in that department. You're right, of course. Someone will have to take over someday. Perhaps not as soon as you'd like, or perhaps a lot sooner than I'd like, but it will happen. And I've made up my mind." Elias hesitated, and Clemmie could feel her heart pounding. "George will succeed me as President and Chairman of the Board of the A & W."

"George! You can't be serious."

"I'm quite serious, Clemmie. And I'll explain why. You've been campaigning for Tom for some time now. Your mother, on the other hand, thinks I've been unfair to Adam. I expect he agrees with her. I expect he also can't understand how I can forgive George for a dozen scrapes and refuse to forgive him for 'marrying the woman he loves.' I believe that's the way he phrased it in one of our arguments. I'll tell you why. I don't approve of George's conduct. Far from it. But I think George will grow up and eventually, once he marries the right girl, he'll settle down."

"George, settle down!" Clemmie scoffed.

"All right," Elias continued in a stern tone. "Perhaps he won't settle down the way I want him to, but he will marry the right girl. I'm going to see to that. Now if his conduct outside of marriage isn't what I'd like it to be, I'm sorry, but that will be a matter between George and his wife. As long as George runs his home and family properly, as long as he and the right girl produce sons and bring them up properly so they can carry things on, I'll be satisfied. If a man can't do that, he can't do anything. And Adam has proved he can't do that. He married a—well, let's just say the wrong woman. A woman who, among other things, could not run her own home or family properly. The woman, their marriage, and everything connected with it smacks of dishonest behavior and broken contracts. I don't have much faith in the prospective children of that marriage either."

"But none of that has anything to do with Tom," Clemmie said. She'd wondered about her father's recalcitrance toward Adam, and now she understood, but it was not what she was after tonight.

"That's quite true," Elias continued. "As far as I can see, Tom runs his personal life in an orderly manner, and I don't imagine that's an easy feat being married to you. He's shown every aptitude for running the railroad."

"Then why shouldn't he take over instead of George?"

"Because," Elias said quietly, "George's last name is Wilder and Tom's is not."

"But mine is!"

"Was, Clemmie, *was.* You're a Hendreich now and more important, your children will be Hendreichs."

Clemmie watched her last trump card disappear. She'd planned to tell her father tonight that she was pregnant. Surely that would throw the balance in her and Tom's favor. They were producing an heir for the railroad. Adam hadn't done that, and if George had, no one was likely to admit it.

"You'll be well provided for, you and your children," Elias added. "You know that. But control of the railroad will go to George and to his sons. The A & W is the Wilder line, and it's got to be run by Wilder men."

"Even if a Wilder woman could run it better?" Clemmie shot back.

Elias smiled for the first time since they'd sat down to dinner. "I thought we were talking about Tom."

"No more whiskey," Porter Lowry pronounced. "A little wine with dinner, but that's all. And you'll have to stop bouncing around in that Marmon. Golf and tennis are too strenuous too, though walking's good for you. You can walk the links with Tom, but I don't want you swinging a number-two iron, or anything else for that matter."

Clemmie groaned. "Why don't you just lock me up for nine months?"

"I don't think we have to go that far, but I'm going to tell Tom what I've just told you. I know you, Clemmie, and I don't trust you a bit, but I can rely on Tom to be sensible."

"Will you stop being so darn pompous, Porter? Just because you've got all those diplomas on the wall doesn't mean you can suddenly start ordering me around. I'm the girl who took away your entire marble collection, remember?"

Porter's face was hollow-cheeked with an ascetic cast to it and when he smiled he looked more sardonic than pleased. "Of course I remember. That's why I want to make sure you take care of yourself. Besides, I can't afford to lose you. I don't have enough patients yet. Keep that in mind next time you start to think about getting the Marmon up over sixty."

Driving home from Porter's office, Clemmie considered his advice. Don't do this. Don't do that. It's as if my life were over just because someone else's is beginning, she thought and pressed her foot down on the accelerator. "I won't," she said aloud, not entirely sure of what she meant.

When she'd first begun to suspect she was pregnant, Clemmie hadn't been displeased. The idea of motherhood held no fascination for her and she hated the thought of becoming thick and ungainly, but the difference a grandson would effect in Elias's plans made everything worthwhile. Her father, however, hadn't seen the matter as she'd expected, and now there seemed to be no point in a baby at all. Especially if she were going to have to go into confinement. The very word struck her as ludicrous, ominous and ludicrous. They were going to lock her up. She looked at the speedometer. Fifty. Her foot began to move down on the accelerator again, then lifted. "Damn," she said to herself.

"A baby!" Tom said. Clemmie looked across the sun porch at him. She couldn't imagine how he could manage to find so much excitement in the idea. "That's wonderful."

"Wonderful for you perhaps—the proud father. But not so wonderful for me."

Tom felt a flash of guilt at his own selfishness. All he'd been thinking of was his pride in having a child. He hadn't considered what Clemmie would have to go through. Suddenly he remembered an event he hadn't thought of for years. He must have been about eight at the time. It was an autumn evening and his mother had put supper on the table for his father and himself, then, without sitting down, had gone to the house next door.

"Why isn't Mama having any supper tonight?" Tom asked his father.

"Because Mrs. Kleiner's going to have a baby," he answered as if that explained everything.

Tom's mother wasn't home by the time he went to bed, but she was there the next morning. She packed his father's lunch pail, put breakfast on the table for them, and left the house quickly. He didn't see her again until late that afternoon when he was playing with two other boys in the tiny arid plot of ground that was their yard. His mother came out of the neighbor's house and shouted at them to go play somewhere else. And then suddenly the most terrible scream came from within the house.

"Quick," his mother said. "Go. Go play."

That night she didn't come home at all to make dinner, and Tom was lying awake in the narrow cot in the kitchen when she finally returned. Although he'd closed his eyes, pretending to be asleep, he could feel her standing over him, just standing and staring for a long time. Finally she walked to the table where his father was sitting with a German-language newspaper.

Tom could still hear the words she'd spoken in German. "Dead. The feet were first, and it was dead by the time it came out. Thirty-seven hours and it was dead."

Tom walked to where Clemmie was sitting and put an arm around her. Without looking up from her game of solitaire, she took a sip from the highball on the table by her side.

"Everything will be all right," he said, certain in the aftermath of his memory that it couldn't possibly be. "There's no reason to be frightened."

"I'm not frightened," she said, turning over a card. "It's just so . . . well, it's just so inconvenient."

Clemmie was not inconvenienced for as long as she'd anticipated. In the beginning of her eighth month she went into labor. Tom expected the worst, but before he could work himself into a suitable state of panic and despair in the drab waiting room of the hospital, Porter was telling him that Clemmie had given birth to a five-and-a-half-pound girl. Although the delivery was premature and the baby small, both mother and daughter were doing well.

Clemmie looked pale and tired, but not unwell, Tom had to admit when he entered her room. She was lying on her back, staring at the ceiling.

"How do you feel?" he asked, taking her hand from the cover where it lay.

"Have you seen her?"

"Just for a moment. She's beautiful," Tom added, thinking it was what Clemmie wanted to hear.

"She's not in the least beautiful, Tom, and you know it. She's an ugly, red-faced baby, just like all the others."

"Well, she won't be ugly for long. She looks just like you. Her hair is jet black."

"Her hair, according to the nurse," Clemmie said, "will fall out."

"Well, I still say she's beautiful." Tom found the child as funny-looking as Clemmie did, but he was surprised to find a protectiveness welling up within him as they talked. He hadn't even held the baby, but he knew she was his and he must protect her. "Or at least she's going to grow up to be that way."

"She might as well," Clemmie said. "If she has to be a girl, she might as well be beautiful." Her voice was fierce.

"Girl or boy, Clemmie, I don't care. She's healthy and she's ours."

"Father would have cared." She was sure the sight of a grandson would have changed Elias's plans.

"I'm sure he'll be very pleased with his granddaughter."

Clemmie said nothing. She was remembering an announcement she'd seen in one of the New York papers just after they'd returned from their wedding trip. ". . . twin sons to Mr. and Mrs. Whitmore Vanderbilt Morris . . . Nicholas VanNest Morris and VanNest Vanderbilt Morris . . ." Damn Alison, Clemmie thought, mousy little Alison whom everyone felt so sorry for. Twin boys. It isn't fair. It just isn't fair. She felt the tears running down her face, into her hair, and felt Tom's hand brushing them away.

"It doesn't matter, Clemmie, really it doesn't," he said. But Tom had no idea what mattered and what didn't.

"I'm worried about Clemmie," Tom told Porter when he ran into him in the hospital corridor late the next afternoon.

"No reason to," Porter said. "They're both fine."

"I don't mean physically, but she's so upset about the baby's being a girl. Too upset."

"Women frequently get depressed after they've had a baby," Porter said. "I wouldn't worry about it. It's normal and, more important, it'll pass."

Tom felt vaguely reassured. In the past year his jealousy of Porter had given way to trust and friendship. He and Porter were as different as two men could be, but in spite of that, or perhaps because of it, they got on well.

Clemmie's room seemed to have turned into a greenhouse overnight. Everywhere Tom looked there were flowers. Dolly, sitting in one corner, was almost hidden by a huge basket of carnations and camellias. Adam stood between an arrangement of calla lilies and one of tulips, and Samantha was rearranging a bowl of anemones. Only George stood apart from the floral arrangement. He had turned one of the bed tables into a portable bar, and was mixing Manhattans.

"It looks like a party," Tom said.

"Either that or a funeral," George answered.

"That's a terrible thing to say," Dolly chastised her son.

"Just meant the flowers, Mother." George turned to Tom. "What'll it be? And let me warn you before you answer, Manhattans are all I have."

"Then a Manhattan is what I'll take."

"We've been discussing names," Dolly said. "Clemmie said you hadn't decided yet."

Tom, in fact, had decided, but he didn't want to discuss it in front of the entire Wilder family.

"I think you ought to name her Clemency," George said, handing Tom his drink. "Then we'd have big Clemmie and little Clemmie. A touching picture, don't you think?"

"Don't do it, Clemmie," Samantha said. "Imagine being known as big Clemmie, then mother Clemmie, then old Clemmie."

"Don't worry, I won't," Clemmie said. "I never could stand women who name their daughters after themselves. It's as if they wanted another try at life."

"What's so terrible about that?" Adam asked.

"Nothing, except there's no point wishing for things you can't have," Clemmie said.

Dolly stood. "Well, right now I'm wishing that George would finish that drink—and not have another—and we'd all leave and let Clemmie get some rest. Except you, of course, Tom. I wasn't hurrying you."

"I've been thinking about names," Tom said when he and Clemmie were alone. "How do you like Elizabeth?"

"Elizabeth. Where did that come from?"

"It was my sister's name."

"I never knew you had a sister."

"She died in . . . when she was very young." They were silent for a moment, each realizing that Clemmie rarely asked Tom about his early life, and he rarely volunteered any information.

"Anyway, do you like the name?"

"If you do," Clemmie said. "Name her anything you like, just so long as it isn't Clemmie."

By the time she was six months old it was clear that, whether or not Elizabeth was going to be a beautiful woman, she was a very pretty baby, as well as a very good one. The child's disposition was marvelous, as marvelous as the nurse Clemmie had found. At times it was possible for Clemmie to forget she had a daughter, although she often remembered she did not have a son.

"What were you and Father talking about, locked in his study like that for half the evening?" Clemmie asked. She and Tom had just returned from the farm, and she was sure they'd finally begun to make progress with Elias. Why else would he take Tom away from the rest of the guests for so long?

Tom was sitting on the end of his bed taking off his shoes. "Your father has changed his will."

The hairbrush stopped in midair, and Clemmie whirled around from the mirror to face Tom. "We won!" Her voice was almost a whisper. "We get the railroad."

"No, Clemmie. He's making some changes in the division of the stock, but George still gets the lion's share."

"It's not fair." Her voice was louder now, and she seemed on the verge of tears.

"It is fair, Clemmie. It's your father's railroad and he can leave it to whoever he wants. Besides, you get more mining stock."

"Mining stock! Who cares about the mining stock? Why didn't you tell him we'd rather have the railroad?"

"Don't you think that would be a little indelicate, telling your father how to draw up his will?"

Clemmie looked straight at Tom, and her eyes were cold. "You didn't get where you are by delicacy."

His eyes held hers. "I got where I am by hard work—and by knowing when to keep my mouth shut as well as when to talk."

"So you just sat there and didn't say a word?"

"I said thank you."

"Thank you. Thank you for what? What sort of changes did he make?"

Tom dropped his eyes and began to remove his cuff links. "He asked me not to talk about it, Clemmie."

"Not even to me?"

"Not even to you."

"But that's ridiculous."

"It's the way your father wants it."

"Well, it's not fair. And it's not right, either. I'm your wife—and his daughter. You have to tell me."

"I can't, I gave him my word."

"Ah, the *gentleman* gave his word. . . ." Her voice was cruel.

"Don't, Clemmie, you'll only be sorry."

She was furious and could feel that her fury was making her foolish in the face of his calm. She was almost grateful when the sound of the heavy brass knocker on the front door interrupted the argument.

Tom reached the door first. When he opened it they found George leaning against a pillar. He was smiling, but it was not the customary smile of confidence, and there was blood on his white silk scarf.

He looked at Tom's open shirt and Clemmie's dressing gown. "Hope I didn't disturb you," he said. It was clear that he had been drinking, but he didn't seem as drunk as they'd often see him. Tom suspected something had sobered him up suddenly.

"What's wrong?" Clemmie pushed aside her brother's apologies. "Were you in a fight?"

"First let him come in, Clemmie," Tom said, leading them both to the living room.

George sank into a chair and closed his eyes.

"Well, what happened?" Clemmie demanded.

"I could use a drink," George said.

"From the looks of you—and the smell," Clemmie added, "a drink is the last thing you need."

George looked at Tom. "Come on, old man. I've had a hell of a night."

Tom poured a couple of ounces of whiskey into a glass and handed it to George. "Okay, now, what happened?"

"Well, to begin with the car is wrecked. Hit a stretch of ice out on High Point Road and skidded right into a tree."

"Are you hurt?" Tom asked.

"I'm okay, but the car's a mess."

"As long as no one was hurt—" Tom said.

"I said I wasn't hurt," George interrupted him.

"Who else was in the car?" Tom asked.

"A girl."

"Who?" Clemmie demanded.

"Just a girl. You wouldn't know her."

"Is she hurt?" Tom asked.

George nodded. "I left her at the hospital. Face cut up and they think she broke some ribs. Maybe more. The doctors don't know yet. She went through the windshield."

"And you just left her at the hospital?" Clemmie said.

"What else was I supposed to do? The doctors said they wouldn't know anything till morning, and the police said I could go."

"The police!"

"Of course, the police, Clemmie. How else do you think I got her to the hospital?"

"Do they know you'd been drinking?" Tom asked.

"If you two spotted it, I imagine they did." George smiled weakly.

"But did they put it in their report?" Tom insisted.

"I don't know."

"Does your father know?"

"Why do you think I'm here? The old man would go through the roof. It's not just the car and the hooch . . ."

"The girl?" Tom said.

George nodded.

"Who is she?" Clemmie repeated.

"Works in that diner near the yards. You've probably seen her, Tom. Cute little blonde." George seemed to remember the accident. "Oh, God, her face was awful. . . ."

"Take it easy," Tom said. "It may not be that bad. They can do a lot with surgery these days. That's one good that came out of the war. For the moment, let's worry about you. We've got to keep the police from pressing charges. I take it they let you go because they knew who you were."

"They drove me here."

"Why didn't you have them take you home?" Tom asked. "A word from your father would take care of everything."

"I'm more worried about him than I am the police."

"He's going to be angry, especially about the girl," Tom said, "but he'll take care of the police."

"Don't be so sure," George groaned. "Not this time."

"This time and every time," Clemmie said bitterly.

"Not after last month."

Clemmie was suddenly alert.

"He didn't tell you?" George looked from Clemmie to Tom and they both shook their heads. "Girl who works in the ticket office in Oil City. Threatened a paternity suit."

"I take it she had the grounds," Clemmie said.

"Hell, it could have been half the guys who buy train tickets. . . ."

"But she said it was you," Tom said. He did not want to encourage George to go into details, especially in front of Clemmie.

"And took ten thousand to decide it wasn't. The old man was pretty mad—as you can imagine. Said he was fed up, and this was the last time. That's when he brought up Cornelia Reed."

"Who's Cornelia Reed?" Tom asked.

"Philadelphia Reeds. About as proper as you're going to get. She probably wouldn't have me, if her old man hadn't lost a bundle in some stock speculation. Miss Cornelia Reed was attached to the ten thousand. I had to promise I'd marry her. That and stop running around. I did too. Hadn't gone near a girl for weeks— except Cornelia. Cornelia the cold. That was the whole problem. I was in Philadelphia today. Had dinner at the Reeds'. On the train home I started thinking about Cornelia, and the more I thought about her the worse I felt, and pretty soon I was feeling so bad that every little while I'd have to take something to cheer me up. I had a flask with me. I knew the Reeds weren't going to give me a decent drink—or at least not more than one. So by the time I got back here I wasn't feeling quite so bad and then I remembered Dorothy. I knew she was on the late shift at the diner tonight."

"How did you know that?" Clemmie asked.

"I'd seen her coming on last night when I left the office. One of the advantages of working late. We stopped to talk for a minute. She's a good kid."

"So you decided to stop in and have a few words with this good kid," Clemmie said.

"Come on, Clemmie. I was feeling rotten after Cornelia, and I figured a little fun wouldn't hurt. No one would have found out if it hadn't been for that damn ice."

"And no one's going to find out now. Except Father. He'll be furious, but he'll take care of it. By the time he's finished Dorothy will have been alone in the car when the accident occurred. And Dorothy will probably have a new face and a nice settlement."

"God, I hope you're right," George said.

"Well, there's only one way to find out. You've got to call him," Tom said.

George looked at him miserably. "Couldn't you do something?"

"You know as well as I do, my word isn't worth anything compared to your father's. I can get small things done for the railroad. He can get anything done."

George dropped it to him easily. "Maybe he wouldn't get so angry if you explained everything to him."

For the first time Tom seemed to lose his patience. Then he caught himself and decided it wasn't worth the trouble. "Sure, George, I'll call him."

"Thanks, Tom, you're a pal. A real pal."

As Tom heard the words, he thought of Clemmie's machinations and his own secret hopes and quickened his steps to the telephone, as if he wanted to escape George's gratitude.

Clemmie had predicted accurately. Elias was furious. He was also efficient. Matters at the police station were taken care of by ten the next morning, and negotiations with the girl's parents had begun by the time Clemmie arrived at her father's office that afternoon.

"I suppose you're proud of your son and heir now," she demanded.

"I'm not proud," Elias said quietly, "but I haven't given up hope. George has been behaving himself for some time now. Last night was merely a lapse. Cornelia Reed will keep him up to the mark. I'm convinced of that."

"To hear George tell it, Cornelia was the one who drove him to it. She'll never be able to reform him, and you know it."

"I think you're in for a surprise, Clemmie. And so is George. He hasn't known enough nice girls, but when he gets to know Cornelia, I think he's going to find marriage to her very pleasant. She's far from homely, you know."

"She still won't be able to hold him. And what was it you said, if a man can't run his personal life, he'll never be able to run the railroad. Well, George is going to make a mess of his marriage, and he's going to ruin the railroad. You know that as well as I do. Giving him the A & W is as good as throwing it away."

Elias looked up from the report he'd been pretending to read while she talked. His eyes showed concern rather than anger. "Clemmie, what's happening to you? What's making you so vicious?"

"I'm not vicious. I'm merely practical. Which is more than I can say for you."

"You're not practical, Clemmie. Far from it. You're obsessed. Obsessed with getting rid of George and putting Tom in his place. Obsessed with having things the way you want them."

"I only want things the way they ought to be. The way that's fair—and makes sense."

When Elias spoke, his voice sounded strangely kind

216

after Clemmie's harshness. "Do you remember that pony cart we had at the farm when you were small?"

"What does that have to do with anything?"

"Do you?" he asked. She nodded. "When I bought it, you were about five, so George must have been eight and . . ." Elias hesitated for a moment, "and Adam ten. I said at the time, and quite rightly of course, that Adam and George could drive it, but you were too young. They could take you for rides, but you were too young to drive it yourself. Well, you were furious, Clemmie. You cried and you screamed. If I remember correctly you even broke a doll in a rage over it. But the most foolish thing you did was refuse to ride in it yourself. Oh, eventually you did, but for the first several weeks you wouldn't set foot in that cart. Adam and George offered to take you for rides again and again, but you refused. It was a silly thing to do. You wouldn't have been in the driver's seat, Clemmie, but you would have had a nice ride."

"I take it that little story was meant to be instructive."

"Yes, it was. I'd assumed you'd grown up since that summer, but in the last year I don't think I like the woman you've grown up to be. What is it, Clemmie? What's made you so bitter—and so determined about this business with Tom and George?"

Clemmie turned away from her father. "I just hate to see you throw the railroad away, and that's what you'll be doing if you give it to George."

"Why don't you let me be the judge of that?" Elias said quietly. "Besides, it isn't as if you won't be provided for, Clemmie. The mines—" Elias was interrupted by a knock at the door. Roberts, his secretary, burst into the room.

"It's number 34, Mr. Wilder. Just outside Cincinnati. Eight cars off the track. O'Rourke's on the phone from Cincinnati. And of course the newspapers."

"Hold the news boys until I talk to O'Rourke. How bad is it?" Elias barked into the phone.

Clemmie watched her father's face, rigid with concentration, as he listened to the report. He'd already forgotten her presence.

"Is the wreck crew down from Toledo yet?" Elias demanded. "Well, get them on it. If these two cars are so damn flammable, I want them out of there. Immediately. All we need is an explosion, and we'll have every do-gooder in Cincinnati on our backs. Keep them working through the night, call in another crew from Youngstown if you have to, just get those two cars upright and out of there."

Roberts appeared in the door again. "The Cincinnati papers are still waiting, Mr. Wilder. And the Chicago ones too."

"Damn," Elias muttered. "Okay, give me something for the papers, O'Rourke. You're sure there are no casualties? What about the cause?" Elias listened for a moment. "They always swear they threw the switch. Sometimes I think the only solution is to make the switchman stand next to the track while the train goes through. Then he'll remember whether he threw the switch or not. All right, no point in looking for a scapegoat now. We'll tell them we're setting up an investigation. Tell those reporters snooping around on the scene the same thing. And get those damn cars out of there. Then get working on the track. I want service restored by this time tomorrow." Clemmie saw her father frown. "If you get another crew and keep them working through the night, it's not in the least impossible, O'Rourke!" As Elias slammed down the phone, he seemed to notice Clemmie's presence for the first time since Roberts had interrupted them. "You'd better run along, Clemmie. You can see what's happening here."

"How do you think George would handle something like this? With two cars about to explode and half a dozen reporters ready to crucify the A & W, who would you rather have running the show, George or Tom?"

Elias's fist crashed down on his desk. He seemed to have forgotten the open door and Roberts lurking just beyond. "Damn it, Clemmie. Are you blind? This is no time for arguments. Now get out of here, and let me get this mess in order."

"It's precisely the time for argument," she shouted. "If this doesn't open your eyes, nothing will. Just think of it, think of George trying to take care of a mess like this. He wouldn't know the first thing to do—that is, if they could find him to tell him about it."

"I warn you, Clemmie . . ." Elias thundered.

"You don't frighten me! I'm not George. I'm not even Tom. I'll tell you when you're wrong, and you're wrong about this."

"Get out, Clemmie, get out now," he shouted. "Because in a minute you won't even get—"Suddenly Elias's face went white, and he fell back into his chair as if someone had pushed him. He looked startled and his eyes were wide with fear. "Clemmie . . ." the thundering voice was a gasp now. "Clemmie," he repeated and then slumped forward on the desk.

"What is it?" she cried. "Daddy, what is it?" She tried to lift him to an upright position, but he was a dead weight she couldn't move. "Roberts," she screamed. "Quickly, call a doctor. Call Dr. Lowry."

Roberts was at her side in a moment. Together they propped Elias up into a sitting position. His head fell back against the chair and his eyes were lifeless now.

"I'll call the doctor," Roberts said quietly, but he felt certain it was too late for that.

When Roberts returned from the outer office, Clemmie was still standing next to her father, her cold hand clutching his lifeless one. "It'll be all right, Daddy, you'll see. It'll be all right," she repeated over and over.

"Excuse me, Mrs. Hendreich," Roberts said. "The reporters are still on the line. Perhaps I might give them a statement."

Slowly she lifted her eyes from her father. "What did you say, Roberts?"

"The reporters. I thought I might give them a statement," he repeated.

"I'll speak to the reporters, Roberts." She took her hand from Elias's and lifted the receiver. "This is Mrs. Hendreich," she said into the receiver. "Mrs. Thomas Hendreich. Mr. Wilder is not available for comment at the moment, but every effort is being made to remove the two cars with flammable materials. Two crews will be working round the clock to that end. There were no casualties, and a thorough investigation will be made as to the cause of the accident. Full service will be restored by this time tomorrow. Mr. Hendreich will issue further statements as more information comes in."

Clemmie replaced the receiver and took her father's hand again, but did not resume her reassurances. There was nothing, she thought, turning away from the eyes that hadn't moved or blinked for several minutes now, about which to reassure him.

Chapter 8

THERE WAS NO formal reading of Elias's will. At ten o'clock in the morning on the Thursday after his death the servants were assembled in the large front drawing room of the farm and Elias's attorney informed them of their various gifts. After that he met privately with Dolly, George, Clemmie, and Tom to explain Elias's bequests and stipulations. Each was given a copy of the will to study at leisure.

Dolly received no shares in the railroad or the mines, but was given the house, a considerable cash sum, and the income of a large trust fund that was to be divided equally between George and Clemmie at her death.

Of the seventy percent of the A & W that Elias owned—the remaining thirty percent was divided between the former owners of three of the railroads he had taken over so many years ago—George was to get three-fourths, Clemmie and Tom one-fourth. It was stipulated, in order that it not be construed as an oversight, that Adam was to receive nothing.

The mining stock was divided between George and Clemmie with a good number of shares going outright to Tom and a large block for Elias's only grandchild, Elizabeth Wilder Hendreich.

"There are," the lawyer said, raising pale eyes from

221

the papers before him to Elias Wilder's heirs, "two stipulations, or rather a single stipulation and an explanation." He turned to George. "Your inheritance, Mr. Wilder, is contingent upon your marriage to Miss Cornelia Reed of Philadelphia. In view of your engagement to Miss Reed I see no problem there."

The lawyer turned to Clemmie. "Your father asked that I give you this at the reading of his will." He handed her a white envelope.

"Now if there are any questions . . . Of course, you'll want time to study the will, and you'll be able to reach me at my office regarding any matters that may be unclear."

"I hope you'll stay and lunch with us, Mr. Anderson," Dolly said. She did not particularly want to lunch with the lawyer, and he would have preferred to dine on the train back to Philadelphia, but custom dictated that Dolly invite him and that he accept.

While the rest of them went into the dining room, Clemmie hung back to read the letter Elias had left her. It was dated a little more than six months earlier, just after Elizabeth's birth.

My dear Clemmie,

At the time I write this you're quite displeased with me. I can only hope that by the time you read it, the years will have intervened to alleviate your anger and disappointment. (As you can imagine, the wish is not entirely an unselfish one.) I have left three-fourths of my A & W holdings to George and indicated to the other stockholders that I expect him to succeed me as President and Chairman of the Board. Though one of them shared your doubts as to the wisdom of such a step, I prevailed upon him by virtue of my past conduct of railroad business. The railroad is, therefore, for all practical purposes, George's to run, and I have every confidence that, with the influence and support of Cornelia—and Tom's help—he will learn to run it well.

George's control of the railroad is not, however, the reason for this letter. If I did not convince you of the rightness of my decision during my life, I do not expect to do so after my death. I am writing instead to explain why I chose to leave the remaining one-fourth of my holdings to you and Tom jointly rather than to you alone.

In my dealings with Tom regarding the railroad I have always treated him as an employee rather than a son-in-law. That was the rule by which I determined to conduct myself during my lifetime, but now I am going to break that rule. I am leaving part of the A & W to Tom not because of his merit—though I firmly believe in that—but because he is married to you.

Tom is a proud man, Clemmie, as proud as you. I believe it would be disastrous for him and for your marriage if he felt you controlled things, including the company that he is instrumental in running. I have therefore left him enough mining stock for a small income and joint interest in your share of the A & W. It can only serve as another bond between you.

> Your loving father,
> Elias

When Clemmie and Tom were alone in the car after lunch, she handed him the letter.

"I've seen it," he said, starting down the long drive that led from the farm to the main road.

"Of course. That night last week when you wouldn't tell me what kind of changes he'd made."

"I told him at the time I didn't want him to do it."

"You told *me* at the time you said thank you." Her voice was heavy with sarcasm.

"I did, later on. He said it didn't matter what I thought, he was going to do it his way, and I said I disagreed, but thanked him anyway. I'm sorry, Clemmie."

"Are you? Are you really so sorry to own a chunk of the A & W, to control part of my inheritance?"

Tom swerved the car to the side of the road and slammed his foot on the brake. "Let's get one thing straight, Clemmie. I don't need your father's stocks to hold up my end of this marriage. I don't even need his money. I can get a job with half a dozen lines right now—Lord knows I've had the offers—and support you and Lizzie. Maybe not the way you'd like to be supported, but I can take care of you both. And as long as I can, I don't need the A & W to shore up my pride."

"The self-made man who doesn't need anyone or anything. Not even me."

"I didn't say that," he answered, staring straight ahead.

She reached over and touched his cheek. "Of course you didn't, darling, because it isn't true. And don't worry about the stock. As Father said, it's only another bond between us."

The wedding was small, limited to the immediate families of the bride and groom. Mrs. Reed had wanted to wait until a sufficient time had elapsed after Elias's death in order to give Cornelia a proper wedding, but when she learned the terms of the will both she and Mr. Reed agreed a small but immediate wedding was best.

As Elias had said, Cornelia was far from unattractive. She had the kind of smooth-browed, haughty-eyed beauty associated with a Gainsborough portrait. Despite her father's prediction, Clemmie was reassured. If any style of beauty could hold George, it was not the sort Cornelia possessed.

The young couple returned from a month in Palm Beach to a house on Walnut Street.

"You can't run the railroad from Philadelphia," Clemmie had said when George told her of the house.

"I don't plan to, but Cornelia doesn't want to leave Philadelphia. I'll spend several days a week here, and get back to Philly as often as possible." George smiled his easygoing smile. "It's the perfect arrangement."

"I trust your bride won't miss you," Clemmie said drily. "And that you won't be too lonely."

"Don't worry about me, kid. Old George is never lonely."

Clemmie went to Philadelphia herself the following week. She told Tom she was going in for the day to do some shopping, and she did manage to pick up a few things before catching the 3:17 back to Scranton. She also managed to pay a brief visit to a small office on the second floor of an old office building on Market Street. There she agreed to pay $8 a day and all expenses incurred in keeping track of the activities of Mr. George Wilder.

"I take it we're looking for anything that might reflect on Mr. Wilder's matrimonial state," Mr. Gillis said. His manner of speaking was formal, and Clemmie thought he reminded her of nothing so much as a minister. We'll do our best, Mrs. Wilder."

"My name is Mrs. Hendreich. Mr. Wilder is my brother. I'm merely interested in sparing his wife any unpleasantness. Address all communications directly to me, Mr. Gillis. No one else is to know about this."

"Of course, Mrs. Hendreich. We respect the privacy of our clients." Gillis did not seem to notice the irony of his statement.

Mr. Gillis's first report, dated a month after Clemmie's visit to his office, indicated that marriage had changed George little. He spent several nights a week in Scranton at the home of his mother, and on those nights he was accustomed to pay a visit to the apartment of a Miss Mabel Werfen. Miss Werfen was a typist with the passenger service division of the A & W.

Clemmie locked the report in the small safe they'd built into the closet of the master bath and mentioned it to no one.

Miss Werfen appeared in the following report, but in the two after that there was no mention of her. There were several other names, however, and several incidents with unnamed women, but after four months there was still, as Mr. Gillis pointed out to Clemmie, no real evidence.

"In cases of this kind, Mrs. Hendreich, one needs hard-and-fast proof. Photographs, the testimony of a witness. The mere fact that Mr. Wilder paid a visit to a lady's apartment is not grounds for divorce in Pennsylvania or any other state. Of course, there are ways of obtaining such evidence. It's a nasty business, I admit, but if Mrs. Wilder wants evidence, we can get her photographs. It will cost a bit more, of course."

Clemmie opened the smooth lizard handbag.

Lock Haven wasn't much of a town, George was thinking, especially on a hot August night, but if you knew how you could have fun anywhere. And Lord knew, he could use a little fun tonight. He'd been in meetings all day, first with the men who represented the local brotherhood, then with the manager of the Lock Haven terminus, finally with the A & W lawyer he'd brought along and the attorney for the brotherhood. They'd gone on straight through dinner, merely sending across the street for something to be sent up. God, how that greasy food lurched around in the stomach, he thought.

George didn't regret the day. The meetings had paid off. Lock Haven was a test case, a test of how much the brotherhood could win and a test of the new president. He'd had to come to the boondocks to prove himself, and he'd done it, by God. George was proud, damn proud. He knew what everyone thought. He knew how they'd talked when his father had left him the railroad, knew that they'd all said he'd never be able to fill Elias's shoes. Well, maybe he couldn't fill his father's shoes, but he could run the A & W. He was sure of it himself, and in the last months he'd begun to prove it to others. Today was merely the most recent in a spate of long tiring days, and there were more ahead. Now that he'd straightened out this business with the brotherhood, he'd leave for Florida. Negotiations down there were already underway, but they couldn't do much more without him. It was going to mean a lot of hard work, George thought, and the exhaustion of the day flooded back over him. There was no question about it, he needed a little fun tonight.

He'd been in Lock Haven once before. It must have been two years ago. There'd been a speakeasy in an old gabled and turreted house not far from the railroad station. George wondered if it were still there. Two years was a long time for a speakeasy to stay in the same place, but after all, this wasn't New York or Philadelphia. It wasn't even Scranton.

He got into the single taxi standing in front of the station. "There used to be a club . . . in an old house . . . the 420 or something like that."

The driver turned and looked him over carefully. The clothes were good, too good for a policeman, even a federal one, and the manner was in keeping with the clothes. "The 421," the driver said, and started the engine.

George didn't recognize the house, but then if he remembered correctly, he hadn't been able to see it very clearly last time he was there. There was a long bar against one wall of what used to be the parlor and a dozen small tables. In the former dining room was another bar, more tables, and a small dance floor. An elderly black man hammered away at an upright piano.

It was a week night and most of the tables in the larger room were empty, but the ones crowded around the dance floor were filled. George stood at the bar and ordered a whiskey and soda. He was hoping the soda would camouflage just how bad he was expecting the whiskey to be.

When he'd entered the room, he'd noticed two women alone at one of the tables, and purposely taken a place at the bar near where they sat. Now, drink in hand, he turned to look at them. They turned away as he did.

The younger one wasn't bad-looking, a little on the skinny side, but not bad-looking. The older one wore a

227

tight red dress to show off a very good figure, but George decided she must be at least forty. Still, they weren't bad—his eyes combed the room—and they were the only women without escorts. He told the bartender to send over two more of whatever they were drinking. When the drinks arrived, both women pretended first surprise, then hesitancy about accepting them. Finally they turned and smiled at George.

"Thank you, kind sir," the older one called.

George took the few steps to their table. "Perhaps you'd permit me to join you," he said, and sat in one of the two empty chairs without waiting for an answer.

George and the older woman exchanged first names. "And this is my daughter, Edna," she added.

"Your daughter! Why, Lois, I don't believe it," George lied. "You can't be old enough to have a daughter like Edna."

Lois giggled wildly. "But I am."

"Well, we'll have to drink to that. To you and your daughter Edna." George ordered a second round of drinks. By the fourth he knew the sad story of Edna's father who had, tragically but conveniently, been killed in the war.

"He was a major," Lois insisted.

By the fifth round he knew how difficult it was for two women alone in a town like this.

"Everyone's so ready to talk about us. Like tonight. Here we are just having an innocent drink, and tomorrow it'll be all over town. It isn't fair."

George agreed that it wasn't in the least fair, and ordered another round of drinks.

When the seventh round arrived, Lois and Edna turned their attention to George. He was from Philadelphia, he told them, a salesman for a wholesale paper goods concern.

When George ordered the eighth round, the waiter announced it was the last. The place was closing.

"Just when the fun was starting," Lois said. Edna merely pouted.

George's mind raced. Drunk as he was, he knew he couldn't risk taking them back to the hotel. The days when he'd try sneaking a girl into his room were gone.

"That's right," George said. Fun's just starting. Have an idea, though. I bet our friend here will sell us a bottle—hell, a couple of bottles—and we can take them back to your place." He saw Lois and Edna exchange glances. "Just a nightcap, then I'll be on my way. After all, you ladies have to work tomorrow, and I've got my paper to sell."

"Well, just a nightcap," Lois agreed.

They lived only a block from the speakeasy, in a small wooden house. The peeling gray paint formed a mosaic across its façade and a broken shutter hung by a single nail from one of the downstairs windows. It was the only shutter left on the house. A bicycle lay rusting in the scruffy-looking front yard.

"It isn't much," Lois said, "but it's all ours."

"That's right," Edna added. "No busybodies upstairs or downstairs like at the last place."

Edna turned on the gramophone, while Lois went for glasses. "I hope you don't mind, but there's no ice."

Edna was moving around the small, cluttered living room in time to the music.

Both women had refused to dance at the speakeasy. "People will talk," Lois explained. Now George slid his arms around Edna's waist, and she did not resist.

When Lois returned with the glasses, they each had a drink and then George and Lois danced. She was too drunk to follow him, and every time they bumped against each other she laughed shrilly.

He danced with Edna again, then Lois, and then after a few more drinks he wasn't sure which of them he was dancing with, but finally he found himself with an arm around each, swaying unsteadily to the music. He bent to kiss Edna, then Lois turned his face to her and her mouth was damp and devouring on his. Edna was moving her body against him as if they were still dancing, and Lois, her mouth still on his, was unbuttoning his shirt. With one hand he felt the thin curves of Edna's body while the other explored the heavy weight of Lois's breasts. They were on the sofa now and he felt Lois's hands fumbling at his trousers and his own working at the buttons of Edna's dress. Edna was on his lap and Lois beside him and they were a mass of tangled clothes and damp flesh, of disembodied mouths and hands and breasts and thighs. Then there was a crash as if a door had been broken in and a flash of light like an explosion followed immediately by three more. Both women sprang away from him, and George realized the flash hadn't gone off in his head. It had really happened.

Edna was clutching her dress to her, and Lois was screaming, and the two men who stood in the door were still setting off those quick explosions of light.

"Make sure you can see his face," one of them yelled. "Get his face in the picture."

George lunged at the man with the camera, but he jumped back and the second man followed through. George felt a fist crash against his jaw, then another in his stomach. He fell backward over the table and the bottle and glasses crashed around him.

Both women were screaming now, and Lois was trying to wrest the camera from the man, but he was holding her off with one hand and laughing. "I never wrestled with a naked whore before," he shouted to the second man. Then he gave Lois a shove that sent her back into the sofa and both men were out the door.

Edna began to put on her clothes, but Lois sat huddled in a corner of the sofa, crying. "All over town, it'll be all over town."

George sat up. The pain shot through his stomach. He couldn't breathe and his jaw was throbbing. Trying to move as little as possible, he reached for his trousers.

"Who would do it?" Lois wailed. "I bet it's that bastard Teddy!"

"Who's Teddy?" George asked, and winced at the pain that shot up through his temple as he spoke.

"My husband, my goddamn husband. He's just been waiting for a chance like this."

"I thought your husband was killed in the war," George said, then realized the absurdity of his statement.

Lois just sobbed.

"Will you cut it out," Edna snapped. "Bawling isn't going to do any good." She turned to George. "Your mouth is bleeding. I'll get some soap and water." She went into the kitchen, came back with a bowl of water and a towel, and began to dab at his jaw. "Does it hurt?"

"Like hell."

Lois had finally begun to put on her clothes, but she continued to sob quietly.

"Listen, Lois," George said, trying to move his mouth as little as possible. "It wasn't your husband. You heard the man. He said be sure to get my face. Whoever wanted those pictures was after me, not you."

"Fine mess you got us into," she sniffled.

"Oh, Ma, leave him alone. Just be glad it wasn't Teddy," Edna said.

"Whoever it was," George said, "I'll make sure no one sees your picture."

"And how are you going to do that? You couldn't even get the camera away from them," Lois said through the tears.

"I'll pay whatever they want."

"Oh, Mr. Moneybags here, the traveling salesman, is going to buy them off," Lois taunted.

As he leaned over to pick up his jacket, George felt another pain shoot through his stomach. He took the billfold from the breast pocket and counted two hundred dollars. "This is all I have with me. I'll send you another three hundred tomorrow. And I'll pay whatever they ask."

Lois took the money and counted it quickly. "Well, I guess that'll be all right."

There wasn't a taxi to be found, and George had to walk back to the hotel. With every step he felt the soreness in his stomach and he was sure his jaw was going to explode. *It doesn't make any sense.* The phrase kept running through his head. He'd heard of incidents like this happening to other people, but there was always a divorce case involved. Cornelia didn't want to divorce him, and even if she did, this wasn't her style. Cornelia had never made the slightest reference to his infidelities. If she suspected them, and George didn't see how she could help doing so, they seemed not to bother her. There had been times in the half-year they'd been married that he'd thought she welcomed his nights with other women since they kept him from bothering her more often. But whether Cornelia knew of George's life—and regardless of what she thought of it if she did know—she would never stoop to detectives. The very idea of a photograph would, George knew, shock his wife's sensibilities. Clearly, Cornelia had not hired the two men who'd broken in tonight, but if she wasn't responsible, who was? George couldn't imagine, and by the time he got back to this hotel room he scarcely cared. He'd sobered up suddenly when the men had burst into the room with cameras flashing, but now his head ached and his body felt as if it had been run over by one of his own trains. He examined his jaw in the mirror. It would be swollen for a few days. He'd have to think of an excuse. And he'd have to make sure he had plenty of cash available. He didn't know who wanted those pictures, but he knew whoever it was would not give them up cheaply.

"The whole idea is ridiculous," Clemmie said. "You ought to be concentrating on building the A & W into a real competitor, George, not building new lines in out-of-the-way places. There are a dozen lines between New York and Chicago that the A & W could use."

"If I'd known I was going to be lectured to, I'd never have accepted your invitation to lunch," George said. "And besides, Cornelia hates railroad talk."

"I don't hate it," Cornelia said, "I'm just grateful George doesn't talk it day and night."

"I'm sure he doesn't," Clemmie said drily. The sting of injustice was as sharp as the taste of the cocktail on her tongue. George didn't care about the railroad and it was his to run as he wanted. She thought of the railroad constantly and had no say in its management.

"I don't know why you're so against this Florida line, Clemmie. Tom and Adam aren't." George walked to the cocktail wagon and poured himself another drink.

"Adam has nothing to do with it," Clemmie answered.

"I trust his judgment—and Tom's," George added.

"But of course not mine," Clemmie snapped.

"Why don't you leave the railroad to us, Clemmie?" George looked at the woman in white who had just entered the room carrying a small, dark-haired child. "And concentrate on Lizzy. I bet that little handful could keep you busy."

The nurse put the child down and she ran on unsteady legs straight into Tom's arms.

"What about old Uncle George?" George said, holding out his arms. Like most easy-going men he liked children. Lizzy clung to Tom's knee and hid her dark curls in his lap. "Daddy's little girl, eh?" George laughed.

"Come over here, Lizzy," Clemmie said. The child toddled over and stood beside her mother. "Now say hello properly to Aunt Cornelia and Uncle George." Her eyes riveted on the rug, Lizzy murmured something unintelligible.

"She's well behaved for eighteen months," Cornelia said.

"Thank you." Clemmie turned to the nurse. "You can take her up for her nap now, Miss Simmons."

"Dadda." The child was not unintelligible now.

"Come on," Tom said. "Give me a kiss before your nap."

Lizzy scampered back to Tom, who lifted her up so the fat little arms could reach around his neck. Then Miss Simmons stepped in and the children's hour was over.

"It just isn't logical," Clemmie resumed her argument when they were seated in the dining room. "Why go all the way to Florida to start a railroad when you've got a perfectly good one right here?"

"Because, my dear little sister, we can't stand still."

"I'm not suggesting we stand still," Clemmie said. "I just think we ought to build what we have. Florida doesn't have anything to do with the A & W.

"Florida's the future," George said.

"This squab is superb, Clemmie" Cornelia broke in. "George adores squab."

"Thank you, Cornelia. What do you mean, Florida's the future?" Clemmie turned back to George.

"There's a boom down there, haven't you heard? Tell her, Tom. Explain it to your wife."

"The state is growing pretty quickly," Tom admitted. "That's because of automobiles, of course— apparently more and more people are driving down there every year—but where there are people there's a need for a railroad too."

"I should think Flagler's East Coast Line could handle that."

George laughed. "Got to hand it to you, Clemmie. At least you know your lines. But as a matter for fact, the East Coast and even the Atlantic Coast can't handle it anymore. The state's growing too fast. Why, for the last six months—and remember, that's only the first half of 1924—what were those numbers again, Tom? How many thousands of new residents?"

"Don't you dare tell him, Tom," Cornelia said.

Don't you encourage him to talk figures and ruin Clemmie's lunch."

"All right, Cornelia." George smiled placatingly. "I may not remember the numbers, but I can tell you they're flocking down there like swallows. Not just the rich, but everyone."

"You aren't going to make money running a railroad for poor people," Clemmie said.

"The trouble with your wife," George turned to Tom, "is that all she can thing about is varnish. She forgets the freight."

"What do you mean, varnish?" Cornelia asked.

"Railroad talk," George said, "for passenger traffic. They're not that poor, Clemmie, and they still need clothes and furniture and a lot of other things. And then there are all those oranges and grapefruits going the other way. I tell you we're going to make a fortune."

"Don't be vulgar, George," Cornelia said.

"You're not in Philadelphia, Nelia," George said. "Out here people occasionally mention money, even at table."

"I still think you're taking an awful chance," Clemmie said.

"Not necessarily," Tom interrupted.

Clemmie shot him a look. "You agree with George about this."

"I'm not sure it's the choice I'd make, but done right, it could be profitable. The way things are moving down there, Flagler can barely keep up, and then there's the whole Gulf Coast. You know what they call St. Petersburg? The poor man's Palm Beach."

"In other words," Clemmie said, "you've both discussed it and made up your minds."

"Not at all. I made up my mind." George flashed a smile. "Tom merely sees the wisdom of my decision. Besides, I like the idea of all those months of negotiations and planning. Pennsylvania's no place to spend the winter."

"Speak for yourself," Cornelia said. "I have no intention of leaving Philadelphia until after the Assembly."

"But Nelia, it's only October. That means I'll be alone in Florida for at least three months." George's face was a mask of disappointment, but he could scarcely keep the pleasure from his voice.

The early news from Florida was predictable. An inside page of one of the local papers carried a photograph of George surrounded by a half-dozen girls in brief-skirted bathing costumes with stockings rolled provocatively below the knee. "Mr. George Wilder, prominent Scranton resident, judges the Coral Gables Beauty Contest."

"What's he doing in Coral Gables?" Clemmie grumbled. "I thought he was interested in the Gulf Coast."

"Leave it alone, Clemmie," Tom answered. "George isn't doing a bad job. And it's his railroad so you might as well let him run it as he likes."

"Run it right into the ground."

But even Tom's confidence began to flag after George had been in Florida for a month and a half. He was buying land, great parcels of it. Tom went straight to Adam's office with the news.

"Why tell me?" Adam asked. "I'm only the chief of motive power. All I do is keep the trains rolling. You're the executive V.P., second-in-command to brother George. I'm only an employee. You're a stockholder."

Tom started to leave the office.

"Wait, Tom, I'm sorry. It's not your fault. Sit down and tell me what's really happening."

"It's all this land. I just don't understand it. I thought he was going to lease land the way we always do, the way everybody does. But he's buying it! And the craziest thing is, he's buying it in places you'd never want to build a railroad."

"Sounds as if the bug that's going around down there has bitten him," Adam said. "The damn fool."

"The railroad wasn't a bad idea," Tom said.

"The railroad wasn't a bad idea, but buying up a bunch of swampland like every damn fool who thinks he's going to get rich quick is a rotten idea. We've got to stop him."

"You think he'll listen?" Tom asked.

"God knows. He never has about anything else." Adam buzzed his secretary and told her to place a call to George. He was not at the first four numbers she tried, and it was six-thirty that evening before they tracked him down.

George did not welcome his brother's advice. "You fellows aren't down here," he told Adam over the phone. "You don't know what's happening."

"We know enough," Adam said, "to realize you don't tie up all your money in land when you're going to need it to build the line."

"Listen, Adam, the railroad's just the beginning. Before we're through we're going to own half the state." In his excitement George seemed to have forgotten that just because the A & W owned something, it didn't follow that Adam did. His brother did not remind him of the fact. "We're going to own cities where old people live and hotels for hotshots and—well, you name it, we'll own it. You're going to love it, old boy. I'll build you a big place on Biscayne Bay, and you and Sam can just lie in the sun and swim all day. What you do with your nights is up to you."

"I don't want to lie in the sun all day," Adam said. "I want to get that line built."

"It's in the works right now."

"And what about all that land?"

Let me worry about the land. After all, who's running this shindig?"

"You are," Adam said evenly. "But do me a favor, anyway. Don't buy up any more of Florida."

George laughed. "Sure thing, Adam. At least not for a while. I've got something better lined up for the next week or so. Fellow I met down here's got a nice little steam yacht—and the cutest collection of these Florida bathing beauties you've ever seen. Been working much too hard. I think it's time I had a vacation."

After Adam had replaced the receiver, he turned to Tom, who'd been watching him throughout the conversation. "He said no more land—at least for a while. He's going off on someone's boat. I never thought I'd be grateful for George's women."

For the next two months the A & W acquired no more land, but late in January George purchased the largest chunk of all.

"As far as I can figure," Tom told Adam, "it's nothing but swamp. What's he going to do with several square miles of swamp?"

"Build another Miami Beach," Adam said. "George probably figures if that guy Fisher could pull it off, he can."

"Well, Fisher did pull it off," Tom said with more conviction than he felt.

"Listen, Tom, I appreciate your fair-mindedness, but you know as well as I do George is no Carl Fisher, or Flagler. For six months you and I kept watch over him, and he didn't do any harm, but now he's down there on his own and he's decided to play mogul. You know what the trouble with George is? He's got one fault and it isn't whiskey or women, it's plain old lack of judgment. One of us better get down there fast."

"You're his brother."

"And you're the V.P. with the stocks and a seat on the board. You'd better go."

When Clemmie finished being outraged that Tom hadn't told her of George's dealings earlier, she insisted on accompanying him to Florida. Tom didn't protest for long. He'd been traveling for a good part of the last three weeks, and did not want to leave Clemmie again. He remembered his train ride with Clemmie the night they were married. "Fine, we'll take the private car."

238

Clemmie barely heard him. She was too busy planning her attack on George.

Tom and Clemmie left for St. Petersburg the following day, but a telegram from Adam was waiting in Washington. George had left St. Petersburg and was staying in Palm Beach.

"I wonder what he's up to now?" Clemmie said.

Tom suspected George was scouting around for some more financing, but said nothing. The news would only set Clemmie off again.

It was late in the afternoon by the time their car was pulled up on the private tracks near The Breakers. Clemmie felt hot and tired and disheveled as Tom helped her down the steps to the platform. There were two other cars on the siding, and next to one of them stood a man and woman. Clemmie noticed them only out of the corner of her eye, but something about the way the man moved as he directed the porter loading the luggage caught her attention. She turned just as the sleek dark head did, and she and Whit Morris were facing each other across the platform. He looked exactly as he had the last time she'd seen him, almost four years ago now. He should look old or unhappy or tired, she thought, but he looked exactly the same.

Alison had followed Whit's gaze and now she was waving and calling to Clemmie across the platform.

"Someone you know?" Tom asked.

"An old friend. And her husband," Clemmie added. She took Tom's arm and started toward them. She couldn't look at Whit, but she felt his eyes on her, weighing, judging, comparing her to his wife. Alison looked pale and fresh in white dotted suisse, and Clemmie was suddenly very conscious of her wrinkled gray traveling suit. She looked at Alison's hair wound around her head in thick neat braids and thought helplessly of her own bob. They'd kept the windows open all afternoon.

"It's so good to see you," Alison said, taking Clemmie's hand.

Of course it's good to see me, Clemmie thought, now that I'm no longer a threat. Clemmie introduced them. Alison Morris. The name tasted sour in her mouth. She watched Whit and Tom shake hands, saw Tom sizing Whit up the way he did every man he met, recognized Whit's special curiosity about Tom. There was a feeling of unreality about seeing them together. Tom was taller by a fraction and more powerfully built, but Whit still had an ease of manner and stance that she'd seen in few other men. His face, browned by weeks in the sun, made Tom look even fairer.

"Whit's just leaving," Alison said.

"Business calls," Whit explained, then remembered the last time he'd spoken to Clemmie and silently cursed himself. He looked at Clemmie, but her face was impassive. She seemed to remember nothing at all.

Clemmie heard the words and wondered if he were taunting her. Then she realized the idea was ridiculous. He probably doesn't even remember. I was never that important to him. Just because you fell head over heels in love with him, Clemmie told herself, doesn't mean he gave a damn about you.

"But I'm staying on for another month," Alison said. "It'll be such fun, Clemmie. We've so much catching up to do."

"I don't think we'll be here for long," Clemmie said quickly.

"In that case, we'll start immediately. You must come have tea right this minute. For my sake—please. I always feel so blue after Whit leaves." There wasn't an ounce of malice in Alison's face, but Clemmie wanted to slap it. "And you must see the twins. They're as brown as nuts."

"I'd love to, Alison, but not right now. We've just arrived, and I want to find George."

"I'll find George," Tom broke in. He'd been hoping

to get some time alone with George, before Clemmie created her scene.

"But the luggage . . ." Clemmie looked pleadingly at Tom.

"Don't worry about a thing, Clemmie. I'll see to everything. Besides, the tea will pick you up."

"Then it's settled," Alison said.

Clemmie felt Whit's hand in hers as he said goodbye, and pulled away quickly. Then she turned and started toward the hotel without waiting for Alison or Tom. She was not going to watch Whit Morris say good-bye to his wife.

Clemmie and Alison found a table in a corner of the veranda. It was tea time, and behind them half a dozen couples moved softly through the dusk in time to the music. Clemmie looked at them and felt suddenly old and sad. It seemed like a lifetime since she'd moved carefree and uncaring from one pair of arms to another at a tea dance.

"Here are the twins now," Alison said, indicating two small boys being marshaled across the lawn by a woman in white. They were, as Alison had said, nut brown. Two dark-skinned miniature editions of Whit.

Clemmie felt a surge of jealousy stronger than anything she'd experienced when she'd seen Alison and Whit together. They should have been her children, hers and Whit's. "They're darling."

"And quite ill-mannered," Alison said, pushing away the small brown hand that had reached for one of the tea cakes on her plate, but it was clear from her voice she thought they were nothing of the kind. "You have a little girl, don't you? Mother told me. She said your mother had written." Alison looked serious for a moment. She told the nurse it was time to get the children ready for dinner, and turned back to Clemmie. "I'm glad you're here, Clemmie. I've wanted to talk to you." Alison hesitated, as if unsure of how far she ought to go. "I wanted to make certain there were no bad feelings between us." She stirred her tea. "Because of Whit."

Clemmie laughed. It was only a fraction too shrill, and not loud enough to be noticed above the orchestra. "Alison, how absurd. Bad feelings? Between us? How could there be? There was never anything between Whit and me."

"But that summer . . ."

"The trouble with you, Alison darling, is that you take everything so seriously. Whit and I were friends, we had fun together, but that was all. You know how I am, Alison. Just because I flirt with a man—or used to flirt with a man—doesn't mean I'm in love with him. Lord, if I were going to fall for anyone that summer, it would have been that Englishman. What was his name?"

"Sebastion Anvers."

"That was the one. So you see, there was nothing to worry about. Besides, Whit was always your beau. Everyone knew that."

Everyone except the three of us, Alison thought. "Tell me about Tom," she said quickly. "You must be very happy."

Clemmie looked at her in surprise. "Why do you say that?" she blurted out without realizing how the words sounded.

"Just the way he looks. He's got the most extraordinary eyes, Clemmie. He looks all 'strong, silent type,' but he's got the kindest eyes I've ever seen."

Clemmie tried to remember the way Tom's eyes had looked when he'd left them this afternoon, but all she could remember were Whit's, dark and piercing beneath the thick lashes.

George was sitting in the living room of his suite when Tom arrived. Through the French doors that were open to the terrace, Tom could see Lake Worth, deep blue in the late-afternoon sun, dotted with small white sails. The peaceful seascape made a deep contrast to the tired-looking man in shirt-sleeves and wrinkled white flannels. George had never looked so worn.

He broke into the old ready smile when he saw Tom, but it was far from convincing. "Why didn't you let me know you were coming? I would have fixed up a welcoming party."

"We tried to, but you're not the easiest fellow to track down. We thought you were in St. Petersburg."

"I was till two days ago, but I had some business over here."

"How's it going?" Tom asked, as if he had no idea.

"Great, just great. We're working on the plans."

"Then we've got all the leases?"

George dropped his eyes. "Not the railroad. I wasn't talking about the railroad. I was talking about *Sans Souci.*"

"*San Souci?*" Tom asked. He knew what was coming, knew now that Adam had been right. Tom had been unable to believe that anyone could be such a fool, but Adam had always known his brother's potential.

"You're going to love it, Tommy boy, you're going to love it." George took a brochure from a table covered with papers, the remains of a half-eaten lunch, and several bottles and glasses. "Just take a look at this. *Sans Souci.* The most luxurious development on the west coast. The best of the new Florida."

"So it says." Tom looked at the sketches of ugly stucco houses, a large beach casino, and golf greens, all peopled by smiling citizens of "the new Florida." He read the copy. "The proposed hotel with an 18-hole golf course . . . salt-water bathing . . . numerous plazas to enhance the beauty . . . a paradise for old and young alike . . ." When Tom looked up from the brochure, he found George watching him with a worried look. "Where is the backing for this 'proposed paradise' coming from, George?"

"Now don't you worry about that, Tommy boy. I've got it all lined up. Just a few wrinkles left to be ironed out, and we're in business."

"What about the railroad? I thought you came down here to build a railroad."

"I did. And it's in the works. I've got leases for half the west coast, just as we agreed. You and Adam were worried for nothing. I wasn't buying land for the railroad. I was buying land for *Sans Souci.*"

"I see. Mizner and Palm Beach. Fisher and Miami." Tom began to count them on his fingers. "Merrick and Coral Gables. DuPont and Boca Raton. And Wilder and *Sans Souci.*"

"What's wrong with that?"

"Nothing, if you can pull it off, but from what I hear it's getting harder and harder to pull off. The market's inflated, George. There are rumors DuPont's pulling out of Boca Raton, and he's no fool. And if he does pull out, think of what it will do to the rest of the market."

George seemed to wilt more with each sentence. He hadn't expected Tom to know so much about the situation, but his brother-in-law had been here for less than an hour and he'd already put his finger on the problem. "It already has," George said miserably.

"How bad is it?"

"I've got all the land. Damn it, I've got miles and miles of land. Or at least binders on it. It isn't the land I'm worrying about."

"What is it?"

"Dredging first, then building."

"Dredging! Christ, George, that's as bad as the jokes that are going around up North about the yokels who come down here and buy a plot that turns out to be under water."

"You can laugh all you want, but it works. Miami Beach was under water till Fisher got there. And what about Flagler's line to Key West? That used to be under water too."

"Fine. Now all we need is money to drain the land and build your paradise. Where are we going to get it, George? I wish you'd tell me that. All I know about is running a railroad, so I wish you'd tell me where in hell

244

we're going to get the backing to dry out half of Florida."

"Just watch yourself, Tom. I'm still running this thing."

"Right into the ground," he heard himself echoing Clemmie's words, but was too angry to care.

"I had the backing."

"What happened?"

"Just what you said. Those rumors about DuPont. The guy got cold feet. He heard DuPont was pulling out, and changed his mind."

"And we're left with every penny we've got tied up in swampland."

"There are other backers, other ways to get money. You just got here, Tom. I've been working on this for months. I've got another prospect lined up right now. A Canadian with a couple of hundred miles of forest. He likes to come South in the winter. Of course, he's talking about a controlling interest."

"Controlling interest! Hell, give him the whole thing. Let's just get out without losing the railroad."

"You know what the trouble with you is, Tommy boy? You're short-sighted. Maybe that's why the old man left the A & W to me and not you. Oh, you know a lot about keeping the trains on time and you've got every foot of track memorized in that steel trap you call a mind, but you've got no vision."

"And this is your vision?" Tom sent one of the brochures sailing across the room at George.

"You're damn right that's my vision. And a year from now you're going to be falling all over yourself to apologize. But don't worry, Tommy boy, I bear no grudges. And just to prove that, I'm going to take you out on the town tonight. We'll celebrate my fat Canadian."

"I thought he hadn't come through yet."

"He will. Now let's forget the whole thing. At least for tonight. I'm going to show you Palm Beach. At least the lively side of it. Wait a minute. I didn't even ask. Is Clemmie with you?"

"She's downstairs with some old friend. A Mrs. Morris."

"Mrs. Morris? Oh, you mean Alison VanNest. I saw her and Whit when I arrived yesterday. So you ran into them. How did Clemmie take it?"

"Take it?" Tom asked.

"Whit. For a while there she was crazy about Whit. Before she met you, of course. No competition after that. Well, let's go get Clemmie. I'm going to take you two out for a night you won't forget."

The Canadian reached George at his suite just as he was leaving for the evening. The man was sorry, but he'd changed his mind. From where he sat, and he admitted he was snowbound at the moment, it didn't look like such a good investment after all. The man hung up before George could marshal his arguments.

George walked to the table, poured himself half a tumbler of whiskey, and downed it. Then he picked up the brochure. The sketch of the opulent hotel with bathing casino had been his idea. It lent a touch of elegance, he thought.

"To hell with it," he said aloud. "There are other backers. I'll find another backer."

During dinner at The Breakers, George did not mention the Canadian's call, and neither Tom nor Clemmie asked about it. They had begun to make other plans, plans that had nothing to do with the Canadian backer.

After dinner George insisted on taking them to a schooner that sat just beyond the twelve-mile limit. "The whiskey's legal and the tables are honest, or so they tell me," George said.

The boat was packed to capacity and most of the gambling tables were filled. "Well, what will it be?" George said. "Baccarat, dice, roulette?"

"Roulette," Clemmie said.

246

George left Clemmie and Tom at the roulette wheel and pushed his way to one of the baccarat tables. He started slowly, not betting every hand, but within half an hour he was thirty-five thousand dollars ahead. It seemed as if he could almost smell when the shoe would turn banker and when it would turn player.

The idea didn't come to George suddenly. It had been growing like the pile of chips before him. To hell with backers. He'd win what he needed. By the time Tom and Clemmie had joined him, he'd won more than a hundred thousand.

"I'm glad somebody's luck is running," Clemmie said. "They cleaned me out."

George said nothing. He was concentrating on the cards before him. He turned over one. Six. The second. Two. I can't lose, he thought as he raked the chips to him. I just can't lose.

"That's quite a bundle," Tom said.

"Just starting," George mumbled.

Three more hands. He was more than half a million ahead now. A crowd had gathered around the table, but George neither saw them nor heard the excited whispers. "Banco," he said quickly. Until now he had not been betting the entire bank, but this was no time for caution.

Tom saw the croupier glance at a dark man standing at the edge of the circle. The man nodded. Two more cards. Six again, then three. A murmur ran through the crowd.

"Banco," George repeated. Again the croupier looked at the dark man. This time he merely closed his eyes. George turned over the first card. "Five of diamonds." Then the second. "Five of clubs." Another murmur from the crowd, a little louder this time, a little more smug. The croupier raked in the chips.

Clemmie groaned. "Now we're both cleaned out. Tom will have to buy the drinks. He's the only one who didn't lose anything. Of course, he didn't gamble anything, but he didn't lose anything."

"I'm not finished," George mumbled.

"Don't be a fool . . ." Clemmie started.

"I said I'm not finished." He motioned to one of the boys for more chips. "Banco," again, and again he won. "I told you my streak wasn't broken," George said, but he lost the next one and the one after that.

"Come on." Tom laid a hand on George's shoulder. "Let's call it a night."

"I said I wasn't finished." George shrugged off Tom's hand.

"You've already lost more than a hundred thousand."

"And I was winning a lot more than that." George motioned for more chips. Now it was the boy with the chips who looked to the dark man at the edge of the crowd, and again the man nodded. Three more hands and he had exhausted his chips again. He motioned for more. The next one would be the one that changed his luck again. He could feel it.

"Come on, George," Tom tried again.

"Leave me alone, Tommy boy. It's my money, not the railroad's." George motioned for another drink. "If it makes you nervous, don't watch."

"George is right," Clemmie said, taking Tom's arm. "It's his money, and he can do what he wants with it. We'll be in the bar when you're finished, George."

"We shouldn't have left him," Tom said when they were seated at a small table in the bar. "At the rate he's going, he'll ruin himself."

"He's already ruined the railroad, now let him ruin himself."

"Clemmie, you can't—"

"I'm not doing anything." Her voice was quiet, but her eyes were bright and hard. "He's doing it himself."

A little after three George entered the bar. They did not have to ask how he'd done. His face, ashen above the white dinner coat, told them.

" 'Fraid you'll have to tip the launch boy," George slurred. It was obvious he'd been drinking as well as gambling for the last four hours. "Cleaned out." He tried one of the old familiar smiles. "Down to my socks."

Back at the hotel, Clemmie and Tom dropped George at his suite and continued down the hall to their own. There was no point in trying to talk to him tonight. There'd be plenty of time tomorrow.

Tom was standing at the dresser removing his cuff links, and Clemmie turned her back to him so that he could undo the buttons of her dress. "You'll have plenty of time to talk to George before your golf date. Now aren't you glad," she added as she walked to the dressing room, "that you can shoot a decent game of golf. It's the only way to get to a man like Jensen in Palm Beach."

Tom said nothing, and she could hear the sound of drawers and closests being opened and closed in the bedroom. When she emerged from the dressing room, Tom was sitting up in his bed reading the early edition of the morning paper. "I didn't know you knew Morris," he said without taking his eyes from the paper.

Keeping her back to him, Clemmie busied herself at the curtains of one of the French doors. "I didn't know *you* did."

"I'd never met him until this afternoon, but I'd heard of him."

"Heard of him?"

"In New York and Chicago."

She moved to the other window. "That's funny. If you said you'd seen his picture on the sporting pages with some horse or sloop, I wouldn't be surprised, but how would you have heard of him in New York or Chicago?"

"Don't underestimate Morris. That's supposed to be one of his advantages. Everyone takes him for a playboy, but as I hear it he's a lot smarter than that. Pulled off a merger a few years ago that was a real coup. Little line called the Dayton Southbound. The way I heard it, the Erie really wanted it, but Morris pulled off the deal so smoothly the Erie didn't even know what happened."

"Not so smoothly," Clemmie murmured.

"What did you say?"

She turned from the window and walked to Tom's bed. "Not so smoothly compared to what you're going to do in the next ten years."

Tom's voice had been casual as they'd talked of Whit, but when he looked up from paper his eyes were hard. "You mean I'm in competition with Whit Morris."

"I mean now that the railroad's ours . . ."

He pulled her down next to him and his hands on her arms, holding her to the bed, were strong. "Forget the railroad, Clemmie." His mouth was rough on hers and his hands moved abruptly at the ties of her negligee. "For once in your life forget it," he repeated, and the harshness of his words matched the fierceness of his movements. There was an edge to his passion, an intensity she'd never felt before. She could sense it in his hands, hurried and hungry against her skin. She could hear it in his breath, short and shallow and urgent. She could even taste it on his tongue, deep and devouring. In the dim light from the lamp his eyes were fierce, as the movements of his body. He entered her suddenly, before she expected it, before she was ready, but then she felt him again and again, and the shock turned to desire, a feverish desire for him fanned by the force of his passion. And behind the passion and desire, behind the dizzying sensations of his body on hers, of him within her, she could sense a power she'd never felt in him before, as if he were determined to overwhelm her, to possess her so completely she would never elude him again.

By the next morning the story was all over Palm Beach. George Wilder had lost more than a million. He still had the railroad and mining stock, but whatever money he'd inherited—and more—was gone. It was rumored he'd have to sell the house in Philadelphia, that and some of his holdings as well. "Poor Cornelia Wilder," the dowagers on the verandas of the Royal Poinciana and the Everglades Club agreed.

George was still in his pajamas when Tom entered his suite. "No lectures, Tommy boy, please. Lectures are the one thing I can do without this morning."

"I'm not going to lecture you. That was your own money—as you pointed out. I just want to know what's happening with your Canadian friend."

George smiled as if he were about to deliver a piece of good news. "Pulled out. Last night."

Last night! For God's sake, George why didn't you tell me?"

"Too busy trying to make some money."

"You thought you were going to win enough for backing?" Tom was incredulous.

"Just as I said, Tommy boy, no imagination. People *have* won fortunes at baccarat."

"And lost them."

"I thought we agreed no lectures."

"What are you going to do about—" Tom hammered at the brochures on the table with his knuckles, "about *Sans Souci?*"

"I've got a couple of people lined up. Got a call in right now to—"

"You know no one's going to come in on this," Tom interrupted. "The rumors about DuPont have cut the bottom right out of the market. And last night isn't going to make it any easier for you to get financing."

"Don't you worry about me. I can take care of myself—and the money boys. If one doesn't come through, there's always another around the corner. The old man couldn't convince Morgan, but he got his railroad without him. And I'll get *Sans Souci* without that damn Canadian. You'll see. I'll have the whole business in shape by the end of the week."

"Look, George, I don't want to fight with you, but

251

it's about time we started looking at this thing sensibly. Clemmie and I have talked it over—"

"You're letting your wife tell us how to run things now?"

"The railroad's part hers, George. She has some rights in this matter."

"Let her attend the board meeting."

"Try to be reasonable, George. Your chances of turning this land thing, this *Sans Souci,* into anything are about zero. Now I think I can find us a buyer. We'll take a loss, I can promise you that, but we'll get out with our shirts—and the A & W. It's our only hope. Let's take what we can get for the land and go back where we belong"

"That sounds like Clemmie, all right."

"That sounds like sense. Listen, George, I wasn't against a railroad down here, but a *Sans Souci"*—Tom pronounced the words scornfully—"is something else. And now your *Sans Souci* has made the railroad impossible. I have a date to play golf with Jensen this afternoon. He represents some of the Flagler interests. They want the land leases for the railroad and they'll take the rest too—at a price. Come along this afternoon, and we'll settle the whole thing."

"You've tied it up pretty neatly, haven't you, Tommy boy? Good-bye land. Good-bye *Sans Souci.* Good-bye a couple of million."

"I haven't tied it up at all, George. That's why I'm here. I want you to tie it up."

"I won't. That land's worth three times as much as Jensen will pay."

"Not to us, it isn't."

"Not to you is right. You and Clemmie and Adam. You all think you've got the answers. And poor George, poor dumb George doesn't know anything. Well, the old man didn't think that. He left me the railroad, and by God I'm going to run it the way I want to. Just as he ran it the way he wanted to. He didn't listen to J.P.

Morgan, and I'm not about to listen to Tom Hendreich, so you can just run along and play golf with Jensen or anyone else. I've got business to do."

Clemmie was waiting for Tom at the Everglades Club. She could tell from his expression that he hadn't been able to convince George.

"I told you he wouldn't listen," she said.

"I feel as if I'm batting my head against a brick wall. I don't know what to do now. George won't sell and he'll never get financing."

"Do exactly what you'd planned to do. Play golf with Mr. Jensen. Get the best price you can, but get rid of that land."

"What good is a deal with Jensen if George won't follow through on it?"

"George will follow through," she said.

"I don't think he will. He's got his heart set on that damn *Sans Souci* thing. *Sans Souci!* Even the name's a joke."

Clemmie smiled into her orange blossom cocktail. "I've known George a lot longer than you have, darling. You take care of Mr. Jensen, and I'll take care of my brother."

"I don't see how."

"You don't have to. All you have to do is play a respectable game of golf. But not too respectable. I hear Mr. Jensen hates to lose."

Clemmie played nine holes of the Everglades' course herself that afternoon, and she was on the terrace again when Tom returned with Jensen. Judging by Jensen's quick invitation to dine with him and his wife that evening, Clemmie knew Tom had pulled off the deal.

"And perhaps you'll have a drink with us now, Mrs. Hendreich?" Jensen added.

"I'd love to," Clemmie said, "but there are a few things I must take care of. Tom, you stay and have a drink with Mr. Jensen, and I'll see you back at the hotel." She turned to Jensen, and flashed a winning smile. "I'm so looking forward to tonight, Mr. Jensen."

George was in his suite when Clemmie arrived. From the look of it and him, she suspected he hadn't left it all day.

"Leave it there," George barked. He was on the telephone and hadn't bothered to turn when she'd entered.

"I'm not the room waiter," Clemmie said. "Though from the look of this place you could use one. And a maid."

When he saw Clemmie, George covered the mouthpiece of the phone with his hand. "Can't be bothered to have them underfoot now. Well, what is it?" he asked impatiently. "I'm busy." George took his hand off the mouthpiece. "Then page him again. I'm sure he's there. Mr. Wickert's home said he was there."

"J.C. Wickert?"

George nodded.

"He's at the Everglades. I just saw him. He was there all afternoon."

"Damn," George muttered to himself.

"You mean he's not taking your call."

"Must be a mistake," George said. "He probably didn't get the message."

Clemmie sat in a chair across the room from him. "Why don't you give up, George? Admit you're beaten and give up."

"I'm not beaten, not by a long shot."

"Then why won't Wickert take your call? I'm not going to argue with you, George. That's Tom's game. I'm simply going to tell you. He made the deal with Jensen this afternoon."

"Well, I won't go through with it."

"So Tom said, but I'm more persuasive than he is. You will go through with it, George. Or rather, you won't have to go through with it because you're stepping down. Or being kicked upstairs, take your choice. But you're going to resign, and Tom is going to take your place."

"I think you've been drinking, kid."

"If you step down now, George, you can go back to your old life. Oh, you lost a lot of money last night, but with Tom running the railroad, we'll be in the black in no time and you'll be able to turn a profit on your stocks. In fact, I'll give you a good price for them now. You'll have your girls and your parties, Cornelia will have her house in Philadelphia, and everyone will be happy."

"You must be crazy."

"But if you don't resign on your own, George, there's going to be a scandal, and the board's going to demand it."

George laughed. "What kind of scandal? The fact that I lost too much last night?"

"A little worse than that, I think." Clemmie opened her bag and took a manila envelope from it. "Newspapers love this sort of thing. And if they blow it up into a scandal, the board will have no choice. Don't forget one of the members is a Quaker. I realize they can't vote you out since you still own fifty-two percent of the stock, but Cornelia will take care of that. She'll have to divorce you. You may not mind that, but you're bound to mind the settlement. Especially after last night. I know Cornelia finds it vulgar to talk about money, but I've noticed she doesn't mind having it." Clemmie leaned over and handed him the envelope. "So I think you'd better resign. Everyone will be much happier in the long run."

George's hands were shaking as he took the envelope from her. He knew what he would see before he opened it.

The detectives had done a thorough job. There were half a dozen photographs, and in each George's face was recognizable even though his body was partially hidden by two naked women.

"You bitch."

"Now, George darling, it's for your own good. You were never meant to run a railroad."

"Does Tom know about this?"

"What difference would it make if Tom did know? It would offend his sensibilities, but that wouldn't stop me from using the pictures."

George dropped his head in his hands. "Why, Clemmie? You don't hate me. We don't hate each other. Why would you do something like this?"

"I'm sorry, George. Please believe me. But I have no choice. You never should have got the railroad in the first place, and now you've come close to ruining it. I can't let you do that."

"Instead you'll ruin me."

"Don't be melodramatic, George. I'm not ruining you. You can go back to your old games, and everyone will be better off. You were working too hard anyway. Now you can take a nice long vacation."

George refused to accompany Clemmie and Tom on the trip North. "Stay around and get some shun," he slurred when Tom tried to convince him. It was not unusual for George to have a drink in the morning, but it was rare for him to start drinking as soon as he got up and to be roaring drunk by lunchtime. Not that he made an appearance for lunch. He hadn't left his suite since the afternoon Tom had played golf with Jensen.

"You got the resig . . . resignation, Tommy boy. Take that back with you and leave me alone."

"You don't have to resign, George," Tom said, feeling the absurdity of trying to reason with a drunk. "All you have to do is follow through on the deal with Jensen."

George looked at him through glazed eyes. "Believe that. You really believe that, don't you?"

"It's true," Tom said.

"Envy you, Tommy boy, envy you little Clemmie. Sure is big help."

There was no point in staying and arguing with him,

Tom thought. If George had been unreasonable sober, he was impossible drunk. He'd come North when he was ready.

George saw no reason to return home, no reason even to leave his hotel room. There was a bellboy who kept him in whiskey. At one point he'd considered asking if he could provide a woman as well—it would be unusual at The Breakers, George suspected, but not impossible—but he'd given up the idea. Memory told him he wanted a woman, but his senses didn't seem to care.

George opened his eyes and looked at his watch. It said four o'clock. He checked it against the traveling clock on the table. One o'clock. The traveling clock was more likely to be right. The maid wound that. Light filtered through the drawn curtains. One o'clock in the afternoon. He wondered what time he'd fallen asleep. The glass on the night table was half full. He took a swallow of the stale whiskey and grimaced, then finished it off.

There was a newspaper on the floor next to the bed. *March 18, 1925,* it said. Was that yesterday or today? He could have been reading the early edition when he fell asleep.

"Eighteenth or nineteenth," George mumbled to himself. "What's it matter?" In bare feet he padded to the table, poured himself a fresh drink, and downed it. Less than half a bottle left, he noticed. He filled the glass again and tried to remember what time the bellboy came on duty.

With a jerky uncertain movement, he opened the curtains. Below him dowagers in large hats and brightly colored umbrellas strolled the grounds. He was holding the glass unsteadily, and some of it spilled. "Watch it, fella," he mumbled to himself. "Don't want to rain on the ladies." George took a long swallow and wondered idly if anyone had ever relieved himself from a terrace of the Breakers. Not worth the trouble, he thought. They'd only make me move.

On the way to the bath he filled the glass again, then

on second thought took the glass and the bottle with him and placed them on a small stool next to the tub. He ran a tepid bath, took off the rumpled white trousers and undershirt he'd had on for longer than he could remember, and eased himself into the tub. The water felt good. He took another swallow. Maybe he'd never leave.

Faintly through the thick walls he heard shouts and the sound of running feet. At The Breakers? Impossible. I must have dozed off, George thought. He took another swallow of whiskey. Now the shouts were unmistakable, and there seemed to be bells and sirens coming from beyond the window. Have to complain, George thought. Call the desk and tell them I'm being disturbed. He leaned his head against the back of the tub and closed his eyes. The sirens and bells grew louder, and now he could make out some of the shouts. "Fire!" a shrill voice screamed over and over.

Slowly, careful not to spill the last of the whiskey, George got out of the tub, wound a towel around himself, and walked unsteadily to the terrace. The peaceful landscape of half an hour ago had turned to bedlam. The lawn was littered with clothing and furs and trunks, bashed and battered from the fall. On a terrace below him a white-haired man struggled to lift a huge Vuitton trunk over the railing, and from another terrace at right angles to George's own a woman threw leather jewelry boxes and small satin bags to her maid on the lawn.

"My ermine, Harry. Don't forget my ermine," an elderly woman screamed, and the white-haired man who had finally succeeded in pushing the trunk over the railing ran back into the room and returned with a long fur that he threw to the woman below. Then he disappeared into the room and did not return.

Gradually George became aware of an acrid smell. He looked up and saw heavy yellow clouds over the hotel. Slowly, deliberately, he walked back into his room and put on clean underwear, fresh trousers and shirt. "Not to panic," he mumbled to himself. "Important thing is not to panic." Dressed, he stood for a moment in the center of the room, wondering if there were anything of value he ought to save. He wore no jewelry, had little cash left. He walked back into the bath and took the bottle of whiskey.

When he opened the door to the hallway he faced a wall of black smoke. "Not to panic," he repeated, and returning to his room, took a fresh handkerchief from a top drawer, ran it under the faucet in the bathroom, and placed it over his nose and mouth. Then he started down the hall. The smoke made it impossible to see anything, and he tried to remember where the stairs were. He was moving faster now, feeling along the wall with one hand. There was a dull noise when the whiskey bottle hit the carpet, but he pushed on, searching the wall with one hand while the other held the handkerchief to his face. His eyes stung and it was impossible to choke back the coughs. The smoke seemed heavier at this end of the hall, and the heat was unbearable. George turned and began working his way toward the other end. He was sure there was a staircase right along here. He pushed a door and it opened, but it was only another room. He started down the hall again, felt a door give way, and saw the staircase through the smoke. One step carefully, then another, and suddenly George felt the stairs give way beneath him. He was falling and the heat was rising toward him, and he felt the flames around him, licking at him like the tongue of a huge vicious beast.

"I don't understand it," Clemmie said when Adam came to the house to break the news. "Everyone else got out. Why not George? A single fatality from the whole terrible thing, and it had to be George. I just don't understand it."

"Don't you?" Tom said. He'd been standing at the window staring out at the snow-covered yard while she spoke. "Don't you understand it, Clemmie?" he repeated, turning back to the room. There was no anger in his voice, but an edge that was worse than anger. Clemmie had never heard it before.

"I'm leaving tonight to bring the body back," Adam said. In fact, he knew there wasn't much of a body to bring back, but he didn't want to go into that. "Cornelia wanted to come along, but Mr. Reed and I agreed there was no need for her to make the trip. We'll bury him here, of course, rather than in Philadelphia. I should be back by Saturday. In the meantime, I wish you'd stay with Mother at the farm."

"How is she?" Tom asked.

"Calm. Too calm, if you ask me."

"We'll stay with her till after the funeral." Tom looked at Clemmie. "We can do that much, can't we, Clemmie?

"Why did George resign?" Tom asked her when they were alone. "All I asked him to do was sell the land, and the next thing we knew, George had decided to give up everything."

She felt Tom's eyes on her, but could not meet them. "I guess he felt he had no choice after the mess he'd made of the railroad."

"Perhaps we should have helped give him a choice," Tom said quietly.

Clemmie remembered George's face that afternoon when she handed him the pictures. It had been white with shock. She could hear his voice. Why, Clemmie? You don't hate me. We don't hate each other. He must have revised his opinion about that. He must have died hating her. Clemmie was sure of that.

She could feel the tears welling up and blinked to hold them back. Tom was standing above her, looking down as if he wanted an answer from her. She wanted to throw herself into his arms, to tell him everything. She wanted to hear his voice, strong and consoling, telling her she hadn't realized what she was doing, couldn't have guessed at the consequences, couldn't be held responsible for George's death. She wanted to feel Tom's arms around her, blocking out the image of

George's face; hear his voice, drowning out the echo of George's words. But she looked up at Tom and knew that Tom would never take care of her in that way, never tell her it was all right when it wasn't.

Well, what did it matter? She could take care of herself. She'd learned how to do that if nothing else. She'd learned to take care of herself and protect herself. She'd learned not to be vulnerable. *Vulnerable.* The very word frightened her.

She wouldn't let Tom see how much she needed him or his reassurance. She wouldn't let him know how she felt about George's death and her own sickening part in it. She couldn't afford to. Once she let Tom see how she blamed herself he would blame her too. And probably leave her. But that was ridiculous. Tom would never leave her, at least he wouldn't as long as she maintained the charade, as long as she didn't give him a chance to see the chinks in her armor.

"Be realistic, Tom." She was fighting to keep her voice even, fighting to stifle the sobs that threatened to break through the words. "We did everything we could. You tried to convince him to play along with Jensen. You tried to get him to come home with us. But he wouldn't listen to reason. Surely we're not responsible for that." Her voice was rising in desperation, and she caught herself. "We couldn't do anything to help George when he was alive," she went on more calmly, "and we can't do anything for him now that he's dead. Except one thing. We can help Cornelia. In view of the way George left things, she'll need cash. I want to buy as many A & W shares as she'll sell."

"Don't you think it's a little premature?"

"Waiting won't do any good. It won't bring George back. And I should think it would be a relief to Cornelia to have that financial mess cleared up."

"Delicacy aside, what do you plan to use for money?"

"That's up to you. You're the businessman. You know how to do these things. Use our own A & W stocks as collateral for a loan."

"They aren't worth much since George's deals."

"They'll always be worth something. Use them, or the mines or this house. . . ."

He was angry now, angry at the futility of George's death, angry at his part in it, angry at Clemmie's insensitivity to it.

"And your jewels? I suppose you're willing to sell those?"

"If I have to," Clemmie said.

"It's nice to know you won't be stopped by anything as frivolous as sentimental value."

"I won't sell the pearls you gave me as a wedding present, or the diamond pin you bought me when Lizzy was born."

"I'm deeply moved, Clemmie—especially since they're not worth as much as the things your father gave you."

A week after the funeral Clemmie took the 9:28 to Philadelphia. She had telephoned Cornelia a few days before, and Cornelia, beautifully mannered as ever, said she was looking forward to seeing Clemmie and they must lunch.

Cornelia made a cool and lovely widow, Clemmie thought as the watched her presiding over the Queen Anne table that had been set for two.

"What are you planning to do about the house?" Clemmie asked when the butler had removed the consommé cups. "It's awfully large for one person."

"Not so terribly large," Cornelia said. "I'm comfortable here. And the family is just across the square."

Clemmie was surprised. She hadn't mentioned the real reason for the necessity of giving up the house, but she didn't see how Cornelia could possibly plan to keep it with the legacy of debts and deflated stock George had left her. "Well, of course, if you feel you can manage it . . ." Clemmie said.

"Oh, there's no problem. I've wonderful help."

"That isn't what I meant." Clemmie waited for the

butler to finish serving the fish. "Cornelia," she began when he'd disappeared behind the pantry door, "I know there are certain subjects you don't enjoy discussing, especially at table"—Clemmie tried to keep the irony from her voice—"but there's something I want to talk to you about and I think now is as good a time as any. I'm willing, that is, Tom and I are willing, to buy as much of the A & W as you're willing to sell. You see, we were with George that night he lost so heavily and . . . well, we feel rather responsible. So we'd like to make things as simple for you now as possible."

"That's very kind of you, Clemmie, but there's no need."

"No need? I don't understand. I know George had nothing left except the shares in the A & W and the mines. You can't expect to keep up this house or or even to live—"

"I don't see that it's your concern, Clemmie, but since you were trying to be kind, I'll explain. I've sold as much of the A & W as I plan to."

"You've sold it! But to whom?" Clemmie demanded.

Cornelia did not try to hide the impatience in her voice. "I have no idea, I'm sure. The sale was handled by a Philadelphia firm. Handled quietly and discreetly," she added pointedly. "Now tell me, how is Lizzy? I was sorry I didn't get to see her while I was at the farm, but of course things were so hectic. . . ."

Clemmie had stopped listening. Someone had bought part of George's interest, bought it for a song since word of George's bad investments had got around, and, more important, bought it quietly and discreetly. As Elias's daughter, Clemmie knew what that meant. Whoever had acquired the stocks did not want her or anyone else to find out who they were.

Chapter 9

WHILE THE FOOTMEN removed the plates littered with oyster shells, Tom watched the heads around the table swing from one side to the other as if they were watching a tennis game in slow motion. Clemmie called it "change courses and talk," but she was good at the nuances of dinner-table maneuvers, better than Tom who recognized their usefulness, but could never quite adjust to their limitations. On the rare occasions when he was engaged in an interesting coversation with the dinner partner on his right, he saw no reason to abandon it for the platitudes of the partner on his left merely because the courses had changed.

"Then you're not one of the West Virginia Hendreichs?" the woman beside him asked, and Tom realized he'd been answering her questions without hearing them.

No, I'm one of the Pennsylvania Hendreichs, the Pennsylvania coal-mining Hendreichs, he wanted to say, but didn't. There was a breed of woman, and Mrs. Singleton was one of them, who could not carry on a conversation without first ascertaining the origins of the person to whom she was speaking. It seemed to Tom that he drew these women as dinner partners with unfailing regularity. Clemmie said he was merely overly

265

sensitive, and he supposed he was, but then Clemmie did not have to truck out her credentials, or hide her lack of them, every time they went to a dinner party.

He glanced down the table to where she was sitting now. She was wearing a blue chiffon dress Tom had never seen before. She must have bought it expressly for the weekend. Unlike the other women at the table, even the younger ones, who were decked out in diamonds and emeralds and sapphires, she wore nothing but the long strand of pearls he'd bought her when they married. Tom had added to them for her last birthday so she could wear them, according to the style of the day, knotted either between her breasts or, when the dress was without a back as it was tonight, at the nape of her neck. She was half turned away from him, but he could recognize a certain suppressed animation as she talked to the man beside her. Tom wondered if their hostess had seated Clemmie next to Maxwell Clinton by chance or if Clemmie had engineered it. He suspected it had been Clemmie's work, but watching the man watching his wife now, Tom knew Clinton could not have been more pleased.

"Do you mean you haven't read *Arrowsmith?*" Mrs. Singleton called him back to his duties. "But you must. They say it's going to win the Pulitzer Prize."

Tom forced his attention back to the woman beside him. Mrs. Singleton was younger than he'd thought at first, probably only a few years older than he was, and she was obviously trying to be friendly—despite the fact that he wasn't one of the West Virginia Hendreichs. The well-cared-for face, marred by only the faintest web of wrinkles around the eyes, was raised to him earnestly. "Gwen must have a copy in the house. I'll see that she gives it to you."

Tom thanked her and said he wouldn't think of troubling their hostess. Mrs. Singleton continued to work her way down the year's best-seller list, but found him wanting again and again.

From far down the table he heard Clemmie laugh at

something Clinton had said and saw the man color with pleasure. "Have you read *Seventy Years of Life and Labor?*" he asked Mrs. Singleton.

"Well, I've heard of it, of course...."

"It's a biography of Samuel Gompers," Tom snapped. "I recommend it highly."

"That dreadful man . . . federations and Labor Day and all that sort of thing. Why, I should think he'd be the last person you'd want to read about, Mr. Hendreich."

Tom smiled. "Not at all. You see, he was my father's hero, which made him one of my boyhood heroes." Let her figure out which Hendreich he was now, Tom thought, but he knew at the same time it had been a foolish thing to say. It was not Mrs. Singleton who was bothering him. He looked down the table to Clinton again. He was leaning toward Clemmie and talking rapidly, as if there were no one else in the room.

"From the looks of things at dinner," Tom said when he and Clemmie were alone in their room, "you must have Trans-American Airlines in your pocket."

"Not exactly, but I'm working on it," Clemmie answered.

"It and Clinton."

"Max Clinton is Trans-American Airlines."

Tom heard the familiar "Max" and said nothing.

"Why else are we here for the weekend," Clemmie asked, "if not to snare Max Clinton and his airline? That's why I got Gwen Byer to invite us."

"I'm sure there are more direct ways of getting to Trans-American."

"More direct, perhaps, but not as effective. You know very well, Tom, that if we approached Trans-American through the usual channels, they'd simply say they planned to go with the Central. But if we happen to spend a perfectly pleasant weekend with Max Clinton, he may see things in a different light. I can get things done on a Long Island house party that would take months in your office. By Sunday night Max will have forgotten he ever planned to link up with the Central."

"I don't see why we don't let the Central have Clinton and his airline and sign on someone else. As long as we have a flight between the overnight to Chicago and the high-speed out of Salt Lake City we cut a day and a half from the New York–California run and we're still holding our own against the Central and the Pennsy."

"I don't want to hold our own, Tom, I want to outstrip them, and to outstrip them we need Trans-American. Why do you think the Central wants TAA? Because they're the best. You've got the reports in your office. TAA has the best record for on-time flights of all the airlines. The fastest trains in the world aren't going to do us any good if the flight between them is late all the time. I want a forty-hour carding, Tom, and only TAA can give us that.

"Besides," she continued, "it will be a real coup if you can snare TAA. It will prove to the board they were right in electing you."

Neither Clemmie nor Tom had forgotten that his election as President and Chairman of the Board after George's death had been probable but not certain. Two of the old stockhoders from Elias's days had talked of bringing in someone from outside, an older man with more experience, they said, still stinging from George's manipulations. But their votes had counted for nothing when Cornelia, who had retained half of George's stocks, voted with Clemmie and Tom—as had, strangely, the buyer of the other half of George's holdings. The stocks, twenty-six percent of the voting share of the A & W, were held by a Philadelphia corporation, and the vote had been cast by proxy.

"It's going to take more than a single deal to prove that to the board," Tom said. "Besides, the Central has already signed up Trans-American."

"That's just gossip. You know as well as I do, nothing's been signed."

"Perhaps Clinton has given his word."

"There are always ways to get around something like that."

"And you know all of them, don't you, Clemmie? All the ways to get around Clinton."

She stopped midway to the bath and turned to him. "You can't be jealous, Tom. You can't seriously be jealous of Max Clinton." Clemmie thought of the round face with the eyes that were too small and the forehead too short and remembered the way he wheezed when he laughed. Trans-American Airlines might be attractive, but the man who ran it was not.

But Tom was remembering a different Maxwell Clinton. Clinton had made a considerable reputation for himself with the Lafayette Escadrille. After the war, when he'd convinced his father to put up almost a million to start a commercial airline, everyone had laughed. Clinton might be an ace, they said, but what did he know about running an airline? Apparently he knew or had learned a great deal in the last seven years, for as Clemmie said, TAA was the best airline in the country. "I'm not jealous," Tom said, concentrating on removing the studs from his evening shirt. "I just don't like using my wife to win a contract."

Clemmie stood looking at him for a moment. She saw the pride, but not the possessiveness. "You're not using me, Tom. We're working for this together. You let someone like Jensen win at golf. I go out of my way to be nice to Max Clinton. It's simply the way things work."

When she came out of the bath a few minutes later, Tom was lying in bed staring at the ceiling, his arms beneath his head. Clemmie crossed the room and sat on the edge of the bed. She traced the line of his mouth with one finger. "I'd say you're still brooding about Clinton."

Tom forced a smile. "Not in the least. I was thinking about where we're going to get the financing for this new air-rail California run you're so set on."

Clemmie let her hand trail down from his face to the buttons of his pajamas. His skin was warm beneath the smooth silk. "You'll take care of it," she said, leaning over till her mouth was on his. "The way you take care of everything." She pressed herself against him and could feel his body hard and familiar in the strange bed. His hands were quick at the ties of her dressing gown, then more urgent when they felt she wore nothing beneath it. They were warm against her breasts, touching, caressing, arousing, and then his mouth was following, and she could feel the soft lips and the tongue like a flame against her skin. Her hands traced the smooth contours of his body, followed the long line from powerful chest to narrow hips, felt the hard muscles of his stomach and the strength of his thighs tangled with her own. And he was inside her again, familiar again, but always new, because there was no memory to this sensation, and he was carrying her further and further into that dark world that grew blacker and blacker until it exploded in a burst of fire.

"I told you," she murmured against his chest, tasting that special taste of him, "you take care of everything."

Except Max Clinton, Tom thought. I leave Max Clinton to you. But he said nothing.

Tom found Clemmie at the far end of the loggia, with Clinton. She'd left the table with him after lunch and they were still together. Tom walked toward them feeling like an intruder and hating himself for the feeling. They were talking quietly and Tom was suddenly struck by Clinton's well-modulated tones. They seemed appropriate to the surroundings, as tasteful as the combination of white wicker and sunny chintz. It was the voice of a rich man, Tom thought, then corrected himself. It was the voice of the son of a rich man. Tom's ears rang with the sound of the hundreds of similar voices that must have flattered and wooed Clemmie over the years. His own sounded strangely ragged when he spoke.

"We'd better get started if I'm going to be in time

for the race." Tom had been pressured into crewing for his host that afternoon, and he wasn't looking forward to it.

"This one doesn't really count," Hollis Byer had said. "Just for fun." But Tom was experienced enough to know that once on the water it was never "just for fun" to a man like Byer.

"You go ahead, darling," Clemmie said, and her voice sounded to Tom like a fluty version of Clinton's. "I'll pass this one up. Max is going to take me for a spin instead. His plane is in a field a few miles from here."

"You're going to fly? This afternoon?" Tom winced at the incredulity in his own voice.

"I've never flown. And I may never get the chance again."

"Perfectly safe," Clinton said, and Tom wondered exactly what kind of danger he was being reassured about, but he did not argue. He would not argue with his wife in front of Clinton.

Mrs. Singleton was leaning against a sleek yellow roadster that had been pulled up before the house. "The others have gone on to the club," she said to Tom. "I said I'd wait and drive you over. And Mrs. Hendreich."

"Mrs. Hendriech isn't going," Tom said.

"Then we might as well get started." She handed him the keys. "I hate to drive."

Tom listened distractedly to her directions to the yacht club. He was thinking of Clemmie. He wished he'd forbidden her to go and knew at the same time it would have done no good. Clemmie would have gone anyway, and he would merely have succeeded in making a scene. Tom had been at enough of these house parties since he'd married Clemmie to know it was bad form to make any show of caring what your husband or wife did, so long as it was done discreetly. But damn it, Tom swore to himself, he did care.

"There's no point in brooding about it, Tom."

He looked at Mrs. Singleton in surprise.

"After all, times have changed. You can't go around locking wives up any longer—much as you might like to."

"I take it you enjoy sailing, Mrs. Singleton," Tom said, keeping his eyes on the road.

Mrs. Singleton would not be so easily deflected from her point. "Call me Nancy. And the only thing I enjoy about sailing is that it keeps my husband at sea—or at least away—for several months every year. He never misses Cowes and I never attend it." She reached over and laid a hand on his arm. "It's not a bad way to run a marriage."

"Is this where we turn?" Tom asked, and as he moved his arm to shift gears he managed to shake off Mrs. Singleton's.

"The yacht club is right around that bend," she said with an edge of anger in her voice that hadn't been there before.

Clemmie had asked Clinton to take her up for purely practical reasons, but the motives behind her request did nothing to diminish the excitement of the flight. They had circled over Long Island Sound and watched the dozens of minute white sails bright and clean against the dark sea. To the west the skyscrapers of New York City shimmered in the sunlight. They looked astonishingly close.

"Had enough?" Clinton asked. Even with the speaking tube that connected the forward cockpit with the rear, he had to repeat himself several times before Clemmie could understand him.

She shook her head. "Not yet," she said, though she knew he could not hear her. She felt the wind buffeting her, whipping the scarf around her head, saw the world miniaturized and distant and crazily unsteady below, and thought she was far from having enough of it.

Clinton executed a dizzying circle that stood Long Island on its side, then headed into the sun. It was several hours from setting but the goggles made the glare bearable.

They were over land again. Clemmie had no idea how long they'd been flying, although her watch told her it was more than two hours since they'd taken off. Below them New York State lay like an unwieldy checkerboard of green and brown patches, each field and farm clearly delineated from the other. It all seemed so neat from this height.

Suddenly there was a loud bang and Clemmie felt the plane shudder. Then there was a terrible silence, and she could hear the wind whistling around them. Clinton did not waste a minute. He picked up the speaking tube again and this time she could hear clearly. "Nothing to worry about. Probably threw a rod. We'll just drop down in that field over there to check things out. Keep calm, and everything will be all right."

He prayed that she'd follow his instructions. The last thing he needed now was an hysterical woman. Then he forgot Clemmie in the face of the problem at hand. The props had stopped spinning and he knew there was no time to reconnoiter the field. He only hoped there were no large rocks. He felt the plane dropping rapidly and cursed the wind. If it had been from the other direction, he wouldn't have to come in over those high-tension wires. Clinton held his breath and watched the plane glide over them. It had been close, entirely too close.

They were coming in quickly, but he had a better view of the field now. There was a deep gulley about a quarter of the way down, but it looked like clear sailing after that. If he could put her down right after the gulley—and if there were no hidden rocks—they'd be all right.

Clemmie could see Max working quickly at the levers, but she was not frightened. The plane was still gliding smoothly and the field below was clear. She had no knowledge of high-tension wires or rocks small enough to be invisible from the air but large enough to send an airplane careening over and over until it shattered into fragments or exploded in a burst of flame.

She saw the ground racing up to meet them, felt the plane hit, then bounce, then hit again with a force that would have thrown her had it not been for the seat belt, and for the first time she sensed the danger. But the plane was skipping and bouncing down the field, throwing them about wildly, and there was no time to worry about what was going to happen because it was already happening. They skidded to a stop a few yards from a road.

Without wasting a minute Max jumped from the forward cockpit and began to pull her from the rear one. Only when he had dragged her some distance away did he ask if she were all right.

"Just a little shaken," she said.

Two men, a woman, and half a dozen children were running down the field toward them, and for the next few minutes there was a great deal of confusion. Finally Max managed to sort things out. He assured the farmer and his family that he and Clemmie were not hurt. He promised he would pay for any damage to the field. He determined that he'd been right—the engine had thrown a rod.

The family, still excited by the plane's landing in their field and the promise of financial remuneration, insisted they come back to the house for some iced tea.

"I could do with something stronger than that," Clemmie whispered, and when the wife left them alone in the small front parlor masked in drab slip covers, Max produced a silver flask and spiked first her drink, then his own.

Clemmie started to raise the glass to her mouth, but found her hand was shaking too badly. Clinton heard the ice clinking against the glass and moved to the sofa beside her. "It's always like that," he said, reaching an arm around her shoulders. "The fear doesn't hit until it's all over."

Clemmie moved a little so that his arm fell away. "Well, it was quite an experience."

"And you held up like a trouper," he said.

The farmer and his wife returned, and Max asked if they had a phone. "There's one in town," the man said. "I'll take you over in the truck, if you want."

"I want to make arrangements to have the plane taken care of," Max said to her. "The landing gear's gone as well as that rod. And of course we ought to call the Byers. There's no getting her back in the air tonight. We'd better tell them not to expect us."

"If you and the missus want a place to stay for the night," the farmer interrupted, "there's a real nice inn down the road. Lots of city folks come up just to stay there. They have real good food and dancin' every Saturday night. I could drive you over." He saw the couple exchange glances. "Well, you folks make up your mind. I'll go bring the truck round."

"It sounds like a good idea, Clemmie. A quiet dinner, a good night's rest, and they could send a car for us tomorrow. Otherwise I can't imagine how we'll get back. It's after eight."

Clemmie smiled. "And we could tell everyone you'd run out of gas."

"Are you worried about what people will say?"

"Not in the least. I'm worried about what we might do. I think you'd better give the farmer some more money, Max, and have him drive us back to Long Island."

"We won't get there till the middle of the night."

"I think that's better than arriving tomorrow morning."

"You're sure you won't change your mind?" His voice was elaborately casual, as if he were offering her a drink or a cigarette.

"Quite sure."

"I was afraid of that. Well, I won't say I'm not disappointed, Clemmie, because I am, but at least we had a good spin."

275

"We did that."

"And there aren't many women who could carry it off. Most of them would have gone half crazy back there when the engine cut out, and they'd still be crying now."

"Maybe I'm just a born aviator."

He took a long swallow of his drink and looked at her slyly. "That's nice to know, Clemmie, because it means there'll be someone in the home office, or at least close to the home office of the A & W, who cares as much about the air part of the high-speed run as the trains."

She looked at him in surprise.

"It would have been nice if you'd decided to stay at that inn tonight, Clemmie, but it wasn't part of the bargain."

"The aviator," Clemmie said, "is a gentleman."

"Now don't get carried away. After all, you're going to have to see a bit of me now that TAA is linking up with the A & W, and I haven't said I've stopped trying." But Clemmie knew from the sound of his voice and the way he joked on the ride back to Long Island that no matter what Max Clinton said, he had given up.

It was close to three when they got back to the Byers', but the whole party was waiting up for them. It would be too good a scene to miss.

Speculation had been rife ever since Clinton had telephoned. Had they really crash-landed or was it just an excuse for a tryst? Max had said the plane was seriously damaged. All the same, what were they doing somewhere over New York State to begin with? The whispering went on beyond Tom's range of hearing, but he was aware of it. He could hardly help being aware of it. They were the same questions he'd been asking himself all evening, only by now he'd found the answers.

He could feel a dozen pairs of eyes on him as Clemmie rushed into his arms, reassuring him she was safe, telling the whole story rapidly, in half-phrases and jumbled sentences that made it sound like a great lark. Then everyone was laughing because, after all, it had turned into a lark, and they were quite safe, and Max was telling what had really happened, and Gwen Byer told the butler to have the cook scramble some eggs and Hollis Byer had him bring up another case of champagne, and it turned into quite a party.

The sun was rising behind the trees on the other side of the bay by the time the celebration broke up and Tom and Clemmie were alone in their room.

"We've got it, darling. We've got TAA."

Tom began undressing and said nothing.

"Well, aren't you going to say anything."

"Congratulations."

"I can just hear the screams at the Central when they find out we stole Max and TAA right out from under them."

"Not we, Clemmie, you. You did all the work on this one. And I hate to think just how hard you were working till the middle of the night somewhere off in the New York countryside."

She'd known downstairs that he was angry, but she hadn't realized how angry.

"But nothing happened, Tom."

He whirled around so he was facing her and his hands were on her shoulders as if he wanted to shake her. "And what if something had had to happen? What if that had been the condition for getting the contract?"

"But it wasn't. It never is."

He dropped his hands from her shoulders and turned away in disgust. He didn't know whether he believed her or not. In his rage it scarcely mattered. If nothing had happened tonight, if nothing had happened with Clinton, it would some other time with some other man. Someday Clemmie would want something, and the man would not behave as well as Clinton—assuming that damn Clinton *had* behaved well—and something would happen. Lying in bed in the dim light that filtered through the windows and watching Clemmie move about the room, he knew that for sure.

He turned his back to her as if by doing so he could turn his back on the image of her with another man. He sensed her weight on the edge of the bed and felt her hand on his shoulder. "Tom," she said quietly. "Tom." He did not answer, and when he felt her hand cool against his back beneath the pajamas he did not move. In a moment he sensed her rising from the bed and knew she had gone back to her own.

After the Byers' house party Tom decided to go straight to Chicago. His instincts told him the conservative New York bankers would be less likely than their Midwestern counterparts to get behind something as newfangled as this train-plane-train route between New York and California. And he welcomed the chance to get away from Clemmie for a while. He was hoping the distance might give him some perspective; since the Clinton incident he'd lost it in regard to her.

Clemmie did not object. She was eager to get the project started. And she thought a few days alone in Chicago might make Tom see things more clearly. It was silly of him to go on sulking about this Clinton business, especially since she had done only what had to be done. And besides, nothing had happened.

One of the business cars was waiting for Tom in Hoboken. He still did not feel comfortable using Elias's private car, although Dolly and Clemmie continued to travel in it. The business car had been added to the two o'clock train to Chicago. It left Hoboken forty-five minutes before the Central's Twentieth Century Limited left New York, but he would still arrive an hour later the next morning. The A & W might be gaining on the Central, especially with TAA on their side in this new high-speed run, but the A & W didn't have a crack train that could compare with the Twentieth Century. At least it didn't yet, Clemmie said.

Tom told her there was no need to come to the

station or even the ferry to see him off, and they'd said good-bye at the St. Regis where Clemmie planned to stop for several days of shopping. "Now don't forget that charity ball tomorrow night," she'd said as she watched him putting the wooden bowl of shaving soap and the brush into the soft leather case she'd bought him at Mark Cross. "It's Jason Wylie's favorite charity. I made sure that Wilcox in the Chicago office got you a ticket."

It was just like Clemmie to know the favorite charity of Chicago's most prominent banker and when that charity would be having a ball. "If you want financing from him, you're going to have to finance his orphans or widows or newsboys or whatever they are. Wilcox will tell you. Just make sure Wylie knows you're there. It'll be worth three hours in his office."

"Maybe you ought to go. After all, the social side of this business is your speciality." If she heard the sarcasm in his voice, she pretended not to.

Tom slept badly that night. That was unusual for him because unlike most people, he slept well on trains, but there were a number of unusual things in his life these last few days. Or so it seemed to him.

A little after midnight, he poured himself a whiskey from the bar in the corner of the business car, and took it back to the stateroom. He lay there for a long time, sipping the drink and watching the countryside and thinking of Clemmie, of Clemmie and Max Clinton. But gradually the countryside racing by his window began to supplant the images of Clemmie and Clinton. He watched it change from dense woods, thick and black in the moonlight, to flat plains and then hills that grew into small mountains, and he thought the same thoughts he always did on these trips. He thought of America, and his ideas about it were, he knew now, those he'd been raised to have.

Karl Hendreich had spoken with a heavy German accent all his life. He had continued to take a German-language newspaper until the day he died two years before. He'd come home from a shift in the mines, eaten his simple dinner, and died quietly in his bed that night. Karl Hendreich had spoken like a German and read like a German, but he had thought like an American. He'd learned to read enough English and had memorized enough American history to become a citizen. And during the war when the homes and shops of so many German immigrants were vandalized, no one had thrown a stone or a nasty word at Karl Hendreich, because no one had ever questioned Karl Hendreich's patriotism. And Tom did not question it now. He watched the rich countryside passing by, felt the breadth and the power of it, thought of the opportunities and gifts it had lavished upon him, and knew that his father had not misplaced his love or his loyalty.

For the first time since Clemmie had started talking about the high-speed New York–California run that both the Central and the Pennsy were instituting, Tom was excited by the idea. He was excited by the thought of his railroad, for it was as much his now as anyone else's, spanning this great nation, carrying its people and its raw materials and its products from one coast to another. It was an aspect of the railroad he'd never considered when, as a smart and ambitious young engineer, he'd gone into it, but it was an aspect that thrilled him now. And as he lay there thinking of his railroad as America rolled by, he realized that his feelings were a legacy not only from his father, but from someone else. He remembered a talk he'd had with Elias soon after he'd married Clemmie. Elias had felt the same way, seen the same connection between the country's greatness and the railroads. "It's what I tried to make old J.P. Morgan see back in '86," he'd said. Tom didn't know if Morgan had ever seen it, but he knew he saw it now and couldn't help being excited by it. He knew tomorrow morning he'd be worrying about Clemmie again, worrying about Clemmie and thinking of the loan he had to get from Jason Wylie and looking after a dozen nagging problems, but tonight he felt only pleasure and pride and excitement.

Tom had only enough time to check into the Palmer House, shower, and change before his meeting with Wylie's assistant. The meeting went well, but Tom knew it was unimportant. This was only the warm-up. The real test would come the next day with Wylie himself.

"Mr. Wylie's looking forward to seeing you in the morning," the assistant said as he walked Tom down the long, thickly carpeted corridor to the reception area.

"Thank you, and please tell Mr. Wylie I'm looking forward to seeing him tonight. At the Red and Gold Ball."

The assistant smiled. He recognized the ploy, but knew its worth to his employer too.

During the afternoon at the A & W office, he managed to forget the evening ahead, but when he returned to his suite at six and found that his freshly pressed dinner clothes had been laid out by the hotel valet, he began to dread the evening again. Charity balls were bad enough with Clemmie. Without her, this one would be unbearable. He took the elevator down to the lobby and entered the barber shop. A shave and a hot towel would relax him, he thought.

At least he did not have to leave the hotel for the ball. When he arrived at the entrance to the Palmer House's main ballroom, it was a riot of colorful gowns and somber black-and-white dinner suits. Tom did not recognize a single face, although the arrogant set of many of them was as familiar as the crystal chandeliers sparkling overhead and the banks of red and yellow flowers. This was exactly like a dozen other benefits except that this time he was without Clemmie.

Waiters circled the room with trays of champagne, but Tom made his way to one of several bars scattered around the perimeter of the dance floor and got himself a whiskey. He'd have one drink, pay his respects to Wylie, and slip away. He had no intention of waiting for the supper. If he were hungry later, he'd have something light sent up to his suite.

He saw Wylie, a small dapper man in superbly cut evening clothes, enter the ballroom, but he was surrounded by people. Clearly it would take some time to get to him. Tom got another whiskey and resumed his vigil. He was watching the party idly and wishing he could reach Wylie and leave when he realized with a start that he'd become almost a connoisseur of these things. He could tell just by looking that this was not a New York or Philadelphia ball. A few years ago they all would have looked the same to him. Now he could spot the subtle differences. In New York the women's dresses and their jewels would be a little more understated. In Philadelphia they'd be considerably more understated. In fact, in Philadelphia there'd be a handful of women, and not all of them old, who looked downright dowdy and were proud of it. Clemmie had shown him the difference, of course. He thought of her and wanted her there beside him, wanted to be able to reach out and touch her. Then he remembered Max Clinton and the desire passed.

It was revived by the girl in white. Tom hadn't realized he'd been staring at her until he found her staring back. The wide brown eyes looked into his own with a challenge, as if she knew how desirable she was in the white satin dress that had no back and moved against her slender body as she danced. The eyes were bold, and the girl was too provocative to be ignored.

Tom turned away abruptly and combed the room for Wylie. He was still surrounded.

"I'm afraid we're not being very hospitable. As one of the sponsors of the Red and Gold Ball, I'd like to welcome you." Tom knew before he turned that it was the girl in white. Her brown eyes were dark and liquid in contrast to the soft blond hair that curled forward on her cheeks—dark and liquid and reckless.

"And since I am one of the sponsors, you're practically obligated to dance with me."

Before he could answer, she'd taken his hand and moved onto the dance floor. "I'm Vanessa," she said moving confidently into the circle of his arm. The dress, as he'd noticed before, had no back, and no matter where Tom put his hand there was warm skin.

"Just Vanessa?" he asked.

"That's the important part."

"Sounds English," he said lamely. She was very distracting.

"Mother had pretensions. She thought the only way she could thumb her nose at Eastern society was by going further east."

"Was she successful?"

"Every time Lord and Lady Webforth pass through Chicago they stay with her and Father."

"Then all I have to do to find out your last name is discover where Lord and Lady Webforth stay when they pass through Chicago." He didn't know how he'd got off on this tack. He wasn't in the least interested in the girl's last name.

"I wasn't trying to keep my name from you." She smiled, and Tom noticed the mouth. It was full and as sensuous as the body beneath the thin white satin. "It's Hodges, Vanessa Hodges. And I'm in the telephone book as well as the blue book."

Tom heard the invitation. "I don't believe I know your family, Miss Hodges, though my wife might."

"That wasn't necessary, Mr. Hendreich. I know you're married." Tom dropped his eyes. He hadn't meant to be so transparent. "And I'm engaged. Recently divorced—it's *Mrs.* Hodges, though I prefer Vanessa—and recently engaged. So you see I'm quite safe." She smiled up at him. "Or at least, equally dangerous."

The music stopped, then, before he could escort her off the floor, started up again in a tango. "I'm afraid I'm at a loss, Mrs. Hodges. I don't tango."

"Good. Never trust a man who tangoes, Mr. Hendreich."

"You seem to know a good deal about it."

"About men, you mean?"

There was the boldness again, and he didn't like it, but he was beginning to sense something else beneath it.

"Except I don't think you're quite what you pretend to be," he added.

"You could take me home and find out for yourself, Mr. Hendreich."

They had moved off the dance floor, but she was standing close to him, and he was still aware of the supple body beneath the white satin and how it had felt in his arms. "That's very kind of you, Mrs. Hodges, but I'm afraid I have to decline. I have an early appointment tomorrow, and I'm going to call it a night."

Tom cut through the crowd to Wylie, made a few appropriate remarks about the ball, and left. When he stopped for a moment at the door and looked back, he saw Vanessa Hodges watching him over the shoulder of her dancing partner. She smiled and lifted her hand in salute. Like everything else about her, the gesture was graceful.

When Tom entered Jason Wylie's office the next morning he felt as if he'd stumbled into the library of an English country gentleman. The prints on the wall were English country prints, the furniture was eighteenth-century English, and the carpet might have been brought back from Delhi by an ancestor in Her Majesty's service. Even the hunt trophies were appropriate except that they bore the insignia of the local hunts.

But Wylie despite the well-cut English clothes and the thin mustache in the English officer tradition, was unmistakably American. He cut the amenities to a bare good morning. "I must say I'm impressed with this plan for a high-speed run between New York and California. The faster we keep things moving—people, products, everything—the faster the economy grows. And I particularly like the link-up with Trans-American." Wylie continued to run through the details Tom had presented to his assistant the previous day. "The plan has promise," he was saying. "It looks like a sound investment, only . . ."

Tom heard the *only* as if an alarm had gone off in his head.

"Only I don't like the idea of lending money to a line that's losing business to another railroad."

"The A & W isn't losing business," Tom corrected him, and began to produce figures that proved the A & W had come out of the Florida business and was back on the road to health.

"Those Toledo branches—the old Toledo Central lines that go east to Akron and west to Fort Wayne—are losing freight traffic to the Lake Erie Southern. And I'd like you to tell me why before we go any further."

There was no point in continuing the conversation. Tom had been caught out. A branch of his own railroad was losing business and he didn't even know it. Either Wylie's contacts were better and more far-reaching than he'd ever dreamed or someone had gone out of his way to make sure that Wylie knew about the problem before anyone else did.

Tom went straight to the A & W office and had Wilcox bring him the latest figures. Someone had gone out of his way to inform Wylie. The figures showed only that two major accounts had cut their shipments last week. It was too soon for it to appear as a loss of business, but it had not been too soon for someone from the Lake Erie Southern to start the rumor.

Tom took the late-morning train to Toledo and got to the office of the Lake Erie Southern just before it closed. He told the clerk he was a furniture manufacturer who was starting a branch factory in Toledo and inquired about shipping rates both east to Akron and west to Fort Wayne. The clerk was happy to provide the information. It shocked Tom. The Lake Erie Southbound couldn't possibly afford to ship at those rates. They'd be out of business in less than a year.

"These seem awfully low to me. Not that I'm complaining," Tom assured the clerk. "Only that I want to make sure I have the correct figures."

"They are low, sir. They were dropped just last week."

"A rate war, eh? I didn't think that sort of thing still went on." Tom laughed as if he'd be only too happy to benefit by another railroad rate war.

"I don't know about that, sir. I only know that those are the rates."

Back in his hotel room, Tom was still mulling over the figures and trying to decide what lay behind them. He had a rate war on his hands, there was no doubt of that, regardless of what the clerk said. But to what end? The Lake Erie Southern was too small to compete with the A & W, let alone hope to starve it out. There was only one answer. Someone bigger than the Lake Erie was behind it.

Tom thought of the rumors that had run rife lately. Even before Clinton had come over to the A & W, it was common knowledge they were planning the New York–California run. They had to if they wanted to keep up with the Central and the Pennsy. And it would also be common knowledge for an insider that they'd need backing for it. Someone wanted to make the A & W look bad to Jason Wylie. But who? The logical candidates were the Central and the Pennsy. Of course, it was more the Central's style. The Pennsylvania Railroad was capable of as many tricks as the Central, but its Quaker and municipal background always made it look as if it wouldn't sink to the notorious manipulations of old Commodore Vanderbilt and his successors. Still, Tom didn't think it was either railroad. He just didn't think the A & W had them that frightened. Not yet, as Clemmie would say.

It came to him suddenly. He was focusing on the wrong part of the country. It wasn't one of his competitors in the East. It was his associate in the West. The Utah Pacific was behind it. Apparently they weren't satisfied with the deal. They didn't want to cooperate with the A & W on the New York–California run. They wanted to take over the A & W, and they were starting here in Toledo and back in Chicago with Jason Wylie.

Tom heard a knock at the door. He hadn't called down for anything and no one knew he was in Toledo. Probably the night maid, he thought, but the small bent man at his door bore no resemblance to a night maid.

"Mr. Hendreich?" he asked. "Mr. Thomas Hendreich of the A & W?"

"You must be mistaken," Tom said. He'd registered under the name of the fictitious furniture manufacturer.

"It's all right, Mr. Hendreich. I knew your late father-in-law, Elias Wilder. Mr. Wilder was very good to me. I owe him my job with the Erie Southbound. I don't want to lose that, but I figure I've got a debt to Mr. Wilder. I won't go into the details, Mr. Hendreich. We don't have time for it. If they find out who you are and that I came here, I'm in trouble. I just wanted to tell you that the Utah Pacific is behind it. And there's going to be more than a rate war. You'd better check into security at your yards. That's all I can say, Mr. Hendreich. Except good luck."

The man disappeared down the dimly lighted hall so quickly that Tom could almost doubt he'd been there. But he had no time for doubts.

He called the managers of the Toledo and Chicago offices and told them he wanted special security on all yards in the area starting that night. He caught the ten o'clock train back to Chicago, stopped in his room at the Palmer House long enough to change to a fresh shirt and collar and toss aside a message that Mrs. Hodges had called, then took the Trans American Airlines morning flight to Salt Lake City. He had to admit Clinton ran his airline well. The flight was not particularly comfortable, but he was in Salt Lake City before noon.

He'd finished his business there by one. There would be no further rate wars and no sabotage. There would also be another Western railroad to complete the last third of the New York–California run.

Tom was exhausted by the time he returned to Chicago, but he put in a call to Jason Wylie immediately. Although it was after five, Wylie agreed to see him briefly. Without telling Wylie any more than he needed to know, Tom explained that the A & W was no longer losing business. Wylie could guess at the details.

"I like the way you handled this, Hendreich. I might as well tell you, that was the final test. If you had called in the government—and the ICC would have been only too happy to get involved—I don't know that I'd have gone through with the loan. I don't like a man who can't take care of his own business. But you've proved you can." Wylie leaned back in his chair. "I'm going to the country for the weekend tonight. A rather long weekend, as you can see, but the hunting's good, and I want to get in as much as I can. I'll be back Monday. Stop by around eleven Monday morning. No, make it eleven-thirty. My people will have all the papers ready by then. In the meantime," he added, easing Tom toward the door, "get some rest. You look as if you've had quite a time of it, Hendreich."

The phone was ringing when Tom entered his room. "Where on earth have you been?" Clemmie demanded before the operator could finish saying that Scranton was calling. "I've been calling since yesterday afternoon."

"Why didn't you leave a message?"

"What's the point of leaving word if you're not there?"

"I was in Toledo. And Salt Lake City."

"Be serious, Tom."

"I am."

"What were you doing there?"

He felt the exhaustion of the last two days wash over him. "I'll explain when I get home. I don't want to go into it over the phone."

"Did you get the loan?"

"Everything wrapped up but the signature. I'm supposed to see Wylie Monday morning. He said he'll have the papers by then."

"Monday. Can't you wrap it up before then?"

He was very tired. "Look, Clemmie, Wylie's going to the country for a long weekend. I can't very well follow him."

"Why didn't you have him sign before he left?"

Tom thought of the last two days again. "It's a long story, Clemmie. I'll tell you all about it when I get home."

"All right, darling, just make sure nothing goes wrong between now and Monday."

"Nothing's going to go wrong." He started to ask about Lizzy, but she'd already told him to have a good weekend and hung up.

"Did you want something else, sir?" the operator asked.

"No, nothing else."

The phone rang as soon as he replaced it in its cradle. "I'm finished with that call to Scranton," Tom barked into the mouthpiece.

"It sounds as if it wasn't very satisfactory," a woman's voice said. Tom knew it was Vanessa Hodges before she identified herself. "I was thinking about how lonely it must be for you down there at the Palmer House, Mr. Hendreich, so I decided to volunteer my services as a tour guide. I know the best restaurants and the liveliest speakeasies in town."

"That's very kind of you, Mrs. Hodges, but at this point the last thing I want is a speakeasy. And I don't think your fiancé would approve."

"My fiancé has nothing to do with it."

"I'm still too tired, Mrs. Hodges. Perhaps another time," he added automatically, then cursed himself.

Another time arrived the next morning. She was in the hotel dining room when he entered. The headwaiter led him to her table.

"You mustn't blame him," she said. "I told him we had an appointment."

"You don't give up easily, do you, Mrs. Hodges?"

She motioned the approaching waiter away with a wave of her well-manicured hand, picked up the china coffeepot with the Palmer House crest, and filled his cup. "It's so rare that I see something I want."

"I told you I'm married."

"And I told you I'm engaged to be married. Besides, I haven't suggested anything more than breakfast, Tom. Although if you're free for lunch, I have nothing planned. And if you're tired again this evening, I can offer you a quiet dinner at my place. I'm a very good cook, believe it or not." She smiled at him, and it was a more ingenuous smile than the one he remembered from the other night. She was wearing a navy blue dress with a white lace collar and not a touch of paint, and she looked almost like a schoolgirl. "After all, you have to have dinner somewhere."

"All right, we'll compromise. I'll take you out to dinner." There was nothing wrong, Tom told himself, with having dinner with her. Just dinner. After all, he had to get through till Monday somehow. But that evening when she opened the door to one of those modern apartments on Lake Shore Drive, he knew there was something very wrong indeed. She was wearing a dark silk dress that was cut very simply to call attention to the soft material and the body beneath it. Tom tried to focus on the room, to keep his eyes on the huge modern paintings that made no sense to him or the view of Lake Michigan beyond the tall windows, but he could not avoid looking at her.

"Where would you like to dine?" He was still standing.

"I thought we'd have a drink here first."

"I thought you knew all the best speakeasies. We can have a drink there."

"Were you in the war, Tom?"

"The infantry, but I never got overseas, Why?"

"You put up quite a battle."

She took him to a small Italian place that she said had very good food and reasonably good liquor. The tables were covered with the obligatory red-and-white-checkered tablecloths and there was a minute dance floor in the middle of the room.

It was better in the restaurant. She was still distractingly beautiful and he noticed that her perfume was one Clemmie wore occasionally and he especially liked, but somehow the beauty and the perfume seemed less dangerous in the noisy little speakeasy. And the fact that the perfume only served to remind him of Clemmie struck him as a good omen.

"They say Al Capone comes here at least once a week, but I don't believe it. At least I've never seen him here."

Tom laughed. She suddenly seemed very young. "Would you know him if you did?"

"Of course, I'd know him, and not just from the newspaper pictures. I even danced with him once."

"You're quite a girl."

"You think so?"

"I meant, there aren't many sponsors of the Red and Gold Ball—Chicago's best ball if my wife is to be believed," he added pointedly, "who are friends of Al Capone."

"I didn't say I was a friend. I merely said I'd danced with him."

"All the same, quite a girl." He didn't want to like her and shouldn't have—he didn't like women who pursue men and she was obviously pursuing him—but he couldn't help liking her. It wasn't simply the lovely face with the wide-set eyes or the long slender body that moved so gracefully, though he was aware of all that. It was something more, a straightforwardness that made the boldness acceptable, a kind of innocent honesty that he found disarming. Innocent honesty, hell, he cursed himself silently. What he found disarming was anything but innocent or honest. What he found disarming was that a good-looking girl was throwing herself at him and in his anger at Clemmie and his loneliness for her, he was being taken in by it.

"He was very nice. Mr. Capone, I mean. Not as nice as you, but nice."

"It's gratifying to know how I stack up against the gangsters."

"Now, don't be a stuffed shirt. There were some similarities."

"I've never killed anyone."

"No, I wouldn't think so." The wide brown eyes looked searchingly into his. "Though I'm not sure you couldn't. All I meant was that you and Mr. Capone are simply two different versions of the same success story."

"You seem to know a good deal about it."

"While you were avoiding me earlier this week, I did my home work. Poor boy from a small town in Pennsylvania. Poor but brilliant, your admirers say. Poor but hungry, according to your enemies, though I'm pleased to report there seem to be more of the former than the latter. Graduated Lehigh University, class of '16. Got ahead quickly, married the boss's daughter and continued to get ahead quickly." She saw the look that crossed his face. "Though the consensus of opinion seems to be that you would have even without her. She's supposed to be very beautiful, but I'd rather not discuss that now. You have a small daughter to whom you're supposed to be quite devoted, a house, comfortable but unpretentious, in Scranton, belong to no clubs except the local country club, though you're up for two in New York and one in Chicago. You're thirty-one years old and, at the risk of turning your head, terribly attractive. Did I leave out anything?"

"Only a few minor details."

"Well, I didn't have much time. Still, I think I was pretty thorough. So you see, we're old friends now, Tom. It seems as if I've known you forever."

"Except that I know nothing at all about you."

"There's little enough to tell. Grew up in Chicago. Was married to a local boy for less than a year. He played the saxophone in a speakeasy. That's why it lasted less than a year. The family does not approve of saxophone players."

"Is that why you married him?"

"Partly, but only partly."

"I take it your current fiancé is not a saxophone player."

"Caldy! That's a laugh. Mr. C. Caldwell Sharply won't even listen to a saxophone. He hates jazz. Thinks it's decadent. But then Caldy's standards are high. I'm constantly amazed that he's lowered them far enough to contemplate marriage to me. But that's another story, and it has nothing to do with tonight. Caldy is the last person I want to think about tonight."

It was after one when they got back to the large modern apartment on Lake Shore Drive. They'd eaten well, as Vanessa had promised, and had several cocktails before dinner and two bottles of wine with dinner. Tom was feeling more relaxed than he had in days.

He opened the door for her and started to hand her back her key but she had already moved into the foyer and he had to follow her into the apartment.

"Brandy?" she asked.

"No, thanks. I think I've had enough for one night."

"Nonsense, one brandy isn't going to hurt you. Besides, it isn't the brandy you're worried about. Haven't I proved myself yet? I've been a good girl all night. Behaved myself admirably." She was already at the cocktail wagon, pouring a brandy for each of them.

"You're very persuasive," he said, and sank into one of the deep upholstered chairs. After all, he told himself, it was only a nightcap. He'd have one brandy and leave.

He was sitting with his back to the cocktail wagon and as she leaned over the back of the chair to place the glass on the table next to him, he heard the rustle of silk next to his ear and smelled the perfume again. He hadn't been able to think of the name before but now it came to him. *Mitsouko.* Clemmie had worn it often when they were first married, but she rarely did anymore. He was trying to think of Clemmie, but he was aware of Vanessa standing behind him and then he felt the long smooth fingers, gentle at his temples.

"Poor Tom," she said. "Such a grueling week and then this dreadful woman who won't leave him alone for a moment." The fingers were stronger at his neck now, then moving out across his shoulders. "You really are tired," she said. "Tired and tense. What you need is a holiday."

What I need, Tom told himself, is to stand up and walk out of this apartment, but he didn't budge and he felt her move around the chair until she was sitting on the arm. One hand was still around his neck and the fingers were gentle again at his temple. She leaned over until her mouth was on his. It was soft and yielding at first, then more insistent as she felt his arms around her.

When she stood, still holding his hands as if afraid that she would lose him, he hesitated, but only for a moment. Then he stood too and followed her down a long hall to the bedroom.

He didn't love her and he knew he didn't love her, and he knew too that what he was doing had no place in his life and nothing to do with everything he believed. But he watched her moving down the hall in front of him, saw the soft white shoulders against the dark silk of her dress, the long slim lines of her body, the loose-limbed athletic movement that was more seductive in its ease than anything contrived to arouse him would ever be, and he knew he could not stop now if he wanted to, though he no longer wanted to.

She closed the bedroom door behind him, put her arms around his neck, and tilted her face up to him. He felt the soft slim body pressed against him and the mouth opening to him and knew again that he would not stop. His hands found the buttons at the side of her dress and it slid from her as if it had been designed only to be taken off. He could feel her breasts soft beneath the thin satin of the chemise, then that too fell from her easily and he touched warm skin, the soft breasts again, and the long line through waist and hip to smooth thighs. Her hands moved deftly at his own clothes although there were more of them and he began to help her now because it had been too long and he was racing instinctively, blindly toward what he'd been avoiding ever since he'd first seen her.

Afterward, when he looked down at the pale body that was still molded to his, he thought she was as beautiful as he'd imagined her to be, as beautiful as Clemmie. The thought struck him like a blow, and he turned away, pretending to search for a cigarette in the tangle of clothes that lay strewn about the floor.

"I suppose you're angry," she said, taking a cigarette from the silver case he held out to her. She could tell from the way he quickly closed it that the inscription within must be from his wife.

"I hardly have a right to be."

"Then remorseful."

He said nothing.

"Poor Tom. Poor darling Tom. Well, if it makes any difference to you, I haven't forgotten that you're married. And this doesn't obligate you to anything. Not that I wouldn't like you to fall crazy head-over-heels in love with me, but I know this doesn't mean you have."

"You're a nice girl, Vanessa." Tom was surprised to find he meant it. He'd expected to dislike her now, just as in the beginning he'd expected to be put off by her wildness, but he found he still liked her very much.

"Ouch. Anything but that. I didn't ask for love, but if you can't come up with anything stronger than nice, maybe you'd better not say anything at all."

He stubbed out the cigarette and sat up. "Maybe I'd better say good night."

She looked up at him questioningly. "Good night or good-bye?"

"All right then, good-bye. I don't think we'd better see each other again."

"That's the silliest thing I've ever heard."

"That's the smartest thing you've ever heard. After all, you're supposed to be engaged to be married."

"Don't go getting dishonest on me, Tom. You know you don't care a fig about my engagement. But you are worried about your marriage."

"I love my wife, Vanessa. I know it doesn't look it" —he glanced around the room miserably—"from all this, but I do."

"The funny thing is, I believe you. But that has nothing to do with us or tonight. I told you before, Tom, you don't owe me anything, and I certainly don't expect you to leave your wife. I might want you to, but I don't expect you to. The point is, you're alone until Monday. And that gives us three days. Surely three days isn't too much to ask."

"It is from a married man."

She started to say something, then stopped. Instead she reached her arms around his neck and pulled his head down to hers until their mouths met. Her hands trailed lazily over his body, drawing him away from everything reasonable and honorable, to a realm where nothing mattered but the smoothness of her skin and the softness of her body and the sheer pleasure of her hands on him.

Tom left Vanessa's apartment a little after midnight on Sunday. He had spent three perfect days with her, and he hated every minute of them. Or almost every minute, because there were moments when she could drive away even his self-hatred.

Saturday morning on his way to her place from the Palmer House—he'd always insisted on going back to the hotel to sleep, though there were few enough hours left to sleep by the time they separated each night—he'd stopped in the small jewelry shop off the lobby and bought an antique locket. He wanted her to have something, because even if he hated himself for this weekend, he didn't hate her. He didn't love her, but he didn't hate her.

When he gave her the locket as he was leaving Sunday night, she began to cry. Then she told him to get out quickly because if there were two things she couldn't stand it was long good-byes and silly women who cried. But she called him back for a moment and threw her arms around his neck and kissed him with more desperation than passion. Then she pushed him out the door again.

On the way back to the hotel Tom tried to reassure himself. What he'd done wasn't so terrible. Millions of men did the same thing all the time and never gave it a second thought. In a way, he told himself, he was even more justified than those other transgressors. The long years of abstinence, the endless years of depriving himself of every pleasure while he struggled to get ahead came back to him now as if his earlier virtue could compensate for his recent sins. But it couldn't because his virtue, if you could call it that, had been amply rewarded. He'd won everything he'd ever wanted. He thought of Clemmie. He'd won more than he'd ever dreamed. And now he'd betrayed her. But hadn't she betrayed him first with Max Clinton? Wasn't that what all this was about? Wasn't that why he'd been so ripe for Vanessa, because of Clemmie and Clinton? The idea made him feel no better.

When Tom arrived at Wylie's offices Monday morning, the secretary showed him in immediately. Wylie was sitting behind the large mahogany desk that was bare except for a telephone, an antique inkstand, and a small bronze statue of a hunter on horseback. He did not rise or extend his hand when Tom entered.

"Good morning, Hendreich. I trust you had a pleasant weekend." The words were hearty but the tone was not. "I had a very pleasant weekend," Wylie continued. "Good weather for the hunt. A little too much wind, but the hounds managed to pick up the scent. Yes, I had a very pleasant weekend, Hendreich, but then I received some very unpleasant news this morning."

Tom raced over the whole Utah Pacific business in his mind. He was certain he hadn't left any loopholes.

"Do you have any children, Hendreich?" Wylie asked. "That may sound like whimsical question, but you must permit an old man a bit of whimsy now and then."

Tom looked across the desk at the steely eyes that were anything but whimsical. "I have a daughter, Mr. Wylie."

"Now, that's a coincidence, Hendreich. I have a daughter myself. Though I expect she's a good deal older than yours. That's the sad thing about daughters. Wonderful when they're young. Nothing in the world more wonderful than a little girl. But then they grow up and sometimes when they grow up they have a way of disappointing you."

The man certainly went to extremes, Tom thought. Last time barely a word of greeting, now a half-hour discourse on family life before they could get down to business.

"I wouldn't know about that," Tom said. "Elizabeth is only two and a half."

"Two and a half, you say. Now that's interesting, Hendreich. Not her age, but the fact that you know it. A good many fathers would have to think for a while before they could come up with a child's age. I can see you're a family man. Fine thing, a family man. I'm one myself. That's why it's so painful when my daughter disappoints me."

"I imagine it is, Mr. Wylie."

"Perhaps someday you won't have to imagine. Hendreich. Perhaps someday your daughter will disappoint you the way mine has me, and you'll know how it feels. Am I making myself clear, Hendreich?"

Tom looked at him blankly. "To be perfectly frank, not in the least."

"Don't try to deny it. Vanessa called me this morning."

"Vanessa! Vanessa is your daughter?"

"Do you mean you didn't know? Well, that explains some of it. I knew you were unscrupulous, but I didn't think you were stupid."

"I had no idea," Tom said as much to himself as to Wylie. "She said her name was Hodges."

"That's the name she uses. She prefers that horn-player's name to mine."

"All I can say is I'm sorry, sir. Terribly sorry."

"Sorry! You're going to be a hell of a lot more than that before I finish with you."

Tom stood. "I said I was sorry, but I'm not going to sit here and be threatened by you, Mr. Wylie. Without going into details, your daughter was not exactly pressured into anything."

"Anything except breaking her engagement."

"I'm afraid you have things wrong. I never asked Vanessa to break her engagement. In fact, we agreed not to see each other again."

"Oh, I know. I know the whole story. She was down here at nine this morning to tell me. Vanessa hasn't been anywhere at nine in the morning since she was a child. And I know you didn't ask her to break her engagement. You didn't have to. All you had to do was teach her what 'real love' was. Love!" He spat out the word. "Apparently it was such an uplifting experience that she can't bring herself to sink to the depths of marriage to Caldwell Sharply now."

"But she never said a word about breaking her engagement."

"No, she wouldn't. She never said a word about you either, if you must know. Just called to tell me that she'd fallen in love and was going to break her engagement. Now I'm not an unreasonable man, Hendreich. I'd rather have Vanessa marry a man she loves, providing he's not a goddamn horn-player, than one she doesn't. So I told her, well, dear, if you're really sure, we'll call this off and in a few months announce your engagement to this new fellow. You know what she said to me, Hendreich? Do you know what she said?"

"I have a fairly good idea."

"She said," he thundered, "that there wasn't going to be an engagement because the man was already married and had no intention of leaving his wife."

"That much is true," Tom said.

"I just wanted to be certain," Wylie said, and Tom was surprised at the calm in his voice. "Certain that you wouldn't marry her and certain that you were the man. You see, Vanessa wouldn't tell me who he was. She knows I have considerable power and I'll use it when I have to. I'm afraid you were far from discreet this weekend. It took my men less than an hour to find out who you were. The only thing I couldn't figure out was why you'd deliberately throw away that loan. God knows you were hungry enough for it last week. But now I understand everything. Let this be a lesson to you, Hendreich. Next time you start fooling around on the side, better find out more about the girl than her name. Though I don't imagine you're going to have much to lose after this, because I'm going to see to it that you can't get a penny from anyone in Chicago. There isn't going to be any backing and there isn't going to be a new high-speed run, and pretty soon there isn't even going to be an A & W. Now get the hell out of my office and get out of my town."

Clemmie knew now she'd been a fool to overlook those times Tom hadn't been in his room. The first time he'd said he was in Toledo; she'd believed him because there had never been a reason not to believe him. And then, when she'd finally reached him early Sunday morning, he'd said he'd been restless the night before and gone to a movie.

She was pacing the living room and as she passed the mantel she struck it with her fist. How could he! She knew their marriage wasn't perfect, but she'd never expected anything like this. She'd never expected another woman. Another woman was something that happened to other wives, not to Clemmie. Only it had happened to Clemmie. She knew that for sure, because in this case the wife was not the last to know but one of the first. She'd had a telephone call from Jason Wylie yesterday afternoon.

When his secretary had said that Jason Wylie was calling, she'd been surprised. Surely if Tom had impressed the banker so strongly that he wanted to invite them for a weekend as well as give them money, it would be more appropriate for Mrs. Wylie to write. But Jason Wylie had dispelled any confusion about that immediately. He felt Mrs. Hendreich would want to know, he said. And if Mrs. Hendreich were interested, he could recommend a good divorce lawyer in Pennsylvania. Clemmie could hear the venom in the man's voice, but it was nothing compared to her own fury.

She heard Tom and the butler in the front hall. They were going through the usual greeting, but there was nothing usual about their voices. The butler knew that Mrs. Hendreich had refused to take her husband's second call last night, and Tom knew the servants must have put it all together by now—his first call to tell Clemmie about the loan, her announcement that she'd already heard directly from Jason Wylie, her hanging up on him and refusing to accept the call when he'd tried again. The butler, the cook, and both maids would know it all by now and would have discussed it, but in front of their employers they would behave as if nothing had happened. And she could tell from Tom's words that he too was doing his best to behave as if nothing had happened. But his voice, low and strangely hushed like the voice of a mourner at a funeral, told her he knew a great deal had happened.

When she saw him standing in the entrance to the living room like a guest waiting to be invited in, she felt almost sorry for him. There were dark circles under his eyes. He obviously hadn't slept any better than she

301

had last night. Then she pictured the mouth, drawn down now in a frown, kissing someone else, pictured the tall powerful body, a little slumped now as if under the weight of his guilt, tangled with another, and she no longer felt sorry for him. She felt nothing but a wrenching pain that was almost physical.

"I'm sorry, Clemmie." The voice that was usually so cool sounded as if it would break with sobs.

"Sorry for what happened or just sorry you were caught?"

He heard the ice in her voice and saw the lovely mobile mouth rigid with fury. He should have known better than to hope. He should have known better than to dream of forgiveness from Clemmie. All the way home on the train he'd been telling himself he could make things right again, telling himself that when he was with her and he didn't have to depend on that impersonal telephone connection that she could sever so easily, he would make her understand, but now he knew he was wrong. "I suppose you want a divorce."

She felt as if she'd been slapped. Then like the old cliché of the drowning man who sees his life passing before him, she saw the sequence of things to come. She saw the maids packing Tom's things, saw the luggage being loaded into one of the cars, saw Lizzy hugging him good-bye as if he were simply going on another business trip, saw herself alone in the living room, listening to their farewells, sitting alone at one end of the long dining-room table, ascending the stairs alone night after night to a solitary bed. "Don't you think it's a little late for that?"

"From what you say it seems a little late for anything else." Then he remembered what would really be bothering her. "If you're worried about the stocks, I'll sign my share over to you. And resign. I'll get a job with another railroad, maybe out West. You won't have to worry about losing your stocks—or being embarrassed by my presence. Though I would like to go on seeing Lizzy. I don't think that's too much to ask. I'll fight for that, Clemmie, I swear I will. I may not have a right to anything else, but I do have a right—"

"Shut up! Just shut up about what you have a right to because you don't know a damn thing about it. You're so worried about whether you'll be able to see Lizzy after the divorce. Did it ever occur to you that there might be another child to worry about? Did that ever occur to you while you were carrying on in Chicago with your . . . your tart? That's why there won't be a divorce, Tom. Not because there's anything left to our marriage, but because I'm pregnant again."

She quickly turned her back on him. He had humiliated her enough. She would not permit him to see the tears that were proof of it.

"Clemmie," he said.

She heard the emotion in his voice and felt his hands on her shoulders, but she shrugged them off violently. "Don't! Don't touch me with those—" she stopped abruptly. She wasn't going to let him think she cared about him enough to mind his being with another woman. "Do you think I give a damn about you and your tawdry little affair? You can do what you what, Tom, but couldn't you have chosen someone else? Did you have to drag the railroad into it? Did you have to throw away this new run just because you felt like taking some girl to bed for the weekend?"

"Oh, yes, the new run. We must never forget the new run." He was shouting now. He'd forgotten the servants or Lizzy or even his guilt. He'd forgotten everything but his own anger. "The one you worked so damn hard to get from Max Clinton."

Clemmie felt herself whirl around, saw her hand moving through space, heard the sound it made against Tom's cheek and knew that she had hit him, but it seemed that it hadn't been her act at all. Even her voice, shrill in her ears, sounded like someone else's. "Don't talk to me about Max Clinton. You have no right to talk to me about Max—or anyone else from now on."

"Is that a threat, Clemmie?"

"That's a statement. Of the way things are. The way you made them." She started out of the room, then stopped for a moment in the doorway. She kept her back to him as she spoke. "If you go in to see Lizzy, please don't wake her. It's late. And you'll find your things in the blue bedroom. I had them moved this morning."

Without realizing what she meant to do, Clemmie stopped halfway down the hall to the master bedroom and opened the door to a small second-floor sitting room. She sometimes read there in the afternoon and occasionally the nurse brought Lizzy in to play. She went straight to a stack of magazines in the corner and had found the one she wanted before she knew that she was looking for it. It was a two-month-old copy of *Town & Country,* and she remembered the picture. She had forgotten it, but she'd remembered it tonight when she'd seen Tom standing abject and apologetic and still attractive in the living room archway. Mrs. Vanessa Wylie-Hodges, it said under the photograph. It was a carefully posed picture that resembled every other formal engagement photograph, but to Clemmie it was unique. The fair hair made a sleek cap that framed the perfect oval face, and the wide-set eyes started out with confidence. Mrs. Vanessa Wylie-Hodges was not smiling in the photograph, and the full lower lip protruded slightly, almost as if she were pouting. Clemmie pictured the mouth on Tom's. She pulled the page from the magazine, crumpled it, and threw it into the wastebasket. Then she took it out and began to tear, once, twice, a third time, a fourth until Vanessa Wylie-Hodges was nothing but a handful of confetti.

A half-hour later she lay alone in the master bedroom, listening to the sounds of the quiet house. She'd heard Tom come upstairs, walk past her room to Lizzy's, then back down to the blue room. She heard the sounds of drawers opening and closing and water running and then when there were no more sounds, she lay quiet in the darkness, holding her breath. She'd had

304

Tom's things moved to another room—there was nothing else she could have done under the circumstances—but she had not locked the door to her own. If he knew her at all or cared about her at all, Clemmie told herself lying there tensely expectant, he would know she had not locked the door. But he did not seem to know, for there was no sound of footsteps in the hall or of a door being opened.

Tom didn't realize she hadn't locked the door because he hadn't bothered to think about it. He simply didn't care.

This time everything went perfectly, or so Clemmie thought. Instead of a premature delivery, the baby arrived on time, to the very day Porter had predicted. The delivery took less than two hours and was even easier than Lizzy's. And this time the mother was troubled by no subsequent depression. The baby was a boy.

When she had slept for some time and was no longer groggy from the ether, the nurse brought the baby into her room and placed him in her arms. He was a small bundle in a blue blanket and looked no different from the other bundles in similar blankets being carried up and down the hall from nursery to private rooms and back, but to Clemmie he looked very special indeed. He was strong and perfect and hers and he would be a vindication of everything. She wasn't sure what she meant by that last—what had to be vindicated and how this small, helpless creature would do it—but the thought kept running through her mind.

"Elias Wilder Hendreich," Clemmie announced the name to Tom when they let him see her.

"Chairman of the board and president of the railroad," Tom joked, but he could see that it was no laughing matter to Clemmie. Nor was Tom particularly amused himself. Ever since he'd returned from Chicago, ever since that terrible night six months ago when he'd learned she was pregnant, Clemmie had been worse than ever about the railroad. It was the only thing that

305

interested her, the single passion that kept her going. Even her joy in the new baby was related to the future and continuity of the A & W. Even their reconciliation—and to be sure, it was fragile enough—had been effected only because he'd managed to turn his defeat at the hands of Jason Wylie into success with the New York bankers. They'd been reluctant to back the high-speed plan at first, but Tom's arguments plus the rumors of New York Central and Pennsylvania plans for similar runs had finally convinced them. Now Clemmie had her high-speed line and her son and heir, and she seemed, for the moment at least, pleased.

"Why doesn't the baby do anything?" Lizzy demanded a few weeks after Clemmie and little Elias had returned home from the hospital. She didn't especially like this small dull thing who lay in a crib all day and still managed to cause so much excitement. People came to see it and barely noticed her. Mummy never had a minute for her. The nurse, Miss Simmons, scolded her more often than ever. Don't touch baby. Don't wake baby. Don't go near baby. Only Daddy seemed to care about her still.

"He doesn't play or anything," Lizzy observed after a month and half. "He doesn't do anything but lie there."

"That's because he's such a good baby," Clemmie said.

"Was I a good baby?" Lizzy asked. They'd told her that once she'd been just like this little thing in the crib, but she didn't believe it for a minute.

"You were a very good baby," Tom said, sweeping her up and carrying her out of the nursery on his shoulders. "And now you're a very good girl."

Tom was glad to get out of the nursery. He couldn't get over the feeling that Lizzy had hit on something this time. When they'd first brought Elias home from the hospital, there'd been no reason to expect him to do anything, but that had been almost seven weeks ago. Now it seemed to Tom that the baby was too passive.

He responded to nothing. At his age Lizzy had followed a finger that came within her range of sight with the avidity of a hunter stalking his pray and had even—Tom would swear to it—reached out for a toy that lay close by. Elias didn't seem to care.

At first Tom had managed to ignore the fact. There was no reason to expect one child to be exactly like another. But soon he began to suspect there was something wrong, and he was fairly sure that Miss Simmons shared his fears. Only Clemmie remained blissfully unaware of any failing in the son and heir to the A & W, and Tom was determined not to wake her from her dream of perfection until he had more to go on than his own suspicions. He stopped in at Porter Lowry's office one morning late in April.

"Lovely day, isn't it, Mr. Hendreich?" the nurse asked as she led him into Porter's private office.

Tom agreed it was with as much sincerity as he could muster.

"Look's as if spring's really here," Porter added as he entered the office from another door that led to the examining room. "Finally."

This time Tom cut through the amenities. "I'm here about the baby, Porter. I'm worried about him." Tom saw the look that crossed Porter's face and knew his fears were not, as he'd hoped, unfounded.

"So am I," Porter said simply. "I didn't want to say anything until I had more proof, but I've been concerned. I had the feeling at the hospital that something was wrong, though it was too soon to tell, and I've stopped in at the house often since then. In fact, I was there yesterday, and I was planning to call Clemmie this afternoon. I wanted to set up a consultation with that new pediatric fellow. Panky's his name. He saw the baby once at the hospital."

"What do you think it is?" Tom demanded.

Porter turned the swivel chair so his back was to Tom. The lot behind his office was dotted with puddles, and bare trees moved in the cool wind. Porter tried to calculate how many weeks it would be before they blossomed. "It's really too early to say. . . ."

"Goddammit, Porter," Tom broke in. "I'm not asking for a final answer. I'm asking what you suspect. You can tell me that, can't you? You can tell me that as a friend if not as a doctor."

Porter turned the swivel chair again so he was facing Tom. The narrow sardonic face was tense now, as if Porter were fighting to keep the muscles from too much movement. "You understand this is only a suspicion. It could be a dozen things."

"I understand," Tom brushed aside the caution and equivocation.

"Well, speaking generally, in layman's terms . . ." Porter saw the impatience gathering in Tom's face, "I suspect brain damage."

As soon as the words were out, Porter regretted them. He'd thought Tom would prefer a little knowledge to total uncertainty, but he looked at the face across from him now and realized he'd been wrong. It was heavy with grief and seemed to have aged ten years in ten seconds.

Tom sat silent and impassive for a moment, then he got up and began pacing the small office, walking from window to bookcase, from bookcase to door. "We'll take him to Philadelphia. Or New York. Who's the best man? You said pediatrician, but shouldn't we see some kind of a brain specialist? We'll see both. In Philadelphia *and* New York. We'll see all of them. Someone's bound to have an answer." He moved quickly around the office, spewing sentences in rapid succession. He was like a high-speed locomotive letting off steam.

Porter let him talk. If Tom kept it all in, he'd explode as surely as that locomotive. Besides, they would see all the specialists. It was the only sensible thing to do, although Porter felt fairly certain the visits would not be particularly productive. As a doctor Porter believed in the powers of modern medicine—and had witnessed the leveling cruelty of disease.

Suddenly Tom stopped his pacing and his plans. "What about Clemmie?" I don't know what I'm going to tell Clemmie."

"There's no point in saying anything until we're sure. I know she's worried, but—"

"But that's just the point, Porter. She isn't. She doesn't see anything wrong."

"But surely she's noticed—"

"Nothing. She's so delighted by the idea of the baby —you know how disappointed she was that Lizzy wasn't a boy—that she barely sees the reality. If I were to try to tell her there was something wrong, she'd say I was making it up."

And indeed, when Tom first suggested to Clemmie that they take little Elias to a Philadelphia doctor Porter recommended, she was surprised. "But why? There's nothing wrong with him."

Tom hesitated. He couldn't bear the thought of listing all the danger signals—the lack of movement, the dullness of the small eyes that had just turned gray, their refusal to focus on anything, the inability of the chubby little hands to grasp at a finger or a rattle, the general lassitude as if he were . . . as if he were a god-damn vegetable, Tom screamed at himself. "Porter thinks there might be something wrong. Nothing really," he added quickly, hating himself for the lie. "Just a little," he groped around in his memory for some of Porter's words, "motor trouble."

"I don't believe it," Clemmie said hotly.

"Now I'm not saying there's anything definite, but Porter is worried."

Clemmie was dialing Porter's home number before Tom had finished. The housekeeper said Dr. Lowrey was dining and couldn't be interrupted. Clemmie insisted he must be. It was urgent that she speak to him now.

"Porter," she began before he could say anything. "What have you been telling Tom? There's nothing

309

wrong with the baby. You know that. I can't imagine how you ever got the idea there was."

"I'm afraid there might be," he said gravely.

"That's absurd."

"I hope you're right, Clemmie. You know how much I hope that, but I'm just not satisfied by the way he's coming along."

"What do you mean the way he's coming along! Just because he's a quiet baby, a good baby, doesn't mean he's a sick baby. And I won't have you implying he is. Or putting ideas in Tom's head."

Tom started to say something, but Clemmie waved him away. "After all, he's my son. Surely I'd notice if there were anything wrong."

"I think he ought to be looked at by a specialist," Porter said simply.

"I absolutely, refuse, Porter. And if you continue to insist there's something wrong with the baby, I'll find another doctor. We've been friends for a long time, but some things are more important than friendship, and my son is one of them." She hung up before Porter could answer.

"I agree with you, Clemmie," Tom said quietly. *"Our* son *is* more important than anything. Anything except our daughter, that is. That's why I'd like to take Porter's advice and see a specialist."

"But there's nothing wrong with him!"

Tom looked at her for a moment. She was closer to tears than he'd ever seen her, closer even than she'd been that night he'd come back from Chicago and she'd told him she was pregnant. This was going to be awful, but he had the feeling it was going to be worse for Clemmie than for him.

"Look, Clemmie, I know you think I have no right to ask. You don't think I have any rights anymore." She turned away from him, but he continued. "But I wish you'd do this for me. I'm begging you to do this for me. If you're right and Porter's wrong, we won't have lost anything. We'll know for sure that the baby's

fine and we won't have to give Porter and his
another thought. But just suppose something is wrong
I'm not saying there is, but suppose there might be—
then it makes sense to see the best man we can find
and to see him as soon as possible. If the baby's going
to need medical care—I don't know, operations, whatever—it makes sense to do things as soon as possible."

Clemmie had kept her back to him, but she could
see his reflection in the dark window that she was pretending to stare out of. He was right, of course. There
was nothing wrong with the baby, but if there were—
just suppose there might be—she'd never forgive herself if it had been her stubbornness that prevented him
from getting the right care as soon as possible. "Very
well. We'll take him to the man in Philadelphia."

They took Elias to three specialists in Philadelphia
and five in New York. The diagnosis was the same each
time, although the manner in which it was offered
varied. Some were sympathetic, others coolly professional. One of the New York brain specialists who was
deeply interested in psychiatry began to explain to
Clemmie that she must not hold herself responsible for
the child's condition. Nothing she had done during or
since her pregnancy could have caused this tragedy.
Clemmie stood and walked out of his office without a
word.

The next doctor they saw, the last, said there was
no hope at all. The baby could not be expected to live
for many years—he would be prey to all sorts of diseases
and infections—but while he did, an institution was the
best place for him. At this, Clemmie merely sat in the
handsomely appointed Fifth Avenue office, staring out
the window at Central Park, cool and green in the June
afternoon.

Both Tom and Porter had expected Clemmie to put
up a fight about the institution. It was a fight, they
agreed, they could not permit her to win, if for no
other reason than that they had to think of Lizzy. Clemmie, however, had been too debilitated by the month and

a half of doctors and diagnoses to put up even a skirmish. Her only protest was silent and came the night before the baby was to be, in the words she'd come to taunt herself with, "put away." She'd gone up to the nursery early that evening and told Miss Simmons to leave her alone with Elias. It was almost eight when Tom came up and found her sitting beside the crib in the darkness. He switched on a small lamp beside the rocking chair. She blinked against the brightness but said nothing.

"Dinner's ready," he said uncertainly. She did not answer. "It won't do anyone any good to sit here this way."

She said nothing.

"At least come say goodnight to Lizzy."

The silence was neither a snub nor a reproach. It was as if she simply didn't hear him.

He left her then to say goodnight to Lizzy, but when he came back three or four times during the evening she was still sitting in the same position, leaning over the crib, staring down at the small sleeping thing. And at seven the next morning when Miss Simmons came in to get the baby ready, she was still there, a gray, haggard statue in the early-morning light. When Tom took her hand to lead her away from the crib, he half expected screams and sobs of protest, but there was nothing but the same wall of silence. She leaned over the crib and touched the child lightly with her fingers, smoothed the cheek that had never broken into a smile. Then she let Tom lead her from the room.

When Tom and Miss Simmons returned from the home, as Porter called it, Clemmie asked no questions, and they did not volunteer any information. Gradually, after a few days, she began to answer Tom's questions with more than a monosyllable. One day he arrived home from the office and found her reading a story to Lizzy. He thought it an encouraging sight.

"Clemmie," he said when they were alone after dinner that night. The butler had brought coffee and brandy into the living room, and Tom had told him that was all for the evening. "It's better for the baby this way, Clemmie. Better for Lizzy, better for us, and better for him."

"I know," she said quietly. He was surprised; he'd grown accustomed to having her leave his words unanswered.

"And there'll be other children. Other sons. As many as you want. The doctors agreed there's no reason to assume—"

She turned suddenly and her eyes when they met his were hard as steel. "No more children!" she shouted as if it were a threat. "I won't have any more children. Do you understand that? I won't! Ever!" She stopped shouting as abruptly as she'd started. Tom waited for the tears, but there were no tears. She merely sat staring into the hearth, filled with flowers in this season, and said nothing, showed nothing until Tom said it was late and they ought to turn in. She went along docilely then to their room, the room Tom had moved back to gradually, almost imperceptibly during the last months.

Before Tom got into his bed that night he sat on Clemmie's and held her gently and quietly without any thought or feeling of passion, and she let him. But it seemed to Tom, as he lay alone later, longing for sleep that would not come, that he'd been holding a corpse.

Chapter 10

A & W LAUNCHES
GREAT AMERICAN

The New York Times had fit the headline into a single column, "Crack New York–Chicago Run to Rival Century and Broadway," the sub-headline read.

Oct. 26. The Great American Limited made its maiden run yesterday between New York and Chicago. The train, number 33 eastbound and number 34 westbound, is scheduled for a 19 hour carding in both directions, 14 minutes faster than its competitor The Broadway Limited and 28 minutes slower than The Twentieth Century.

Both east- and westbound trains arrived on schedule today, the eastbound leaving Chicago at two o'clock Central Time yesterday afternoon and arriving in New York at 8 A.M. Eastern Standard Time, the westbound departing New York at 1:15 P.M., E.S.T. yesterday and arriving in Chicago at 9:15 this morning Central Time.

In case of delay during future runs of

> The Great American Limited, the A & W
> has initiated a policy of fare repayment.
> Travelers will receive a rebate of one
> dollar for each hour the train is late, an
> hour being computed as anything more
> than 55 minutes. A train arriving fewer
> than 55 minutes late will be considered
> on time. The New York Central and the
> Pennsylvania have similar policies re-
> garding The Twentieth Century Limited
> and The Broadway Limited.

Clemmie flung the newspaper across the drawing
room in disgust. "Why do they keep comparing it to
the Century and the Broadway? As if it couldn't stand
on its own."

"Isn't that what you had in mind? A rival to the
Century and the Broadway?" Tom said. At first he'd
welcomed Clemmie's interest in the new train. They
had talked of the idea for a long time, and she'd been
full of plans for it. Most of them, he had to admit,
were good, and even Adam, sensible Adam, now second-in-command to Tom by the latter's choice, agreed.
Then, after the baby, The Great American Limited was
a godsend. For months after they'd put the child in the
home Clemmie had shown no interest in anything. Only
recently, only when the idea of the Great American
Limited had become reality, had she begun to emerge
from the cocoon of apathy in which she'd wrapped herself. At first Tom had been delighted that she could find
something to care about, but as Clemmie became more
and more obsessed with the train, overseeing every
stage of the planning, meddling in every detail, driving
him and Adam and everyone at the railroad mad with
The Great American Limited and her need to overtake
the Century and the Broadway, he'd begun to wish
they'd found another cure.

"What I had in mind," Clemmie said, "was not a
rival to those trains, but something superior to them.
That's why I wish they'd write about The Great Ameri-

can without comparing it in every other sentence to the Century and the Broadway."

"Here, read this article. Not a word about the Century or the Broadway." Tom handed her a Chicago paper. That peculiar little man, the one who wore flashy jackets and talked too loud and called himself a *publicity man,* that peculiar little man whom he and Adam had said they didn't need but Clemmie had insisted on hiring, had seen that all the papers were delivered to their drawing room this morning. Tom and Clemmie had made the maiden run west on number 34 yesterday and were returning to New York on number 33 today. They'd participated in all of it, but Tom watched Clemmic devouring the newspapers, and it seemed to him that those accounts had more reality for her than their own experience.

Tom was not entirely correct about Clemmie's response. She was eager to read the news reports, but she'd enjoyed every minute of yesterday as well. She'd enjoyed the experience of the past twenty-four hours more than she had anything in the last six months. For the first time since Porter had spoken to her about the possibility of something being wrong with the baby, the pain was, if not vanquished, then dormant. She hadn't forgotten the son who'd turned out to be not a son at all, but for a moment she had stopped grieving for him.

From the instant they'd arrived at the A & W level of the Pennsylvania Station with reporters' lights flashing all around them and a band playing and politicians, dignitaries, and fashionable people jostling to board The Great American Limited, Clemmie had known the train would be a success. She felt herself the center of attention, or at least one of the centers of attention, walking down the red, white, and blue carpet, her arm securely in Tom's. It's my train, she kept telling herself, and as the train pulled out at exactly a quarter past one, the rhythm of the wheels picked up the chant. My train, my train, my train.

There were a great many people to see and a good

many parties in various suites and much champagne that would not be mentioned in the newspapers. By the time she and Tom returned to their own stateroom that night, she'd forgotten everything but the triumph of The Great American Limited—or almost everything, because Tom was there beside her, his hand around her waist steadying her as they walked the narrow aisles of the Pullman cars back to their own suite. It was the same thing really, Tom and The Great American Limited. Tom and the railroad were always linked inextricably in her mind.

"We," she pronounced when Tom had closed the door to the stateroom behind them, "are a smashing success."

He looked at her and smiled. He knew she was high, but he didn't mind because beneath that she was very happy. "Almost as good as winning the ship's pool?" He was remembering something he'd almost forgotten.

"Much better than that." She crossed the few steps between them and put her arms around his neck. "Much, much, much better than that." She lifted her face to his and he bent until his mouth was on hers. She felt the familiar stirrings. "You taste," she murmured against his mouth, "like Dom Perignon."

"I could have sworn," he whispered without taking his mouth from hers, "it was plain old New York State bootleg."

She dropped her head back and looked up at him. "It may have been originally, but you wrought a definite improvement." She lifted her face to his again and his tongue was sharp with the champagne. She felt his arms tighten around her, pressing her to him. She clung to him, dizzy with the champagne and the motion of the train racing through the night and her own desire. His hands had begun to work at the buttons of her dress and she kept her mouth on his, her arms about his neck as he slid her clothing from her, layer after layer until finally she was naked, feeling the warmth of his hands on her skin and the roughness of his jacket against her breasts. She unbuttoned the jacket and reached her arms around him, holding him close. Now she felt the smooth silk of his shirt against her and she was impatient and clumsy with his tie and buttons and he laughed quietly, but it was no more than a choked sound. He was tugging at his own clothes and she felt the smooth skin and hard chest against the softness of her own body, felt the waves of excitement they sent through her, and began to work hurriedly at his trousers. And then they were both naked, and he drew her down to the narrow bed where the sheets felt cool against bodies warm with desire, warm with touching and tasting and savoring.

Her hands trailed over him slowly, feeling the network of muscles and tendons beneath the smooth skin, feeling the power of his shoulders and the strength of his chest, and the hardness of his wanting her.

"Clemmie." It was a moan in the half-darkness, an urgent plea and her body responded to it, moving more rapidly now against his, in rhythm with his, racing heedlessly, hungrily through dark mindless sensation, like the train racing through the black countryside, toward some destination of pure explosive ecstasy.

But that had been last night and now their passions had been put away as neatly and efficiently as the folding berths of a Pullman car; the dark intimacy had disappeared in the bright light of the brisk autumn day. Clemmie still looked happy, Tom thought, glancing across the stateroom at her, but she looked self-contained as well. She was not the same Clemmie who'd stood clinging to him the night before, turning her naked body slowly, maddeningly so his hands could explore every inch of it. The slim supple body was hidden beneath a severe black suit and the eyes that had grown wide with passion were focused on the Chicago newspaper he'd handed her.

The by-liner's name looked familiar to her. The columnist was one of those the publicity man had insisted on inviting on the maiden run with all his expenses paid by the A & W. Tom hadn't seen the necessity for it. "If the train's as good as we think it is, word will get out. Besides, we've run enough advertisements about the Great American already." But Clemmie had immediately recognized the wisdom of the publicity man's suggestion, and apparently it had paid off. A column like this was worth a dozen ads, and a good deal more than the columnist's fare on the train.

I arrived at the Dearborn Street Station at 1:30 in the afternoon. A cold rain pelted the city, and as I hurried toward the train shed my mood was as gray as the overcast day. I was about to travel east on the maiden run of The Great American Limited, and I was certain that I was in for a disappointment. Traveling on this new train we've all heard so much about in the last months couldn't possibly live up to expectations, mine or the Allegheny and Western's. I was sure of that. But I was wrong. The news is that The Great American Limited is everything the A & W has promised and more. I can hardly wait for my next trip. The excitement begins as soon as you set foot in the train shed. A handsome red, white, and blue carpet runs the length of the platform, and the crowd traversing it, hurrying toward their suites and staterooms, seeing others off on this delightful trip, was as fashionable as any I've seen strolling up the first-class gangway of the great ocean liners or hurrying to those other two high-speed trains with which we're all familiar.

Among the worthies embarking on the maiden run of The Great American Limited yesterday were Mr. Samuel Insull, the international financier; Mr. John Henry Mears, who just set another flying

record and reported that travel on The
Great American Limited was almost as
fast and a lot more comfortable; Mr.
George Gershwin, who was headed east
for the opening of his new show *Treasure
Girl;* Mayor James J. Walker, who announced he was pleased to return to the
greatest city in the world on the finest
train in the world; and Mr. Theodore
Dreiser, the writer. Among the Hollywood luminaries heading east were Mr.
Al Jolson, Miss Gloria Swanson, Mr.
John Gilbert, and Miss Janet Gaynor.

"Quite a sailing list on number 33 yesterday," Clemmie said when she finished the paragraph.

"I only wonder if any of them paid or if that darn
publicity man gave them all free rides."

Clemmie smiled at him. "You just won't admit you
were wrong. People will read this piece and decide The
Great American is the most fashionable train to ride."

"Especially if they don't have to pay," Tom said,
turning back to the *Wall Street Journal.* She was right—
about the usefulness of the article and about his reluctance to admit it.

Clemmie went back to the newspaper.

Once inside my luxurious stateroom I
knew why all these important people
were riding The Great American Limited. The accommodations are both opulent and in the best taste. The color
scheme of the A & W is, of course, royal
blue and white, and on this, its best train,
touches of crimson have been added in
keeping with the patriotic motif. The
appointments are handsomely streamlined with deeply upholstered sofas and
bright chrome fixtures. In fact, my stateroom was so pleasant only the pangs of
hunger drove me from it.

The dining car on this fine new train is, once again, handsomely decorated in red, white, and blue, and softly lighted. And the menu—if there is a restaurant in Paris that can rival the delicacies turned out by The Great American's cooks, I haven't found it on my many trips abroad. After much deliberation I decided on some *canapés* of genuine Russian caviar, a saddle of lamb *en casserole,* and the finest rice custard I have ever tasted. The fresh whipped cream for the custard comes, the steward assured me, from the A & W's own dairy farms in Pennsylvania.

"I adore that about the cream," Clemmie laughed.

"What about the cream?" Tom asked. He hadn't bothered to read beyond the first paragraph.

"It says the cream on The Great American comes from our own dairy farm in Pennsylvania."

"Where on earth did he get that idea?"

"From the publicity man, I imagine. After all, if the Century uses butter churned on a family farm, we must have cream from our own cows."

"We'll have to cut back a bit on that menu once The Great American gets into gear," Tom said. "It's too expensive."

"You're not going to start that again. You know as well as I do that dining cars always lose money. It doesn't matter what you serve, they still run in the red."

"They don't have to run quite as red as this one's going to."

"We've been through this a hundred times. I want only the best on The Great American. There'll be no through dinners. Everything fresh and everything local. If it costs a few pennies more to add Lake Michigan whitefish west of Buffalo and bring fresh strawberries up from St. Louis for breakfast on number 33, it's worth it." That seemed to finish the conversation for Clemmie, and she went back to the article that continued to enumerate the delights of traveling on The Great American—the pleasures of the club car, the convenience of the barber shop, the efficiency of the stenographer, the smoothness of the ride, the speed of the trip. It closed by calling the train, once again, "the finest train in the world," a challenge obviously to the Twentieth Century's claim to being "the greatest train in the world."

Clemmie tossed the paper aside with satisfaction. "That settles it."

"That settles what?" Tom asked without looking up from his paper.

"It's time we moved. To New York." He was looking up now, but she went on quickly before he had a chance to say anything. "The A & W isn't a local railroad anymore. And we're not local gentry. We're running . . ." She caught herself. "You're running one of the three greatest lines in the East and you can't run it from Scranton. It's time we moved to New York. Anyway, it will be better for Lizzy," she added.

"I can't imagine how it will be better for Lizzy."

"I told you, we're not local gentry anymore." We're as good, she thought but did not say, as anyone, as Whit and Alison Morris with their impressive New York connections, as Vanessa Hodges and her dreadful father who controls half the midwestern banking interests. Clemmie still hadn't forgiven Tom for Vanessa Hodges. She behaved as if she had—what else could she do if she were going on with him?—but she couldn't forget that he had preferred another woman to her, that he had betrayed everything she had given him and everything they had shared by his preference for that woman. Whatever else she had done to Tom, she had never done that.

"It's never too early to start Lizzy on the right track."

It isn't Lizzy you're concerned about, Tom thought, but merely said, "Scranton's home. For both of us, Clemmie. That area has always been home."

Clemmie laughed. "If I remember correctly that was

the subject of one of our first conversations. That time I asked you to dinner. Mother said you were a Pennsylvania boy at heart and I teased you about it and later you said I was darned rude."

"And you were too." The memory of that night aroused as well as offended him.

"Well, I'm not being rude now, I'm being practical. We ought to be in New York."

"I suppose you've already chosen a house."

"As a matter of fact, I have looked at one."

He was surprised. He'd been joking, but the move was no joke to Clemmie. She'd already chosen a house.

"It's on Fifth Avenue. Now don't look that way, Tom. It's several blocks too far uptown to count as part of Millionaire's Row. It's really quite unpretentious. And we can certainly afford it. You've said yourself the railroad's making money as it never has before. And the value of the stocks has tripled in the last two years."

"That doesn't mean a thing, Clemmie. Unless you want to sell them tomorrow, and I'm sure you don't want to do that."

"Of course I don't want to do that. But the point is, we don't have to in order to buy this house. I told you, it's really quite simple." She moved to the other sofa and sat beside him. The gesture was affectionate but not seductive. He had to give Clemmie that. She wouldn't use the previous night to get what she wanted today. Many women would, but not Clemmie. "Just take a look at it, Tom. I know you'll fall in love with it as soon as you do."

He didn't fall in love with it at all. The house was about as unpretentious as the Italian Renaissance palace after which it was modeled. The white limestone façade with the elaborate carving, the heavy grille front door, the five stories, the huge center stairwell with the great winding marble staircase that climbed three of them in dizzying grandeur, and the small elevator that had been installed only recently were imposing rather than inviting. And he didn't like the lack of space inside and the noise and traffic outside. Tom didn't like any of it, but he bought it. He'd known he would the moment Clemmie had mentioned it on the train.

It made sense, he told himself. Most A & W business was carried on in New York and Chicago, and now he'd be spending less time away from home taking care of it. They decided to keep the house in Scranton. "It can be our country place," Clemmie said. At least he'd won that round, Tom thought. Or had never had to fight it. He'd been prepared to veto any suggestion of a place on the north shore of Long Island.

Now that the main office of the A & W would be in New York in name as well as fact, Adam decided to move too. Samantha was delighted. It seemed to her she was finally moving back into the main arena. She was delighted, that is, until they began to look for a place. She knew she couldn't hope for a house like Clemmie and Tom's, but perhaps a smaller brownstone around Gramercy Park. It would be pleasant to be on the park. Adam, however, had something even more modest in mind. He found a pleasant seven-room apartment on Park Avenue.

"But it isn't even a duplex," Samantha said.

"We don't need a duplex, Sam. There's only the two of us."

"But we can afford a duplex. Or even a house. I'm sure we can."

Adam's smile was tired. "Perhaps we can, but I don't think we need one."

"I can't imagine where the money goes."

"Can't you? It's not cheap to keep you neck-in-neck with *Vanity Fair,* you know."

She did know that, but she knew something else as well. Adam was making a great deal more money than she was spending.

Tom signed the papers on the house two weeks after Clemmie took him to see it. They moved in before

Christmas. "Of course I want to make changes," Clemmie told him, "but it's really quite habitable as it is."

They had bought the house from the widow of the heir to what had once been one of old New York's solid fortunes. The man had managed to spend most of what was left of the fortune during his lifetime, and his widow was only too glad to sell the house and most of the furnishings—quite good things, really—along with it. Not only was she in need of the money, but she had no sentimental attachment to the house or anything in it. Her late husband had been a philanderer and a drunkard as well as a spendthrift and she had few pleasant memories of their chaotic life together in the handsome townhouse. So Clemmie and Tom and Lizzy moved into the twenty rooms—actually only twelve were used by them; the rest were for the servants and their household functions—filled with the excellent Sheraton and Duncan Phyfe, Queen Anne and George III, Louis XV and XVI, Indian and Chinese carpets, and even the less valuable pictures that had been amassed by the late spendthrift's ancestors.

Clemmie was enchanted with the house. Tom was reserved about it. Lizzy was miserable. She missed her friends, the freedom of the fields surrounding the country house, the small stable, and the numerous dogs and cats. She hated having to keep Pinwheel, her pony, across the park where she could visit him only if someone took her. Pinwheel was, in fact, her greatest worry since they'd moved. She was sure he missed the other two horses that had been left behind and old Billy who came over from Grandmother's stables every day to take care of things. She was sure he was lonely among all those strange animals belonging to strange people and disconsolate without her frequent visits and lumps of sugar. She was sure Pinwheel hated New York as much as she did and commented on the fact frequently. ·

Her complaints did not go unheeded. On an uncommonly mild day in late January, Miss Simmons' day off, Clemmie agreed to take Lizzy riding in Central Park.

She'd left her own horse in the country but could rent one.

Clemmie had promised that morning that they'd go riding as soon as she returned from her appointment at one of the half-dozen galleries that were scouring Europe for pictures to adorn Mrs. Thomas Hendreich's new town house. When she entered the foyer at three-thirty, she found Lizzy looking excited and impatient in her fawn-colored jodhpurs and dark riding jacket. The small peaked cap cast a shadow over her lively eyes.

As Clemmie removed her fur coat, the child looked at her silk afternoons dress balefully. Clemmie laughed. "Well, I couldn't very well lunch in my riding habit, could I, Lizzy?"

"Hurry, Mummy. Please hurry and change. Pinwheel is *waiting*." The accent on waiting, a blend of indignation and despair, were enough to have Clemmie changed and ready to leave in ten minutes.

It was a warm day for January but still cool in the park and the bridle paths were almost deserted. Overhead the bare trees made a dark mosaic against the winter sky. It was the kind of gray, forbidding day that Clemmie, for some reason she didn't understand, always found exhilarating. She was enjoying their ride almost as much as Lizzy whose expression, as she sat erect on Pinwheel, was blissful.

As they emerged from a dense glade into full view of Central Park West and the line of new apartment houses there, Clemme noticed a man and woman stopped some distance ahead of them on the path. Even from this distance she could tell they were arguing. Obviously a tryst gone *triste,* she thought without any particular interest. Then something about the way the man leaned forward in his saddle, bending toward the woman, something in the tilt of his head caught her attention. Of course. Why not? What could be more logical than Whit Morris riding in Central Park? Only the woman, Clemmie could see even from a distance, was not Alison. She wasn't sure if the fact pleased or infuriated her. She

327

wasn't sure if she should go on or turn back, but Lizzy, oblivious to the presence of anyone but Pinwheel, cantered ahead. When they were only yards away, Whit, suddenly aware of other people on the path, looked up and saw them. Even in argument, he'd appeared at ease Now he looked suddenly uncomfortable. And still unbelievably, achingly handsome. A hundred memories, more sensations than conscious thoughts, flooded over Clemmie. She'd told herself she'd forgotten Whit Morris, but he was not so easy to forget.

Seeing him there, only yards away, sitting a horse as few men could, brought it all back. She remembered an afternoon in Newport when he'd taken her riding. "I know you prefer fast cars or speedboats," he'd said when they'd stopped in a quiet woods to rest the horses, "but there's something to be said for a slower pace." He was half leaning, half sitting in the deep vee of a gnarled old willow tree and he reached an arm around her waist and pulled her to him. "For example," he joked, "I find it darn near impossibe to kiss you at ninety miles an hour." And his mouth had been soft on hers but urgent too, and through the thin material of her blouse and the smooth fabric of his jacket she could feel the strength of his body and the force of his wanting her. Now, watching Whit, looking into the dark eyes as bright and compelling as star sapphires, it all came back to her. She felt his mouth on hers again, and his body pressed to hers, and the terrible, inescapable desire to reach out and touch him.

"Clemmie," he said in those deep, smooth tones that made her name in his mouth sound different and strangely exciting. "What a surprise. Though of course I'd heard you'd moved."

She barely heard the meaningless words, but was acutely aware of the mouth that spoke them, the mouth that had tasted her body, she remembered, and flushed at the thought. She watched him as he spoke. He was still Whit, handsome, elegant even with his vital animal appeal, but something was different. She realized with

328

a start it was the mustache. He'd grown a mustache. The youthful rakishness was gone. He looked debonair.

He was introducing the woman now and Clemmie heard the name with a shock, although she supposed she should have expected it. Beautiful actresses with reputations for wildness would be just his speed. "How do you do, Miss Bankhead," Clemmie said coolly.

The actress seemed no more pleased at meeting Mrs. Hendreich. Her low throaty voice acknowledged and dismissed Clemmie with a single syllable. "Then I won't expect you at the theater tonight," she added abruptly to Whit, and with a motion of the long slender hands with their blood-red fingertips she turned the horse and started back to the stable.

Clemmie heard the anger behind the words and knew she'd interrupted an argument and prevented a reconciliation. She felt a current of perfectly irrational pleasure run through her.

Lizzy managed to tear her attention away from Pinwheel long enough to acknowledge her mother's introduction to the strange man with the dark mustache. "She's very lovely," Whit said. "Exactly like her mother," he added as he spurred the horse gently and they started along the path side by side with Lizzy trotting on ahead. Clemmie heard the words and found herself holding the reins tightly as if to slow her mount. She wanted the ride to go on forever.

"I didn't know," Clemmie began, partly as a wicked joke, partly as a test, "that you took such an interest in the theater."

The dark eyes darted sideways at her. "I've backed several plays." There wasn't a trace of embarrassment in his voice. He was the old Whit she thought, entirely sure of himself.

He couldn't look at her, Whit told himself, and fought to keep his eyes straight ahead. It wasn't only her beauty, though that was dangerous enough, but he couldn't meet her eyes as he answered her question. Of all the times to run into her, this was the worst. He'd heard that

329

Clemmie Wilder—no, he had to stop thinking of her that way—Clemmie Hendreich had moved to New York, and he knew he'd be seeing her regularly now at dinners and dances and charity balls. His only hope, he'd decided when Alison had first told him the news in a tone that struggled to sound pleased, was to keep his wife and family between them. He would not see her alone, although he wanted to see her no other way, and he would convince both himself and her that he was a devoted husband who had never looked at another woman. That pose would scarcely be convincing now. Devoted husbands did not go riding with notorious actresses. Devoted husbands were not surprised while arguing with mistresses whom they were trying, politely but firmly to drop. He'd had enough of the fiery Miss Bankhead. Riding now with Clemmie, intensely aware of her presence beside him, he wondered how he'd ever found the obvious and self-dramatizing actress so irresistible. He had no difficulty in remembering how he'd thought the same of Clemmie, though that had been further in the past. Still, he had to stop himself from thinking about it.

"I imagine your husband," he said the word as if it were a talisman against her, "will find it convenient being here in New York. Though why I should want to make things more convenient for the head of the A & W"—he laughed—"I can't imagine."

"Oh, come now, Whit, you're not going to tell me the Central is worried about the A & W. Why, you don't even consider us a competitor."

He laughed again. "Who told you that? Max Clinton? I have to hand it to you, Clemmie. On Friday TAA was in our pocket. By Monday it was in the A & W's."

"Why, Whit, are you calling me a pickpocket?"

"Just Elias Wilder's daughter. You always did get what you wanted, Clemmie." He was thinking of Tony Bayliss, now, and the memory gave a harsh edge to his words.

Clemmie heard the words with surprise. He couldn't

330

really believe them. He must know that he was the only thing she'd really wanted, and she'd lost him to Alison. Until now. Now she was being given a second chance at Whit Morris.

"And I have a feeling," he went on, trying to make his voice light again, "that the next thing you're after is the Century's reputation. I hear the Great American's doing well. Too well as far as the Central's concerned."

They'd reached the stables and she smiled down at him as he walked around his horse and reached up to help her down from hers. "It isn't doing well, Whit, it's doing stupendously. You might as well face it. You're in danger."

He looked up at her from under the long dark lashes. "From the Great American, you mean?"

"Why, what else would I mean?" She laughed a little breathlessly as she felt his hands around her waist and the strong arms helping her down, the arms that held her once and would hold her again.

She was sure of it.

Samantha had not lost her flair. She could still attract the most sought-after and wittiest people to her parties, still knew how to get the bootlegger to provide his best whiskey and champagne, still managed to find the most fashionable cook for half of what other women paid. Samantha wasn't frugal, but she was clever, and a few years in the provinces had strengthened her determination without dulling her ingenuity. She received only four refusals to the party she gave at the new apartment the first week in February, and those four would have come if they hadn't already been in Palm Beach for the season. In fact one guest came back from Florida expressly for the party.

"An awkward time for a party, the first week in February," several of Samantha's detractors whispered among themselves. "Everyone's getting ready to go away."

"What a splendid time for a party," her friends said.

"Leave it to Samantha to know just when everyone needs a bit of cheering up."

Although the apartment on Park Avenue wasn't as large as Samantha would have liked, it accommodated the hundred guests quite comfortably. Adam moved among them feeling more like a guest than the host. Cocktail parties, he decided, watching a pretty girl spill her orange blossom down the front of her short beaded dress and onto the carpet without noticing, were the worst invention of the last ten years. Everyone drank too much and talked too loud and nobody ever listened. Even if you wanted to carry on a sensible conversation, the din of other people's voices and the noise of the music made it impossible. He saw the Athertons bearing down on him and wished he could get away. Ever since Adam had married Samantha, Tim Atherton had been uncomfortable around him, as if he were constantly remembering their conversation at the Yale Club and thinking that Adam was remembering it too. Well, Adam supposed he was, although he didn't blame Tim for trying to warn him—especially not now.

"Smashing party, old man," Tim said without looking directly at him.

Polly had less time for the amenities. "Is that really Philip Barry over there?" she demanded.

"I don't know. Never met the fellow myself."

"It must be. I've seen photographs of him. I must meet him. You must introduce me, Adam. I just adore his plays. They're so sophisticated, so *soignée.*"

"So *risqué.* Don't forget *risqué,* Polly," Adam laughed.

"Oh, Adam, you've always been a suffed shirt. I don't know how Sam puts up with you."

"Why don't you ask her? At the same time ask her to introduce you to Barry," he said, and moved off toward one of the waiters carrying a tray of champagne that cost, Adam knew, three dollars a bottle. He hadn't meant to be rude to Polly, if only for Tim's sake, but she was such a fool.

332

He looked at the man Polly had said was Philip Barry. Adam had to admit he rather liked his plays himself. There wasn't much to them, light as froth, but they were awfully good for what they were. And Barry was the toast of the town. Trust Sam to snare him. Adam wondered for a moment how she had, but there was no force to the old jealousy. Anyway, he suspected Sam had learned her lesson. Barry had fame, but not a great fortune, and Samantha obviously needed a great fortune. The days of penniless tennis instructors were long gone. He looked across the room to where she was standing with Clemmie and Max Clinton. Clinton was neither a dashing young sportsman nor a sought-after playwright, but he had other attributes Samantha might find attractive. A few years ago the idea would have been like a knife going through him; now it was no more than a pinprick to his peace of mind.

Adam joined the group more out of curiosity than anything else. Clinton was having the time of his life, falling all over himself being nice to Clemmie and Sam. Well, Adam couldn't blame him. They were both very desirable women, even if he had never desired one and no longer desired the other.

". . . and Clemmie had no idea," Max was saying, "the trouble we were in. There were rocks all over the field and a gulley halfway down it. It was a miracle we made it."

"Nonsense," Clemmie said. "It was the sheer skill of the pilot."

"Ah, she says that now, but she wasn't so flattering that afternoon. Practically broke my heart."

"Oh, I'm sure your heart is more durable than that, Max."

The banter went on for a while, and then the conversation drifted from broken hearts to broken marriages. It was, Adam thought, typical cocktail-party talk without meaning or morality. Marriages were wrecked verbally, reputations ruined on the basis of a groundless rumor. Clinton was telling a story and Samantha was laughing before he'd even finished it, and Clemmie was looking over his shoulder the way people tended to at cocktail parties when they were eager to get away.

Would he never arrive, Clemmie was thinking as she listened halfheartedly to Clinton. Then she saw Alison's smooth blond head bob into view across the room. He was here! She wanted to sing it, to shout it, to stop the party in recognition of it.

Alison was snaking her way through the crowd toward Samantha. Whit seemed to be taking an interminable amount of time with their coats. Clemmie thought.

". . . and he's simply heartbroken," she heard Alison saying to Samantha. "He was so looking forward to your party, but he couldn't get back in time."

The words came to Clemmie dimly, as if from a distance, and she felt the exhilaration go out of her like air out of a child's balloon. For the last two weeks, ever since she'd seen Whit in the park, she'd thought of nothing but seeing him tonight. She'd held a hundred conversations with him in her head, dreamed a dozen ploys for getting off alone with him, dressed tonight with only him in mind. And he "couldn't get back in time." He couldn't manage to make the party even though he must have known she'd be here. The disappointment washed over her like a wave of nausea. She pulled her hand away from Alison's cool grasp and fled from her words to the privacy of Samantha's bath.

When Adam entered the master bedroom a few minutes later he heard the water in the bath running full force but not the sobs it was meant to cover. Another drunk, he thought, and wondered if there were any place in the apartment he could hide from his wife's party.

Clemmie slept little that night and was up early the next morning. She rang for her coffee while Tom was in the bath. The maid brought the tray with the morning mail and the papers. Clemmie went through the mail quickly. There were the usual invitations, solicitations for contributions to worthy causes, requests for her presence on the board of this or that charity. She was on her second cup of coffee and halfway through the first paper by the time Tom emerged from his dressing room. He looked, as he always did on these mornings, ready to take on the world. The dark pin-striped suit, custom-tailored in England, the stiff white collar, the Turnbull and Asser tie, the black waxed calf shoes polished to perfection. He'd even learned about his hair. He had it trimmed often and carefully, so often and so carefully that it never had that just-trimmed look. Clemmie tried to consider him coolly, as if he were a stranger. She supposed other women found him attractive. She pulled herself up. Of course other women found him attractive. Vanessa Hodges had found him irresistible. Well, he might be attractive, and he might have learned to dress well, but he'd never have Whit's style, that inbred grace that couldn't be acquired. The idea did not soothe her. She was as angry at Whit this morning as she was at Tom when she remembered Vanessa Hodges.

"Tom," she said, glancing at the paper opened to an inside page, "who do you suppose is the most famous writer in America today?"

He was surprised. It was not the sort of thing she usually asked him. "The most famous? I don't know. I kind of like Sinclair Lewis."

"No, not Lewis. I want someone more fashionable."

"Well, I don't know how fashionable he is, but I think he's a darn good writer." Like most of his colleagues Tom had little time or inclination to read, but at some point he'd picked up *Main Street* and he'd never forgotten a long passage about railroads, about how they were the lifeblood of the nation, the arteries that could keep a town alive or let it wither and die. He'd never forgotten the passage, but he'd never mentioned it to Clemmie. "And didn't he win one of those prizes a year or so ago? The Pulitzer, I think."

"Won it and turned it down. That's what I mean. I

335

want someone who leads society, not someone who thumbs his nose at it. I want someone with *cachet*."

"What do you want him for?" Tom remembered the playwright he'd been introduced to the night before. It wasn't like Clemmie to go out of her way to capture some current literary lion for a party. And she'd certainly never cared about outdoing Samantha.

"It's this thing in one of the columns. Michael Arlen. You know, *The Green Hat*. 'I take the Century because I want very little in this world, only the best and there's so little of that.' "

"So you're going to find another writer to say something equally witty about The Great American?"

She thought of Whit's absence last night. "A better writer to say something wittier."

"Let it go, Clemmie. The Great American's making more money than we expected. She's taking business from the Century and the Broadway. Isn't that enough?" But he knew even as he asked the question that it was not enough for Clemmie.

"I want more than business. I want the reputation of being 'the greatest train in the world.' Lord, how I hate that expression. I want *cachet*."

He was annoyed now. She was on that single track again. And he remembered something from last night's party: she'd spent a great deal of time with Max Clinton. It seemed every time he'd looked around the room to find her she'd been talking to Clinton or laughing with Clinton, and once, after she'd disappeared for a time and returned looking strange and laughing far too much, dancing with Clinton.

"Why don't you get that fellow they keep writing up in the papers and magazines? The one they keep asking what he thinks of 'flappers' and 'the jazz age' and all that? You know the one I mean. F. Scott Fitzgerald. But—" Tom stopped at the door and looked back at her. His eyes were not especially kind. "You may have some trouble, Clemmie. I hear he's very much in love with his wife." He was down the hall on his way to say good-bye to Lizzy before she could answer.

Tom heard the familiar "all aboard" echo through the train shed and felt the train start forward smoothly without the usual jerks and stops. He took out the pocket watch his parents had given him when he'd been graduated from college. Clemmie had said he ought to have a better one, but he said as long as this one continued to keep time, he'd carry it. It was precisely two o'clock. "We're pulling out on time, he said to Adam, who was sitting across from him in the drawing room.

Adam laughed. "The Great American always leaves on time. It's the arrival we have to worry about. But fortunately that's been good too. We've only paid rebates twice since we put thirty-three and-four on. A pretty good record for four months."

"It went well," Tom said, referring to the two days of meetings in Chicago they'd just been through.

"Hell, it went better than that. If things keep on this way we'll have control of that line west of Chicago by summer. The only question is how far west. Or rather how long it's going to take us to get to California." Adam looked out the window at the Englewood Station as the train came to a stop. "Think of it, Tom. We'll be the first line to run coast to coast. Even the Pennsy and the Central stop at Chicago."

"They won't for long."

"But we'll be the first. No more imitations, no more second best."

"I think there's some hereditary disease in your family."

Adam knew what he meant. "Not on your life. All I want is the richest and most powerful railroad in the country."

"That's all?" Tom laughed.

"But you're right about Clemmie. She's got an—I don't know what you'd call it—almost an obsession to outdo the competition. I want the A & W to be the greatest, she wants it to be greater than."

Tom looked out the window and said nothing.

"She's been driving me crazy about the carding lately. I got a telephone call last week. No "hello." No "how are you, how's Sam." Simply 'a nineteen-hour carding is too slow for The Great American.' That was your wife's greeting to me. I told her it was too dangerous to try to cut it, but she insisted it could be done. You know the argument, I'm sure. If The Century can make it in less time, we can. Especially since our routings are more direct. She doesn't seem to take into consideration the fact that they don't have the mountains to worry about."

Adam was silent for a moment.

"They can drive you crazy, all right," he finished.

Tom didn't understand for a minute. Then he realized that by "they" Adam had meant women. It startled him. He had never been able to think of Clemmie in generic terms.

"I don't know if it's worse before you marry them or after." Adam was looking out the window again, and although he was trying to make his voice sound as if he were still joking, Tom knew he was not. "Before you marry them, you can't think about anything else. I was sure I couldn't go on living without Sam." If Adam realized that he had switched from third person to first, his face, still turned thoughtfully to the countryside speeding by the window, did not indicate as much. "And now I can't even remember feeling that way. Or rather I can remember it, but I don't quite believe it. It doesn't seem that it was me, Adam Wilder, who felt that way. Or that I felt that way about Sam—the Sam I know now." Adam stopped abruptly, as if he'd suddenly realized what he was saying—more than he'd meant to say, but still only a small part of what he was working out in his mind. He'd been worried about so many things when he'd married Samantha. Some of the worries had been justified—the worst of them had been. He'd lost

338

the A & W. The others no longer mattered. He'd been afraid of Samantha's past, had tortured himself with images of her rumored affair and fears that it would happen again. There had been a time, just before they'd married, that Adam had sworn to himself that he'd kill Sam, actually kill her, if she were ever unfaithful to him. And now he found that he simply didn't care. He didn't really give a damn what this Samantha, the Samantha he was married to, did. As for that woman he'd wanted with such fierce passion, she'd turned out to be nothing more than a figment of his imagination. The Sam he was married to was as beautiful as that imaginary woman and as stylish and could be as charming, especially to strangers, especially when she wanted something, but she didn't have that woman's spirit or honesty or delicacy. The Sam he was married to was a grasping fortune hunter, just as his father had said. It amazed Adam that he had not been able to see as much.

"I don't suppose that kind of passion ever lasts," Tom said, calling Adam back from his thoughts. He was not being truthful though. He knew from experience that it did last.

Adam smiled at the polite words that pretended he hadn't revealed himself.

"And I guess there's no point in complaining about it." Adam made the proper, meaningless answer and stood. "Well, I think I'll pay a visit to the barber—I could use a hot towel—and then the club car. I'm supposed to meet Wolfson for a drink."

"Wolfson?"

"You know, that short man, brown as a nut, who was on the observation platform when we boarded. Though I admit he was pretty hard to see surrounded by those four blondes. Those are his starlets. I mean it. That's what they call them in Hollywood these days. Starlets. The ones who make a success of it get to drop the *let* and become stars; the ones who don't—well, we can imagine what they become. Anyway, Wolfson's a producer and he's taking his four little starlets East. And that has to be at least two starlets too many, even by Hollywood standards. Care to join us? We can forget Clemmie's my sister for the evening."

Tom yawned as if he were simply tired and wanted to get a good night's sleep, as if his reluctance had nothing to do with Clemmie or the fact that he'd learned his lesson with Vanessa Hodges. "Thanks, but no thanks."

Adam had not been fooled. "You know, I envy you. I know it sounds stupid. It ought to be the other way around. After all, I'm going off to an evening with four starlets and you're going to stay here alone. But I envy you. I envy your having someone who makes you choose to stay alone."

Memories of Vanessa flooded over Tom and he turned away from Adam. "I'm no saint, Adam. I'm just tired."

"The hell with that. Listen, if you don't want to dine alone, why don't you join us later? There's no harm in dinner. Even you have to admit that."

"Sure," Tom said, but Adam knew he would not join them.

"Oh, one more thing," Tom said as Adam was about to open the door. "I almost forgot. That Philadelphia corporation, the one I'm sure is a front, has been buying up stocks again. I know Cornelia sold some of hers —she says she feels more comfortable owning Pennsy stock like everyone else in Philadelphia—and that Quaker friend of your father's sold some of his. Funny, I could have sworn that if anyone could resist cashing in on this market it would be a Quaker, but I guess I was wrong. Anyway, I don't think it's anything to worry about, but I just wanted to let you know."

"Why let me know? You're the millionaire. I'm just a salaried employee—a well-salaried employee, thanks to you, but still an employee."

"Hell, Adam, you're second in line. If someone's trying to get control of the A & W, it affects you as much as it does the rest of us. Besides, if people are selling, I thought you might be interested in buying some stock."

Adam had looked almost angry for a moment, but now he burst into a wide grin as if Tom had just told a very funny story. "Buy A & W stocks. With Samantha for a wife? You must be kidding, Tom."

Tom dropped his eyes. "If you want a loan . . ." he began nonchalantly.

"Forget it," Adam broke in before he could finish. "In your words, thanks, but no thanks. He straightened his tie though it was still in place. "I'd better get going. If I wait much longer one of them may turn into a star and then she'll be too busy with her public to care about me." The door closed quickly behind him, biting off the end of the sentence. It was as if he couldn't wait to get away.

Clemmie read the invitation again. Mrs. Whitmore Morris wanted them to dine on Thursday, the twenty-eighth Of course there was no doubt that she'd go. Especially when she remembered that Tom would be out of town that night. She'd go to Alison's dinner party, all right. Wild horses couldn't keep her way.

"You never should have invited her," Grace VanNest said as she handed her daughter's guest list back to her. Alison had been married for seven years, but Mrs. VanNest still harbored the misconception that her daughter could not give the simplest lunch without her aid and supervision.

"We'll have to see them sooner or later."

"I can't imagine why. It isn't as if Clemmie married anyone of importance. You can get along quite well without entertaining Clemmie Wilder or that upstart husband of hers.''

"I like Tom," Alison said. "I don't know him very well, but I like what I've seen of him."

"If you have any sense, Alison," Grace said, dropping her voice so that the twins, who were playing with a huge electric train set that occupied half the playroom, would not hear, "you won't get to know Mr.

Hendreich any better. I'd spend as little time with Clemmie and her husband as possible. You haven't forgotten that summer before you married, have you?"

Alison blushed. "If I had, Mother, I'm sure I could rely on you to remind me of it."

"Don't be impertinent, Alison. I have only your interests at heart."

"Don't you think the baby's looking well?" Alison called her mother's attention to the small girl in a playpen at their feet. "I was afraid she was coming down with a cold, but fortunately it turned out to be nothing."

Grace looked at the child. She reminded her very much of Alison at that age. "Alexandra is not the one I'm worried about at the moment. Closing your eyes to the problem won't make it go away, Alison."

Alison could see that there was no avoiding the discussion. Her mother had her heart set on it. She looked at the twins. "Why don't we have tea downstairs, Mother. I'd rather not be lectured in the nursery."

"I'm not going to lecture you, Alison," Grace said when they were alone in the second-floor sitting room. "I'm merely trying to warn you not to be foolish."

"Do you call having an old friend to dinner foolish?"

"Friend! Really, Alison, you're either an angel or a fool, and neither fares very well in the real world. Clemmie Wilder—Clemmie Hendreich—is no friend. She'd as soon take Whit away as . . ." Grace did not have a chance to finish her comparison. The butler had entered with the tea tray. "I'll pour, Hennings," she said peremptorily. "Marriage hasn't changed Clemmie," Grace continued when Hennings had left the room.

"Perhaps it's changed Whit."

Grace looked at her daughter incredulously. Had she really heard none of the rumors? Just a few months ago there had been something about an actress, and two summers before that, when Alison took the children to Newport, there'd been talk about the Billings girl who was divorcing that Russian count she'd married. Whit was sufficiently discreet to conduct his affairs at a dis-

tance from his family, but Grace hadn't thought that
Alison was simple enough not to have heard of them.

Alison felt her mother's eyes on her now and kept
her own steady as she poured cream into her cup. "I
know what you're thinking, Mother. I've heard the
rumors. There's always some well-meaning friend who
can't wait to tell me—for my own good, of course. I've
heard them and I've ignored them because the only
way I can keep Whit is by ignoring them. You're right
about that, Mother. I want very much to keep Whit.
I'll do anything to keep him. But I don't think avoiding
Clemmie—even if I could, now that they're living in
New York—is the way to keep Whit. In fact, seeing as
much of Clemmie as I can may be one way to keep
from losing Whit to her."

"You think you can keep your husband by throwing
him together constantly with a woman he obviously
finds attractive? I don't understand you, Alison."

"He does find her attractive, Mother. I'll give you
that. Incidentally, she's looking lovelier than ever."
Alison reported the fact calmly, but she felt a surge of
jealousy when she remembered how Clemmie had
looked that night at Samantha Wilder's party. It seemed
to Alison she hadn't aged at all. Her skin was still
smooth over the fine bones and the jet black bob gave
her a youthful air. She'd been wearing a thin silk dress
with a short beaded skirt. It was very stylish, and Alison
never would have had the nerve to wear it, not at her
age, not with three children, but Clemmie had looked
exactly right in it. Alison fought to shake off the thought
of what Whit might think of Clemmie in the striking
silk dress with the short skirt.

"But I can't keep Whit from every beautiful woman
in the world, Mother. Surely even you will admit that.
And that's exactly the point. If Whit's going to . . ." she
couldn't bring herself to say the words, "well, he'll do
it a little farther from home. He won't like the fact that
Clemmie's a friend of mine or that he sees Tom all the
time."

343

"Your friendship with Clemmie didn't seem to stop him that summer at Newport."

Stop turning the knife, Alison wanted to scream. Even if you are my mother, you don't have the right to torture me this way. Instead she simply smiled at Grace calmly. "We weren't married then, Mother. Whit owed me no loyalty then. He does now, and he knows it. Whit may have certain weaknesses, but the lack of a sense of honor is not one of them."

The morning of Alison's party Clemmie awakened to a mostly clear sky, but high clouds hinted at snow. From her bedroom window she could see women swathed in fur and men holding onto their hats as they hurried down Fifth Avenue. In the park across the street the trees, still winter-bare, were buffeted by the brisk wind.

Clemmie rang for her coffee and got back into bed beneath the warm satin comforter. She debated what to do with the day. There was nothing to buy. She had a new dress for the evening. Black satin that fell from two narrow beaded straps straight to the single strand of beads about her hips, then flared out gracefully in a skirt that stopped just at the knee. It was very simple, very sophisticated, and very flattering, she thought. The dress had been fitted perfectly. She had shoes and gloves. There was nothing she needed. Anyway, she didn't feel like shopping today. Clemmie could never understand how so many women could spend so much time shopping. Unless you were looking for a particular article, shopping struck her as a very boring pastime. Of course, there was the hairdresser at three. She wondered idly if Alison's personal maid did her hair. Well, that was all very well if you still wore your hair piled on top of your head like something out of a prewar magazine, but for a bob that had to be marcelled there was no one like that man in the French salon on Forty-eighth Street. Still, it wouldn't take all day. She had until three o'clock.

Clemmie looked out the window. From her bed she

could no longer see the people hurrying back and forth on the street below, only the tops of the trees and, across them, the buildings of Central Park West. She'd take Lizzy to the park. And to the Plaza for lunch. Lunch would be a treat for Lizzy. And a morning in the park would give Clemmie some color.

She jumped out of bed and was in the bathroom in seconds, fiddling with the faucets, too impatient to wait for the maid to run her bath, too impatient and too cheerful. I must be a monster, she thought, as she regulated the water until it was as hot as she could bear it. Going off on a lark with my daughter while I'm planning an affair, taking Lizzy out for the afternoon so I can get through to tonight—and Whit more quickly. But as she pulled off the silk nightdress and eased herself into the steaming tub, she didn't feel like a monster at all. She felt happier than she had in a long time.

By the time Clemmie left for Whit and Alison's that evening there was an inch of snow on the ground and it was still falling heavily. "Have you put the chains on the tires, Wilson?" she asked the chauffeur as he helped her into the car. "Mr. Hendreich said they've had half a foot in Chicago," she continued when he'd gone around the car and settled in the front seat. "He said not to forget the chains."

Wilson assured her he'd put the chains on that afternoon. Good Lord, couldn't the woman hear them? And Mr. Hendreich should have known he wouldn't forget. He took care of the cars as if they were his own babies.

The butler let her into the high-ceilinged foyer of the Morris house and took her furs. She saw Alison coming toward her and, beyond her in the drawing room, Whit standing in front of the fireplace with two other men. Even the way he held himself, erect with that patrician air, yet entirely at ease with himself and those around him, made her feel warm with wanting him. She had to have him, no matter what the cost.

When he turned and saw her, he stood for a moment,

staring across the room filled with his guests. Then his manners must have triumphed over his feelings, whatever they were, and he excused himself and crossed the room to her.

"Look who's here, darling," Alison said as Whit joined them. "It's Clemmie."

Clemmie looked up into the dark eyes, saw her own reflection there, and wanted to laugh and shout at Alison that Whit could see for himself who was here.

"I was just telling Clemmie," Alison went on in her fluty voice, "how sorry we are that Tom couldn't make it."

"He'll be lucky if he gets back by the weekend," Clemmie said, her eyes still holding Whit's. "He said they're having a fearful storm out there."

Whit had taken her hand in greeting and now he relinquished it, as if he'd been holding it too long and had suddenly realized the fact. "Tell him to take the Century," Whit laughed. "Little bit of snow can't stop the Century."

"Now you mustn't tease Clemmie," Alison said, taking her arm and leading her into the room. "You must meet Lord and Lady Webforth. A delightful couple."

Must I really, Clemmie thought, or must you simply get me away from Whit? Well, she couldn't blame Alison for trying, but she wasn't worried either. There was a long evening ahead.

As it happened, the evening was interrupted considerably earlier than Clemmie had expected. As the plates for the beef Wellington were being removed, Clemmie noticed the butler bend over Whit's shoulder and whisper something to him.

"There's a call for you, Clemmie." She was sitting three places down the table from him and he spoke so quietly that only the guests in their immediate vicinity could hear him. "You can take it in the library." He stood and led her out of the dining room and across the hall to the dark-paneled library. "There's been an accident, Clemmie. Outside of Newark. They tried to

346

locate Hendreich, but he's not at his hotel." Something
flashed through her mind, something about not being
able to find Tom in Chicago, but it passed quickly.
There were too many other things to think of now.
"Apparently they can't track down Adam either." He
handed her the telephone. "Do you want me to wait
outside?" She shook her head, but said nothing. She
was already listening to the voice at the other end of
the line. Number 22 had been trying to make up time
lost in Pennsylvania because of the snow. Number 22
was the crack Pittsburgh–Harrisburg–New York train,
or at least it used to be. It had been late too often recently and couldn't spare the hour and a half it had lost.
It had run a signal and crashed into an eastbound
freight train. No one knew how extensive the damage
was, the man at the A & W office said, but there was
plenty of damage. He knew that not only from the
preliminary reports, but from the way the reporters were
swarming around him already.

Clemmie wasted no time in speculation. She said she'd
be at the site of the crash within the hour.

"Bad?" Whit asked.

Clemmie nodded. "Would you have my car brought
around, please?"

"I'll go with you," Whit said.

She looked at him in surprise. "And have an executive of the Central presiding over an A & W crash?"
But there was no humor in her voice, and Whit did not
even smile. They were both racing ahead in their minds
to measure the magnitude of the disaster.

It took more than an hour to get to Newark. The
roads hadn't been plowed and the few automobiles that
had ventured out skidded and frequently stuck. Whit
had been right—the new Holland Tunnel was faster
than the ferry—but the highway, once they got to New
Jersey, was treacherous.

They didn't reach the accident until after eleven. It
was a hundred yards or so from the road to the tracks
and as they crossed them hurriedly Clemmie felt the

snow seeping into her satin evening shoes, but she was barely aware of the cold. Whit pushed his way through the crowd roughly, pulling her along behind him. He turned once to ask if she were all right, and didn't wait for an answer. The police had set up a cordon to keep the crowd of curiosity-seekers from the wreckage, but Whit broke through with a few words to one of the officers.

Clemmie had never seen such destruction. It went on and on down the track. Where they stood, four freight cars had run off the track. They lay on their sides in the snow, spilling forth coal and crates of produce like great wounded animals with their intestines torn out. The real animals from the overturned livestock cars moaned and lowed in a cacophony of suffering. Farther down the track, a passenger car, or its remains, lay mangled with another coal car as if two beasts had fought and died. A clearing had been plowed from the road to the tracks and several ambulances were drawn up. Whit headed directly for them.

"Out of the way. Out of the way." Two men carrying a stretcher pushed past them. Clemmie saw a woman, her face white in the moonlight, as white as the sheet covering her body. The sleeve of a red bathrobe hung limply from the stretcher. At first it looked as if the woman were merely trailing her arm over the side of the stretcher. Then Clemmie realized that there was no arm, only a sleeve. The red dye of the bathrobe was blood. Without realizing it, she let out a cry. Whit followed her gaze to the stretcher, then turned her head and held it for a moment against his shoulder. "Don't look," he said quietly, then hurried on, keeping her turned from the stretchers. One of the ambulance drivers was carrying a small boy who sobbed loudly. A man sat in the snow on the embankment and stared ahead vacantly. Workmen, police, stretcher-carriers ran up and down in front of him, but he didn't even blink, only continued to stare ahead of him as if into a great void. Finally one of the men from the ambulances came and led him away.

A little beyond the ambulances they found Paxton, the chief engineer. At least he had been available. Clemmie introduced the two men briefly. Paxton looked surprised, but Whit began to fire questions at him rapidly and the surprise vanished in the exigencies of the moment. The death toll stood at six and was bound to go higher. One wreck crew had already arrived from New York and was working at clearing the cars off the track. More men were on the way.

They stayed at the site for more than three hours, until all the passengers were evacuated and a second crew had arrived from New York. After the ambulances had gone Wilson pulled the Bentley into the cleared area and Whit made Clemmie get into the car.

"I'm not cold," she insisted. It was taking every ounce of control to keep from shivering visibly, but the fact of her cold seemed absurdly trivial in the face of the suffering around her.

Whit looked down at the lovely mouth that was tinged with blue beneath the remains of her lip rouge and knew that she was freezing but would not admit it. That was the real Clemmie, he thought. That was the Clemmie he loved. The idea had crept into his mind like an intruder who waits until the gatekeeper, exhausted from his vigil, dozes off. *Had* loved, he corrected himself. He didn't love her now. He merely respected her strength.

"Your catching pneumonia isn't going to help any of the wounded," he said, and handed her into the car. He poured her a brandy from the bar in the back, drank off one himself, then went back to Paxton. Half an hour later he returned to the car accompanied by a reporter from the *Times,* another from the *Tribune,* and a third from the *Newark Star.* Clemmie was standing beside the open door. Her own comfort, she'd felt after five minutes in the car, was an affront to the injured.

"These gentlemen would like a statement from you,

Mrs. Hendreich." It was clear he'd kept them from finding out who he was.

Whit stepped back a little and listened while Clemmie spoke to the reporters. She was a pro, he thought. Said all the right things in exactly the right way. "A great tragedy . . . too soon to be sure of the cause . . . certainly no fault in the equipment . . . though a thorough investigation will be made. . . ." She repeated the same stock phrases he'd said himself more often than he'd wanted to, the same meaningless but necessary phrases. And throughout the ordeal no one could have guessed how frightened or horrified she was by the disaster. No one, that is, except him. Whit caught himself again. He had to stop thinking that way. He had to stop assuming there was some special bond between them.

"That's all, gentlemen," Whit moved back into the group. "I'm sure you can appreciate that Mrs. Hendreich has a great deal on her mind now."

The reporter from the *Tribune* was watching Whit carefully. He knew the face, but couldn't connect it with a name. He ran through the roster of A & W officials he knew. The man wasn't Hendreich. If Hendreich were here, his wife wouldn't have had to make a statement. Anyway, he'd seen Hendreich. He was bigger than this guy and fair. Who was the second-in-command? Wilder. That's who it was. Adam Wilder. "Do you have anything to add to Mrs. Hendreich's statement, Mr. Wilder?" the reporter asked.

Whit looked startled for a moment. "No, nothing to add, gentlemen. You'll have a full report after the investigation."

"Who's Wilder?" the man from the *Star* asked the *Tribune* reporter after Whit had helped Clemmie into the car and closed the door behind them.

"Christ, Malloy, don't you boys out here in the sticks know anything? Adam Wilder. Son of the original owner. Second to Hendreich now."

"If he's the son, how come he's only second-in-line now?"

The *Tribune* reporter laughed. "Hell, I'm not going to do all your work for you. Go look it up in your morgue."

"Thank you," Clemmie said when the car was back on the highway heading toward the city. "For everything."

Whit looked over at her. Her head was resting on the back of the seat and her eyes were closed. He'd seen her look the same way once before. An image of that night in his Uncle Quentin's beach house flashed through his mind. He rubbed his eyes as if by easing their stinging exhaustion he could banish the memory of that night.

"It was nothing," he said automatically.

"It was a great deal, and I'm grateful." There was a long silence before she spoke again. "Do you ever get accustomed to it?"

He knew what "it" was without asking. "It loses the power to shock, but not to hurt. Whenever you can measure the loss in human terms, not human terms as you read them in the paper—eleven dead, thirty-seven wounded—but human terms as you see them at the scene, it still hurts."

There was another long silence. "Thank you again," she said finally. "I don't think I could have stood it alone."

She'd been staring out the window as she spoke, and he looked at her profile silhouetted against the faint light of false dawn. The features were finely molded, but strong. "You could have stood it alone, Clemmie." There was no harshness in his voice, only a hint of something like admiration.

The words came floating to her across the dark privacy of the car crawling through the emptiness and freedom of those strange hours just before sunrise. It was the hour when anything might happen and so much often did. "Well, I'm glad I didn't have to," she said quietly. "I'm glad you were there to help."

"So am I."

It had stopped snowing but progress was still slow, and after a while Clemmie dozed off. Her head fell gently against Whit's shoulder, and he sat very still, feeling her hair against his cheek, inhaling the scent of her perfume, listening to the sound of her quiet breathing. When the car rounded a curve he could feel the weight of her body pressed against him.

Back in the city, heading crosstown to Fifth Avenue, he looked down at her in the light from the street lamps. Despite the exhaustion of the evening she looked young. She looked more than young. She looked innocent. Hell, Whit told himself, everyone looks innocent in sleep, but he couldn't stop thinking of the flashes of Clemmie he'd seen tonight. She'd been strong, but she'd been vulnerable too, frightened and deeply moved. It reminded him of the girl he'd known that summer in Newport—the girl he'd thought he'd known, Whit corrected himself—but still he kept going back to those months so many years ago. Disjointed moments that he'd forced himself to forget, raced through his mind. And always he came back to that night at the beach house.

As if aware that he was staring at her, she opened her eyes and looked up at him. When she saw his face above her in the half-darkness, she didn't sit up or pull away. She merely smiled. She was no longer asleep and she still looked innocent and she was still smiling up at him. She moved her head a little so that her mouth was close to his, tantalizingly within reach. Then the car turned onto a crosstown street and the first rays of the sun came streaming down from beyond the East River. They flooded the car with light and intimations of the coming day. The spell was not broken, merely revealed for what it was. Whit drew himself up and away from Clemmie.

The buzz of the speaking tube seemed to indicate that even Wilson had sensed the change. It was none of his business whether he took Mr. Morris to his own house or home with Mrs. Hendreich—it was none of his business, although he couldn't help thinking about it because he respected Mr. Hendreich—but he had to have his orders.

Mr. Morris gave them. He would appreciate being dropped at home.

By the next day Tom and Adam were in control of things again, and Clemmie was able to put the accident out of her mind—if not the incidents surrounding it. She and Whit had been so close. Until he remembered himself.

Tom, it appeared a week after the accident, had his own memories of that night. He came home from the office and, stopping only long enough to get himself a drink, went up to the nursery where Lizzy was having her dinner.

"Why do you always have that?" Lizzy asked after she hugged him hello, and he sat down at the small table with her.

"What?" Tom asked absently. He was more than a little preoccupied tonight.

Lizzy pointed to the drink in his hand. He put it down defensively, then picked it up again as if it were more offensive on the nursery table than in his hand.

"I don't *always*, Lizzy, but I often do when I get home in the evening. You have your supper and I have my drink."

"I'd rather have supper. That smells awful. Like spinach or liver. I'd hate to have that every night."

Tom stayed in the nursery for only a few minutes that evening. He kept his face averted as he hugged her goodnight, hoping she wouldn't smell the whiskey on his breath and knowing she would.

On the way down from the nursery he met Clemmie coming up the stairs. "You'd better hurry and dress," she said.

"I didn't know we were going out." It was what he always said these days although he knew that more often than not they would be going out. Tonight, however, he was more than a little annoyed with the new life Clemmie was building for them.

"We're dining at the Marshes', then going on to the theater."

"I should have known."

If she heard the sarcasm in his voice, she pretended not to. "Yes, you should have. I mentioned it to you this morning."

"I was looking at some of the news clippings from the accident today," he said as he followed her into the bedroom.

Clemmie kept walking into her dressing room. "I trust I didn't say anything impolitic," she called over her shoulder. She did not want to discuss that night with Tom.

"You were fine. I was just wondering . . ." He heard her opening and closing drawer and closets. "How did the papers get the idea Adam was there?"

She emerged from the dressing room wearing a blue silk robe. "You know how papers are, Tom. They're always getting names mixed up." She had not looked at him while she spoke and as she passed the chair where he was sitting he reached out and put a hand on her arm to stop her.

"Really, Tom, my bath will get cold, and I'm not going to ask Belle to draw me another."

"That's what she's paid for, isn't it?"

The statement was uncharacteristic. Tom was scrupulously considerate of those who worked for him.

"I suppose it is," Clemmie said, "but I don't see why she should have to a second time just because some newspaper reporter made a mistake."

"What I'm wondering is, if Adam wasn't with you that night, who was?"

Clemmie turned away and started toward the bath again.

"Whit Morris, of course. I thought I'd told you."

"You know damn well you didn't tell me."

"Well, I guess it slipped my mind. It wasn't exactly

354

a matter of importance in view of everything else that happened that night," she added, then closed the door to the bath behind her.

When she came out he was still sitting in the chair, staring into the glass that was almost empty.

"If you don't want to go, Tom, say so and I'll make some excuse for you, but if you're going, you really ought to hurry and dress."

Was that what she wanted, for him to stay home and let her go alone, the way she'd gone to the Morrises' the night of the accident? "I don't understand what Morris was doing at our accident."

She laughed grimly. "Don't be so possessive, Tom. I'm sure he wasn't trying to steal any of the publicity for the Central."

Tom looked slowly from the glass to her. He'd never forgotten George's words that afternoon in Palm Beach. *For a while there she was crazy about Whit. Before she met you, of course.* Tom gave more credence to the first sentence than the second. "You mean he was there because of you, not because of the accident?"

"He was there," she said more calmly than she felt, "because I was a guest in his house when I heard about the accident, and he offered to go along and do what he could."

"And exactly what was that, Clemmie?"

Suddenly she was furious. She didn't know about what or whom—Tom's accusations, Whit's refusal to justify them, herself for the situation—but illogical as it was, she could feel the cold blind fury rising within her.

"I'll tell you exactly what Whit did. He went with me to the accident and took care of things and people you should have been taking care of except that you weren't there."

"That's right, I wasn't. I was in Chicago."

"But where in Chicago, Tom? That's the question I've never asked, and you certainly haven't answered. Exactly where were you that night? Because if they'd been able to find you, you know, they never would have called me, and Whit never would have had to go with me to New Jersey."

He was shocked. It had never occurred to him that she had wondered where he was that night. It had never occurred to him that she might care. "I was in a speakeasy, Clemmie. Alone." He did not add that he had been there because he'd been unable to sleep worrying about her, and her growing coolness.

"What about the lovely Mrs. Hodges?" she wanted to shout, but she would not give him the satisfaction.

"I don't care where you were or with whom," she said as she started for her dressing room. "But I scarcely think you're in a position to go around shouting simply because an old friend helps out when you can't be found."

"An old friend?"

"The husband of an old friend."

"How nice," Tom said, standing and heading for his own dressing room. "We're all just one big happy family."

In the weeks after the accident Clemmie began to live for chance meetings with Whit—he would be at this dinner, at that charity ball—but when Whit did not appear at any of the gatherings where she'd expected to find him, she began to scheme for ways to see him. On the day of the twins' birthday party she gave Miss Simmons the afternoon off and went to collect Lizzy herself. She had to linger for some time having tea with Alison and comparing notes on the children until Whit arrived, but when he walked into the small second-floor sitting room and found her there, his look of surprise and then sudden naked pleasure was all Clemmie had hoped for. All the way home in the car she kept remembering the way his eyes had come alive when he'd seen her and the feel of his hand holding hers while he muttered the polite words of greeting.

When he'd offered to see her to the door and Alison

had said she'd see them out, Clemmie wanted to scream. Still, she thought as the car crept up Fifth Avenue, Alison wouldn't always be able to head them off. She wanted Whit, fiercely, desperately, and she knew after this afternoon that he wanted her too. It was only a matter of time until they belonged to each other again.

"It must be funny having Mr. Morris for a daddy." Lizzy's words roused her from her own thoughts.

"Why do you say that, Lizzy?" Clemmie asked, almost as if the child knew something she couldn't.

"Think of hugging him goodnight. With that bristly mustache. Ugh. I'm glad Daddy doesn't have a mustache. Aren't you glad he doesn't have a mustache, Mummy?"

"Yes, dear," she said absently, remembering that night in the car, remembering what it had felt like to sit beside Whit in the quiet darkness, to sleep against Whit, to wake up finding his face there only inches from hers.

Tom was in the front hall taking off his hat and coat when they came in, and Lizzy ran straight into his arms.

"I'm glad you're not like Mr. Morris," she said when he released her. "That's what I just told Mummy."

"Did you?" Tom said, looking at Clemmie over the child's head.

"It would be awful to have a daddy like Mr. Morris. Every time you hugged him you'd feel that awful mustache. I'm glad you don't have one, Daddy. And so is Mummy. She said so." Lizzy looked up and saw her father and mother staring at each other. He didn't seem to be listening to her anymore. "Don't you want to see my treat, Daddy?" She tugged at his hand. "I got a treat and I won a prize too."

A month later, at a cocktail party at Polly and Tim Atherton's, Clemmie saw Whit again. Strange what children notice, she thought as she stood in the crowded, noisy room saying hello to Whit and Alison. She wanted to reach out and stroke the soft dark mustache.

The Athertons, like everyone else, were closing their apartment and going to the country for the summer, and the party was to celebrate their departure. It seemed every night this month there was some kind of going-away party, although the guests would all go on seeing each other in the country or abroad or wherever they were headed. Even Clemmie planned to spend enough weekends on the North Shore to make Scranton bearable. Especially since Whit and Alison would be in Glen Cove. The parties, nevertheless, were as fiercely jubilant as if none of the guests would ever see each other again.

The party was like a dozen others, but for Clemmie it was special. Whit was there, and it seemed to her that every time she looked up, she found him watching her. With what, she wondered. Affection? Desire? Surely it was more than curiosity. Sometime around midnight when she was standing on the terrace with a small group that included Samantha and Max Clinton, she felt Whit beside her.

"I was just trying to convince Mrs. Hendreich," one of the men in the group said to Whit, "to come cruising in Nova Scotia this August. You come too, Morris. Clinton here and Mrs. Wilder have signed on. It's what we'll all need by August. A little quiet cruising and clean living." They all knew those were the last things they'd be likely to get on the proposed cruise.

"We'll make it a scientific expedition," Clemmie said. "Can you promise us any newts? Whit loves discovering new species of newts."

Whit looked at her sharply, but she merely smiled. It was a slow, secret smile that shared nothing with anyone else in the group.

"What's a newt?" Samantha asked.

"Salamander, kind of," Max answered.

Dimly, as if she were in another room, Clemmie heard Clinton explaining about newts to Samantha and the proposed host telling them they'd find whatever they wanted in Nova Scotia. Clemmie murmured an excuse and started down the terrace. She prayed Whit would follow. He had to follow.

At the far end of the terrace the shrubbery grew tall and thick and formed an artificial grove. Polly's landscape designer had done a superb job. Clemmie turned and rested her arms on the ledge. Behind her the trees formed a dense wall shielding her from the guests on the terrace, from the party going on beyond the windows to the apartment. It was quieter here, and she could hear her own breathing and faintly from below, the sound of the traffic.

"I didn't think you remembered the newt." Whit's voice was quiet behind her.

"I remember everything," she said simply.

He took a step so that he was standing beside her at the wall. They remained that way for a moment, looking out over the lights of the city, feeling the cool spring breeze against their faces, standing only inches from each other, without touching.

"The weighing chair?" Whit asked.

"And Lancelot."

"The picnic at Breton's Point when you terrified Sebastion Anvers."

"Poor Sebastion."

"Poor Sebastion! You stood me up for him."

"Only once."

"Once was enough. I still remember that day."

"So do I," she said quietly.

"And that night?" He was staring out at the lights of the city and his voice sounded strained in the darkness.

"And that night," she whispered.

"Clemmie," he said, and turned to her abruptly. His mouth was warm on hers at first, then hungry, and she felt his body hard against hers, strange after all these years yet familiar too. She pressed herself against him, clinging to him as if she could become part of him again, as if they could become part of each other, as if their physical closeness could wipe out the years and the distance that had come between them. She felt his mouth tracing a line over her cheek. His breath was warm against her ear, murmuring her name over and over, then his mouth was on hers again, tasting, devouring, promising.

The sound of footsteps on the flagstone path came to her as if from a distance, then a loud forced cough. "Excuse me." They sprang apart guiltily. "I'd say I'm sorry to interrupt you," Adam said, "but I'm not."

"Listen . . ." Whit said.

"I'm listening," Adam answered.

"You see . . ." Whit began, then stopped.

"I see perfectly, Morris. You'd better get back to the party." He smiled grimly. "I think Alison's looking for you."

Whit's eyes met Clemmie's for a moment. What was in them? Apology, regret, promise? She couldn't be sure.

"Wasn't that a pretty scene?" Adam said.

"I'm not going to listen to lectures, Adam. I'm a grown woman. I don't need a big brother anymore, thank you."

"Oh, you'll listen all right, but not now. You don't have time to listen now. Tom was on the terrace with me a few minutes ago. He's probably left the party by now. If you have any sense, you'll follow him."

"I'm not ready to leave," she snapped. Not now, she added silently, almost as if the words were a prayer. Not without Whit.

"Don't be a fool, Clemmie. Or a bigger fool, I should say, after what I've just seen. Tom isn't as sophisticated as you and your fashionable friends. He doesn't take these things lightly. In fact, he was angrier than I've ever seen him. If you have any sense you'll try to find him. After all," he added with a snideness that was meant to shock her into sense, "you don't want to lose Tom before you have Whit, do you?"

"If you weren't my brother—"

"If I weren't your brother—and Tom's friend—I

wouldn't give a damn about any of this. Don't waste your time arguing with me, Clemmie. Save it for Tom."

Twenty minutes later when she entered their bedroom and found Tom flinging clothes into a suitcase, she knew Adam was right. He didn't even look up; and she could tell he was in no mood to listen to argument or reason.

"Going somewhere?" she asked innocently.

"I'll send for the rest of my things tomorrow."

"Do you intend to tell me what all this is about, or are you just going to storm out of the house?"

He whirled on her. "You mean you want to know how much I know."

It was, of course, exactly what she wanted to know. Calmly, as if she were not in the least upset, she removed her evening cape and draped it over a chair. "I don't know what you're talking about."

"Ask Whit Morris. Maybe he'll be able to explain it to you."

"You mean because I had a few words with Whit alone on the terrace."

He was stuffing shirts into a suitcase violently. It was not the shirts he wanted to hurt, she knew.

"It was a little more than a few words."

"Good Lord, Tom. All right, Whit kissed me. It was one of those noisy drunken parties where everyone and everything gets out of hand, and Whit kissed me. That sort of thing happens all the time."

"Not to my wife."

"Well, it just did, and I think you're making too much of a fuss about it. After all, it was only a kiss. Nothing else happened."

He slammed the suitcase closed and looked at her for the first time. She had never seen his eyes so dark with anger and it frightened her.

"Maybe what you say is true, Clemmie—"

"It is," she said, hotly, guiltily, because she knew it was only a matter of time until it wouldn't be.

"—but if it is true, it's probably no thanks to you.

After all, your friend Morris is a *gentleman*." He spat out the word. "And gentlemen have standards about these things. A wife's friend, a friend's wife—as if I were his friend. But you'll break them down. I'm sure of that. And when you do, I feel sorry for the poor bastard."

"That's a horrible thing to say," she shouted.

"Are you objecting to my language, Clemmie? Because it seems to me you always found it too polite. Well, I've learned. You've taught me a lot." He picked up the suitcase and started toward the door.

"It isn't true. None of what you said is true," she screamed as she followed him down the hall.

He turned and grabbed her arm. "Every word is true and you know it. You've wanted him all along, only I was too much of a fool to see it. Well, I may have been a fool, but he's a bigger one. Morris and his standards! If he had any sense he would just take you." He dropped her arm abruptly and pushed past her as if in flight from his own words.

"The way you did Vanessa Hodges?" she shouted after him, but he kept walking, and in a moment she heard the front door open, then close behind him.

Chapter 11

CLEMMIE HAD SWORN she wouldn't talk to Adam. She was not going to put herself in a position to be blamed. What of Tom's conduct? What of the rumors about Adam's own wife? No, she was not to be blamed, and she wouldn't permit Adam to act as if she were. But after three days alone in the house without word from Tom or Whit, she welcomed Adam's call.

"I'm inviting you to lunch, Clemmie," he said over the phone. "But I ought to warn you that it won't be a pleasant one."

"Are you always so charming, Adam, or are you rising to the occasion?"

"I have no intention of being charming. I'll meet you at the Ritz at one."

"I'm not sure I can make it at one. . . ."

"You'll make it, Clemmie. If for no other reason than you want to know where Tom is."

It was true. He hadn't sent for his things and she had no idea where to reach him. He might be at one of the two clubs he'd joined in New York. He might be in Chicago or Philadelphia. He might be anywhere.

She dressed quickly in a navy blue linen suit with a white silk blouse and a blue straw hat. "Very somber," she told her reflection in the mirror. "Very contrite." She removed the hat and chose a red cloche from the boxes that lined the shelves of her dressing room. "If it's flaming sin he wants, then I'll give him flaming sin."

She arrived at the Ritz roof, which was of course not

the roof at all but the first floor, half an hour late, but Adam had just sat down. He knew his sister wouldn't heed his summons without making some protest.

"I hope I didn't keep you waiting," she said as she joined him.

"Not at all. I just arrived."

"Do you suppose you could order me a cocktail or are we upholding all the laws this afternoon?"

"I've already ordered you one. The law doesn't mean much if you've bothered to cultivate the maître de'."

"Does that mean I'm going to need a drink?"

"Argumentative, aren't you?"

"You set the tone, Adam darling. It wasn't exactly the most charming invitation I've ever received."

"I'll leave the charm to Whit Morris."

"You used to like Whit."

"I still do. I just don't like Whit and you together."

"You used to like Whit and me together too."

"That was before Tom."

She took a sip of the Manhattan that had just been set before her. "Do you know where he is?" she asked casually.

Adam looked at her over the rim of his glass. "Why? Do you want to call him? I'll be happy to tell you where he is if you promise me you'll call him."

"He's the one who slammed out of the house."

"After he saw you kissing Morris."

"He said horrible things. Things he had no right to say."

"In this case, I imagine they were deserved."

She pushed back her chair to stand, but he put his hand over hers to stop her. "Clemmie and her pride. You never learn, do you?"

"Whose side are you on, Adam? You're supposed to be my brother."

"That's right, I am. I'm your brother and Tom's friend, as I said the other night, and I don't want to see the two of you do something stupid."

"I scarcely think you're in a position to cast the

first stone." She wondered if she dared go on. Would he think she was merely referring to him, or had he heard the stories about Samantha?

"If you're talking about Sam and me—don't look so surprised, Clemmie. Of course I've heard the rumors about her and Clinton. How could I not hear them? I only wish he'd marry her, but I suppose that's too much to hope for. The point is, you and Tom are different. At least I always thought you were."

"Just shows how wrong you can be, my darling brother."

He finished his drink and signaled the waiter for another. "Maybe I'm wrong about you, but I'm not about Tom. He never looks at another woman. I know."

She slammed her glass down. "You know nothing. Absolutely nothing."

Adam remembered that evening coming back from Chicago with Tom on the Great American. It hadn't been the only incident of its kind, only the most obvious. "Perhaps I know more than you do."

"Do you know about . . ." Clemmie caught herself. She'd almost asked if he knew about Vanessa Hodges. She'd almost given herself away.

"Do I know about what?"

"Nothing." She picked up the menu and began to study it. "Nothing at all."

"I know Tom loves you, and I think you love Tom, but for some reason you won't let yourself love him. And for some reason you won't let that thing with Whit Morris die."

"That thing with Whit Morris, as you call it, died years ago," she said, keeping her eyes on the menu.

"It didn't look that way the other night on the terrace."

"That was nothing."

He took the menu from her and forced her to meet his eyes. "You know, Clemmie, I think you're right. I believe it was nothing. I just don't think you believe it."

*   *   *

Two weeks later Clemmie closed the house and took Lizzy to Scranton. Alison had gone to the country a week earlier, but Clemmie still had not heard from Whit.

There was something peculiar about the move. All those trunks and all those servants and only she and Lizzy in the main saloon of Aries. So much fuss for one woman and a small child. Tom had written a week earlier saying he'd be traveling on business a great deal this summer and would stay at one of his clubs when he was in New York. He hadn't mentioned coming to Scranton.

After a week she felt as if she'd been there for a month. The days dragged by without anything to differentiate morning from afternoon or afternoon from evening. As June passed she played golf and tennis at the club, dined with Dolly and had Dolly to dine, saw old friends for bridge, and let Porter Lowry escort her to the club dances.

Lizzy adored it. She loved the freedom of being able to romp about the grounds without having to wait to be taken to Central Park. She loved old Billy and the familiar stable and the fact that she could see Pinwheel every day and didn't have to wear her stiff jodhpurs and itchy coat to ride him. She loved the long picnics out by the lake where, if you were very quiet about it, you could swim without waiting the obligatory hour after eating because Miss Simmons wasn't along and the adults were too busy with each other to notice. She loved everything about being home again, except the fact that Daddy wasn't there too, but she'd stopped asking where he was because every time she did, Mummy had looked angry and been snappish for hours afterward. And having Uncle Porter around helped. It wasn't as good as having Daddy, but it was fun.

She'd wait a little longer, Lizzy decided, then make him go for a swim with her. If she asked him now, Mummy might notice that she'd just finished lunch and shouldn't be in the lake at all. Anyway, she didn't want to go near them now. They were still sitting beneath the big willow where they'd had lunch, and Uncle Porter looked much too serious, and Mummy looked angry.

"I thought Tom would have come out by this time. At least for a weekend," Porter said. "It's been more than a month."

"He's been busy."

"So busy he can't get away to see his wife and daughter for a few days? It's not good for him, Clemmie. No one ought to work that hard."

"Well, I certainly can't stop him."

"Have you tried?"

She shot him a look. "Has Mother been speaking to you?"

"She didn't have to, Clemmie. I'd be blind if I didn't see what's going on."

"It's none of your business, Porter."

"It's my business as your family doctor, but more important it's my business as a friend. What happened, Clemmie?"

"Nothing happened. Tom's working and I brought Lizzy out for the summer."

And it would take wild horses to keep Tom away from the two of you. Either that or your intransigence. Why don't you give him a call, Clemmie? Ask him to come out for the weekend. It'll be good for Lizzy and for you too."

She started putting the picnic things back into the hamper. "Why is everyone suddenly so ready to tell me what I ought and ought not to do? First Adam, then Mother, now you."

"You can't be happy the way things are, Clemmie. I can see you're not happy."

"Damn you, Porter! Who are you to tell me what to do?" She had turned away so he couldn't see her face, but he noticed that her hands were trembling as she folded the cloth and put it back in the hamper, and he could hear the repressed sobs behind her words. "Since when did you become the great authority on marriage? Porter Lowry, the family doctor! Porter, the family friend! The kindly old observer, wiser than Solomon and twice as pompous." She whirled about to face him. "What do you know about Tom or me or anything, locked away in that antiseptic office of yours, untouched by anything or anyone? What do you know?"

He turned away from her as if he'd been slapped. "Nothing, Clemmie. You're right. I don't know the first thing about any of it."

A few days later a letter arrived from Tom. It said only that he'd like to take Lizzy to the seashore for the weekend. He would pick her up Saturday morning at ten if that was all right with Clemmie. He did not suggest that he might stay at the house and did not ask if Clemmie might like to join them.

At ten o'clock Saturday morning Lizzy, doll-like in her new white dress with the smocked bodice, sat on the front porch, frantic with anticipation. Seeing Daddy again was wonderful. Having a whole weekend with Daddy at the seashore was more than she had dared hope for.

Clemmie remained upstairs in her room, listening to Lizzy's yelps of pleasure mingling with Tom's words of greeting. The sound of their mutual happiness seemed to linger on the front steps long after the noise of the automobile had died away down the road.

Of all the unbearable weekends Clemmie had spent in the last month and a half, this was the worst. She drove over to the farm and found when she arrived that she could not go into the house. Dolly's polite words masking the unasked questions, the unspoken accusations—she'd finally given up arguing—were more than Clemmie could face. She backed the car out of the drive and headed for the club where she took out her anger and her loneliness on a tennis ball and Porter Lowry.

"I'd prefer to lose to a civil partner than win over a surly one," he said afterwards. "I suppose you'll bite my head off if I offer you a drink."

"No time for a drink," she snapped, heading toward the clubhouse.

"No time?" he repeated.

Furious at the implication, she didn't even bother to turn.

She thought of calling Whit that weekend, thought of it while she sat alone at the long dining table, pushing unwanted food around on her plate, thought of it later that night as she tossed and turned, trying to find sleep, awakened thinking of it the next morning. But she knew she was not going to call Whit. She'd deluded herself for too long. He didn't want her. That moment on the Atherton's terrace had been nothing more than blind, drunken groping. It had been entirely without significance. Adam had been right about that if nothing else.

Strangely enough, Tom got through the summer more easily than either his wife or her reluctant lover, who had vacillated as often about phoning her as she had about calling him. It wasn't that Tom was less unhappy than they, only that no one had ever told him he could have everything in life, and it came to him as no surprise that he could not.

He took a room at one of his clubs, took it with a kind of grim self-mockery. After all, how else did a gentleman leave his wife? Perhaps if there were no clubs, there would be fewer divorces. He thought of his own parents. They had fought rarely, but when they did it was with an intensity that had frightened the small boy feigning sleep in the cold kitchen. Was the only thing that had kept his father home the fact that he'd no place to go? The advantages of the lower classes, Tom thought.

He worked hard all summer, but that was not unusual, and there was a certain pleasure to be found in the work. Not only did it keep his mind off Clemmie, but it paid more direct dividends as well. The A & W was thriving, not simply in paper value as so many companies were that summer, but really thriving. Freight revenues were up twelve percent over the previous year, passenger revenues nine percent. They had acquired another line stretching southwest of Chicago to Bloomington and Springfield. It was a very profitable line.

On the surface there was nothing unusual about Tom's life that summer. Even his separation from Clemmie appeared no different from the summer arrangements of many people in their set. Among the men who couldn't afford to take off two or three months, summer bachelorhood was an accepted—and for some of them, welcome—way of life. Tom developed only one unusual habit during those weeks. He took to reading the obituary pages. In the morning on his way to the office, after he'd finished the financial news in the *Wall Street Journal* or the international news in the *Times* or the *Tribune,* in the afternoon when he stopped at a speakeasy for a drink, or sat with the *Sun* in the lounge of his club in preparation for solitary dinner, he'd turn to the obituaries. It was a perculiar thing for a man of his age to do, but he could not stop himself. He found himself reading through all the longer pieces, weighing and evaluating the men whose lives had been reduced to a column or two of newsprint. One man had invented a gadget that had changed every housewife's life, another had built an industry that spanned three continents, a third had written a book that had opened a whole new area of inquiry. Tom considered their achievements carefully, but it was always the small paragraph, either at the beginning or the end of the obituary, that intrigued him. Mr. Blizen is survived by a wife, three sons, and five grandchildren. Mr. Quinn is survived by a brother and two sisters. Mr. Leighton is survived by a daughter and four grandchildren. Statistics that never told the real story. Did Mrs. Blizen grieve or was she relieved to be free of her husband after all these years? Was there a woman he'd never married who mourned for Mr. Quinn? How had Mr. Leighton felt when Mrs. Leighton had gone to her heavenly reward? The facts gave no clue to what was behind them—except one. It was the obituary of a well-known attorney. Maquin was the name. Janius Maquin had married the former Belle Locke in 1861. Sixty-eight years ago, Tom calculated rapidly. Mrs. Maquin had died four months ago, and Mr. Maquin had followed in short order. Tom smiled sadly at the obituary, then cursed himself for being a rank sentimentalist.

One night late in August, Adam caught him at his new pastime. Tom had been in Philadelphia for the day and they had arranged to meet for a drink at a speakeasy on Forty-sixth Street. Tom had arrived early and worked his way through the two lead obituaries before his brother-in-law arrived.

"Someone you know?" Adam asked, taking the chair across the table.

Tom looked up furtively as if caught in some forbidden act. "No, just passing time."

"Kind of a morbid way of doing it, isn't it?" But Adam did not press the point. There were more important things on his mind this evening. "Samantha came back to town last night."

"Wasn't she planning to go to Nova Scotia?" Tom asked without interest. It was not Samantha's return to the city that interested him.

"Couldn't wait to talk to me. Couldn't wait to tell me the good news. Of course, she didn't know I'd think it was good, but it is. I can assure you of that. Samantha's divorcing me. She's going to marry Max Clinton. She didn't tell me that part of it, but I know Samantha. She wouldn't let me go unless she was sure she had Max. And she really must have the poor bastard. Sam never makes the same mistake twice. She learned one lesson after that business with . . . with Baldwin." Cynical as he'd become about his wife, Adam still couldn't bring himself to speak of the tennis player. "And another with me. This time she found someone who already has the money. She isn't taking any chances on being disinherited a second time."

"I'm sorry," Tom said.

"Hell, there's no need to be. I'm relieved. Really I am. If someone had told me this was going to happen when I first married Sam, I would have sworn I couldn't live through it, but now I just don't seem to care. We killed everything there was, or everything I thought there was, the first year or two, and since then we've just been caretakers at the grave. On her birthday I'd lay a flower there, on anniversaries she'd put a wreath, and then we'd go off to our own lives. And in Sam's case that means Max Clinton. I think I ought to take the poor bastard to lunch. It's the least I can do."

Tom tried to laugh, but he didn't find the situation nearly as amusing as Adam did. And he certainly couldn't picture himself feeling sorry for Whit Morris, no matter what he'd said to Clemmie.

"Well, so much for the domestic news," Adam said. "How was Philadelphia?"

"Everything's under control." The statement was only partially true. Tom had seen the son of one of Elias's former stockholders that afternoon. He'd heard the man was willing to sell his holdings in the A & W. The man had said that Tom's information was correct, but Tom was too late. He'd sold a few days ago. Like Cornelia, he didn't seem to know or care to whom. Tom had planned to discuss the matter with Adam, but in the face of Adam's personal problems, regardless of his protests that they were not problems at all, it didn't seem fair to worry him about stock takeovers.

Clemmie did not return to town that fall, and Tom did not ask her to. It was absurd, each swore, to let things drift on this way, but neither of them would approach the other. He could have asked to see me when he came to get Lizzy that weekend, Clemmie told herself. All she had to do was come downstairs that Saturday morning, Tom reasoned. Each blamed the other for not writing.

There was another reason for Clemmie's reluctance

to return to New York that fall. She knew she'd have to see Whit eventually, resume the old social pattern as if nothing had happened—and to be sure, little enough had—but she wasn't ready to yet, not while the hopes he'd fired and never fulfilled were still so fresh, not while her marriage was in such an unresolved state. So she lingered in the country waiting for Tom to ask her to come back to New York, and Tom remained in New York waiting for word of Clemmie's return.

Then the world fell apart, as the ministers had been warning that it would ever since the war had ended—or, more to the point, the peace begun—and an era came to an end, as historians would begin to say in the years ahead. On October 24, 1929, Clemmie and Tom stopped thinking of their grievances and began worrying about survival.

That Thursday was the beginning rather than the end. It was the day that the small investors, the get-rich-quickers who bought on margin and sold on whim, went bust. It took another week to do in the more solid representatives of the financial community, but by October 29 the job was almost complete.

Clemmie took the afternoon train to New York and went straight to Tom's office. She had not telephoned, but she knew he'd still be there.

The large general office was deserted. Here and there a light had been left burning, but that did little to lift the cavernous gloom of the vast space cluttered with desks and chairs, typewriters and adding machines, and bereft of any humanity at this hour. Clemmie opened the door to Tom's outer office without knocking. The books, papers, pencils, and telephone on his secretary's desk were arranged neatly, and the typewriter had been covered. Not even the destruction of the economy could introduce disorder into Miss Blatty's carefully organized world. Clemmie crossed to the half-open door to Tom's inner office. The shades of the windows behind him had not been drawn and Tom in his shirt-sleeves was a pale wraith against them. The windows faced uptown, and behind him she could see the lights of Manhattan glittering in the autumn night as if nothing had happened.

When Tom looked up, it was apparent a great deal had happened. His face was as white as his wrinkled shirt, and the circles under his eyes and two-day growth of beard did nothing to improve his appearance. She could tell he hadn't left the office for some time.

"Hello, Clemmie," he said when he saw her. His face showed no emotion, not even surprise. It was as if he had spent all his feelings and had nothing left to draw on. He was as bankrupt as the economy.

"How bad is it?" Clemmie asked.

"It's too soon to tell."

Clemmie thought that from the way he looked he had a pretty good idea of how bad it was, but she didn't want to say as much. "You can give me an idea."

"A & W stock has dropped a hundred and fifty-seven points in the last week, but that doesn't mean anything. Except that on paper we're worth about a quarter of what we were a week ago."

"What else?"

"We're bound to lose that new line southwest of Chicago."

"Any others along with it?"

"I told you, it's too soon to tell. Loans will be called in. We won't be able to pay a dividend this quarter." And God knows for how many quarters after that he thought. "And revenues are bound to fall off. Last week they were saying it was only a Wall Street panic. Now nobody's saying anything because they know it's worse than that, but they're afraid to guess how much worse."

"We've got to hold on to the railroad. That's all that matters."

He looked at her for a long time before he spoke. "Yes, I suppose it is."

"I'll make whatever sacrifices are necessary. We'll sell the house here or at least the one in Scranton."

374

He laughed, but there was no humor to the sound. "I doubt you'll find any buyers after today."

"Then we'll close down part of it and live very simply."

This time he did not even smile, but looked at her carefully. "Are you asking me to come back, Clemmie?"

She hadn't expected him to put it in quite those terms and was caught off guard. "I'm saying we ought to do anything we can to save the railroad."

"What about Morris?"

"What about him? I told you last spring that nothing had happened."

"Or almost nothing. But that was last spring. You've had a lot of time to make things happen since then."

The injustice of it all infuriated her. How dare Tom talk to her this way, after what he'd done. Clemmie had conveniently forgotten how hard she'd worked to make something happen with Whit and remembered only that nothing had. "I won't apologize to you, Tom."

"No, I didn't expect you would."

"I have nothing to apologize for," she said hotly. "Besides, we were talking about the railroad, not about us. The railroad is all that matters now," she said again.

He had stood when she entered his office and remained standing throughout the conversation. Now he sat again as if he were too tired to go on with it. "All right, Clemmie," he said, offering a resignation rather than a promise, "we'll forget about us. We'll forget about everything except the railroad."

To Clemmie the words were clear. Tom would come back, and if they were not going to start over, at least they were going to pick up from where they'd been. Tom had meant nothing of the sort, she realized later that night. She'd brought two of the maids to town with her and sent them to the house to open a few rooms for the night. When she and Tom arrived home a little after midnight, he went straight to one of the guest rooms on the third floor.

Clemmie did not have to be struck more than once to feel the pain. The next morning she told the maid to move all of Mr. Hendreich's things to the guest room.

That Christmas they stayed with Dolly at the farm. It was simpler and less expensive than opening their own house in Scranton. It had, as Tom predicted, proved impossible to sell. When Clemmie had called the broker late in November, he'd merely laughed at her.

Dolly was delighted when Clemmie wrote to say that all three of them would be down for the holidays, and Clemmie's request that they put Tom in another room did not entirely dispel Dolly's pleasure in the reconciliation. She'd grown up in a world in which such arrangements were the norm rather than the exception.

There'd been some talk of reviving the old open house in the tradition of Elias and his father, but they'd finally decided against it.

"It's a needless expense," Clemmie said when Tom brought the subject up over Thanksgiving dinner with Dolly and Adam. "I don't see the point of having hundreds of people in just when we're trying to cut down in every way possible. Maybe we'll do it again eventually, but it's simply the wrong time."

"It might be exactly the right time," Tom said. "We've had to let men go already and there are going to be more casualties. Adam's been talking about cutting wages."

"I don't see how we're going to get around it," Adam said.

"In view of all that, this might be exactly the right time to revive the open house."

"You aren't going to make the men any happier about losing their jobs or taking a cut in pay by giving them a free drink or a Christmas dinner," Clemmie said.

"No, I don't suppose we are," Tom answered. "But it might be a nice gesture anyway. Show them the A & W is still the kind of railroad that cares, even if it is located in New York."

"That's another reason," Clemmie pointed out, "for not having the party. Most of the A & W office people are in New York."

"A lot of the old-timers are still in Pennsylvania, Tom said stubbornly. "Of course, it's really up to you, Mrs. Wilder, since we're not going to open the house, and we'd have to hold the reception at your place."

"Well . . ." Dolly said slowly, wondering if the servants would be pleased at the revival of the old custom or merely annoyed at the extra work, wondering if they were still up to it and if she were.

Clemmie did not give her a chance to finish. "You see, Mother's as reluctant as I am. That settles it. We'll skip the open house this year."

"There's nothing like the democratic process in action," Adam said to no one in particular.

The gathering at the farm on Christmas Day was small but still festive. Adam was there, of course, and Porter Lowry. "Poor Porter," Dolly had taken to calling him. "I keep hoping he'll marry, but he shows no signs of it," she told Clemmie on Christmas Eve.

"Oh, Porter will never marry," Clemmie said airily. "If he hasn't done it yet, he never will."

"Don't be so sure," Tom said. "He isn't exactly an old man. He's younger than I am."

"Yes, darling," Clemmie said, "but you're not exactly a young man."

"Thirty-five is still young for a man," Dolly told her son-in-law.

"But not for a woman, is that what you mean, Mother?" Clemmie was not as light-hearted about the matter as she sounded. That experience with Whit had made her feel her own loss of youth acutely.

Lizzy was the first to hear Porter's car on the drive outside the house and she scampered out to meet him. She'd opened the last of her presents hours ago, already broken several pieces of the miniature china tea set, and was eager for another round of gifts. Uncle Porter looked appropriately laden down.

"May I help you carry them, Uncle Porter?" she demanded, running to meet him.

"Only this small one. It's for your mother." Lizzy was disappointed—she wanted to carry the big one wrapped in red and white like a candy cane, to see how heavy it was—but took the small package he handed her.

"What did you get Mummy?"

"Not on your life. You'll run right into the house and tell her. I know you, Lizzy, you're not to be trusted with Christmas secrets."

Lizzy looked indignant. She could be trusted with secrets. Only not with hidden gifts. She'd found the big box in Daddy's closet weeks ago and hadn't been able to resist opening it. Still, the doll house was wonderful enough not to have to pretend to be excited this morning.

It seemed to Lizzy the grown-ups took an unbearable amount of time greeting each other, and then Grandmother said Uncle Porter had to have a glass of eggnog before they could open presents.

Porter put all the presents except one under the tree in the front hall and followed Dolly and the others back into the living room. There was a fire in the hearth and garlands along the wainscoting and over the mantel. Everything was perfect, Porter thought, even the piece of wrapping paper on the Indian rug and the fragments of ribbons over the chairs, remnants that the maids had missed cleaning up after this morning's orgy of giving. The room was not only beautiful, it was lived in. He thought of the house he'd just left, the house he'd grown up in and inherited at his mother's death two years earlier. He'd put up a tree and his housekeeper had seen that there were greens in every room so that it smelled like Christmas, but the house didn't feel like Christmas. It was too empty for that.

"I think," Porter said, taking a glass of eggnog from Dolly, "I ought to give Lizzy at least one of her presents first. I don't think I could enjoy a drink with that sad

378

face hanging over my shoulder. Do you want to start with the biggest or the smallest?" he asked Lizzy, although he knew the answer and had not bothered to put the huge red-and-white striped box under the tree.

"The biggest." It was as heavy as she'd expected and inside was a handsome new saddle, all polished leather and fine tooling.

"It's really for Pinwheel," Porter said, "but I imagine he'll share it with you."

Lizzy giggled. She knew the saddle was for her. Finally Uncle Porter finished his eggnog and the adults began exchanging the kinds of things they always did. Mummy told Uncle Porter that *Shalimar* was her favorite scent and Grandmother said the scarf was lovely and Daddy and Uncle Porter and Uncle Adam all looked a little embarrassed for a minute and said they'd had been wanting to read this book or had really needed a new pen. Lizzy didn't pay much attention. There was several packages from Uncle Porter still left to open. In the last were three miniature passenger cars, sleek and streamlined replicas of the latest Pullman models painted the A & W's colors.

"They'll fit that set of yours we used to play with, Adam," Porter said. "At first when I saw them, I thought what a shame Lizzy wasn't a boy. Then I remembered that Clemmie used to have as much fun with your electric trains as we did, so I decided Lizzy ought to have some of her own."

"I had forgotten that set," Clemmie said.

"So had I until I ran across these cars last week. Of course, they're not as splendid as the set you used to have."

"Elias had those specially made for the children," Dolly said, looking at the small cars sadly. "And each year he'd add to it. He'd get very angry when you and George used to stage wrecks, Adam."

Suddenly everyone in the room was quiet, Lizzy noticed, the way they always were when anyone mentioned Uncle George. Although she was dying to know where the electric trains were, she was afraid to ask.

"Where are the trains now?" Uncle Adam came to the rescue. "Lizzy can't play with her present without tracks."

"In the attic," Dolly said, "but you're sure to get all dusty if you go after them now."

"Nonsense, Mother. Come on, Tom. Wait till you see this."

It took them almost two hours to set the whole thing up, although Lizzy thought things would have gone faster if everyone hadn't kept stopping to get another drink, and at one point even Mummy was down on the floor in her velvet dress helping Lizzy attach the new cars to the old-fashioned engine.

"Your mother's only helping now, Lizzy, so you'll let her run the trains later."

"You're just jealous, Porter, because I was always better at the switches than you were."

"You had more experience. You lived with them, I only got to play with them on visits."

"Did you have a train like this when you were little, Daddy?"

"I had something better, Lizzy. I had a real train that ran through my back yard."

"A real train of your very own? In your back yard?"

"Well, not exactly of my very own."

"I don't understand," Lizzy said.

"Daddy's teasing you," Clemmie interrupted. She gave Tom a long look. "He didn't have one like this when he was little, but now that he's big he has a much better one, doesn't he? Now he really does have a train of his very own. Many of them."

"I think," Dolly said quickly, "that you'd all better go clean up. "Dinner will be ready in a moment."

Lizzy was so exhausted from the excitement that she could barely hold her head up through the main course. The turkey with dressing and Naomi's cranberry jelly lay untouched on her plate, and the child didn't murmur a word of protest when she was carried off for a nap before the plum pudding arrived.

"Everything was wonderful, as usual, Mrs. Wilder," Porter said when they'd moved back to the living room for coffee and brandy.

"Naomi always outdoes herself when she knows the children are coming home."

"The children," Adam laughed.

"You know what I mean," Dolly said. "You should have heard her. She's been lacing 'Mr. Adam's' fruit-cakes with brandy for months now. I'm sure she's made a considerable dent in your father's supply."

"I'll see you get some more before next Christmas, Mother," Adam said.

"Do you think Prohibition will still be around by next Christmas?" Clemmie asked.

"Absolutely. People have more serious things to worry about now. Any politician who wants to get elected these days is going to promise the people food, not whiskey." Adam turned to Porter. "Just how bad are things around here?"

"I'd say as bad as they could be, but people keep telling me—Tom for one," Porter added, gesturing toward Tom, "that they're going to get a lot worse. You know about the mines, of course. Your own number two is closed. The steel mill has laid off a lot of men. Why bother going on? It's the same all over. Only the details are different. Around here the Dutch farmers are beginning to dip into their savings. You know what that means."

"At least it means you're still getting paid," Adam said.

"Only intermittently. The rich never bother to pay their bills and now the poor can't. All the same, I'm not complaining. I'm better off than most. I'm not sure who's in worse shape, the people who never had much or those who had everything and lost it all. I keep hearing about some of your big Wall Street friends. That fellow you brought home from Yale one year, Adam. What was his name? Henley?"

"Hendry. He shot himself in the mouth two weeks ago."

"Terrible thing," Porter continued. "And I hear that airline friend of yours, the one who ran the Chicago–Salt Lake City flight for your high-speed run, is the latest casualty."

"Financial casualty, you mean?" Adam asked quickly. "You haven't heard that he's done anything, have you?" He didn't want Samantha a widow before she was a wife, and his reasons were not entirely unselfish.

"Clinton's all right," Tom said. "Or at least he was last Monday. I ran into him on Broad Street. He looked awful, but he seemed calm, or as calm as anyone could be in his position."

"I didn't know Max was in trouble," Clemmie said. "Why doesn't anyone tell me anything. You didn't even mention you'd seen him downtown, Tom."

Tom saw no reason to remind Clemmie he had a perfectly good reason for not mentioning Max Clinton to her. She might have forgotten that weekend on Long Island, but he hadn't. His current hatred of Whit Morris did nothing to alleviate his earlier suspicions of Max Clinton.

"How badly was he hit?" Clemmie asked.

"Apparently he was overextended," Tom said. "Like everyone else. When things were hot, he couldn't set up those new routes fast enough. Then things cooled off, to say the least, and he was in way over his head. I don't imagine that deal with us helped much either. Anyway, Trans-American went into receivership and Clinton lost everything."

"Everyone lost money on that high-speed California run, Tom. The Pennsy and the Central and their airlines too," Clemmie said defensively. "Still, poor Max."

"Poor Samantha," Adam said. "She doesn't seem to have much luck, does she? First me, now Max. It's beginning to look as if my lovely wife—ex-wife—is a financial jinx."

"I doubt she'll go through with it now," Clemmie said. "The marriage, I mean."

"Oh, she'll go through with it, all right. Sam's got too much style not to. No morals and worse luck, but plenty of style. Imagine what people would say if she didn't, and Sam is very concerned about what people say. She doesn't mind their gossiping about her affairs —I'm sorry, Mother—but she can't stand being called a gold digger. Samantha will hold on to Max—at least for a while. She'll have to in order to save face."

"How's Tom?" Porter asked when he and Clemmie were alone for a moment in the front hall as he was leaving.

"What do you mean? You've been with him all day."

"That's why I asked. He looks tired. And he seems . . . I don't know, worried, tense."

"I suppose he is," she said impatiently. "Most people are these days."

"There are more important things than holding on to a railroad, Clemmie."

She handed him his hat. "I wouldn't expect you to understand, Porter."

He looked at her gravely, almost as if he were sorry for her. "And I guess I shouldn't have expected you to."

Things did get worse, as Tom had predicted, although not for the A & W. The railroad did not pay any dividends during the first three quarters of 1930, but it was still solvent. Tom saw to that. He worked untiringly all that winter and summer. Tom had always thought of his days in college and the early years with Elias as arduous, but they'd been nothing compared to the time and effort he was putting in now. He'd been away at least half of the time for the last nine months and when he was in New York, he never left his office before nine or ten. More often, he was there till after midnight. It seemed to him that all he saw of Lizzy these days was a glimpse of a child on her way to school. He saw Clemmie almost as infrequently. It was an impossible situation, but a necessary one. He didn't think about it much. He didn't have time to. Until that night in Pittsburgh.

He'd been with the steel men all day and they'd finally worked out a compromise on rates, more than they could afford, the men said, less than he could break even at, Tom countered. It was after ten when he got back to his hotel. He gave the bellboy a two-dollar bill and sent him out for some whiskey. Tom knew he was drinking too much, but if he didn't drink he wouldn't sleep. His exhaustion lowered his defenses enough for him to give himself over to worry and depression but not enough for him to give himself over to sleep.

It was some of the worst whiskey he'd ever tasted, but after the first drink it didn't matter. It never did. "Medicinal," Tom said to the empty room. It seemed to him he was always talking to empty rooms these days. He poured himself another drink and downed it in a single gulp. It had less taste that way. He thought of putting in a call to Clemmie, then decided against it. It was too late to talk to Lizzy and midnight telephone conversations with Clemmie were rarely a success, especially if he'd had a few drinks. The alcohol would send him looking for something, but he could never find it in those cool talks. He had two more drinks and fell asleep in his shirt and trousers a little after one.

Tom awakened with a start. He could hear his own breathing, sharp and shallow in the silent room. His body was covered with a film of perspiration, but he was shivering as if in a terrible chill. And there was a pain in his chest. He was terrified.

Easy, he told himself. Just take it easy. He took several deep breaths and tried to relax his body. The pain lessened, but now fear sat on his chest like a great lead object, weighing him down, holding him to the bed.

Moving only his arm, he fumbled around on the night table until he found his cigarettes and lighter. He inhaled deeply two or three times and could feel the lead weight beginning to dissolve in the smoke.

Just a nightmare, he told himself, though he couldn't remember dreaming of anything. He sat up and swung his legs over the side of the bed. Nothing was wrong. There was no dizziness, no pain. He crossed the room to the table where he'd left the bottle of whiskey. It was still a third full and he began to pour himself another drink. He slammed the glass down suddenly, spilling the whiskey on the cheap wood table.

"A nightmare," he said aloud. "Like hell it was a nightmare." He crossed the room to the mirror over the bureau. His eyes looked out at him from deep sockets. You're mortal, he told himself silently. You're going to die.

"Hell, so is everybody," he answered aloud.

But not without living, the silent voice told him.

Tom took care of a few remaining matters the next morning and finished up in time to have the business car added to the Pittsburgh Day Express. It made more sense to travel overnight and arrive in New York in the morning, but he was impatient to see Clemmie. And he could work on the train, where there would be no interruptions.

He arrived at the Pennsylvania Station a little after seven that evening and went straight to the house. Clemmie was surprised to see him. She had assumed he'd go to his office first and hadn't expected him for dinner.

When she heard his voice in the hall, she went out to meet him, lingered there giving James instructions about dinner, then followed him into the rear drawing room. It was smaller and more intimate than the large front one they used for guests.

"I told James to bring the cocktails in here," she said. "Or would you rather go upstairs first?"

She meant, he knew, did he want to go upstairs to bathe and change, but the words could so easily have held a different meaning. There had been a time just after they were married when they might have. He'd been away for a week and it would have been logical for him to go upstairs, not to his room, but to their room, for her to follow him. It would have been logical after a week's separation for him to want not a drink or dinner, but Clemmie, his wife. And it would have been logical for her to want him in return. It would have been logical for them to go upstairs and make love, urgently, impatiently, not caring that he was tired and disheveled from the journey or that she hadn't expected him, or about any of the other proper, conventional excuses that kept people from making love when they wanted to. It would have been logical if the times or their marriage or they themselves had been different, but they weren't and he hadn't touched Clemmie in almost a year, not since months before that night they'd agreed to go on together to save the railroad.

"I'll have a drink with you first," he said. He'd promised himself last night that he'd cut down, but one cocktail before dinner couldn't hurt. And he felt he needed it now. If he were going to talk to Clemmie, he needed it.

"You look tired," she said automatically. It was what she always said these days. "I hope the trip was worth it."

"We reached an agreement." Tom turned to the butler. "You can leave the things, James. I'll mix the drinks." He did so in silence, wondering how to begin. "It's not working," he blurted out as he handed her a drink.

"What do you mean?" There was no mistaking the startled look on Clemmie's face. It infuriated him.

"I don't mean the railroad." He watched the relief spread over her features and relax them. "I mean us." There was no expression now. Her face was a mask.

"We agreed we'd forget about ourselves and concentrate on saving the railroad," he went on.

386

"Is that what we agreed?" It was not exactly what she'd meant that night in his office, but he'd forced her into making it sound that way. Had he expected her to come to him begging for his return? Well, perhaps she had done just that, but she'd been able to blame it on the railroad's needs rather than her own.

If Tom heard the sarcasm in her voice, he pretended not to. "I'm going back on my word, Clemmie. I can't forget myself, and I can't forget you. I'd rather have a marriage than a railroad. I'd rather have you than anything. I still love you." His voice was hoarse, as if the words were painful to him. "In spite of everything."

She heard the words with a shock. If only he'd said them at any time during the last year. If only he'd said them that night she'd gone to his office and asked him to come back—or a hundred other nights since then. If only he'd said them when she could believe that he meant them, that he was not merely pretending to care for her in order to keep her from knowing how much he cared for someone else. And she was sure now, after the previous night, after her meeting with Vanessa Hodges, that Tom cared very much for someone else.

Vanessa Hodges. For years now Clemmie had hated the very sound of her name, but it had been only a name, the disembodied sound of her own betrayal. Last night the name had become a woman, a beautiful, vital woman who had taken Tom from her.

Clemmie hadn't planned to go to last night's charity ball at the St. Regis. Everyone was cutting back these days, supporting only their favorite causes, but Gwen Byer had refused to take no for an answer. Without Clemmie's support, she'd insisted, the new hospital wing would never be built. Clemmie had decided it was easier to buy the ticket and attend the ball than to withstand Gwen's daily assaults. At least she'd thought it would be easier until she was introduced to Vanessa Hodges.

Hollis Byer had brought them together saying that Mrs. Hodges had asked to meet her. The nerve of the

girl, Clemmie thought, but she would not give her the
satisfaction of turning away. She would not give Vanessa
Hodges the satisfaction of knowing how she'd been hurt.

"I met your husband in Chicago," Vanessa said.
"Some years ago," she added, and smiled. There was
no mistaking her meaning. Clemmie was sure of it. The
girl said they'd met a few years ago—what else could
she say under the circumstances?—but the implication
was that they still saw each other. And she was flaunting
the fact.

Clemmie wanted to reach out and slap the beautiful,
fine-featured face. "Did you?" she asked coolly, as if
Tom and his activities held little interest for her. Then
the music started and two men appeared at Vanessa's
side. She moved off in the arms of one of them, and
Clemmie couldn't help noticing that the girl had more
than beauty. She had an animal grace that many men,
Clemmie suspected, would find exciting. Certainly Tom
did.

Clemmie slept little that night. She kept remembering
the smug look on Vanessa Hodges' face when she'd
mentioned Tom's name and the seductiveness of her
movements as she danced off with another man. Now
she understood why their arrangement was so painless
to Tom, why he didn't miss her as she did him, although she'd never admit as much. Tom didn't need
her because he had Vanessa Hodges. And it was so
simple to arrange, with all his traveling. Her here in
New York. Vanessa in Chicago. Clemmie wondered if
there had been someone last night in Pittsburgh. Was
that why Tom looked so tired, not because of work,
but because of some cheap woman he'd found for the
night? No, that was not like Tom. He had no taste for
cheapness. Indeed, Vanessa Hodges had turned out to
be a very expensive girl. She'd cost them the loan from
Jason Wylie and possibly a good deal more that Tom
had never mentioned.

Clemmie looked across the sitting room at him now.

He still loved her, he said. In spite of everything, he said.

"You mean in spite of Vanessa Hodges."

Tom rubbed his eyes as if the exhaustion were too much for him. "How long are you going to go on holding that against me, Clemmie?"

"How long are you going to go on seeing her?"

"I haven't seen her in years. I told you I wouldn't see her again, and I haven't."

"Well, I have." He didn't look tired now. He was suddenly alert. Getting ready to defend himself, Clemmie thought. "She was at the hospital ball last night."

"I don't see what that has to do with me."

"Apparently everything about you has to do with Mrs. Hodges. Even your wife. She asked to meet me. Perhaps she meant to be flattering, Tom, but I think your mistress's curiosity is in rather poor taste."

For the first time in all the years since he'd seen her, Tom felt a surge of hatred for Vanessa as well as himself. "What did she say?" he asked warily.

"I thought you might be interested. Only that she knew you. She didn't mention your affair. Even Mrs. Hodges is too discreet for that."

"We're not having an affair, Clemmie. You know that."

"How would I know that?" she said sharply. "I wouldn't have known about it the first time if Jason Wylie hadn't told me, and now I imagine the two of you have enough sense to keep it from her father as well as your wife." Clemmie put her cocktail glass down on the table and stood. "And I am your wife, Tom. I have no intention of changing that for the moment. I need you. Not just your stocks, but you," she said coolly. "You've done a superb job with the railroad this year. Even Adam couldn't have done as well."

The implication was clear. It stuck Tom like a sharp blow. If Adam had been able to do as well, she wouldn't need him. That's all he was to Clemmie, all he'd ever been. The railroad.

After Clemmie left the room, Tom crossed to the cocktail wagon. The pitcher of martinis he'd mixed was still half full. One cocktail before dinner, he'd told himself. So much for resolutions, he thought as he refilled his glass. So much for all last night's resolution. He'd planned to start over with Clemmie, but there was no starting over because Clemmie didn't change. She didn't forgive, and she didn't change.

He could leave her, of course, but for what? For whom? He didn't want Vanessa. Oh, he'd want her if he saw her, he supposed, just as he had wanted that nameless, faceless girl he'd taken to his hotel room in Chicago several weeks ago and the two or three others who had done nothing more than punctuate his loneliness over the last year, but he didn't love Vanessa Hodges. He loved Clemmie. Maybe it was only a vestige of his youthful longing. Maybe it was only the memory of the few good moments they had shared. Whatever it was, there was no point in trying to define or explain it. It was not something logical and manageable, something that could be understood like his ambition or the success he'd fought for. It was something without reason or sense or even sanity. His love for Clemmie had become part of him. If he could rid himself of her as he had that summer before the crash, he could not rid himself of his love for her. Last night he'd promised himself he wouldn't go on this way, but he knew as he downed the second martini and poured himself another, that he would go on this way as long as Clemmie let him. And the sound of the key to Clemmie's door being turned later that night, a sound he'd never heard before in all their nights of arguing, did nothing to undermine that knowledge.

Tom didn't arrive at his office until after nine the next morning. In terms of the hours he'd been keeping for the last year, he was at least an hour late.

"Mr. Wilder has been in to see you twice," his secretary said as he came through her small outer office.

"He asked me to let him know as soon as you arrived."

"Well, I've arrived, Miss Blatty, and you can tell Mr. Wilder I'm ready whenever he is."

"Yes, Mr. Hendreich," she said quickly, but her eyes followed him into his office, and she did not turn back to her desk until he'd closed the door behind him. Lila Blatty was plain, with asymmetrical features and an unremarkable if somewhat nervous manner. She would have been a perfect mouse of a woman if she had not been twenty-five pounds too heavy to be called anything so diminutive. But Miss Blatty had a secret life. From eight-thirty till five-thirty five days a week, eight-thirty till one on Saturdays, she was an engine of efficiency. After hours she was a wild romantic. Lila Blatty was thirty-seven years old and had never been kissed by a man, but in her after-hours fantasies she reached heights of passion with Thomas Hendreich that most of her married friends never dreamed of. Tom, of course, had no inkling of Miss Blatty's other nature. He knew only that she was admirably efficient as a secretary and blessedly undistracting as a woman.

" 'Morning, Miss Blatty," Adam said as he crossed her office toward Tom's a few minutes after she'd called him. "I see the boss is finally in." Miss Blatty said nothing. She would protect Tom against intruders but she would not defend him against his colleagues. She had enough sense to know that would only make her the laughingstock of the office.

"I won't ask what's up," Tom said as Adam took the chair across from him, "because I know it's trouble. That's all it ever is these days."

"It's the brotherhood. The word went out last week that we were cutting crews on all freight runs, and now they're squawking."

"What did you expect?" They'd been over the problem at length. Tom hadn't wanted to lay off men, but Adam kept coming back to the figures, the bottom line he called it.

"Would you rather lay off a few men or have the

whole line go under?" Adam had asked more than once. It was not, of course, a question to which he expected an answer.

"I knew they'd make a fuss," Adam said, "but I was hoping we'd get by without a strike."

Tom had been looking over the mail Miss Blatty had arranged on his desk while they spoke, and now he raised his eyes to Adam's quickly. "Are they hinting at a strike or threatening one?"

"Threatening. Full crews reinstated by midnight Thursday or they go out."

"Goddammit."

"We can keep the trains running, at least for a while, with supervisory people."

"I wish to hell we could keep them on somehow."

"There's no way, Tom. You know that. We're barely breaking even now."

"Those men we let go aren't going to be breaking even at all. They'll be lucky if they can get their hands on an apple to sell."

Adam kept his eyes on the floor and allowed Tom to talk himself out. The argument was familiar by now, but Tom never tired of going over it. It was, Adam thought, the last vestige of his background. Tom Hendreich had come a long way. The penniless son of an immigrant miner was now a power in the world of transportation, industry, and finance, and no one knew that better than Adam. There were few traces of the boy that Tom had been. Neither his speech, nor his manner, nor the hundreds of small things that might have given away a man like Tom remained from his past. Tom's quickness and Clemmie's ambition had seen to that. And yet every so often Adam would see Tom stray from a hard-nosed business problem to the murky questions of how the workers would live or eat or clothe their children. The first few times it had happened, Adam had tried to reason with Tom. Now he merely let him talk himself out. The forces that had conditioned him to care for the workers had also driven him to care for himself. Tom would cut the crews and keep the trains running during the strike, but he would have to wrestle with his conscience before he did.

"I hear there's going to be a strike," Clemmie said when Tom arrived home that night.

He never knew how she got her information so quickly. Did she hound Adam, pump Miss Blatty? He knew it rarely came from him. He disliked discussing railroad business with Clemmie, almost as much as she enjoyed it. "Midnight Thursday everything stops."

"You're not going to let them stop!"

"No, we're going to try to keep them running with supervisory people."

"That ought to teach them."

"I don't want to teach them, Clemmie, I only want to keep the trains running."

"Well, they ought to be taught a lesson," she said indignantly. "How do they expect us to keep our heads above water while they're saddling us with enormous crews?"

He looked around the sitting room. Clemmie hadn't bought anything for the house since the crash, but the combination of what had been there when they arrived and what she'd added in the first year was splendid, more splendid than he'd ever dreamed. "I imagine they have more on their minds than whether we keep our heads above water, as you put it, or keep the railroad solvent."

"Well, I can't be bothered by what they think."

"You know, Clemmie, you should have been a Vanderbilt rather than a Wilder." The words were out before he remembered that Whit Morris was in fact Whitmore Vanderbilt Morris, and when he saw the look of alarm that flickered in Clemmie's eyes he went on quickly. 'The public be damned,' old Billy Vanderbilt said. I don't suppose that's a far cry from the workers be damned."

The men went out at midnight on Thursday, but the

trains, at least the passenger trains, were still running quite comfortably and efficiently, Porter Lowry reported when he arrived that Friday afternoon. Porter always stayed with Clemmie and Tom when he came to New York.

Clemmie had a few people in for dinner and afterward they went to the Music Box to see *Once in a Lifetime*. Porter laughed a good deal. "It's a shame Tom couldn't make it," he said to Clemmie afterward. "I think it would have done him good."

"He promised to meet us later," Clemmie said, but when they arrived at the speakeasy on Fifty-fourth Street Tom was not there and by the time they left he still had not arrived.

Tom left the house before either Clemmie or Porter had come down on Saturday morning and he returned a little before four to report the second day of the strike had gone smoothly. "Where's Lizzy? I promised to take her riding in the park."

Clemie looked at her watch. "Porter took Lizzy out after lunch. They should be back any minute."

Tom looked at his own pocket watch as if she must be mistaken. When he saw she was not, he sat heavily in the chair opposite hers. "Well, I'll take her tomorrow. I'll be sure to get home in time tomorrow. After all, it's Sunday."

They sat in silence for a while, Clemmie leafing through a magazine, Tom staring into the fire. Once he got up to put another log on, but said nothing. Finally they heard the excited sounds of Lizzy's voice in the front hall telling James what a wonderful ride they'd had and how Uncle Porter had taken her for tea afterward. She was still chattering when she reached the door of the small back sitting room, but when she saw her father, she stopped. Tom thought the small face looked at him reproachfully.

"I'm sorry I got held up, Lizzy, but we'll go for a ride tomorrow. I promise." The child said nothing.

"Run along now, Lizzy," Clemmie said, "and tell

Miss Simmons you're to have your bath before dinner. If, in fact, you can eat any dinner after Uncle Porter's tea."

Lizzy left the room with what Tom could only describe as considerable dignity for a seven-year-old. "I apologize to you too, Porter," he said when the child was out of hearing. "You must have better things to do on a weekend in New York than take Lizzy riding."

"Not at all," Porter answered. "I got my fill of night life last night—though I'm sure Clemmie has something planned for tonight—and I enjoy being with Lizzy. If you don't mind my saying so, Clemmie, she's more interesting, or at least more refreshing than that woman on my right last night. What was her name? Stage?"

"Paige, Porter. Sally Paige. And she's really a perfectly nice woman except when she's between husbands as she is now. That's why I put her next to you."

"Thank you, but no thank you. I prefer Lizzy."

"Well, Porter, can I offer you a drink?" Tom asked. "Or did you stuff yourself on cream puffs, too?"

Porter started to say that he'd love a drink, but there was a strange sound from outside the house and he stopped to listen to it. So did Tom and Clemmie. At first it sounded like the rumbling of traffic on Fifth Avenue, but there was a more noticeable rhythm to it. It was growing louder and seemed to be getting closer and soon it was recognizable as the sound of men's voices. They were chanting something, and although the words were unintelligible the anger in their voices was unmistakable. Clemmie, who had been about to ring for James, dropped the bell cord and turned to the window. It faced the side street, but afforded a partial view of Fifth Avenue, and when she held the draperies aside, she saw an army of men marching up the broad avenue, chanting as they marched. Some of them were carrying signs, others torches though it was barely dark, but most were simply marching and chanting. She felt Tom and Porter behind her, and just had time to read one of the signs—A & W UNFAIR—before Tom pushed her away from the window.

"Get back," he barked at her. "Go tell Miss Simmons to keep Lizzy in the nursery. Don't let her come to the front of the house under any circumstances."

Tom had never spoken to her so abruptly and she followed his orders without thinking. When she came downstairs again he and Porter had moved to the front drawing room and each of them was standing at a window holding the draperies back only an inch.

"I think you ought to call the police," Porter said.

"The amazing thing is that the police let them get this far. They couldn't have come up Fifth Avenue," Tom answered.

"What does it matter how they came?" There was more anger than fear in Clemmie's voice. "Porter's right. Call the police."

"All that will do is turn an angry mob into a violent one," Tom said.

The chants had become intelligible now. They were calling for Tom. Against the sound of his name being repeated over and over was the counterpoint of individual shouts.

"We know you're in there."

"Come on out, you yellow bastard."

"Come on out or we'll come in and get you."

"If you don't call the police, I'm going to." Clemmie started out of the room, but the sound of glass shattering stopped her. A rock had come through the window and knocked over the Chinese lamp on the end table. Before she could react, Tom was pushing past her. "Stay away from the window," he shouted angrily over his shoulder. "And the telephone."

"Where are you going?" she screamed after him, but the door had already closed behind him.

At first the sight of Tom on the steps before the massive grille door only enraged the crowd. The insults and threats grew louder. Tom did not try to shout above them. He merely stood there with his back to the splendid limestone façade, facing down a couple of hundred enraged men. His face was impassive, but he could feel his heart racing and he knew he was trembling. He had never feared a single man, or even two or three, but this mob was different, and it wasn't only a matter of numbers. They weren't two hundred men, they were a single seething animal, an angry unthinking beast that might do anything if provoked. Tom knew that and feared it, but he continued to stand there without movement or expression, and gradually the noise began to die, until it was nothing more than an occasional angry shout from here and there in the crowd. The noise had died, but Tom could still feel the anger of the crowd, sense the menace that might explode into thoughtless unchecked violence at a single wrong word or even an arrogant look.

"I guess I know why you're here," he said finally.

"Damn right."

"Sure as hell do."

The irate answers came to him from different corners of the crowd.

"And I guess I know what you want."

"Everybody works or nobody works," shouted an older man in the front of the pack.

Tom knew the man from the old days in Scranton. He was a good brakeman, but something of a troublemaker. He'd been with the railroad for twenty years and Tom was sure he hadn't been let go. Then, a true godsend, the man's name came to him. "You haven't been laid off, Kronig."

The man looked a little shamefaced at being addressed by name in front of the others. "I ain't but others has. Everybody works or nobody works," he repeated, and others took up the chant. When it died Tom spoke again.

"If everybody works today nobody will work tomorrow."

"Liar."

"Bastard."

"It ain't your kids that's starving."

For the first time Tom held up his hand as if to silence them. "We're doing our best to let only men without families go."

"So you starve alone without a wife and kids," a young man near Tom shouted, and grim laughter rippled through the mob.

"And it's only a temporary measure."

"That's what they always say," the man named Kronig shouted.

"I don't know what they always say, but you have my word it's true. The brotherhood leaders have seen the figures. They will go on seeing them. As soon as we can afford to reinstate full freight crews, we will."

There was angry muttering at this, but no shouted arguments. Tom pressed ahead. "I've never lied to you or your brotherhood before, and I'm not lying now. Full crews . . ." Tom began, but his words were drowned out not by the shouts of the men but the sound of sirens in the distance. Tom continued to talk but the noise grew louder, shrieking toward them up Fifth Avenue. Suddenly police cars were driving into their midst and men on horseback came thundering out of the side street, wielding clubs wildly in all directions. Tom saw Konig fall under a clubbing, then the man next to him went down. All around him men were scuffling with their fists and clubs and the signs they'd carried. Futilely, absurdly, he called for the police to stop, but no one was listening to him. Then he was no longer shouting or watching the mass of fighting men, because one had lunged at him and another followed and he felt a fist against his jaw and another against his nose. He tried to fight back but he was being pulled and pushed and pummeled by too many hands, and he felt himself going down on the front steps, felt a heavy boot drive into his side, and then Porter was fighting toward him and a policeman was charging through, his club swinging against the men, driving them back, and Porter and James were helping him back into the house.

They took him to the library because Porter didn't want Tom to climb the stairs until he'd had a chance to look at him, and the small elevator had never worked as smoothly as it might.

"You never should have gone out there," Clemmie kept repeating, as if her words could prevent Tom's beating after the fact.

"I'm all right, really I am," Tom said, although he could taste the blood in his mouth as he spoke and his side was throbbing. "Everyone's making a fuss about nothing."

"Nothing! Look at you," Clemmie almost shrieked.

"That's enough, Clemmie," Porter said sharply. Then he sent her off to speak to the police officer and told James to bring hot water and soap and any antiseptic they might have in the house.

"It really is nothing," Tom repeated when he was alone with Porter. "I was in worse fights as a kid. And took a worse beating."

"I daresay you did—as a kid." Porter had made Tom take off his jacket and shirt and now his hands were moving expertly over his ribs. "Well, nothing's broken. We have that much to be thankful for."

"I could have told you that."

"Yes, but from you it would have been bravado. From me it's medical expertise." James entered with the things Porter had requested and he began working at Tom's face. "Well, I guess you're right. A nasty cut near your eye—fortunately it didn't come closer—but nothing serious."

"Clemmie called the police, didn't she?" Tom asked.

Porter pretended to be concentrating on the cut at Tom's temple and said nothing.

"You're right, Porter. I shouldn't have asked you. This is between Clemmie and me. It has nothing to do with you."

"She only did what she thought was right. She was worried about you." Tom raised his eyebrow, but Porter was insistent. "She was, Tom, whether you believe it or not. She may have acted on impulse, but it was an impulse that she believed was right."

"She always does. Believe she's right, I mean."

Porter stepped back. "You can get dressed now. The patient will live, and I prescribe a hot tub and a stiff brandy."

Clemmie called the Dabneys and told them they could not dine, and she and Tom and Porter had a quiet dinner at home.

"What's going to happen now?" Clemmie asked at dinner.

"The strike will go on. And the trains will keep running," Tom said. He did not want to mention the men who'd been jailed or the fact that now there would be a bitterness to the negotiations, a hostility on the part of both labor and management, that had been absent before. He did not want to mention any of it to Clemmie.

If Clemmie felt the unspoken accusation, she did not answer it. She was, in fact, unusually quiet all evening. A little after ten she stood and said she was going to bed. "You ought to get some rest too, Tom."

Porter heard the abrupt way she spoke and, knowing Clemmie, wondered if the words were an invitation to her husband, but the thought did not even occur to Tom. She left the two of them before the fire in the small drawing room. There was a quarter of an inch of amber in the bottom of Tom's brandy glass. He drained it, then got up and returned with the bottle, which he put on the table between them. Porter said nothing. He'd ceased being a doctor as soon as he'd ascertained that Tom had not been seriously hurt, and it was not friend's place to comment on drinking habits.

Tom had two more brandies, but they did not make him better company. His conversation, Porter thought, was hesitant and distracted, as if he were thinking of something else, something he didn't want to talk about.

"I guess I'll call it a night," Porter said finally.

Tom merely mumbled and reached for the brandy

bottle. He barely noticed that Porter had left the room. His mind was a kaleidoscope turning the vivid images of the afternoon into fainter ones from a long time ago. He saw the crowd pressing toward him on the sidewalk like an ominous wave surging up the beach and men falling before police on horseback, but they weren't the men who'd fallen this afternoon or the police who'd supposedly come to his rescue. They were larger than those because they were seen through the eyes of a ten-year-old boy.

His mother had told him not to go near the mine that day, or any day while the strike lasted, but he'd been drawn there by a sense of imminent drama. The miners, Tom knew from the snatches of conversation he heard on the street and the way the other boys in school talked, were getting angrier, and suppers were getting smaller—they never had meat anymore—and Billy Mausur said his father swore something had to break soon. Tom could still see the police on horseback storming into the crowd of miners, see the men trying to scatter, running desperately and uselessly in front of the horses. He saw Billy Mausur's father trampled beneath the hoofs of a huge chestnut animal and felt a man's hands pushing him, dragging him, heard a man's voice screaming at him in German to run faster, faster.

He and his father hadn't stopped running till they had reached their own house and then, gasping for breath, his father had pushed him inside and bolted the door behind them. His mother had neither screamed nor cried, but simply stood there in silence listening to his father's terse account of what had happened. When she'd heard the whole story, she turned to Tom, and he knew he was in for something bad.

"I told you not to go to the mines, Thomas."

Tom stood with his eyes on the floor, holding his breath in anticipation. How bad would the punishment be?

"Leave him alone," his father said in German. "It's better that he saw."

He'd seen, all right, Tom thought. He'd seen it then and he'd seen it this afternoon, but he'd seen it from a different side. That afternoon the police had chased the German miner and his scruffy kid. This afternoon the police had protected Mr. Thomas Hendreich of the A & W.

He poured himself another brandy. There had been no need to call the police. He had been winning them over. He was sure of it. Another five minutes and they would have dispersed. He took a long swallow of the drink and felt the anger at Clemmie turning to rage at himself. She'd been a damn fool to call the police, but what kind of a man was he that he couldn't keep his wife from acting like a damn fool?

No man at all, came the answer. Only an overbred lap dog, an emasculated servant. Why else did he stand by when his wife went flying with Max Clinton or kissed that goddamn Morris? Well, he hadn't stood by then, but he hadn't done anything either. Clemmie meddled with the railroad and toyed with whomever she chose and manipulated him. Like that business about Vanessa. She knew damn well he wasn't seeing Vanessa, but it was a convenient excuse. An excuse for what? To put him in the wrong, to get her own way, to lock her goddamn door.

He poured himself another brandy, downed it, and refilled the glass. Well, she wouldn't get away with it. Not anymore. He was going to have it out with Clemmie and he was going to have it out now. He drained his glass and stood, then he was moving up the stairs too quickly to realize how unsteady he was. He started to knock at her door, then dropped his hand. To hell with manners, he told himself, and pushed it open roughly.

She was sitting up in one of the twin beds reading. The other bed had not been turned down. The sight of the bed that should have been his, pristine under the blue satin cover, infuriated him.

"I've had enough!" he slurred.

Clemmie heard his speech and saw the way he stood swaying at the end of her bed. "I should say you have. Go to sleep, Tom. You're drunk and upset and you'd better sleep it off."

She got out of her bed, walked around to the other one, and began to turn down the spread. She kept her back to him and her voice was casual. "You might as well stay here. I doubt you can make it to your own room."

"Goddammit, Clemmie"—his hand was rough on her arm as he turned her to him—"don't patronize me."

"You're hurting me," she said more calmly than she felt.

"Hurting you! It hurts you just to have me touch you. But not Whit Morris. You don't mind Morris touching you, do you?"

She started to turn away, but he held her arm tightly. First he was shaking her in fury, then suddenly he was pulling her to him and his mouth was rough on hers. She was not struggling but in his impatient rage he seemed not to notice. He was tugging at the straps to her nightdress avidly, blindly, then she heard the sound of cloth tearing, and felt his hands hot and urgent on her breasts.

"Tom." She was not sure whether it was a protest or a cry of excitement, but he did not hear. He pulled her down on the bed and held her to him with one hand while the other fumbled at his belt. They were a tangled mass of clothing and limbs, and she felt the buttons of his shirt pressing into her skin. His hands fought furiously through the yards of satin that formed the skirt of her nightdress and then she felt them rough against her thighs. He entered her abruptly and his body was moving angrily, savagely against hers, and she felt her own responding as if it had no will beyond this. Finally, finally, finally. The words thundered in her head, a frenzied echo of their movements, and there was no thought that he was drunk or angry or violent, but only that he wanted her again, wanted her with a fierceness that broke the dam of his reserve and threatened to drown them both in the flood of long-denied passion.

Clemmie slept well that night. She awakened only once and heard Tom's heavy breathing in the next bed. Between the alcohol and the beating he was going to feel just awful tomorrow. Clemmie smiled to herself in the darkness, but it was not an unkind smile. She decided she'd be very gentle with Tom the next day.

She slept later than she'd expected to, and when she awakened the first thing she noticed was that the other bed was empty. She hadn't expected Tom to go to his office after last night, but she should have known he would.

The bells from the church a few blocks away chimed, and she looked at the small gilt clock on the night table. Eleven. She'd ring for breakfast first, then call the office and insist Tom come home for lunch. Better yet, she'd have the car brought around and take Lizzy down to get him. Lizzy loved to go to Tom's office, and Porter wouldn't mind being left alone for a while. He was a self-sufficient houseguest, especially when there were plenty of Sunday papers.

When the maid entered with her breakfast tray fifteen minutes later, there was a long white envelope on it. Someone must have delivered something. There was no mail today.

"Mr. Hendreich left this for you, ma'am," the girl said.

Tom's apology was brief and businesslike. "It," as he put it, would never have happened if he hadn't been drinking. "It" would not happen again. He had planned to go to Chicago later in the week, but he was leaving this afternoon instead. He would be back in a few days. He hoped by that time she would have forgiven him and they might go on as they had before.

Clemmie crumpled the letter and hurled it across the room. It bounced off the wall and fell to the carpet where it lay like a mangled dove in the bright sunshine filtering through the windows.

Chapter 12

By THE SPRING of 1931 a good many small railroads were in trouble. The downward spiral of failing banks and failing businesses led to reduced freight revenue. There was not enough business to keep many of the small lines healthy, but there was still enough freight—especially coal—to keep them alive, if terminally ill. The local lines struggled on, reducing service, cutting rates, and watching the value of their stocks plummet. It was the perfect time, Clemmie pointed out to Tom and Adam, who'd come to lunch one Saturday, to consolidate the A & W's holdings in the Tidewater and Western. Five years ago when the economy was thriving and the Tidewater and Western couldn't get the coal east to Norfolk and Newport News fast enough, they'd paid dearly for several thousand shares of the small Virginia line. Now the shares were valued at less than a fifth of what they'd paid, but the railroad was still hauling coal, Clemmie pointed out.

Tom was surprised. He'd been sure Clemmie's next project would be electrification. The Pennsylvania was electrifying its entire New York–Washington run. Tom had been toying with the idea himself. Electrification was an expensive proposition, but in some ways the time was ripe for expensive propositions. Revenues were down, but so were labor and material. On the other hand, Tom wasn't sure the A & W ought to electrify at all, at least outside the cities. The Pennsy's New York–Washington run was a high-speed, highly urbanized one. The Central, for its part, had electrified nothing but a few commuter lines since it went underground during the first decade of the century and transformed Park Avenue above Forty-second Street from a noisy, filthy railroad yard into a fashionable residential district.

Tom had considered the problem at length and finally decided to hold off for a while, to see just how much worse things were going to get. Certainly they weren't going to get much better for a long time. He'd made his decision, but it did not necessarily follow that Clemmie would accept it. Tom had been prepared for a battle over electrification; he hadn't expected a word about the Tidewater and Western. Clemmie had never shown much interest in the mines or in any of the other investments that consumed so much of his time, but she was showing interest in the Tidewater and Western now and he had to admit her idea was a good one. Consolidating their interests there made sense, although he'd never expected Clemmie to think so.

"It's not a bad idea," Tom admitted.

"It's a good idea," Adam agreed. "But I doubt we've got the patent on it. The Baltimore and Ohio and the Central both own blocs of Tidewater and Western stock, larger blocs than the A & W does."

"We don't have to be the only ones with the idea," Clemmie said. "All we have to do is get there first. I'm planning to leave for Richmond the day after tomorrow."

Adam was watching his brother-in-law carefully. He was fairly sure the news came as a surprise to Tom just as it did to him.

"It's a good idea," Tom said coolly, "but I think Adam and I can handle it from here, Clemmie."

"I'm sure you can," she answered easily, "but I can

help. Who owns the controlling interest in the Tide-water?" she went on quickly.

"Middleton Sharp, of course," Tom said.

"That's right. And I went to school with Lydia Hennings before she was Mrs. Middleton Sharp."

"I didn't know you'd stayed at Miss Plymouth's long enough to make friends," Adam joked.

"I resent that. If you remember I wasn't fired from Miss Plymouth's until my third year."

The expression still struck Tom as peculiar. Men were fired from jobs. Young girls were not fired from finishing school. But apparently in his wife's world they were.

"The point is," Clemmie continued, "I know Lydia and I've even met her husband, and that may just be more than anyone at the B & O or the Central has done. I'll turn up in Richmond on some pretense or other and simply give Lydia a call." She looked at Tom. His face was impassive. "I'll merely lay the groundwork. You'll take care of the stocks." Her voice was smooth as butter. "It's the fastest and most logical way to do it. Why, I bet I can get things done during a weekend in Richmond that would take months in your office."

The words struck Tom as familiar. *I can get things done on a Long Island house party that would take months in your office.* And she had, of course. Clemmie had accomplished a great deal that afternoon she'd gone up in Max Clinton's plane. She'd won Trans-American for the A & W and planted the first seeds of suspicion in their marriage.

"I don't suppose," Tom said after Adam had left, "that you'd consider not going." He'd almost said "not going simply because your husband asked you not to," but he'd stopped just in time. He knew how his voice would have sounded, bitter and begging.

"Not unless there's a good reason to prevent my going."

There were a dozen reasons but Tom produced only one, and it was the least convincing to Clemmie. "Because I prefer to do these things through normal channels."

"Your normal channels aren't necessarily everyone's normal channels, Tom." She stopped abruptly.

"Of course. I'm not a member of the old boys' club."

"All I meant was that it's silly not to take advantage of these old friendships."

"Or new ones. Like Max Clinton that time. I'm assuming you never went to school with Clinton."

The fact that he'd still bring that up, bring it up without reason or justification after all these years, infuriated her. "I've heard enough about Max Clinton. Nothing ever happened with him—"

"So you say."

"—but if it had, at least I'd have won something for the railroad, which is more than you did with Vanessa Hodges!" Clemmie slammed out of the room before he could answer, and in fact Tom had no answer. They'd both said all they could about Vanessa and Clinton and a good many other subjects. They'd both said entirely too much—and perhaps not enough—but for the next thirty-six hours until Clemmie left for Richmond, they exchanged no words at all.

Lydia Sharp said she was delighted to hear from Clemmie. She said she never would have forgive Clemmie if she'd come through Richmond without calling. There had been Christmas cards, of course, but how long had it been now? Since that time they'd run into each other on Fifth Avenue and that must have been five years ago. Well, they had a lot of catching up to do, and Lydia insisted they begin immediately. They were having a few people to dine that night. Wouldn't Clemmie join them? Clemmie said she'd love to.

Both the Hennings and the Sharps went back a long way in Virginia, and as Clemmie drove up in the Sharp car that had been sent for her, she felt as if she were moving back into the antebellum South. Magnolia and honeysuckle and fragrant blossoms of every color and description rioted around the broad front veranda. An elderly black man in livery shuffled down the stairs to hand her out of the car.

Although Clemmie hadn't seen Lydia for years and had met Middleton Sharp only once at a large ball, they made her feel as if she were the one guest they'd been waiting for, the one guest they'd really wanted to arrive this soft spring evening. There was something to be said for Southern hospitality, Clemmie decided, as Lydia led her from the broad entrance hall to a large drawing room that, despite the twenty guests in evening clothes, still seemed comfortable and rather horsy. The Tidewater might not be doing terribly well, but life at the Sharp home—or did they call it a plantation, she wondered—would go on as before.

Lydia had begun introducing Clemmie to a group of guests standing near the entrance to the room. Clemmie was cataloging names and smiling into faces she would never see again and murmuring appropriate platitudes when a figure at the far end of the room caught her eye. It was impossible. But it was true. Whit Morris stood talking to two men. He was turned a little away from her, but now, as if feeling her gaze like a hand on his shoulder, he glanced across the room and saw her. He looked startled, as if someone had played a joke on him that he didn't find amusing.

Of all the people, Whit thought. Of all the places. He'd got accustomed to seeing Clemmie in New York, and he'd learned to control himself, for the most part. There'd been that night on the Athertons' terrace, but he wasn't going to think about that. He was glad nothing had come of it. Or he'd thought he was glad until he turned and saw her standing across the room in a pale chiffon dress that was cut perfectly to reveal the slender body beneath it. He told himself as he crossed the room to Clemmie that he wished Alison had come down with him just this once, but he knew he was lying to himself.

"How are you, Clemmie?" Her hand felt cool in

his—as if she were completely unruffled by his presence, Whit warned himself.

"This is beginning to look like a stockholders' meeting," Middleton Sharp said. His eyes were canny, and a funny smile played around his mouth.

The Sharps moved off to greet arriving guests and Whit turned to her, closing the two of them into a corner, separated from the rest of the party.

"I never dreamed you'd be here," he said.

"Does that mean you wouldn't have come if you'd known?"

His tone was light, as if he were speaking to anyone. Was she really that unimportant to him? She hadn't thought so a year ago, after the accident, after the night on the Athertons' terrace, but the months that followed had taught her differently.

"I'm down here working," Whit continued. "It's foaling time. My breeding farm's fairly close by." He gave her a wicked smile. "But I imagine you're here on a different sort of business entirely. Something to do with the Tidewater and Western perhaps?"

"Not at all. I went to school with Lydia Sharp." As soon as Clemmie mentioned school, she remembered that Alison had been at Miss Plymouth's with them, but Alison was not here tonight. Was she back at the farm? Or was she still in New York?

"So your being here tonight has nothing to do with the Tidewater or the A & W's holdings in it?" Whit laughed.

"About as much as yours does with the Central's holdings, I imagine."

"It won't do you any good, Clemmie."

The words sounded like a warning in her head, but she fought to keep her tone casual. "You mean I'm too late?"

Whit laughed again. "It would serve you right if you were. We're not even yet for Max Clinton."

Clemmie made her voice ingenuous. "Why, Whit, I never knew you were interested in Trans-American."

410

"About as interested as you are in the Tidewater, but as I said, it won't do any good."

She was getting annoyed. "You're gloating, Whit."

"I only wish I were. You're not too late, Clemmie, only too optimistic. You see, Middleton Sharp has no intention of selling."

"Or at least you couldn't convince him to."

"But you think you'll be able to."

Clemmie's face became a mask of innocence. "Why, I never said that."

"But you were thinking it."

"Well, I might consider giving it a try."

He looked down at her and the dark eyes were serious as if he were making a decision about something, something more important to him than control of the Tidewater and Western. "Just how sure of yourself are you?" he asked finally.

She pretended to think for a moment. "Mildly confident."

"Well, Clemmie, in this part of the country when a man—or a woman—is mildly confident of something, he's generally willing to wager on it. The horse influence, I imagine. Are you willing to bet on Sharp? On whether you can convince him to sell?"

"Of course," she answered without a moment's hesitation.

"You haven't heard the stakes yet."

"As high as you like."

"I won't hold you to that, though I'd like to."

"You can."

"I'll bet you time, Clemmie, not money. Spend the weekend with me."

The words shocked, then delighted, and finally confused her. Spend the weekend with me. It might mean everything—or nothing.

He was still smiling down at her, but he no longer seemed amused. "You needn't worry. I said I wouldn't hold you to it."

"And I said you could."

"You're really that sure of yourself?"

Clemmie started for a moment. She'd forgotten what they were betting on. She'd even forgotten that they were betting. She'd forgotten everything but the fact that Whit still wanted her.

Later that night when Lydia Sharp said she'd have the car brought around to take Clemmie back to her hotel, Whit said there was no need to. "I'll be happy to see Mrs. Hendreich home."

"But it's at least forty-five minutes out of your way," Lydia said.

"No bother at all," Whit said, hurrying Clemmie into her evening cape before anyone could say more.

"It was only a joke," Whit said when they were alone in the car. "The bet, I mean."

"Was it?"

"You don't stand a chance with Sharp. He came right out and told me he wouldn't sell at any price. He said the shares may not be valued at much these days, but the Tidewater's still worth a lot to him."

"And you're too much a gentleman to bet on a sure thing."

"I'd like to think," Whit said, and his voice sounded strained, "I'm too much a gentleman to bet those stakes."

Clemmie took a deep breath. Her hands were clasped in her lap, because she knew if she did not clasp them Whit would see they were shaking. "Then I propose another bet. If I win"—she was careful to use the same words—"you'll spend the weekend with me. You can show me the countryside," she added.

He wondered if she'd really thought sightseeing was what he'd had in mind, but then he'd never known what Clemmie really thought about anything. He considered telling her what he'd meant. He considered pulling over to the side of the road and taking her in his arms and telling her it hadn't been only a bad joke, it had been no joke at all, telling her just how much he wanted her after all these years, after everything that had happened, after everything they'd done to each other. He considered it wildly, irrationally, desperately for a moment, then pushed the thought from his mind. "Tomorrow's Friday," he said as if the terrible joke were still going on. "That doesn't give you much time."

"I don't need much time." She tried to laugh, but she wondered if Whit could hear that it was a thin sound without the old bravado.

By two o'clock the next afternoon Clemmie knew Whit had been right. Sharp was determined not to part with his railroad. Middleton Sharp's intransigence was not, however, what was bothering her. Whit's words were. Whit's words and what he was going to do about them. Or what she was going to do.

It had been spring in New York, but it felt like summer in Virginia. Clemmie was hot and disheveled after her unsatisfactory meeting with Sharp and the anti-climax of lunch with Lydia. On her way through the hotel lobby, she stopped at the desk. There were no messages for her.

She went to her room and took a long shower. Then she dressed slowly and thoughtfully, her mind waging its own war all the while. Finally, when she had nothing else to do in the room, she crossed to the phone. She'd made up her mind to call Whit, but when she heard the operator's voice asking if she could help, Clemmie lost her nerve. She abruptly replaced the earpiece in the cradle.

She went down to the desk with the intention of finding out about train schedules that night, but suddenly, without thinking, she was asking about hiring a car. No, no driver, she told the man, only a car, one that could take country roads.

It seemed to Clemmie when she thought of it that Whit had made a point the previous evening of telling her where the farm was located, and with the aid of a map and the directions given by a filling station attendant, she had little trouble finding Wingate Farm. Rolling fields stretched back from the road for acres and acres, and the long rows of stables, as well as the large porticoed house half hidden by a dense wall of willows, stood white and fresh against the deep green meadows. Clemmie turned the car into the drive and continued toward the house. The air smelled rich and verdant, and the breeze was soft against her face.

She brought the car to a stop in a shaded area before the house. In the distance she could see two men standing just outside the paddock, watching a magnificent chestnut mare. She could not see their features, but she knew from the way one held himself, the way he leaned against the wooden fence, one leg resting on the bottom rail, that it was Whit. He was watching the horse carefully and talking to the other man, and she was halfway to the paddock before he turned and saw her. He looked surprised, then suddenly happy. Clemmie was sure of it.

He closed the distance between them in a few steps and took her hand. He didn't say anything, just stood there with her hand in his looking down at her. She started to stay that he'd won after all, started to pick up the now familiar joke, but something in his eyes stopped her.

"I'm glad you came," he said finally. He wondered if she knew that if she hadn't driven out, he'd have come into town to get her. All day long he'd been telling himself he wouldn't, but he'd known ever since he'd awakened this morning, thinking of her, still seeing her the way she'd looked the night before, still feeling her presence beside him in the car when he'd driven her home, that he would not be able to stay away from her today.

He was still holding her hand, and now he began leading her to the house. Inside, it was spacious and comfortable without being in the least stylish. In the living room an Irish setter lay sleeping in the sun that filtered through the window. When they entered the room he came over and sniffed at Clemmie, then brushed against Whit a few times, and returned to his place in the sun.

"Lazy old thing, isn't he?" Clemmie said.

"Lazy ancient thing. He's been here ever since Quentin had the place."

Quentin. Again. She wondered if the name meant as much to Whit, but of course it couldn't. To him it represented a flesh-and-blood man he'd known all his life. To her it meant only a deserted beach house.

"Quentin left the place to me because no one else in the family was interested in breeding horses anymore. I'm the only one who ever comes down here."

Is he trying to tell me that Alison never comes here, Clemmie wondered.

Had he been too obvious, Whit thought. Had he made too much a point of the fact that this was his place and had nothing to do with Alison?

"Well, I imagine you could use a drink. It's a long ride out here." Whit excused himself for a moment. There was no butler. All the men at the farm worked outside the house. Clemmie heard him in the pantry telling the woman to bring a tray for mint juleps. "And there'll be two for dinner," she heard Whit say.

She watched him at the sideboard as he mixed the drinks. He was wearing a tweed jacket, flannel trousers, and riding boots, and the costume looked as old and worn and comfortable as the room. And Whit looked absolutely right in it.

He walked toward her with the tall glass. She took a sip. It tasted sweet and sharp at the same time.

He took the chair across from hers, but said nothing. It was as if he were content to sit and look at her. She shifted a little under his gaze. His eyes were like hands on her.

"The gentleman farmer," she said. "In his domain."

"I resent that. This is a serious breeding farm, and I'm a serious—if only sometime—breeder. Why, I was up all night two nights ago trying to save a colt who'd had a premature delivery from a dying dam."

"Were you successful?"

"I'll show you after this drink. He's a little gem."

The colt was a beauty, a small satiny thing with long

legs and woeful eyes. Clemmie watched Whit stroking the animal. She'd forgotten how gentle he could be. Which was strange, because she had thought she remembered everything about Whit.

On the way back to the house they stopped at the paddock where Whit had been when she arrived, and he introduced her to Keller, the man who ran Wingate Farm for him. Keller greeted her politely, but he was more concerned with a mare who was sure to foal in the next forty-eight hours. Clemmie could tell from the conversation that Whit had not lied. If he were a gentleman breeder, he was a serious one. His own words and the way Keller listened to them proved that.

When they returned to the house Whit showed her to a room and bath upstairs where she could freshen up before dinner. He hadn't asked if she'd stay. He'd simply assumed she would.

When she came downstairs again he was sitting in the same room, no longer sunny, but still inviting in the gathering dusk. He handed her another mint julep. Her hand brushed his as she took it from him. His touch was electric.

When she thought about that weekend afterward, she could never remember what they'd talked about, but she knew talk had come easily and there had been neither strain nor embarrassment. There were a hundred topics they didn't dare mention, but none of them came up. They talked and they laughed a great deal, and in the warmth of the wine and the summer evening and the presence of Whit, Clemmie grew rosy and drew nearer to him.

After dinner they went into the library. It was filled with trophies.

"I'm overwhelmed," Clemmie said.

"Only a few are mine. Most of them go back to Quentin or my grandfather."

Quentin again. He said it so easily, he must have forgotten.

"It seems," he said, sitting next to her on the deep

leather sofa, "that we spend a good deal of time in Quentin's houses."

"I thought you'd forgotten."

"I told you that night on the terrace, Clemmie. I remember everything. Every moment of that night. The way you looked in the moonlight." He raised a hand to her cheek. "The way your skin felt. The way your voice sounded in the darkness. The way it sounded when you said you loved me. I can remember the way it felt to say the words and the way it felt to hear you say them. I thought you meant them."

"I thought you did," she said softly. There was no anger in her voice, only sorrow.

"I did." His finger traced the contour of her cheek. "I still do."

Then why, she wanted to ask, but his mouth on hers banished every question, all words. She felt his arms around her, holding her to him, binding her to him, and she clung to him feeling the strange body against hers, and the familiar current of desire. His fingers worked quickly at the buttons of her dress, but when they found skin they slowed, and she felt his hands warm against her, as light and intoxicating as the soft magnolia-scented breeze that came from the open windows. And then it was not his hands but his flesh that was warm against her, his body hard against the softness of her own, and she felt herself falling, falling, falling into the deep soft sofa and Whit rising above her, and the slow dance of expectancy quickened so that his mouth was avid and his hands urgent and she felt herself racing to that moment of pure, midnight black ecstasy.

"Clemmie." His voice sounded soft after her own cry of pleasure that still echoed in the dimly lighted room. "My Clemmie," he said. If there was an irony to the words, neither of them heard it.

He raised his head a little to look at her. The dark eyes were softer than she'd ever seen them. "I won't let you go, you know. I've found you again, and I won't let you go."

After a while they dressed, and Whit poured a brandy for each of them. Finally they went upstairs, not to the room Clemmie had used before but to the large front bedroom with the high, old-fashioned canopied bed, and they undressed again, slowly now, methodically, and she felt Whit beside her beneath the light linen comforter, felt his skin smooth against hers and his mouth soft on her breast and his hands moving familiarly over her body like an explorer who knows the terrain but never tires of it, and she trembled with the excitement of his touch and the ecstasy of her own fulfillment.

She slept fitfully during the night because she was no longer accustomed to a man beside her in bed, but each time she awakened and heard Whit's breathing or saw the outline of his profile against the moonlit window, she would touch his arm, brush the hair from his face, or rest her cheek against his shoulder, and the gesture would banish all thought and every fear.

When they came down to breakfast the next morning, Clemmie was sure the servants would be scandalized, but the huge black cook seemed only delighted that she and Whit consumed vast quantities of hoe cakes and eggs and ham and her daughter who waited table kept her eyes down while she served.

"You forget you've come South," Whit said quietly when both women were out of hearing. "The war may have made it impossible to get decent servants in New York, but down here the only war that changed anything was the Civil War.

"What do you say," he asked when they'd finished breakfast, "to a little riding?"

"In this?" She indicated the yellow silk dress she was wearing, the same one she'd driven out in the day before. She'd been thinking that she had to go back to town to pick up some clothes, but she didn't want to think about leaving the farm yet, even briefly.

He seemed to read her mind. "Let's not drive back

to town yet," he said, and reached over to take her hand.

"I don't want to." Town was outside, town was the world beyond, town was the future.

He was thoughtful for a moment. "My cousin Lucille, Quentin's daughter, used to stay here all the time before she married and went back to France. I say 'back' because her mother was French. Anyway, I know she left all her riding things here. Apparently they weren't splendid enough for the French countryside. I'll bet they'd fit you."

With the help of the cook and another of her daughters who took care of the upstairs cleaning, they managed to find Lucille's things. "Lucille never looked half as good in them," Whit said when Clemmie came downstairs wearing a pair of twill jodhpurs and a close-fitting dark pink jacket.

"I feel a bit formal for a simple ride. It seems as if I ought to be after the fox."

Whit crossed the room to her. He opened the jacket and reached his arms around her waist. Through the thin silk of the blouse she could feel his hands drawing her to him. "As soon as we're out of sight," he said, his words soft against her ear, "I promise to see that you are as informal as possible. Disarray," he whispered, "is what I have in mind."

It was the most beautiful countryside Clemmie had ever seen. The land stretched out in gently rolling fields that lured them on and on—just to that fence, just to that stream, just to that glade, I must see that glade—and the woods were thick and quiet and darkly private. On the way back to the farm they stopped at a stream that ran through a densely forested area a few miles from Whit's property. The mossy river bank was like a deep carpet and Clemmie sank to it gratefully. Whit stretched out on his back beside her, his fingers laced together under his head.

"When I was a boy," he said, "and used to come down to visit Quentin, this was my favorite spot."

"I should have thought that would be the stables."

"I spent a lot of time there too, of course, but when I wanted to get away, I used to come here. That stream looks shallow but it's just deep enough for a good summer swim. It was a lot more fun swimming here than at the club, where there were governesses and rules and those awful itchy woolen suits." He looked up at her from under the thick lashes and smiled. "I told you I had disarray in mind."

"Here?"

"Here, back at the house, in the tack room, wherever I happen to be with you." He sat up and began to untie the stock of her shirt.

"And what if we're discovered?" She laughed. It was the old challenging laugh.

"We won't be." He had undone her blouse and his hands were working at the buttons of her jodhpurs while her own fumbled at his clothing. Then suddenly they were naked in the cool shade of the sweet-smelling trees. He held her for a moment and she pressed her body against his and felt the excitement in him and the desire.

"I thought we were going to swim," she whispered.

"We are." His voice sounded hoarse against her ear. "Later." His mouth was hungry on hers, whispering her name and words of love until she could taste them and Whit, and she watched him above her, watched him clearly and avidly in the midday light, his eyes wide with pleasure, his shoulders broad and smooth against the dark trees above them. She saw him bend to her breast, saw the dark fringe of lashes against the whiteness of her own skin, and felt the pleasure of soft mouth and hard teeth, a pleasure so exquisite it made her cry out with wanting him. He was rising above her again, and she could read the fierce desire in his face, see the power of his body above hers, the long clean lines descending from strong shoulders and smooth chest to the two of them locked together in ecstasy.

Afterward they swam and the water felt cool and fresh against her skin that was still hot with pleasure. Whit's hands were tender now rather than urgent. She knew they could arouse her again at any moment, knew they were capable of stirring her deeply and wildly, but they made no attempt to stir her now, only to hold her to him as the cool water swirled around them.

The mare that Keller had worried about foaled late that night, and at dawn the next morning one of the boys came to the house for Whit. In half-sleep Clemmie felt him kissing her good-bye. She opened her eyes to find him dressed and leaning over her in bed. "I'll be back," he murmured against her mouth.

"Hurry," she sighed, and turned to hold the pillow where Whit had been sleeping.

When she awakened a little after nine, he had not returned, but the servants must have heard her walking about the room because in a few minutes there was a knock at the door and the girl entered with a tray.

"Mr. Whitmore still in the stable, ma'am. He say he'll be up soon as he can."

Clemmie breakfasted lightly. The cook's hoe cakes weren't nearly so irresistible alone. Then she dressed in another of Lucille's riding costumes and left the house. The mist hadn't lifted entirely and the fields looked wet and green and lush in the morning coolness. She was just in time to find Whit emerging from the stable. He was smiling broadly. "That Keller's a godsend. It was touch and go there for a while, but he pulled them through."

"I imagine you had something to do with it. What time did you get up? I swear it was still dark."

"Not quite. It was almost five."

"An unconscionable hour, if I ever heard one. And an unconscionable thing to do, leaving me all alone."

"Well, you have my full attention now. What would you like to do?"

She looked directly into the dark eyes and read the message there. "Go back to bed, of course."

It was after noon by the time they came down again, after noon on Sunday, and they both knew what that meant. "I have to go back to New York," she said on the way back from the stable. The foal was colicky but still all right.

"I know," he answered without looking at her.

They were silent on the way back to the house, and when they got there Clemmie went straight upstairs and changed into the yellow silk dress.

Whit was in the large front room where they'd first had drinks Friday evening, standing with his back to the room, looking out the window. She hesitated in the doorway for a moment, watching him that way, without his knowing she was there. All the sensations of the past two days came flooding back, and she felt the taste and touch and excitement of Whit washing over her like a great wave. Then the wave receded and she felt parched and empty.

"I'm ready," she said. Her voice sounded foolishly bright, like that of an ingenue in a play trying to make the most of her single line.

"Let me drive you back to town."

"No, I have the rented car. Anyway"—she held her breath for a moment—"I'd rather say good-bye here."

He was across the room in a moment, and his arms were around her, holding her to him. "Not good-bye, Clemmie. We're never going to say good-bye again. I told you that Friday night."

They were the words she'd been waiting for, praying for. He wanted to see her in New York. There were no longer two Whits; there was only the one who loved her and wanted her regardless of anyone or anything else.

On her first night at home Tom was colder than ever, but Clemmie scarcely noticed. Her mind was too full of Whit to perceive the absence of Tom.

He asked about Middleton Sharp, but didn't seem much disappointed by her terse, distracted answers. Clemmie was too preoccupied to say much, and she heard almost nothing. Only one thing Tom said cut through the haze.

"I can understand Sharp's wanting to hold onto his stocks. We may own some interest, and the Central and B & O have some, but it's still Sharp's railroad. He's still running the show. It's like the A & W, Clemmie. There are other shareholders, but we're still running the show. As long as you and I stay together, we hold the largest single block—and virtual control. Of course, if we were to split our holdings for any reason, things would be different." His eyes caught hers as if to make sure she was paying attention. "Then each of us would be just another stockholder. Although," he added, "I imagine the board would keep me on. I've done a good job, Clemmie—as you pointed out."

Whit called Wednesday morning. He'd just got in, he said. Could she see him this afternoon? It never occurred to Clemmie to say no.

He gave her the address of a friend's apartment just off Gramercy Park. She said she'd be there at one.

Whit had planned to speak to her first. There were things he wanted to say. He'd even thought they'd lunch. There was champagne cooling in a bucket and he'd had something cold sent up from the nearby hotel. But when he saw Clemmie standing in the doorway of the apartment, the three days they'd been apart seemed like three years, and there was no time for talk or food or wine.

Whit had drawn the shades of the bedroom windows and it was all cool shadows and quiet privacy. At first it felt different because they were both dressed for town and there were more clothes, but then the clothes were gone and it was the same, the same taste of his mouth on hers, the same electricity of his skin against hers, the same maddening excitement of his hands bringing her body to life. And her own were familiar on him, beginning to be schooled by him, guided by him to his own desires, and then they were not hands or mouths or bodies but pure sensation climbing, mounting, soaring to an intense, trembling explosion.

After a while Whit got up and went into the other room to get the champagne. She watched him as he returned with the bottle and two glasses. He was lean and slender and very graceful. Tom was taller and more powerfully built, but Whit had an elegant ease that could not be rivaled. The observation shocked her. Why was she thinking of Tom when she was here with Whit?

He got back into bed and poured two glasses of wine. "Would you like some lunch?" he asked, handing her a glass.

Clemmie shook her head. "I am utterly and absolutely contented." Her hand trailed a lazy pattern on his chest. "There's nothing more I want in the world."

"Nothing?" he asked tracing the line of her mouth with his finger. It was hard to keep from touching each other.

"Nothing," she whispered against his fingers.

His hand stopped. "Not even permanency?"

"We are permanent. Forever and ever."

"Forever and ever on Wednesday and Friday afternoons perhaps and an occasional night when . . ." He'd been about to say when she could get away from Hendreich and he could leave Alison, but he wouldn't mention his wife and he couldn't bear to think of her husband. "No, Clemmie, not that way. I've been thinking about it ever since you left on Sunday."

She felt herself go cold. He was going to break it off. He was going to say this was the last time. They were back in New York and he was a different man again.

"For once in my life I want to do things cleanly."

A clean break, she thought.

"I've had enough lies and equivocations and—and, damn it, Clemmie, enough affairs. That's not what I

want with you. I want more with you. I want to marry
you. I suppose I always have."

She couldn't believe she was really hearing the words,
those same words she had prayed for so many years ago.
It seemed impossible that Whit was finally saying them.

"I know it will be messy. People will be hurt. . . ."

She was no longer listening to the words. He was
talking of asking Alison for a divorce, of her getting one
herself, and he'd broken the spell. To say he wanted
to marry her was one thing. To discuss the details of
the divorces was something else entirely. Because the
divorces, Clemmie realized with a start, were unthink-
able. Or at least her own was. It wasn't the scandal that
worried her, although she could hear Whit talking as if
from a distance and knew it was worrying him a good
deal. Clemmie didn't care about the scandal. She cared
about the railroad, her railroad. If she divorced Tom
she'd lose the A & W.

There had been a time when the A & W had been
nothing more than a means to get back at Whit, or so
she'd thought, but that time was long past. She'd put
too much of herself into building it, she had too much
of Elias in her to relinquish it. As Mrs. Whit Morris
she'd be the wife, and the second wife, at that, of one
of the many stockholders and several vice presidents of
the Central—hadn't Elias always said the Vanderbilts
had been fools to divide it and subdivide it with each
generation?—but as Mrs. Thomas Hendreich she was
the moving power behind the A & W. Together with
Tom she was the A & W. And the A & W, Clemmie had
learned in the years since Whit Morris had first taken
her and then abandoned her, since Elias had died and
the baby had turned out to be less a child than a curse,
since she and Tom had grown farther apart, the railroad
was all she had. Clemmie Wilder Hendreich had learned
to depend on two things in the world—herself and her
railroad. She couldn't give the latter up, not even for
Whit.

Especially not for Whit, some calculating corner of

her brain reminded her. He betrayed you once. The night in Quentin's beach house had been perfect, as perfect as the past weekend in Virginia or the past hour in some anonymous friend's apartment. But the night in the beach house had been followed by Whit's departure and his subsequent engagement to Alison. He might talk of divorce now—it was easy to talk of divorce here alone in the borrowed apartment, fresh from wanting each other and having each other, but back in the house on Fifth Avenue, back with Alison and the children—she mustn't forget the children— would he still want to sacrifice it all for her? The hard, practical edge of Clemmie's mind cut through Whit's picture of the two of them finally and blissfully married, and imagined another scene. She saw Whit hesitating, equivocating, finally changing his mind because he couldn't bear to hurt Alison and the children, but it would be too late for her, because she would have told Tom and she'd be alone, without the railroad, without Tom, with nothing but the leftovers of Whit's life, the shards that remained for the mistress of a married man who was not married herself. She'd been a reckless girl and she was a daring woman, but she wasn't a fool.

"I'll tell Alison tonight," Whit was saying. "And you've got to tell . . . him."

They were still beside each other in the rumpled bed, and she moved closer to him beneath the sheets. She must do this very carefully. "Won't it be a bit of a shock to—to Alison? Coming so suddenly."

"The words aren't going to sound any better in a week or a month or a year, Clemmie. There's no way to lead up to something like this."

"I suppose you're right, darling. All the same, it seems we might go on this way for a while—just until everyone gets used to things."

He pulled away from her and sat up. Christ, didn't he ever learn! "You mean until we get used to it. And then once we're used to it, there'll be no need to change things. Isn't that what you mean, Clemmie? You don't want a divorce. All you want is a nice convenient affair."

"I want you, Whit."

Something menacing flashed in the dark eyes. "When it's convenient."

"Whenever you want."

"As long as it isn't always. As long as it doesn't interfere with your marriage."

"I love you."

"But it's more convenient to be married to him." He'd got out of bed and was putting on his trousers. She could read the anger in his movments. "Clemmie was bored. Again. And I just happened to come along. Again." He straightened from the pile of clothing he'd been searching through furiously and looked at her. "Like Tony Bayliss."

"Who are you to blame me for Tony Bayliss? You were the one who left that morning, left with nothing more than a phone call."

"But at least I called. I called to say I had to go to New York on business and would be back in a few days. You didn't say a word. Just went off with Bayliss." He spat out the name as if it disgusted him.

"Nothing ever happened with him!"

He laughed but there was no mirth to the sound. "Would you tell me if it had?"

"But I never cared for Bayliss."

"In view of this afternoon, Clemmie, I'm beginning to think caring or not caring is beside the point for you."

Without stopping to think, she was out of bed and across the room. She heard the sound her palm made against his face and saw the look of surprise in his eyes Then they turned icy. "I apologize if I offended you, Clemmie." His voice was as cold as his eyes and heavy with irony.

"I'm sorry," she said without looking at him. She'd begun to dress, and they were both silent. "I'm sorry I struck you," she said finally, "and I know you're sorry for what you said. Can't we forget the whole unpleasant incident?"

He sat on the end of the bed and looked up at her, but there was no reading the emotion in his eyes now. "Pretend it never happened?"

"That's right."

"And go on from there?"

"I don't see why not."

"A nice neat affair. We make love twice a week, three times if we're lucky. Usually in the afternoon, I imagine. Then you go home to your husband. Tell me, Clemmie . . ." He stopped for a moment. "No, that would be an indelicate question. Rather like talking about Bayliss."

"You're trying to argue."

"As a matter of fact, I am. I told you before I wanted to go on cleanly. I meant I wanted us to marry. But if can't have that then I'd rather end it cleanly."

"But we don't have to end it, Whit. That's what I'm trying to make you see. The way things are now may not be perfect, but it's better than nothing."

He stood. "No, Clemmie. It isn't. Nothing is better. Or at least more bearable."

It was not yet five o'clock when Clemmie arrived back at the house that afternoon, but Tom was already home. He came out of the small rear drawing room to greet her in the foyer.

"Well, this is a surprise." Her voice sounded unusually shrill in her ears.

"Come have a drink before you go up to dress, Clemmie." His own voice was polite and innocuous, almost like a stranger's, but his face was rigid, as if he were struggling to control some emotion.

"I'm tired, Tom. I'd like to lie down for a while. We're dining at the Byers, you know." She started past him. She had to get away. She had to be alone.

"And I'd like to talk to you."

"I'm sure it can wait. . . ."

His hand on her arm stopped her. They both looked down at the strong fingers gripping the silk of her dress, then looked back at each other guiltily. That night of the riot was still fresh. Tom dropped her arm. "It can't wait. Not anymore."

Inside the drawing room he went straight to the cocktail wagon. "I don't want a drink," she said.

"You're going to."

The tone, no longer polite, was as ominous as the words. Clemmie heard it and refused to be intimidated.

"Really, Tom, I wish you'd stop being so melodramatic and simply say what you have to say."

He handed her the drink and continued to stand over her chair. His face in the light of the damask-shaded lamp did not look kind. "You want me to dispense with the preliminaries, Clemmie? I thought you liked all that polite fencing. I thought you and your friend Morris were very good at all that innuendo and whatnot."

"I don't see what the Morrises have to do with anything."

"Not the Morrises. Just Whit Morris. Very well, Clemmie, we'll go straight to the point. Where were you last weekend?"

She laughed as if the question were silly, but she could feel herself beginning to tremble. "You know where I was, Tom. In Richmond. Or rather just outside it. I saw the Sharps. Though I wasn't very successful. I thought you seemed rather smug about that part of it. About my failure."

"Oh, I'm not smug. I'm anything but smug. Furious. Disgusted. Fed up with you and with myself. But not smug."

"I wish you'd stop being so mysterious and just tell me what you're talking about," she said, although by now she was sure she knew.

"I called your hotel last weekend, Clemmie. It's not something you and I often do anymore. After all, we so rarely talk to each other at home, why should we bother to telephone when one of us is away? But I did call Friday night. I guess it was foolish of me, but I wanted to know when you were coming home. Home to New York, not home to your hotel room. But pretty soon I started to wonder about that, too, because the operator kept calling every half-hour until after three and there was no answer in the room. I tried again Saturday, all day and half the night, and again on Sunday. You know when I reached you, of course. Sunday evening."

"But you didn't say you'd been calling all weekend."

"I guess I ought to apologize for that, Clemmie." He gave her an unpleasant look. "Devious of me, wasn't it?"

"I don't know if it was devious, but if you'd mentioned it I could have explained that I was at the Sharps' for the weekend and saved you all this worry. They asked me—"

"Stop it!" His voice was a harsh bark. "I called the Sharps on Sunday. I wasn't being devious then, merely stupid. You see, I was worried about you, Clemmie. Mrs. Sharp said she hadn't seen you since Friday afternoon."

Clemmie stood and walked to the cocktail wagon. She hadn't finished the drink he'd given her, but she busied herself freshening it. She kept her back to Tom while she spoke. "I went off for the weekend, Tom. To the country. Just some inn. I felt perfectly rotten about that Tidewater business—darn it, Tom, I knew you were going to gloat—and . . ."

"Goddammit, Clemmie, don't lie to me. I'm sick of your lies. You were with Morris."

The anger in his words had forced her to turn back to him and she stood staring at him dumbly, aware of her own breathing in the room that was suddenly quiet after his outburst, aware of the glass that felt icy in her trembling hands. "That's ridiculous," she said slowly. "How could you possibly . . . what would Whit be doing? . . ."

430

"I ran into your friend Alison today. I had to come uptown to lunch with the attorneys from . . . what does it matter where they were from. I saw Alison. We were very polite. She asked about you and I asked about her husband. She said he was just back from Virginia. Taking care of his horses."

She had no choice. She had to brazen it out. "And that's what all this is about. Just because Whit Morris and I happen to be in the same state on the same weekend, you accuse me of . . . of I don't know what."

"Oh, surely you can guess what I'm accusing you of, Clemmie. And if you went to an inn, why didn't you check out of your hotel? Stop playing games. I can get more evidence, if I have to. There are agencies for that sort of thing."

Clemmie remembered the pictures of George and those women, only this time there would be servants' reports on Whit and herself.

"I could go to one of those agencies, but I don't have to, Clemmie. You and Morris spent the weekend at his farm. Incidentally, if it makes any difference to you—and I doubt that it does—I didn't tell Alison you were in Virginia with her husband. She's a nice woman."

"Which I, of course, am not! Tell me, Tom, while you're judging all of us—Alison is nice, I'm not—where does Vanessa Hodges fit into this spectrum of virtue? How do you rate your mistress?"

"Sit down, Clemmie." He saw her begin to say something. "Sit down and listen to me, and don't say a word till I'm finished.

"You're never going to mention Vanessa Hodges to me again. It was a single weekend that happened years ago. And it never would have happened if it hadn't been for you and that damn Max Clinton. Well, it did happen and it's over and I've paid for it. Oh, you've made me pay for it all right, but I'm not going to pay anymore. The matter is closed.

"Now for your friend Morris. It's up to you, Clemmie. Either you stop seeing him or I walk out of here, tonight, for good. And I might as well tell you, I won't do it like a gentleman. I won't do it the way Morris would. I would have at one time, but not now. I'm too damn angry now. For one thing, I'll take Lizzy. No court in the country is going to give her to you after they find out about that weekend in Virginia. And I'll take my half of the stocks. Not a very civil thing to do, but I'm not feeling very civil. The idea of you and Morris rolling around in bed all weekend makes me feel damn uncivil. So there it is. Either you promise never to see him alone again—and you'd better mean it, because I'm going to watch you like a hawk—or I leave, with Lizzy and with the stocks."

"You aren't giving me much of a choice, are you?"

"I'm giving you a clean choice. Something you've never been willing to make, Clemmie."

A clean choice. A clean break. Damn these men with their finalities. Was anything ever that simple? Well, she supposed it had been for her at one time, but it wasn't any longer.

"If I had half a brain, I wouldn't even give you a second chance." His voice was still full of anger, but now she heard something else in it as well.

"Then why are you?"

He looked at her for a long time before speaking. "Because I still love you, Clemmie. I don't want to, but it isn't something I have a choice about."

"And what if I say I'll never see Whit again?" It wasn't much of a sacrifice in view of this afternoon. "What kind of a marriage are we going to have after this?"

Again he was silent for what seemed a long time. "I don't know. I honestly don't know. I said you're not going to mention Vanessa again, and I won't mention Morris, but that doesn't mean I won't be thinking of him and hating him and hating you for what you did with him. Maybe in time I won't. Maybe that's our only hope, Clemmie—time."

She had no answer. Any more than she had a choice.

She'd stay with Tom, but the question of what kind of marriage they'd have hadn't been an idle one. She knew they had to go on, but she didn't see how they would manage to. "You said before that you love me, Tom. You don't like me very much though, do you? I don't mean hating me about Whit, I mean simply not liking me very much."

It was not the sort of question he'd come to expect of her. "I can't answer that," he said finally.

"You mean you've suddenly decided to be kind and you won't answer it."

"Kindness has nothing to do with it. I told you, I hate you for the Morris business, and I don't like a lot of things you've done, but I can't *not* like you, Clemmie." His tone was gruff and he was not looking at her. "Any more than I can *not* love you."

Tom's words, Clemmie thought, promised more than she'd dared hope, but later that evening, when she took his arm as she was stepping into the car and he started as if stung by her touch, she wondered if there were any hope at all.

BOOK
THREE

Chapter 13

By the early months of 1941 the Depression was a thing of the past, there was a war in Europe and perhaps in America's future, and the A & W, thanks to both conditions, was flourishing. So were Clemmie and Tom. She'd been wrong about starting over, or at least partly wrong. It wasn't a blissful marriage, but it was a satisfactory one. And what more could she expect at her age, though sometimes when she met Whit Morris at one of the large parties or balls where he could not be avoided, she thought that age had nothing to do with it. She kept her word, though. She had not seen Whit alone since that awful afternoon at the apartment on Gramercy Park, since that afternoon Tom had given her the ultimatum. And she had to admit Tom had had been as good as his word. He'd never mentioned Whit or that weekend in Virginia again. If things hadn't worked out exactly for the best, Clemmie thought, they had worked out a good deal better than she'd expected them to eight years ago on that awful afternoon.

She heard Lizzy and Porter Lowry in the entrance hall. They were laughing about something. Clemmie couldn't understand the words, but the sounds were familiar. Lizzy and Porter were always laughing about something. Lizzy loved Tom, but she adored Porter.

"You should have come, Mother," the girl said as she entered the sitting room in her easy long-legged stride.

There was no doubt about it, everyone said, the girl looked exactly like her mother—the jet black hair, worn in a pageboy rather than a bob according to the fashion of the day, the fine-boned features, the flawless skin, and the long legs and slender body as graceful on a tennis court as on a dance floor. She looked exactly like Clemmie except for the eyes. Her eyes were Tom's. They were velvet brown, large and wide-set, and when she was excited they danced with green lights.

"Your mother," Porter said, following Lizzy into the room, "doesn't like anything that was painted after 1900."

"It's simply," Clemmie said, "that I prefer to know what I'm looking at in a picture."

"Don't be so old-fashioned, Mother. Porter isn't old-fashioned. Well, will it be tea or cocktail? After the crowd at the exhibit, I think we deserve cocktails."

"You'd better have James put out plenty of ice," Clemmie said. "The twins called. First Nick, then Van. I gather they'll both be turning up any minute. Really, Lizzy, you ought to choose one or the other. It's unfair to keep the two of them dangling." It was what Clemmie always said, but she didn't really disapprove of Lizzy's indecision, at least she didn't for the moment. The idea that her daughter could choose between Whit Morris's two sons was enormously satisfying.

"How can I choose between Nick and Van?" Lizzy asked. "They're the same person."

"Well, you're going to have to eventually," Clemmie said.

"Eventually isn't now and certainly not before next spring. I'm permitted my indecision at least until I come out. Don't you agree, Porter? Don't you think I'm entirely too young to have to make the momentous choice between Nick and Van?"

438

"You're a heartless little thing," Clemmie said, but there was no rancor behind the words.

"Me! Porter, what were you telling me about Mother when she was a girl? How many broken hearts? Be careful, Mother, I have access to an authority." But the bantering was cut short by the doorbell and the sound of James greeting the Morris twins.

They were, as Lizzy said, identical, although when she said as much she was speaking of their personalities rather than their appearances. Both young men were tall and slender with Whit's coloring—and his grace, Clemmie thought, as they came into the room. They had the VanNest nose and the VanNest chin, narrower than Whit's and more aggressive, but they were unmistakably Whit's sons, just as Lizzy was unmistakably her daughter. The observation gave her more pleasure than it should have.

Both boys were polite to her and patient with Porter. They didn't know what Lizzy saw in the sardonic old duffer, but they knew she saw something, and neither was taking a chance on alienating a possible ally, any possible ally.

"I didn't think you were coming down this weekend," Lizzy said.

"He wasn't," Nick answered. "Until he heard I was."

"A blatant lie," Van said. "I got the two-thirty out of New Haven. Our heroic flyboy couldn't leave for another hour. ROTC needed him."

"Just because the navy isn't bothering to train you fellows. . . ."

All their lives Nick and Van Morris had shared things—rooms at school, summer holidays, friends, even Lizzy—but now at college they had finally gone in different directions. Among the students an eagerness to get into the war was a constant; only the means varied. Nick had signed up with the army in hope of getting into the air force, and if he didn't make pilot he'd never forgive himself. Van had joined the navy. Let Nick have the glamour of the air. He wanted the excitement of sub service.

"All the same," Nick said, "it was my idea to come down this weekend, so you ought to have dinner with me."

"Only if you want to be bored to death," Van said. "Come on, Lizzy, we'll go down to that little Italian place in the Village."

Sometimes it seemed to Lizzy that after years of competing on every front, the twins had settled on her as the final battlefield. Occasionally she wondered if either of them cared for her at all.

"I'm having dinner with Peter Fowler," Lizzy said.

"Peter Fowler!"

"Harvard!"

"But not even Hasty Pudding Harvard." Nick and Van ran the litany between them. They were united now.

"But I'll see you at Cynthia Byer's dance afterward," Lizzy said.

The girl was good, Clemmie thought, as good as she'd ever been. And for the same reason. She simply didn't care, about Nick, about Van, about Peter Fowler, about any of them. Clemmie looked at Whit's sons sitting on either side of her daughter. She wondered what would happen when Lizzy finally came to care.

"Mother," Lizzy asked the next day, "why didn't Porter ever marry?" They were in the library with a tray of coffee and the Sunday papers. Porter and Tom had gone off for a game of squash.

"Do you good," Porter had said. "Do us both good. Have to keep in shape. The way things are going Uncle Sam may need us."

"God help him if he does," Clemmie said, and told them not to have too many drinks at the club when they'd finished because they were lunching with friends.

"He just didn't," Clemmie said.

"Was it because he was in love with you?"

"No, that wasn't it."

"I didn't think so, though I admitted it was a possibility. But if Porter had been in love with you, I don't think he and Daddy would be such great friends now. That's why Daddy doesn't like Nick and Van's father, isn't it? Because Mr. Morris was in love with you once."

"Lizzy, where do you get these ideas?"

"Just by watching all of you. Oh, you're all very discreet, but you're all very transparent too. You adore the twins, but Daddy doesn't really like them. Oh, he pretends he does—you know how fair he is—but I can tell. I like to think there was a huge scandal years ago with everyone being wildly and shamefully in love with everyone else."

"Lizzy!"

"Oh, Mother, I was only teasing. Heaven knows you're all such towers of virtue, I can't imagine a single scandal between the whole bunch of you. But I can imagine Mr. Morris being in love with you and then Daddy carrying you off on a white horse, or I guess in those days it would have been a red Stutz."

"Mr. Morris was the one with the Stutz."

"That's even better. You threw over Mr. Morris and all his filthy money for true love."

"I did nothing of the sort, but if it makes you happy to think so, go right ahead."

"But you still haven't answered me about Porter."

"I don't know why he never married, Lizzy, but I remember you once told him you were glad he hadn't."

"I did?"

"You were about ten at the time." Clemmie did not add that it was the winter that the baby—she had stopped thinking of him as having a name after they'd put him in the institution—had finally and mercifully died. Respiratory failure, they'd told her, as if the cause of death mattered. As if he'd ever been alive. "We went to the farm for Christmas, as usual, and Porter showered you with gifts, as usual, and you said you were glad he didn't have his own children because then he wouldn't care about you."

"Selfish little tyke, wasn't I?"

"Oh, I don't know. Perhaps just straightforward."

James knocked at the library door then and said Mr. Morris was on the phone for Miss Elizabeth."

"Which Mr. Morris?" Clemmie asked.

"Does it matter?" Lizzy laughed on her way out of the room.

Clemmie sat alone in the library thinking of her daughter's words. *You're all such towers of virtue.* Children knew so little. Only their own generation could feel desire or passion. But they weren't blind. That business about Tom's not liking the twins—how could he like Whit's sons? He did, as Lizzy said, try to be fair. They were good catches, and if Lizzy fell in love with either of them Tom would give his blessing. Tom approved of the twins but he didn't like them. And he still hated Whit, although he'd kept his word and never spoke of his hatred.

In the beginning he hadn't had to. Clemmie had felt his hatred there, something palpable between them. She'd seen it that first night when she'd come back from Whit and Tom had given her his ultimatum. She'd seen it that night when she'd put a hand on his arm and he'd stiffened at her touch, and she'd seen it dozens of times in the following months, the way she'd look up sometimes and find him watching her, not with affection, but with curiosity as if trying to find out what went on behind the cool façade they maintained. He'd treated her as formally as if they were strangers who'd just met, rather than husband and wife, and he'd gone on sleeping in one of the guest rooms. They'd said they were going to forget, but apparently Tom could not forget what had happened between her and Whit. It was that, Clemmie knew, that sent him to the guest room every night. She knew he wanted her but the shadow of Whit Morris, the shadow she had brought into the house and Tom kept there by the force of his own pride and jealousy, would not let him have her. Until that night at the lake.

They'd gone to Pennsylvania for the summer. They had both known, although neither had admitted it, that things might be easier between them away from New York. Tom was always happier in Pennsylvania. And in Pennsylvania there was no Whit Morris. So they'd closed the house in New York for the summer and returned to the one they'd started their marriage in, and Tom came out as often as he could. In the first weeks at the house, when Clemmie looked up and found him watching her, she would see desire on his face more often than distrust, but still he kept his distance, kept it so perfectly that Clemmie thought she would scream with wanting him. For the first time she realized that Tom was stronger than she. She was more willful perhaps, but he was stronger.

Still, despite her loneliness and longing for Tom, Clemmie had not actually planned to do anything that night. At least, she hadn't until well into the evening.

There'd been a picnic at the lake and it had been fun to see the old crowd, as Clemmie called them—the old crowd that she'd grown up with and Tom had come to know and ultimately outstrip. There had been the usual old-fashioned supper and lots of beer because the previous March had brought 3.2 repeal. More than one flask made the rounds as well. With the exception of Porter, another bachelor, and a woman who, as the youngest of five daughters had stayed at home to keep house for her widowed father, they had all been married for a decade or more, yet they felt very young and irresponsible that night. There'd been a good deal of splashing and dunking and singing of old songs. Porter had threatened to throw Clemmie in as retribution for a story she'd told of his childhood, but Tom prevailed on him not to since Clemmie had borrowed his sweater to ward off the evening breeze. She felt Tom's arm around her, rough because of the horseplay, but protective still, felt it pulling her away from Porter to him, holding her close against his body. Perhaps it was the strength of Tom's body, perhaps merely the courage she'd derived from the whiskey, but suddenly she knew what she was going to do.

"Come on, Tom, I'll take you for a row. Get you away from all this drunken riffraff."

"I like that," Porter said.

"You might like it, but you're not invited," Clemmie tossed over her shoulder and started toward the rowboats pulled up on the beach. They pushed one into the shallow water. "Get in the stern," she said. "I'll row."

"Don't be ridiculous."

"Nope, this is my ride. I'm taking you." She stood holding the oars until Tom climbed in, then she followed him, placed the oars in the locks, and started across the lake. The oars made soft rhythmic ripples in the water, first one side, then the other, right, left, right, left. It was pleasant and utterly peaceful and Tom leaned back in the stern. The night was clear, and the full moon and stars bright overhead, but he didn't watch them for long. He kept looking up, trying to pick out stars and constellations, but soon he'd find his eyes drawn back to Clemmie facing him in the small boat, rowing steadily and smoothly across the still water. Her face was serious, as if she were concentrating on something, but she moved easily. As she pulled each stroke of the oar through the water, he was conscious of her breasts beneath the open sweater and thin blouse, and each time her legs, stretched out to brace her, touched his thigh, he felt as if he'd received an electric shock.

"Want me to take over?" he asked.

"Nope, we're almost there. You can row back."

"Where's there?"

She gestured behind her. "Only that cove." She took the last few strokes smoothly and they felt the bow bump against the shore.

Tom climbed out and steadied the boat for her.

"I wonder why nobody ever comes over here?" she said.

"Not enough beach."

It was true, of course. It was what she'd had in mind. The trees were thick here and there was barely a clearing.

He stood for a minute, watching as she walked up to the small beach, then pulled the boat up out of the water.

"Did you bring cigarettes?" she asked as he dropped down next to her on the sand. He produced a silver case from his trouser pocket, offered her one, took another for himself, and lighted them both, then he lay back on the sand. From across the lake they could hear bursts of laughter and occasional snatches of songs. Now the crowd had begun "Poor Butterfly".

"'. . . 'Neath the blossoms waiting . . .'" Clemmie joined in softly, then laughed. "They've worked their way back through the war, and now they're on the prewar stuff."

"Nineteen-sixteen. Summer I was graduated from college. Summer I went to work for the A & W. The summer everything began."

"No, that was the summer—or rather the fall—of '21. That was the first time I saw you, really saw you, I mean. The first time we saw each other. You never looked at me before that day."

"Oh, I looked at you, all right."

"A gallant statement if not exactly a truthful one."

"I'd been looking at you since you were a spoiled kid throwing a tantrum on the ninth hole because your governess wouldn't let you play the entire eighteen." He rarely mentioned those memories, but for some reason he didn't mind talking of them tonight. "And then there was the time I took some papers out to your father and you were on the terrace with two very proper-looking Philadelphia types. I think you were probably rougher on them than the governess."

He was still on his back, looking up at the sky while he talked, and now she leaned over him so it was her face he saw rather than the moon and stars. "And you were insanely jealous. Wild with desire for me and insanely jealous."

He heard the light tone of her voice and tried to match it. "I might have felt a touch of that, but only a touch, you understand."

"And you swore then and there you'd have to have me. And," she added, her mouth on his, "now you do. Only," she lifted her head and looked into his eyes, "you don't seem to want me anymore." Suddenly she was no longer joking.

He heard the change in her voice and couldn't believe it. For a moment he even thought he saw tears in the wide gray eyes, but of course the moon was behind her and it was hard to tell. He reached up and touched her hair. "I want you, Clemmie. I've always wanted you, and I always will."

And then he was drawing her head down to his and his mouth was soft at first and almost hesitant, then gradually more forceful until it was avid on hers. The dam had broken, unleashing the flood of their passion, submerging the long arid months of loneliness. He was tugging at her clothes, almost too impatient to stop for buttons or clasps, and she felt his hand urgent beneath her skirt, hurrying through folds of material until he found warm skin and slowed, not out of slackening desire, but out of the pure joy of the sensation. They were beside each other and in the soft moonlight she could see his features taut with wanting her. She raised her face to his again and felt his mouth on hers and tasted whiskey on his tongue. He had opened her blouse and his tongue was like fire now against her skin and she held him to her, feeling the strength of his body and the force of his hunger as it stirred her own.

"Please." Her voice was a desperate whisper. Then "Tom," then "please," again.

And he heard her dimly through the haze of his own need, not comprehending the words, but knowing the sense of them, knowing she wanted him as fiercely as he did her, and they were moving together wildly, savagely, unthinkingly, free of every restraint, rushing headlong to an ending that could only be a beginning.

It had been the beginning, Clemmie thought now, putting the papers aside and getting up to poke the fire. She looked at her watch. Tom and Porter would be back from their squash game soon.

To be sure, that night hadn't blotted out everything, but it had marked a fresh start. They'd rowed back to the party in silence. Porter had looked at them strangely, perhaps a little enviously, Clemmie had thought, then forgot his look immediately. She was not thinking of Porter that night.

Tom had been solicitous on the drive home, not the impersonal politeness of the last months, but a real concern and a tenderness she hadn't seen in years.

When they got back to the house, Clemmie said she was going to have a quick shower before bed. She felt tired but perfectly content and the warm water streaming over her body lulled her into a pleasant daze. She closed her eyes and leaned against the tile wall. She didn't know how long she'd been standing that way, but suddenly she felt Tom's arms around her and his body hard against hers. She opened her eyes and saw him smiling down at her. He didn't say anything, just took the soap and began lathering her body. She'd felt drugged by the water, but now she felt his hands smooth and slippery against her body, caressing it, coaxing it, and she felt herself coming awake, her body coming alive, and she clung to Tom as if he had saved her.

Saved her from what, Clemmie wondered and poked at the logs a last time before sitting down again. She was being melodramatic. She hadn't been lost and Tom hadn't saved her. They had simply worked out an accord. Sex was a big part of that accord, she knew. It was, she supposed, the only area in which she and Tom had never had problems. They might quarrel, they might stay away from each other for long periods of time, but whatever mutual desire bound them together, was always there when they returned. Perhaps it was not enough. Her mother's generation, Clemmie knew, would have been certain it was not enough. But it was, Clemmie felt sure, more than most people had. It had kept them together. It and the railroad.

Clemmie looked up from the paper she hadn't been reading as Lizzy returned to the room. She wondered about Lizzy and the twins. She wondered what happened when she was not fending off two of them, but alone with one. She remembered herself and Whit so many years ago. But that was foolish. Hadn't Clemmie seen only last night that Lizzy cared, really cared that is, for neither Nick nor Van? She was too young, Clemmie supposed. Why, she wouldn't turn eighteen for another two months. But Clemmie knew, age had nothing to do with it.

Lizzy came out that spring. The imminence of war should have made the balls and dinners and teas seem more frivolous than usual, but it only lent them a certain intensity. How many of the men would not dance their way through another season?

"How's the debutante?" Tom asked Clemmie as he walked into the master bedroom late in the afternoon on the day of Lizzy's ball.

"Resting. And cool as the proverbial cucumber. I've given up trying to predict what Lizzy is going to do. She has high spirits about the most unexpected things, but when it comes to her own coming-out party or the twins fighting over her, she's absolutely unflappable. And clever. Van sent orchids. Nick gardenias. You can imagine the problem that caused. We tried putting them together, but both boys went all out, and the result was overbearing. So she's decided to carry Porter's roses.

They're simple and appropriate, and neither Nick nor Van can possibly mind her carrying Porter's flowers."

"A diplomatic resolution if ever I heard one."

"Well, she oughtn't to be so diplomatic, and mature. It makes me feel ancient." Clemmie was standing before the full-length mirror in a corner of the room and she looked at her face carefully. "I don't think I like being the mother of the debutante."

Tom crossed the room to where she was standing and slipped his arms around her waist. "You look more like the debutante."

She looked at his reflection in the mirror. "You're being charming tonight."

He laughed. "You say that as if I'm not usually."

"Well, you must admit you're not one for extravagant compliments."

"That wasn't an extravagant compliment, simply an observation." The statement seemed true to him, or at least the sentiment that prompted it did. He'd been thinking about it all day, about Clemmie, about Lizzy, about himself.

It had been a peculiar day for Tom. The morning had been ordinary enough. He'd gone to the office, then lunched with Adam at a downtown club as they did once or twice a week.

"I hear my former wife is giving a dinner before Lizzy's dance tonight," Adam said over coffee. Apparently Clinton's doing fairly well over at Pan Am. Terribly civilized of her. She even invited me."

"Are you going?" Tom asked in surprise. He could never adjust to the attitude that kept them all meeting no matter what happened.

"Fortunately I can't. Promised to be one of the old fogeys—what we used to call chaperones—at Alison Morris's dinner for the kids."

Oh, they were civilized all right, Tom thought, but he couldn't maintain the flash of anger he'd felt. It wasn't that he'd forgotten what Whit Morris had done, and certainly he hadn't forgiven him or Clemmie, only that it had happened a long time ago and he had other things on his mind today.

Once outside the club, Adam started back toward Broadway, but Tom did not fall in step. "I think I'll leave you here," he said.

Adam looked surprised. "You mean you're not going back to the office?"

"There are a few things I want to take care of this afternoon." Tom wasn't entirely sure what they were, but he knew he had to get off by himself for a while.

"My God, maybe you're human after all." Adam gave him a light slap on the arm and started off in the direction of the A & W office.

Tom knew Adam had meant the comment as a joke and wasn't troubled by it, but he kept thinking about it. As he hailed a taxi and told the driver to take him up to Cartier's, he found he was weighing himself and the life he'd made. The early poverty and the early dreams were not as vivid as they'd once been, but he still remembered them. He could still stand off and look at his success and summon the awe of the small boy or the ambitious undergraduate who had been Tom Hendreich. The judgment was clear in that area. He'd achieved everything he'd ever dreamed and more. Oh, to be sure there were minor problems. There would always be minor problems. That was the price, and part of the thrill of it, Tom supposed. There was talk that if America got into this war, and it was bound to, they'd nationalize the railroads again just as they had during the Great War. And there was that business about the Philadelphia company that was after more A & W stock, but he'd been dealing with that problem ever since he'd taken control. And he was in the market for more stock of his own as well. His and Clemmie's holdings amounted to forty-eight percent of the voting stock. He was just a hair's breadth away from complete control. All things considered, Tom didn't have a single complaint as far as his professional success was concerned. He weighed it all in the scales of his own judgment and found the balance more than satisfactory.

But what of the rest of his life? What of the human side, the side Adam had joked about? There was Lizzy, of course, and it had been Lizzy who'd set him thinking today. He remembered his sister Elizabeth, who hadn't lived to see the Statue of Liberty, who'd died in steerage from heaven only knew which of poverty's evils. And now her namesake was "coming out" at a splendid dance in a splendid Fifth Avenue mansion, his splendid Fifth Avenue mansion. She'd be in all the papers to-morrow, and she'd already been acclaimed the debu-tante of the season. With good reason, Tom thought. A father's prejudice notwithstanding, Lizzy was a beauty. There'd been enough young men hanging around the house for the last year or so to leave no doubt on that question. But it was more than the spectacular debut that showed he'd arrived and Lizzy's beauty and popu-larity that made it all storybook perfect. He was proud of the girl herself, not just her beauty but her kindness and decency and the young woman she was becoming. She was as frivolous as all young girls, he supposed, caught up in a swirl of parties and clothes and young men, and she could be stubborn too. He'd wanted her to go to college—it wasn't as important for a girl as it was for a boy, but he still thought it was important—but Lizzy had refused. "I'd feel like such a sap," she'd said, "sitting around in Poughkeepsie or Northhampton reading Greek and Latin while people are dying in Eu-rope."

"I don't see how your not going to college is going to help anybody's war effort," Tom had answered.

"At least if I stay in New York and roll bandages or work for the Red Cross or a hospital or . . . or any-thing, I'll be doing something useful." And he'd had to admit that since she'd been home from boarding school, she'd gone at her war work with a vengeance, but without losing an ounce of her sparkle or innocence or boundless good spirits. Lizzy looked like Clemmie

and she'd inherited a good many of Clemmie's super-
ficial traits, but she had one thing that Clemmie had
always lacked. Lizzy had balance. Tom loved her and
admired her and knew he could count on her.

And what of Clemmie? Still beautiful, still irresistible
to men—others as well as himself, he knew from simply
watching—still without a sense of balance or of responsibility to anyone but herself. Oh, she'd stuck to their
bargain, all right. Tom was certain of that. Maybe she'd
stuck to it for the wrong reasons, out of fear rather than
honor, out of her need for the railroad rather than her
love for him, but she'd stuck to it, and he didn't suppose
he could complain about that. Marriage to Clemmie
hadn't turned out the way he'd sometimes hoped it
would when he'd been young, but it had turned out as
well as he had any right to expect, he realized now that
he was no longer young. He knew women who were
better wives than Clemmie, women who were kinder and
easier to live with and could be relied on, but he didn't
want those women. He wanted Clemmie, and the only
answer to the problems she presented was that he
had Clemmie.

The taxi pulled up in front of the handsome building
on the corner of Fifth Avenue and Fifty-second Street,
and the doorman came rushing down to open the cab
door for him.

"Good afternoon, Mr. Hendreich," he said.

Tom laughed to himself. How do you like that, Ma?
Think of that, Pop he mused. The doorman at Cartier's
knows me. It was only a small part of what he'd been
thinking all the way uptown, but it was a pleasant foot-
note.

Lizzy's pearls were waiting for him. The perfectly
matched white globes glowed dully against the black
velvet lining of the case. The jeweler watched Tom
gravely, as if daring him not to appreciate such magnifi-
cence. Tom murmured his approval, and the man's
face relaxed. He slipped the case into his breast pocket
and was at the door of the small private room when he

thought of it. He almost hadn't. My God, maybe Adam was right. Maybe he was inhuman. He closed the door he had begun to open.

"Is something wrong, Mr. Hendreich?" the man asked quickly.

"I'd like to see some"—Tom thought for a minute—"some emeralds."

The man smiled in delight. He appreciated his pearls, but he adored his emeralds. "Just a moment, Mr. Hendreich," he said, and scurried out after the gems.

An hour later in his own bedroom, Tom had removed the long case with Lizzy's pearls from his pocket, but the smaller one with the emerald pendant was still there. He wondered if Clemmie could feel it pressing against her shoulder as he held her to him. She was no longer examining her reflection in the mirror, but smiling at his. His hands moved from her waist to her breasts. She was wearing nothing beneath the silk robe.

"There are a thousand things I ought to be doing," she said quietly.

"Of course," he agreed, turning her to him.

"Last-minute details."

"Absolutely." His hands worked at the tie of her dressing gown.

"And you ought to be checking the liquor. And the champagne."

"Mmm," his mouth on hers agreed.

"And there are servants and hired people all over the house."

"So there's no need for us," he said, leading her to the bed.

"None at all," she agreed, drawing him down beside her. She began to undo his clothing and the small jewelry case fell out of his jacket pocket. Clemmie did not seem to notice it.

"I brought you something," Tom said, indicating the small black box that lay next to them on the bed.

"Later," she murmured, her mouth warm and eager on his.

They were out of their clothes quickly, with the speed of experience, and she felt his hands on her body, and his body responding to her own, to the things he'd shown her and the things she'd learned about him. And it was familiar but it was new too, because the memory of sensation was never the reality of sensation, and each time she tasted his mouth on hers or felt his hands on her skin or thrilled to his body responding to her own, it was new again.

"I think," Clemmie said, stretching and feeling the length of Tom's body still molded against hers, "I'd like my present now."

It took Tom a minute to locate the small box in the pile of clothing that had fallen to the floor. He handed it to her without a word.

When she opened the case she let out a small gasp. He could tell it was more than she'd expected. He was glad and a little proud.

"It's magnificent," she breathed.

"Now don't say I shouldn't have."

She smiled up at him. "I had no intention of saying anything of the kind. Thank you, darling." She took the brilliant green pendant on the platinum chain from the box and fastened it around her neck. Then she looked up at him and smiled again, as if she knew how beautiful she looked in the emerald and nothing else. "Thank you," she repeated, her mouth on his, and he could feel the softness of her breasts against him and the sharp gem he'd given her.

Porter Lowry was alone in the library a few hours later. He'd gone there because it was one of the few quiet rooms left in the house this evening. The doors between the large front drawing room and the smaller rear one had been opened and the furniture and rugs removed. Hired servants hurried back and forth at James's bidding, and when Porter had come downstairs a few minutes ago, James had given him a long-suffering look that said "What can one expect from help that can be rented for an evening?" and told Dr. Lowry he'd set up the cocktail things in the library.

Porter had only just settled down when Lizzy joined him. She looked radiant in her white dress with its sweetheart neckline and the yards and yards of skirt that made her waist look as if his hands could encircle it. The green lights were dancing in her eyes and her color was high.

He stood as she entered the room. "You look lovely, Lizzy."

She laughed. "You oughtn't to sound so sad about it."

"Just awed."

"I'll forgive you for teasing me because your flowers are so beautiful. Thank you." She crossed the room and kissed him lightly on the cheek.

"I wasn't teasing you. And I'm glad you like the flowers." He smiled, a more comfortable smile now. She was familiar again despite the white dress. "And it does save you from having to choose between the Messieurs Morris." He looked at her slyly. "At least for the moment. Where are the sterling fellows? I expected them to be cooling their heels on the doorstep by now."

"I'm early. Disgraceful thing to be at your own coming out, but there it is. Mother and Daddy are still dressing, but James said you were in here. I came to share a cocktail."

"Do you think you ought to? They're going to be plying you with champagne all night."

"I think I ought to do exactly as I please tonight."

"Lord, I pity the twins." But he mixed another drink and handed it to her.

She settled back in the sofa, holding the glass in one hand while she arranged the yards and yards of white silk around her with the other. "Where are you dining tonight, Porter?"

"With your parents. Someone called Mrs. Renfrew."

Lizzy laughed. "You'd better be careful. Mrs. Renfrew's daughter never married. Mother and her friends don't give up, do they?"

"I think it's instinct or the force of nature or something like that. I represent a void to them, and they feel obligated to fill it."

"Perhaps you ought to let them. Holly Renfrew's really quite pretty. For someone over thirty."

Porter let out a bark of laughter. "Oh, the arrogance of youth. Someday I'm going to make you pay for that statement."

Lizzy blushed. "You know what I meant."

"Yes, Lizzy," he said as he heard the twins' voices, loud and exuberant, in the entrance hall. "I know exactly what you meant."

Samantha Clinton had taken special pains dressing for Elizabeth Hendreich's dance. She was wearing a deep green satin dress that Max said was a "knockout." He was always using words like that these days, as if appropriating the language of the hungry young men on his heels at Pan American Airlines could prevent them from appropriating his position.

"It's no fun," he'd said to Samantha a year or so ago, "working for someone else," but he'd seen the look of alarm in her eyes and never mentioned the matter again. At least he was working, Max told himself, recalling those three and a half awful years after the Crash. He could still remember how long the days had seemed without anything to fill them, how powerless he'd felt being not Max Clinton the war ace or Max Clinton the head of TAA but only Max Clinton, and how shamed he'd felt when he'd realized that old friends had begun to avoid him at his clubs or cross the street when they saw him, not because they thought he wanted to borrow money or ask for a job but simply because he represented failure and in those days everyone was too busy running from failure to take the chance of greeting it head on.

Well, he'd made it through those years, and now he

was back on his feet, not the way he had been, of course, but well enough, and the important thing was not to worry, because once you started worrying about the future, it was sure to become a self-fulfilling prophecy. He would not worry about it, and more important, he would not allow Samantha to think he worried about it.

Samantha for her part was not in the least concerned about her husband's mental state. She cared only about his future, and she could guess what that would be. Max might stave off the young Turks for a while, but only for a while. Then it would be polite retirement on a modest income. Samantha hadn't spent years keeping herself young only to grow old so suddenly and abysmally. She might have railed that it simply wasn't fair, but Samantha had never been one to rail against fate. She merely took it into her own hands.

Mr. and Mrs. Maxwell Clinton and their party arrived at Lizzy's dance a little before eleven. It took Samantha less than ten minutes to locate Adam. She could have done it more rapidly—after all, the house wasn't that large—but she'd gone upstairs to make sure the elements hadn't played havoc with her appearance during the time she'd spent traveling between her house and Clemmie's. The blond hair, lifted in a sleek upsweep, was still perfect. And it looked natural, Samantha told herself.

Adam was standing with a group of men in the large second-floor sitting room where one of the bars had been set up. Samantha joined them, and the men welcomed her as she had known they would—everyone except her former husband. There was something mocking in Adam's smile, but it did not seriously trouble her.

"We missed you at dinner," she said to him quietly after a few minutes of general conversation.

"We?" She saw the smile again and was beginning to be annoyed by it.

"All of us," Samantha said. They'd moved a little

457

away from the rest of the group. "But especially me. You always were a good conversationalist, Adam."

"That's funny. I can remember one night—after a dinner at the Thornbys', I think—when you told me Max Clinton was the most fascinating dinner partner you'd ever had. You said he could talk on any subject under the sun. Of course, that was when Max owned TAA. Owning something like TAA always does a lot for a man's powers of fascination."

She looked up at him with those eyes he'd found wild so many years ago. Now they struck him as canny. "You don't own the A & W, Adam, and I still find you fascinating."

He smiled again, but this time smugly, as if he were laughing at something that had nothing to do with Samantha. "I'm touched, Sam, truly touched."

"You're not in the least, but you ought to be, and just to make sure you are, I think we ought to have one dance together. For old times' sake."

"Why, Sam, I never knew you were so sentimental. About some things, perhaps." He touched the gold necklace they'd argued over so many years before. Apparently Max hadn't been any more successful in outdoing J.P. Morgan than he had. "But not about me."

"That, Adam darling, is exactly where you make your mistake."

They went downstairs to the two drawing rooms crowded now with young couples and a few older ones moving briskly to the strains of the latest songs. Here and there a uniform stood out against the soft pastels of the girls and the somber black and white of the men. It was a prophetic scene, but neither Samantha nor Adam paid much attention to it. They were thinking more personal thoughts.

It was strange dancing with Sam again. Years ago, before they'd married, the touch of her small voluptuous body against his, the feel of her hand against his neck or her hair against his cheek as they danced had driven Adam half mad with wanting her. And in the first months of their marriage, he'd gone on responding to her that way. But then he'd come to know Samantha, to understand the woman inside the body that could arouse him so quickly, to hate the woman who'd thought she could use him so easily. At first the hatred had existed along with the desire, and Adam had found it an unsettling experience. He was accustomed to purer emotions. Then gradually he'd come to see the complexity of human relations, not only his own but everyone's, and for a few years he'd lived with the peculiar mixture, but only for a few years. It hadn't taken long for the hatred to strangle the desire. But that had been more than a decade ago, and now the hatred was as much a memory as the desire, and he felt the small body against his, the casual touch of her hand against the back of his neck—oh, so casual, because after all Sam was a pro about things like this— and a familiar current of desire ran through him. Then he remembered not only what Samantha had done to him, but what she'd cost him, and he was angry. He took a step back to put an inch of space between them.

She looked up at him and smiled as if they understood each other perfectly. "You see, it's still there."

"What's still there?" He could hear the tension in his voice.

"What we had. Nothing's changed, Adam."

"Except that you're married to Clinton."

She moved in again until her body was pressed against his. "How I must have hurt you," she whispered against his ear. "What a fool I was, Adam. To throw away what we had for—"

He moved away again. It seemed important to keep even this small distance between them. "For a man who was going to go bust in less than a year?"

"I never loved Max. You know that."

"Let's say I'll believe that. But I think you had a considerable affection for TAA."

She looked up at him and her eyes were clear, as if daring him to contradict her. "Perhaps I did, but I had more than that for you, Adam. I loved you. I've never stopped loving you."

"I'm touched." He repeated the discouraging words he'd used upstairs, but now they had a hollow ring.

"I know you don't trust me, darling. Why should you? But I can make you trust me again. I know I can." She looked around furtively, as if to make sure Clinton were not in the room, but Adam knew it was a gesture made entirely for his benefit. She didn't give a damn about her husband. "Let me talk to you alone, Adam. We can slip away. No one will notice. I know I can make you understand if we can just be alone."

Adam's mind raced ahead. She'd been demure the first time she'd gone after him, but she wouldn't be now, not after they'd been married, not after her affair with Clinton. She'd use the same battle plan she had used with Clinton. First the affair, then the divorce and re-marriage.

Well, why not, Adam asked himself. Why the hell not? Not remarriage, of course, but why not take advantage of what Samantha was offering him? He didn't owe her anything, not even honesty or decency. He could still feel her warm breath against his ear when she'd murmured to him a moment ago. You'd be a fool to refuse her, he told himself. Sleep with her tonight. Have an affair with her. Hell, if you want retribution, lead her on, let her leave Clinton, then leave her. The idea, with the exception of the part that involved his own body tangled with Samantha's, repulsed him. Who ever said revenge was sweet? It was as bitter as betrayal, more bitter perhaps, because after you've been betrayed you still have your own honor or decency to hang on to. No, he wouldn't revenge himself on Samantha. He'd leave the whole thing dead and buried as it had been for a long time now. As for the desire he'd found still alive, he'd slake that with someone else.

He looked down at Samantha. Her eyes were fastened on him, and a half-smile played about her mouth. It was at once smug and seductive.

"Just slip away," he said.

"It's the simplest thing in the world."

"Perhaps a quiet drink. At my place."

"Everything will be just the way it was. Only better. Do you remember that night at Bar Harbor, darling? We'd been married less than a week."

He remembered it all right, just as she'd known he would. He remembered the way she'd looked in the moonlight and the way her skin had tasted and her mouth had repeated his name, wanting him, pleading for him, welcoming him. Or at least he'd thought she had, and he hated her now for reminding him of that night, of his vulnerability then and the fact that it was still able to move him now.

"Only we're not married now, Samantha. Perhaps that makes it better for you—it seems to me you always did have a taste for forbidden fruit—but not for me. So if you don't mind, I'll pass up your offer. It was an offer, wasn't it? And I'll just turn you over to your husband." He looked toward Clinton, who was making his way across the room to them. "It was a pleasant dance for old times' sake, Sam, but old times are past. Thank God." He handed her over to Max and cut across the dance floor to a young woman barely a few seasons ahead of Lizzy who'd already been through her first marriage and divorce. Adam did not have to turn to know that Samantha was watching him, and he knew without looking that her eyes would be hard with anger. He felt sorry for Clinton, but not very sorry.

Clemmie took a house on Long Island that summer. Pennsylvania was no place for a girl who'd just come out. It was, for one thing, too far from the Morris twins. In that respect, Oyster Bay had been the right choice. They'd been underfoot all summer, sailing and swimming and and playing tennis during the day, escorting Lizzy to club dances and parties and movies in the evening.

Lizzy joked that she couldn't choose between them

461

because there was no difference between them, and in fact Clemmie still had trouble telling them apart physically. Often when she stumbled across her daughter these summer afternoons at the club or on their private beach below the house or the veranda, she wasn't sure which twin was in attendance, but Lizzy, recognizing her mother's predicament, always provided a helpful "Nick says" or "Van wants to know." Lizzy, however, was nowhere in sight on the afternoon Clemmie returned from the club to find one of the twins waiting for her on the terrace. James had brought him a gin and tonic and he was sprawled in a wicker chair sipping the drink and staring out across the bay, reflectively. He had not heard her step on the Oriental carpet and Clemmie stood just inside the screen of the French window, watching him for a moment. He might be either Van or Nick, but he looked exactly like Whit. The sight of him there in white trousers and blue blazer—he'd obviously dressed carefully for the visit—took her back twenty years. She saw Whit on the VanNest terrace, looking young and sleek and handsome in a similar costume, heard the words, the key phrases young people use among themselves, and the jokes and the songs of that summer. She saw the young man on the terrace and heard his father's voice and felt the old attraction. Then the young man turned and saw Mrs. Hendreich watching him and the spell was broken. He looked embarrassed for a moment, but stood quickly, gracefully, just as his father would have, and Clemmie pushed open the screen door and walked toward him, holding out her hand.

"How nice to see you." The greeting sounded incomplete. It should have been followed by a name, but she didn't dare. "Of course, you know Lizzy's not here. She's gone to her grandmother's in Pennsylvania for a few days."

He looked relieved. "So that's where she went. She just said she was going away. She wouldn't tell Nick or me where."

Clemmie felt a wave of her own relief. This was Van.

"I guess she wouldn't say where she was going because she wanted to get away from us for a few days," Van said. He looked bleak at the idea.

"I wouldn't worry about it too much, Van. A few days of quiet and she'll be dying to see you. Both of you," Clemmie added. She had to be scrupulously fair.

"Do you really think so, Mrs. Hendreich? Maybe I'll drive down there tomorrow. She's been away for two days. I could drive down and bring her back on Sunday."

And win a day without Nick, they both thought but did not say.

"I don't see why not," Clemmie said. "I think she's planning to come back Sunday evening." It wasn't that she was encouraging Van over his brother, Clemmie told herself, but if the boy showed initiative, she didn't see why it shouldn't be rewarded.

Late the following morning Lizzy and Dolly sat on the terrace of the farm. Lizzy had a book in her lap that she hadn't opened, and Dolly was gazing peacefully at her garden that sloped down from the house to the woods beyond. The wrought-iron table with the glass top was set for three for lunch.

"It's kind of you to stay with me, Lizzy. I know the farm isn't very exciting for you."

"It's as exciting as I want it to be, Grandmother. I like staying with you. I love it here. You know that. Long Island is all right. Mother adores it, and of course there's always plenty to do, but this always feels . . . I don't know . . . like home."

"You must get that from your father. Heaven knows your mother doesn't feel that way. Neither does Adam. He comes to visit regularly enough—Adam's always been a dutiful son—but he starts thinking about leaving the minute he gets here." Dolly was silent for a while, looking out over the garden. The old groundsman, Joe, still tended it, despite his age and his arthritis, but she'd selected every flower and knew the history of each plant.

"How would you like it, Lizzy, if I left this house to you? Your mother can't wait to get rid of her own house here, and Adam would sell this one in a minute. Of course, you can sell it too, if you chose to, but I don't think you would."

Lizzy felt the discomfort of the young for the realities of the old. "Oh, Grandmother, you mustn't talk about such things."

"Of course I must. I'm going to die sooner or later, and I'd like to do it as neatly as possible. And it strikes me that the sensible thing to do with this house is to leave it to you. The Wilders aren't exactly old, Lizzy, at least not by New York or Philadelphia standards, but they've lived in this house for two generations, three if you count your mother and uncles growing up here, and if you were to live here, if only for part of the year, it would make four generations. I know it isn't a fashionable spot, but it's peaceful and you might find that attractive if you're going to live in New York. I can't imagine where else you'll live if you marry one of the Morris boys."

"I'm not going to marry either of them, Grandmother."

Dolly looked at the girl to see if she were serious or merely trying to put her off the scent. She thought Lizzy was serious, but she was also young and could be expected to change her mind. "Have you told your mother that?"

"Again and again, but she refuses to believe me. I guess she just can't believe anyone would pass up a husband as eligible as Van or Nick Morris."

"And yet she passed up their father." Dolly was watching the girl out of the corner of her eye, and noticed that she looked surprised, but not overly so.

"I knew there'd been something there," Lizzy said with satisfaction. "Then she ought to understand. If she preferred Daddy to Mr. Morris with all his millions and all his social credentials, she ought to understand how I feel. I like Van and Nick, but I don't want to marry either of them."

"She won't understand, Lizzy. Your mother passed up Whit Morris, but in her own perverse way, she doesn't realize she did. And I suppose it was a good deal more complicated than I make it sound."

Lizzy waited for her grandmother to go on, but the old woman seemed to be thinking of something else. "Curious thing about the Wilder women—though I wasn't a Wilder then, I was a Lovington—and the Morris men."

"You, Grandmother? You and the twins' grandfather?"

"Their great-uncle, dear. Nick may be a nice young man, but Nicholas, after whom he's named, was a perfect stick. He had the instincts of a minister without the requisite humility. I don't think I ever met a more pompous man than old Nicholas Morris. Fortunately neither Whit nor his sons take after him. They're more like Quentin. Quentin was quite a charmer."

"Were you in love with him?"

"I thought I was at the time."

"Why didn't you marry him?"

Dolly's eyes moved from the garden to her granddaughter. Why hadn't she married Quentin Morris? At one time the reasons had been emblazoned on her mind with a brilliant and painful intensity that revealed her shame. Now she could barely remember. Oh, she still knew the story, but she couldn't believe it had really happened. "Because he wouldn't have me."

"I don't believe it," Lizzy said. She'd seen pictures of her grandmother as a girl. She'd been lovely.

"I'm flattered, dear, but it's quite true. You see, I didn't cut much of a figure, at least not in comparison to a French duchess. I was poor as a churchmouse, though the Lovingtons went back as far as the Morrises and a good deal farther than the Vanderbilts, but I was just a poor country mouse caught in the Newport rat race, if I may use one of your more modern terms."

465

"But certainly the Morrises didn't need money. I mean, this Great Uncle Quentin must have had his own fortune."

"He did, but things were a good deal more complicated in those days—or perhaps a good deal more simple. One made the most spectacular marriage one could even if one didn't have to make a spectacular marriage. If Quentin had married Dolly Lovington, his standing might not have gone down, but it certainly wouldn't have gone up. When he married Gabrielle, the Duchesse of Saville, his rating definitely climbed. Quentin Morris could have married me if he'd chosen to, Lizzy, but he chose not to. For all his youthful scrapes— he was what was called a rake in those days—Quentin was a very practical young man."

"He sounds dreadful."

"Well, I don't know about that, but in retrospect I can say he wasn't half the man your grandfather was. Not that your grandfather didn't have his faults."

"Uncle Adam and the railroad, you mean?"

"Among other things. Still, he was a good man. Perhaps that's the secret, Lizzy. Don't look for perfection, only a good man." Dolly laughed. "Heavens, but I'm running on." She looked about as if she were embarrassed, and Lizzy could see the pretty young girl of the pictures in the faded face. "I wonder where Porter is. Thank heavens I told Naomi cold salmon. I wouldn't want a hot lunch spoiling."

They heard the sound of a car on the gravel drive. "That must be Porter now," Dolly said, but Lizzy knew it was not. She was familiar with the ragged sound of Porter's old station wagon. The engine she heard now purred like a sleek animal. Van had a green LaSalle convertible. Nick had a Tuscan red Packard, also convertible.

The sound of the well-tuned engine died, then Lizzy heard the familiar station wagon on the drive. "That's Porter," she said.

Porter and Van emerged together from the house onto

466

the terrace. Dolly watched her granddaughter greeting the two men and believed what she'd told her earlier about having no intention of marrying either Morris boy. Lizzy seemed no more excited by Van's arrival than she was by Porter's. Dolly had another place laid at the table and hoped there was enough salmon.

"What a nice surprise," Dolly said as they sat down to lunch. "It seems I never have trouble filling the house when Lizzy's here. Of course, you'll stay overnight," she added to Van. "After that long drive."

"Thank you, Mrs. Wilder. I'd like to." He turned to Lizzy. "Actually, I thought I might drive you back tomorrow. Your mother said you were planning to go back then."

"I've been thinking of staying longer," Lizzy said. "At least until Wednesday."

Van looked bleak and a little annoyed. He couldn't imagine what held Lizzy here. Well, even if she didn't drive back with him tomorrow, he'd still won two days without Nick. "I'd offer to wait and drive you back then, but I've got to be in New Haven."

"Surely it's too early for school to start," Dolly said.

"Too early for school but not for ROTC."

"Army?" Porter asked.

"No, that's my brother Nick. He wants to fly. I'm in the navy. Hope to get into subs. That's were the real action will be. The flyboys will have all the glamour, but we'll be the ones who clean up the Atlantic. Did you see the latest figures? The Germans have sunk more than seven million tons of shipping."

"And you can't wait to get in there and stop them?" Porter asked, but his voice was not unkind. He just wished the kid didn't sound like such an eager young fool going off on a lark, but that was the way all the kids sounded these days.

"Someone has to," Van answered.

"Well, you're right about one thing," Porter said. "It isn't going to be glamorous. None of it—not even the air war—is going to be glamorous."

Van recognized the tactic. All the fellows who were too old for this war liked to frighten you with horror stories from the last. It was as if they knew power was slipping out of their hands, that once he and his contemporaries went off to war, they'd have no control over them, and this was their last attempt to keep the next generation in its place. Well, if the old boy wanted to jaw about his own feats in the Great War, Van would let him. "Were you in the last war, sir?"

"Just missed it."

"That must have been tough on you," Van said.

"On the contrary. It was tough on the men who went over."

"I mean, you must have felt you missed out on something."

Porter looked across the table at Van. Did he really think it was going to be a great adventure? "I only hope that you and others like you will miss out on it as well. I don't suppose you will, the way things are going, but I wish you could."

"Well, I for one wouldn't want to," Van shot back. He was no coward.

Porter caught himself. There was no point arguing with the boy. He'd have to learn the hard way. Most men did.

After lunch Dolly told them not to worry about her. She'd be happy just sitting here in her garden, but the young people ought to go off to the club for a game of tennis. As soon as the words were out, she was sorry she'd said them. Porter wasn't a young person, at least not by any standards but those of an old woman.

"We'll have to find a fourth," Lizzy said. "How about Linda Shron? I'll take you, Porter, and Van can take Miss Shron. That ought to even the sides up. Providing you're in good form today. You were slow as molasses yesterday."

"I like that! I made you work for every point, and you know it."

"About as much as Grandmother would have," Lizzy said, bending to kiss Dolly's cheek.

"Don't you think you're a little hard on the old boy?" Van asked when they were in his LaSalle following Porter to the club.

"What do you mean?"

"All that business about being slow on the court. It's obvious he likes to think he's young. Maybe it's because he never married or had kids of his own. I don't know, but you can see how he takes that kind of thing."

Lizzy looked at Van from behind her dark glasses as if he were a little mad, then she began to laugh. "Just leave Porter to me, Van. I'll take care of dear old Porter."

There was a dance at the club that night. Lizzy was cut in on every few minutes, or so it seemed to Van, but he was happy to see that she did not dance with any one man more than the others. His rival was still his brother, not some country joker who'd turned up from her youth.

The house was dark when they returned home that night. Lizzy switched on the light in the front hall, but Van, following her in, switched it off again immediately. He caught her around the waist and pulled her to him. His mouth was avid on hers but she neither responded to it nor pushed him away. Then his mouth began to trace a line down her neck and she pulled away.

"Don't, Van. Please." She switched on the light again and could read the familiar anger in his eyes.

"Don't, Van. Please," he mimicked. "I love you, Lizzy."

"You don't love me. You just want to beat Nick."

"That's not true." He pulled her to him again as if he could prove his words by physical force. "I love you, and I want to marry you. Don't you understand that? We don't have much time. We're going to be in this war before you know it."

469

"I don't think that's much of a reason for getting married," she said, disengaging herself from him.

"The hell it's not. I'd rather have a month with you than nothing at all."

She felt as if she were caught in a vise that was being drawn tighter and tighter. It wasn't fair to use the war against her all the time. "Look, Van, maybe there won't be any war. Maybe you won't be sent. . . ."

"What you mean is you don't want to marry me."

"I don't want to marry anyone."

"Not even Nick?"

"God, there you go again. All I am to you two is one last trophy to compete for. Well, I'm not going to marry you, war or no war, and if it makes you feel better, I'm not going to marry Nick either."

"It does make me feel better, but not for the reason you think. Only because as long as you haven't decided to marry him, I still have a chance." She started to say something, but he stopped her. "Don't take that away, Lizzy. The least you can do is send me off to war with some hope." He was half joking, she knew, but only half.

"Send you off to war! Don't be melodramatic, Van. What I'm sending you off to is sleep. And no more arguments upstairs. I don't want to wake Grandmother."

Lizzy was impatient for Van to leave the next afternoon, but after he had, she felt no better. Dolly was upstairs resting, and after pacing first the living room, then the terrace for twenty minutes, she started out for Porter's house. She had to talk to someone.

The housekeeper told her Dr. Lowry was in the library. She did not bother to show Lizzy in. The girl had been popping in and out of the house for almost as long as she could walk.

Porter looked up from the book he was reading when Lizzy entered. She noticed the dust jacket. *Berlin Diary.* "I thought you were one person who wasn't obsessed with the war, but I can see I was wrong."

470

"I'm not obsessed, Lizzy, but I'm not an ostrich either. And don't take your bad mood out on me. I'm sure whatever you're angry about has nothing to do with my reading matter."

She flopped down in a chair across from him. She was wearing a white sleeveless dress with a pleated skirt, and her arms and legs looked sleek and brown against the pale linen. "I'm sorry. I'm not angry."

"Then what?"

"I don't know. Maybe guilty."

"I take it that has to do with Mr. Morris. Which Mr. Morris was it yesterday anyway? Nick or Van?"

"You know very well it was Van. Porter . . . what am I going to do about them?"

He'd closed the book when she entered the room and now he put it on the table beside him. "Do you have to do something about them?"

"They're both driving me crazy to. So's Mother, for that matter. Everyone says I have to choose between them."

"Then I guess you'd better choose between them."

"You mean you don't think I have to."

He rose and walked to the window. When he spoke his back was to her and he sounded angry. "I can't tell you what to do, Lizzy. This isn't a matter of choosing between two cakes for tea. You're choosing between two men. And if you're old enough to do that, you're old enough to do it by yourself."

"But what if I don't want either of them?"

He turned back to her, and now he looked as well as sounded angry. "Then for God's sake, don't choose either of them. But don't expect me to tell you to marry one or the other or neither—or both, for that matter."

"But, Porter, if I can't talk to you about it, whom can I talk to?"

"Well, you can't talk to me about this, Lizzy, and if you don't know why, then you're not as bright as I've always thought you were."

She had stopped thinking of Van and Nick. Another

471

problem confronted her now, the one that had lay beneath her words all along. She'd sensed something all summer, but she'd been afraid to believe it. It had been too impossible to believe. And now she was afraid to speak in case she might have misunderstood him, in case she might make a fool of herself. Yet she knew that she'd come over here complaining about Nick and Van only because she wanted to make Porter speak.

"You're not a child anymore, Lizzy. And I don't feel about you the way a man feels about a child. So don't come here asking me about Nick and Van. Or anyone else for that matter." He was speaking quickly now, and his voice sounded strange and harsh. "The only thing I'll say is—don't marry any of them, but I have no right to say that."

She looked up at him from under dark lashes. The uncertainty was gone. The abrupt half-angry way he'd spoken, his inability to look at her as he did, gave force to his words.

"You could say, 'Don't marry any of them, Lizzy, marry me.' "

He laughed grimly. "To use a cliché, I'm old enough to be your father."

"But you're not my father. And I don't feel in the least daughterly to you. I haven't for some time now."

"It's impossible."

"Are you going to force me to beg you, Porter?"

"You'd be sorry within a year."

"Why? I've loved you for longer than a year. First one way, then another. I don't see why being married to you should suddenly change that."

"There'd be a thousand problems."

She stood and crossed the room to him. "Probably a million." She put her arms about his neck and raised her face to his.

"Lizzy," he said. It was a protest, but her mouth on his changed it into an endearment and then a promise.

*   *   *

Nevertheless, Porter was not so easily convinced. He could not get over the feeling that marrying Lizzy was somehow unfair to her. He agreed that they would begin seeing more of each other on these new terms. But she must also, he insisted, give herself every chance to fall in love with someone her own age.

"But I'm already in love," Lizzy protested. Porter, however, was adamant, and so that autumn Lizzy agreed to go to the Harvard weekend with Nick Morris. It was only fair, she explained to Van, since she'd gone to the Princeton weekend with him. Van pointed out that fairness had nothing to do with it, but Lizzy was firm and it was Nick who met her at the New Haven station that Friday night in late November. The town was covered with a thin film of snow—a definite improvement, all the undergraduates joked—and spirits were high. They sank somewhat the next afternoon when Harvard trounced Yale 14–0, but it was hard to remain depressed when there were so many cocktail parties to attend after the game, and soon the score was only a mistake to be remedied the following year.

The parties after the game were a familiar blend of old graduates and undergraduates. Rarely did the generations meet with so little hostility and such complete understanding. Of course the whiskey helped, but there were times when whiskey only served to drive the two groups farther apart, so it was clearly more than that. It was the feeling of shared experience and comaraderie and sheer sentimentality. Lizzy looked from the twins to their father. Both Whit and Alison had come up for the game. The three men looked alike and they sounded alike, rehashing the game, greeting friends, teasing her and Mrs. Morris about their imperfect understanding of the sport. They even stood the same way, glasses in one hand, the other hand resting easily in gray flannel pockets. She thought of her grandmother's story about her mother and Mr. Morris. She wondered if her mother had really been in love with him. She wondered why she couldn't manage to fall in love with either Nick or Van.

473

It would be so much easier if only she could choose one of them, but she knew she couldn't. Even after several drinks she knew she couldn't.

The parties dragged on and Lizzy was late getting back to the Taft Hotel to change for the evening. Nick opened the door to the room she was sharing with another girl, then, instead of handing her the key, followed her in.

"If you don't get moving," she said, "I'll never be dressed in time."

He flopped diagonally across one of the twin beds and smiled up at her. He was terribly good-looking, she thought, and fairly drunk at the moment. "And if I'm not dressed in time we'll miss the dance."

"Terrible thing," he said. "Couldn't stand to miss the dance." He caught her hand as she walked past the bed and pulled her down beside him.

"I mean it, Nick."

"Sure you do. You always mean it." He laughed but did not let her go. She felt his mouth hungry on hers and the length of his body pressed against her own. She tried to pull away, but he held her to him with one hand while the other was gentle but insistent against her sweatered breast. She wrenched away from him and stood. "No!" she said. It was almost a shout.

"Christ! What's wrong with you anyway? Elizabeth Hendreich, ice goddess. Elizabeth Hendreich, modern man's monument to frigidity."

There was a time when the words would have terrified her, but they didn't anymore. She turned away from him and straightened her sweater and skirt.

Nick sat up and took a package of Lucky Strikes from his pocket. "Don't you know what you're doing to me, Lizzy?" His voice was filled with misery rather than anger now.

"*I* wasn't doing anything."

"You're damn straight you weren't." He lit the cigarette and inhaled deeply. "Listen, Lizzy, maybe I had too much to drink. Maybe I pushed you too hard. But

474

I wasn't just fooling around. I love you. I want to marry you. I don't want to go off to this thing without marrying you."

"That's what Van says."

"I don't give a damn what Van says."

"Don't you?"

"I didn't mean that. Of course, I do. And I feel sorry for him, but he'll find someone else."

"You'll both find someone else because I'm not going to marry either of you."

He was still sitting on the bed and he looked up at her with eyes that were not particularly kind. Lizzy saw the look and thought that perhaps she was wrong. Perhaps there was some difference between Nick and his brother.

"Does that mean you're waiting to see which one of us comes home after this thing? You're the spoils and you'll belong to the victor—or at least the survivor."

"That's a rotten thing to say."

"Sorry, but I'm feeling pretty rotten at the moment." He started for the door. "Don't worry, Lizzy. I'll take a cold shower before I dress and by the time I come back for you I'll be good as gold."

And he was. Perhaps it was simply the resurgence of the Morris manners. Perhaps it was the knowledge that if he fought with her, Van would be only too happy to step in and take his place.

Chapter 14

ON THE AFTERNOON of December 7 Lizzy was in her room listening to the radio. She raced downstairs with the news of Pearl Harbor, but her parents had already heard. The servants had been playing the radio in the kitchen, and James had come upstairs with word.

Both Nick and Van had tried to call all afternoon and evening, but they hadn't been able to get through. The following day she received two letters from New Haven. Both begged her to reconsider, to agree to marriage before they were shipped out. Nick's plea was only a little more demanding than Van's.

The following weekend Porter came to town and she told him about the letters. "Are you sure you don't want either of them? They're both good enough sorts." They were in the Palm Court of the Plaza Hotel, Lizzy's favorite spot even in the days when Porter had taken her for cocoa and disgracefully rich pastries rather than cocktails.

She reached over and put her hand on his. Out of the corner of her eye she saw two matrons watching them disapprovingly, but she didn't care.

"I don't want anyone but you, darling. I've been telling you that for months, but you refuse to believe me. Personally, I think you just like playing hard to get.

Well, I was perfectly willing to let you. I was perfectly willing to spend time with all sorts of men I don't care about to prove to you how much I do care about you. Or at least I was until last Sunday. Until they bombed Pearl Harbor and you went off and enlisted—like some fool undergraduate."

"Well, when you're in love with a younger woman . . ."

"You know perfectly well that I had nothing to do with your enlisting. You didn't do it to prove anything to me, darling. You did it because of the kind of man you are. And that only brings me back to my point. I love you for the kind of man you are and I have no intention of losing you. I have no intention of sitting here while the navy sends you off heaven only knows where. So you might as well give in, because if you don't marry me and take me with you, I'm going to follow you anyway." She smiled at him across the table. "I'll become a camp follower. But a very selective one, you understand."

"You know it's what I want, Lizzy. There's nothing I want more. Only, I feel so . . . I don't know, guilty about wanting it."

"You're supposed to feel blissfully happy."

"Oh, I feel that, all right. I can't help feeling that. But every time I think of those upstanding fellows you ought to marry . . . not only Nick and Van but all those brilliant young men with brilliant futures . . ."

"Are you telling me you have a past, darling? Well, I'm broad-minded. After all, you had to do something while you were waiting for me to grow up."

"I can see you're not going to be serious about this."

"Do you want me to be?"

He smiled and placed his other hand on top of hers. "Not in the least. I keep feeling I ought to give you a chance to change your mind, but I don't know what I'd do if you did."

"Well, I won't."

"They're going to put up a fight, you know."

"Of course I know. That's why I don't want to tell them until the last minute. If it were up to me I wouldn't tell them until afterward—confront them with a *fait accompli*—but you're so scrupulous. So we'll tell them before, but only just before. I still remember that story Grandmother told me about Consuelo Vanderbilt. The way they locked her up until she agreed to marry the Duke of Marlborough."

"I don't think they'd go that far."

"Of course they wouldn't, but I'm not giving Mother a chance for any other schemes. I'll tell her next Saturday and we'll leave for Grandmother's house that night. That will give them time to get to the wedding on Sunday, but not time to stop it."

"You've worked out everything."

"Almost everything. There's still one thing that bothers me. What if they send you overseas?"

"At my age! I'll be lucky if they let me staff a base hospital."

"Do you mean that, or are you only saying it to make me feel better?"

"Have I ever lied to you, Lizzy?"

"Not that I know of."

"The answer is no. I've never lied to you, and I'm not going to start now. Marriage may change me, but it's not going to change me that way." He signaled for the check. "And now I'd better take you home or you're going to have to tell a lot of lies yourself."

They emerged from the warm lobby into the crisp December night. Across from the hotel the lights of the fountain, already dressed for Christmas, glittered in the darkness. The doorman held the door of the taxi open for them.

Porter gave the driver the address, and the taxi circled the plaza past the store that had replaced the old Vanderbilt mansion. The windows were filled with costly gifts for what was expected to be, until a few weeks ago, the last peacetime Christmas for a long time. Lizzy dropped her head on Porter's shoulder. "I'm going to be a Christmas bride." She lifted her face to his, and his mouth was warm on hers and his arms strong around her. She tasted the whiskey on his tongue and smelled the familiar fragrance that was Porter and reached up to touch the soft hair. She felt happy in his arms and secure and then something more, something urgent and exciting as she felt his hands inside her fur coat holding her to him.

She turned her head until her mouth was at his ear. "Tell the man to turn around, darling," she whispered.

He looked down at her in the shadowy light of the cab. "Tell him to turn around and go back to the hotel. Another week and a piece of paper aren't going to make any difference. I love you, and I want you to make love to me. I think it's about time, darling. I think it's more than time."

"Lizzy," he murmured. "Lizzy." Then he kissed her once more before telling the driver to go back to the Plaza.

The following Saturday, the day Lizzy had chosen to tell her parents she was going to marry Porter Lowry, began badly. First, in the early hours of the morning, there was that business between Nick and Van Morris at someone's dance on Long Island. Clemmie had heard about it before Lizzy was up the next morning. Fighting in the snow like two young animals. It was flattering in a sense, Clemmie admitted to Tom over breakfast, but really, the time had come for Lizzy to put an end to all this foolishness. They'd both be going overseas soon, and she couldn't let things drag on.

"She says she doesn't want to marry either of them," Tom said, "and I don't see why she has to just because they're going off to war."

"Of course, she's going to marry one of them."

He smiled down the table at Clemmie. "Because you want her to?"

"Because it's the logical thing to do. They're both in love with her, and she couldn't find a better husband

480

than either of them. It's her age, Tom. She's young and
indecisive and can't make up her mind. If it weren't
for the war, I wouldn't force her to. If it weren't for the
war she could take all the time she wanted deciding
between them, but with the war it isn't fair to either
of the boys to keep them dangling this way. And I'm
going to tell her so as soon as she's up. I've been telling
her all along, but this time she's going to listen." That
seemed to finish the issue for Clemmie. She had something else on her mind this morning and she knew Tom
wasn't going to like it.

"I was thinking of going to Washington tomorrow
afternoon." He looked up from the paper in surprise.
"Just for a few days."

"What's in Washington?"

"These days, everything. There's too much talk about
nationalizing the railroads again, and we can't let that
happen. I remember the way Father complained during
the last war. They let everything go to pieces—the
tracks, the rolling stock, everything—and it cost a
fortune to get things back in shape. We can't let it happen again."

"We're not going to. We have someone down there
representing us. You know that, Clemmie."

"McSorley," she said disparagingly. "He isn't worth
the money you pay him. I told you that when you and
Adam hired him. He doesn't have the right connections."

Tom was still watching her, but he was no longer
amused by her determination. He had a feeling they'd
had this conversation before. "But you do, of course.
Have the right connections, I mean. Are you going to
tell me you went to school with Eleanor, just as you
did with Lydia Sharp?"

"I knew you were going to bring that up. And I think
it's awfully unfair of you. Just because I didn't succeed
with Middleton Sharp before doesn't mean I won't this
time."

They were both thinking not of her failure to win control of the Tidewater and Western but of the rest of that weekend, but neither would mention it. "For one thing I do know Ralph Budd. We both do, if it comes to that. You've been buying equipment from him for years, but I bet McSorley has never even met the man."

"What you don't understand, Clemmie, is that Budd was in charge of transportation for the Defense Advisory Commission, but that was before December seventh. There are new men down there now setting up new agencies and you won't even know where to begin."

"I'll begin with Budd. Things can't be moving that fast." Her voice was cool and her movements, as she refilled Tom's cup and her own from the silver pot, were relaxed and confident. Her face looked smooth, without a line of distress or anger. Clemmie had made a decision. It was that simple to her. Tom remembered the day of Lizzy's debut, only a little more than six months ago. He'd wandered around town that day toting up his life as if it were a finished product. He'd considered the pluses and minuses as if he were at a final reckoning, reading one of those obituaries he'd been addicted to the summer he'd been separated from Clemmie. But nothing about his life was fixed or final, and the old bitterness could be summoned easily.

"Why bother with Budd?" he shot back. "Why waste your time on any of the subordinates? Why not go straight to the President? He's supposed to have quite an eye for the ladies, and that's what you're counting on, isn't it, Clemmie?"

"What if I am? Does it matter how we avoid nationalization, as long as we do?"

"It does to me. It does if it means my wife has to run around Washington selling herself to every politician in sight."

"You're exaggerating. As usual."

He stood abruptly and Clemmie watched the coffee spill over the Lenox saucer and on to the Irish linen place mat. "No, I'm not exaggerating, Clemmie, and we both know it. I won't dredge up the past because we agreed a long time ago we wouldn't talk about that. And I won't tell you not to go to Washington, because I know it won't do any good. But I'm asking you not to go. Begging you not to go. And I'll tell you one thing, Clemmie. This isn't a threat, just a statement. If you do, it will make a difference between us. I've managed to forget—not forget perhaps, but bury—a lot of things. I guess we both have. But I'm too old to begin forgetting new things." He started out of the dining room.

"Is that an ultimatum?"

"I told you, Clemmie. Only a statement."

It was nearly noon when Lizzy came down. Clemmie heard her in the front hall telling James she'd be back late that afternoon. Clemmie hurried out of the library to catch her, but the girl was already in her nutria coat, fastening her galoshes.

"I want to talk to you, Lizzy."

"Can't now, Mother. Hopelessly late."

"Late for what?"

"Lunch . . . friends . . . I'll explain everything later." In one swift movement she managed to plant a kiss on her mother's cheek, put on her hat, and sweep out the door.

It was after five when she returned. Clemmie and Tom were in the small rear drawing room. He'd gone to the office that morning even though it was Saturday, and spent the afternoon at one of his clubs. A game of squash with Tim Atherton had done little to drain the anger he'd felt this morning, but he had not mentioned Washington when he'd returned home and hour ago, and Clemmie had not raised the subject either.

"It's freezing out," Lizzy said as she came into the room in her easy athletic stride. Her cheeks were flushed and she held two icy hands against Tom's face.

"You're in a good mood," he said. He was glad someone in the family was.

"I'm in a stupendous mood."

"Well, Nick and Van aren't," Clemmie pointed out. "Not after last night. They've been calling here all day. So have all your friends. The phone hasn't stopped ringing. How you can cause something like last night and then just disappear? . . ."

"In view of the fuss, it seems disappearing was the best thing I could do. And you're really making too much of last night, Mother. They'd both had too much to drink, and when Van tried to cut in, Nick wouldn't let him. The next thing I knew they were saying absurd things to each other and Nick demanded they go outside to settle it—as if the two of them will ever settle anything. Anyway, before I knew it they were rolling around in the snow like a couple of polar bears. And having a perfectly good time, if you ask me."

"What a *femme fatale*," Tom laughed.

"It's not a joking matter," Clemmie said.

"Of course it is, Mother. It's exactly the sort of thing Nick and Van love to do. And I don't believe it has a thing to do with me."

"Then why were they both calling here all day? And you still haven't told me where you were," Clemmie added.

"I was with Porter."

"Porter. I didn't even know he was in town."

"He doesn't always stay with us when he is, Mother. He was having his uniforms fitted."

"His uniforms?" There was no mistaking the surprise in Tom's voice.

"He's enlisted."

"At his age," Clemmie said. "Don't be ridiculous."

"He's not old, Mother. And he's a doctor. They always need doctors."

"Have to hand it to him," Tom said.

"Well, I think he's being foolish, but Porter is not the one who concerns me now," Clemmie said. "You must make up your mind about the twins, Lizzy."

Lizzy had been sitting on the arm of Tom's chair,

and now she moved to the ottoman in front of the fireplace and looked from one parent to the other. She was smiling as if she were about to deliver a piece of good news, although she knew they would not consider it such. "I've made up my mind, Mother. I've been telling you that for ages. I'm not going to marry either of them. I'm going to marry Porter."

"Lizzy, this is no time for jokes," Clemmie snapped.

Tom was watching his daughter carefully. "You're not joking are you?"

"Not in the least, Daddy."

Clemmie looked at her daughter for what seemed like a long time to both of them. "But he's old enough to be your father."

"That's what he said at first, though he's four years younger than Daddy. Porter is forty-two, Mother. I'm nineteen. Isn't that shocking?"

"You'll be nineteen this spring."

"The point is, I'm old enough to marry without your permission. I don't want to do it that way, but if I have to, I will."

"The point is that he's much too old for you," Clemmie shot back.

"I imagine it looks that way to you, but age has nothing to do with it. I love Porter and he loves me and when we're together everything seems right." Lizzy turned to her mother. "You must know what I mean. It doesn't have anything to do with how old anyone is or how good a catch or any of the logical things. I don't think there's anything logical about it. Oh, you can talk about having things in common and that sort of thing, and I guess you'd say Porter and I have all that. We like the same things and we laugh at the same things and Lord knows we go back far enough together, but it's more than that. It's just that suddenly, or maybe not suddenly but little by little, you begin to realize you're unhappy when you're apart and happy when you're together and you keep saving up things to tell each other and pretty soon other people don't matter so much because you have your own world."

"You feel all that about Porter?" Tom asked quietly.

Lizzy turned to him gratefully. She'd been trying to convince her mother, but it was her father who'd seen what she was trying to say. "I really do, Daddy. And that's why the age thing doesn't matter at all."

"You'll be a widow before you know it," Clemmie said.

"That's a horrible thing to say," Lizzy cried. "And a silly one. Would I be any safer with Nick or Van? Neither of them can wait to see action."

"What about Nick and Van?"

"What about them, Mother? They're my friends, but they're not my responsibility. I can't marry them just because everyone expects me to. And if you think of it, this is the best way out. This way I don't have to choose between them."

"I don't understand it," Clemmie said. "They're both young and handsome with good futures. When I think of the Morris name and that fortune . . . and you want to throw it all away to marry a country doctor twice your age."

"Didn't you throw over the Morris name and all that money to marry Daddy?"

Clemmie was shocked. She couldn't imagine where Lizzy had got that idea, but there was nothing she could say in front of Tom.

"If you married for love, I don't see why I can't." Lizzy pressed what she believed was her advantage.

"I don't think," Tom said, standing and walking to the cocktail wagon, "that your mother and I—or at least our marriage—have anything to do with it." He freshened his drink and turned back to them. "This concerns only you and Porter."

"Exactly," Lizzy said.

"I can't say I'm pleased," Tom went on. "There will be problems that you don't even dream of now." He saw Lizzy begin to speak and went on quickly. "You don't see that, but I'm counting on the fact that Porter does. Porter's no fool. He knows what he's getting into and what he's getting you into. He'd never do anything to hurt you. I'm sure of that. I can't say I'm pleased about all this," he repeated. "But I don't see any real reason to be displeased either. I guess it's just going to take some time for me to get used to it."

"Oh, Daddy, you're a darling." Lizzy was across the room and in his arms in a moment. "I knew you'd understand."

"Well, I have no intention of understanding or getting used to it," Clemmie said. "I have no intention of letting you go through with it."

Lizzy turned from her father to Clemmie and she was no longer smiling. The soft brown eyes were grave now. "It's not up to you to let me or not let me, Mother. I told you that. Porter and I are going back to Grandmother's tonight. We're going to be married there tomorrow."

"Tomorrow!" Clemmie cried.

"You might have given us more notice," Tom said.

"Porter wanted to. Honestly he did, but I wouldn't let him. It would only have meant more time for arguing about it, and there's no point in arguing because I've made up my mind. We're being married at Grandmother's tomorrow and I hope you'll both come."

"It seems," Clemmie said, "that if you told your grandmother, the least you could have done was inform your parents."

"I didn't mean to tell Grandmother, but she guessed. I spent a lot of time at the farm last fall and I imagine I was pretty transparent."

"And does she approve?" Tom asked.

"About the way you do. She was shocked at first, but she's so crazy about Porter, she can't help but approve."

"It seems I'm the only one left in the family with any sense," Clemmie said, but the doorbell rang before anyone could contradict her.

"That will be Porter."

"I don't want to see him. I won't have him in my house. Not after what he's done."

"Mother," Lizzy began but Tom interrupted her.

"This is *our* house, Clemmie, and Porter is as welcome in it as he's always been."

Porter entered the room looking a little shamefaced. His eyes darted from one to the other of them rapidly, as if reconnoitering the situation. He assessed it correctly. "I don't have to ask if Lizzy told you."

Lizzy crossed the room to him and put her arm in his.

"She's just told us," Tom began in a neutral voice, but Clemmie broke in.

"How could you! How could yo do such a disgraceful thing?"

"I didn't expect you to be pleased, Clemmie, but it isn't a tragedy."

"It isn't a tragedy for you," she snapped. "It is for Lizzy. For all of us. It's more than a tragedy. It's disgusting. A man your age ... taking advantage ..."

"That's ridiculous, Mother, and you know it."

Clemmie whirled on her daughter. "Be quiet. You know nothing about it. You're a child." She turned back to Porter. "And you ought to know better than to get mixed up with a child. The daughter of your oldest friend. And behind our backs. It's disgusting, I tell you. A man your age with an eighteen-year-old girl. You must be mad. Or sick. Or degener—"

"Clemmie!" Tom cut in. "That's enough."

"It's not nearly enough."

"I said it is!" Tom's voice was like steel, and his eyes warned her not to go on.

"I suppose you're going to stand by and let him get away with this," she said to Tom.

"A little more than that," he answered quietly. "I'm going to give the bride away. If she wants me to, that is."

"You're as bad as they are," Clemmie hissed. She

stood there for a moment staring at Tom, then left the room without a glance at Porter or Lizzy.

"Now that the histrionics are over, perhaps we can get on with the celebration." Sound pleased, Tom told himself. Smile. It's what they both want. He crossed the room to Porter and shook his hand. "Congratulations. And good luck." The smile was beginning to stiffen on his face, and he felt awkward. "And all the rest of it. Darn it, we need some champagne. Lizzy, ring for James. We've got to celebrate this thing properly."

Tom was not quite as cheerful as he sounded and both Porter and Lizzy knew it, but he was putting a good face on it, and they were both grateful to him for that.

Clemmie was sitting in a chair before the window when Tom entered the bedroom an hour later. There was a magazine on her lap, but it lay there unopened. She had been looking out the window at the traffic crawling through the slush of Fifth Avenue. She'd been looking out the window and she'd seen Lizzy and Porter leave only a few minutes earlier. Her arm had been tucked in his and when they'd reached the sidewalk they'd turned and waved toward the doorway below. Then Tom must have closed the door because they'd turned back to each other and Clemmie had seen the expression on Lizzy's face as she looked up at Porter. It was young and trusting and absolutely naked with love.

"I suppose you're going to let her go through with it," she said as Tom entered the room.

"It's not up to me, as Lizzy pointed out."

"Of course, it's obvious that he's a father figure to her."

"Have you been reading watered-down Freud in the fashion magazines again?"

"Sneer if you want, but it's obvious."

Suddenly he was exhausted. That business about Washington this morning. Her refusal to yield an inch now, even though she'd have to be blind not to see that Lizzy was in love.

"Maybe she does want a father," he said. "Maybe her own father was too busy worrying about her mother, trying to please her mother, trying to placate her mother all these years to have any time for her. Maybe he was too busy with her mother and the railroad to think much about Lizzy. I don't know, Clemmie, and at this point I don't care, because for whatever reason, Lizzy does love Porter and he loves her, and if you ask me, which you aren't now and never have, there aren't many men who can hold a candle to him."

"You've never liked the Morris boys."

"And you simply can't get over the fact that she doesn't want to marry one of Whit's sons. She was supposed to realize your dream. Wasn't that it, Clemmie?"

"She couldn't have made a better match than the Morris boys."

"So you never tire of saying. I don't agree with you, but I'm not going to argue the point anymore. Are you coming with me to the wedding tomorrow?"

"I'm going to Washington tomorrow," she answered, and opened the magazine on her lap.

Adam arrived at the house half an hour later. He'd called that afternoon and said he wanted to come by to speak to Tom.

"Did you hear the news?" Tom asked, meeting him in the front hall. "Lizzy's marrying Porter Lowry."

"You're joking."

"That's what Clemmie said."

"How's she taking it?"

"If she comes down, you'll see. If she stays upstairs, you can guess."

"She's going to have to come down," Adam said. "I want to talk to her too, but I wanted to see you alone first."

Tom led him into the library and poured a whiskey for each of them. "To Lizzy and Porter," Adam said, lifting the glass in salute. They talked for a few minutes about the match, but Tom could tell that Adam had something else on his mind. "I guess this is a day for surprises," he said uncomfortably.

"Don't tell me you're marrying some debutante. Or that you've enlisted. Porter's done that too."

"Well, I'll be damned," Adam said. but it was clear that he was not paying attention. "It's going to be in the papers Monday, Tom, but I wanted to tell you myself. It's about the railroad stock. You know, the last bloc that belonged to the daughter of that Philadelphia fellow."

Tom mentioned the name of one of the three men who had taken A & W shares from Elias in return for their own small railroads so many years ago.

"That's the one. Well, she finally decided to sell, and I bought them. The whole bloc."

"That's fine. I've been telling you all along that you ought to be buying stock." Tom was genuinely glad for Adam, but he was a little annoyed as well. He'd spoken to the woman only a few months ago, but he hadn't been able to convince her to sell. He'd have liked to been able to buy those few extra shares that would have put him over the fifty-percent mark, but he supposed having Adam own a bloc of shares that could be added to his and Clemmie's was the next best thing.

Adam was turning the glass of whiskey nervously in his hands, and now he looked down into it as if he did not want to look up at Tom. "It's a bit more than that. That Philadelphia firm, the one that's been buying stocks all along . . ." He stopped as if he couldn't bring himself to go on.

Tom looked across the room at his brother-in-law. His head was still down and his shoulders were hunched forward. It came to him with a sudden shock.

"You're that firm," Tom said.

Adam nodded.

"From the very beginning? From Cornelia?"

This time the movement of Adam's head was barely perceptible.

"And now you've got fifty-two percent of the voting stock."

Adam did not even move.

Tom felt his hand tighten around the crystal glass as if he were going to crush it. "Christ!"

"I'm sorry, Tom."

"You're sorry! If you were sorry, you wouldn't have done it. What I don't understand is why you had to do it. I've been offering you stock all along and you kept refusing it."

"I had to do it my own way. I had to prove something—to myself, to Father. You see, he'd always had faith in me. Until Samantha. Then he gave up on me. And it didn't help much that he turned out to be right. And I turned out to be the ass of the century. So I had to prove myself all over again. And the only way to do that was to take over my own railroad. Just as Father had. Don't you see, Tom, I couldn't take it from you as a gift. I could have at one time, from Father, but I couldn't from you now. I had to prove I was smart enough and strong enough to win it on my own.

"It won't change anything, Tom. I want you to stay on. We've been running things together all these years, and I want us to keep running them together."

Tom drained his glass, stood, and crossed the room to refill it. When he turned, the broad handsome face was taut with rage. "You know there's something wrong with your whole damn family, something about that railroad that makes you all a little crazy. George went off the deep end as soon as he inherited it. He ended up losing everything—including his life—because of it. Clemmie's always been obsessed by it. And now you. I thought you were the sane one, but I was wrong. You're as bad as the others. Worse. I wanted you to buy stocks. I wanted to share the railroad with you. But that would have been too simple, too straightforward. Why buy stocks openly when you can maneuver an underhanded takeover?" His voice had been rising with each sentence, and now his anger incited Adam's. The new owner of the A & W was through apologizing.

"Don't be so damn holier-than-thou, Tom. It doesn't suit you. After all, you weren't exactly the logical heir to the railroad."

"Whatever I bought, I bought openly. And I never asked to inherit those stocks in the beginning."

Adam stood and refilled his glass. When he turned back to Tom his smile was cruel. "No, you never *asked* for anything. You just married the boss's daughter. . . ."

Before he knew what he was doing, Tom felt his arm moving through space and his fist connecting with Adam's jaw. It made a loud smacking sound that drowned out the dull thud of the glass striking the carpet. Adam fell back into the chair with a surprised look on his face. He sat that way for a moment, then his hand moved to his face and he rubbed his jaw gingerly. He hadn't expected the response, but he wasn't sorry it had come. "I guess that evens things up."

"The hell it does. That finishes things. I've had it. With you. With Clemmie. With the whole damn railroad. You can tell Clemmie I'll sign all my stocks over to her. Then the two of you can fight it out. I'm just glad I won't be around to watch."

"To watch what?" Clemmie was standing in the doorway.

Tom turned at the sound of her voice. "Adam will explain it to you. Adam will explain everything. I'm leaving."

"Don't be a fool," Adam said.

"I'm not. For the first time in a long time I've stopped being a fool."

"I don't understand," Clemmie said.

"I'm leaving, Clemmie. I'm leaving here tonight. Don't worry, I'm leaving you the railroad. Or at least part of it. You'll have to fight Adam for the rest."

"But where are you going?"

"Tomorrow I'm going to our daughter's wedding. While you're in Washington trading your charm or your body or whatever the hell is necessary for a little political consideration, I'm going to give Lizzy away in marriage—a marriage you'll never forgive because it isn't the one you wanted, because she isn't marrying the son of your—" He stopped abruptly. He'd almost forgotten Adam was in the room. "After that, I don't know. Maybe I'll go to work for another railroad. Maybe I'll take a cue from Porter and enlist. I don't know where I'm going or what I'm going to do, but I know one thing. I'm getting out of here. I should have left years ago. Instead of sitting around and letting you walk all over me, I should have got up and walked out years ago."

"And all this," Clemmie said coolly, "just because I refuse to go to Lizzy's wedding?"

"All this because all your life you've gone your own way and done exactly as you pleased and said to hell with the rest of us. All this because you'd rather see Lizzy make a marriage that pleases you than find her own happiness. All this because all I've ever been to you is a hired hand to run the railroad, someone to be used when he was convenient and ignored when he became inconvenient—and I was inconvenient when I started making sounds like a husband, wasn't I, Clemmie? All this because you and Adam are two of a kind and I don't want to be around either of you anymore. I guess I just haven't got the stomach for it." He started for the door. "Do what you want, Clemmie. Divorce me or not. It doesn't matter. Just as long as I don't have to see you again."

Chapter 15

HE'LL BE BACK, Clemmie told herself the next day as she boarded the Washington express. He was just blaming her for Adam's actions. She was furious herself. It had been an unconscionable thing to do. They'd been handing power to Adam all these years, and he had to steal control. Still, she could adjust to it. She'd run the railroad through Tom and now she could run it through Adam. Thank heavens he was more reasonable than George. Or even Tom, for that matter. Adam had seen the wisdom of her going to Washington immediately. And Tom would get over it, just as he had all the other disagreements. She decided she'd call him from the hotel tonight. It wouldn't hurt for her to take the first step this time, even if Tom were in the wrong.

Clemmie telephoned the farm that evening, but Dolly said Tom had already left. So had Lizzy and Porter. "It was a lovely wedding," she added pointedly. "Lizzy seemed so happy."

"Did Tom say where he was going?"

"No, he didn't." Dolly was silent for a moment. "But I got the feeling it was not New York. You shouldn't have gone to Washington, Clemmie."

"Adam shouldn't have done what he did."

"I'm not defending Adam, but Adam isn't married to Tom. You are."

"That's right, Mother, take everyone's side but mine. Adam's right, Lizzy's right, Tom's right, but I'm wrong."

"You're headstrong, dear. You always have been."

"I'll call you from New York when I get home," Clemmie said abruptly, and hung up.

During the next two days Clemmie's connections turned out to be no better than McSorley's. Neither her charm nor her old friendships went far in wartime Washington. Everyone was busy, everyplace was crowded, everything moved according to military rank. Of course, Mr. Budd who was in charge of the transportation division remembered her, his secretary said, but he really couldn't see her today. Perhaps next week, she said in that tone that told Clemmie next week she'd be put off to the following one.

She'd reserved a room at the Shoreham, but found when she arrived that it was occupied by one of those self-important dollar-a-year men who could not be ousted. The desk clerk finally found her a small second-floor room that Clemmie swore must have been the noisiest in the entire hotel. When she queued up for a taxi or a public telephone, she found that men no longer stepped aside to let her go first. Even those not in uniform seemed to think she had all the time in the world while they had not a moment to spare. And as if all that were not enough, she still couldn't reach Tom. When she called home, James said Mr. Hendreich had come by Monday and packed some of his things, but had left no message. She telephoned Adam on Tuesday night. He hadn't heard from Tom at all.

"He'll turn up, Clemmie. Don't worry," Adam reassured her, although he was beginning to worry himself. "He just needs time to think things through. How's it going down there? Any word on what they're going to do to us?"

"I'd be the last one to know. I can't get in to see anyone. I need a uniform, or at least an official title."

"Well, you tried."

"I'll give it one more day. Then I'm coming home." Clemmie hung up the phone and looked around the small room. The blond furniture of no particular period or style was as ugly as the pale green walls and the standard pictures of Washington street scenes. She couldn't stay here all evening. She'd go crazy if she stayed here.

The lobby was crowded with people in a hurry. Everyone had a destination but her. As she passed the telephone booths she overheard a marine who'd left the folding door open to make room for his long legs. "Come on, baby. I've only got an overnight pass. You tell that swabby to get lost." He rubbed the broad expanse of neck that looked raw and vulnerable under the newly shorn hair. "Tell him the marines have landed."

At the front desk a man in a navy officer's uniform was signing the register. The girl next to him was wearing a corsage and looking a little embarrassed and impossibly proud. They must have been married for all of an hour, Clemmie thought. She remembered the way Lizzy had looked up at Porter as they left the house. The world was at war and suddenly everyone was in love. Damn Tom! Damn him for doing this to her.

The revolving door from the street never stopped turning. Officers, enlisted men, girls in furs that looked bulky over long expanses of leg, men in somber business suits with tired faces, women determined to meddle where they were not wanted. Like herself, she supposed. The door turned again and impossible as it seemed, she saw Whit Morris coming in out of the cold December night. Instinctively she started across the lobby to him, then stopped when she realized he was not alone. The girl looked far too young for him, young enough to be his daughter, she thought, and remembered Porter and Lizzy. What was it about these men and their infuriating desire for youth? The girl looked up at Whit and smiled, tossing her silky blond pageboy as she did. Clemmie saw him bend to the girl to say something, then they both laughed.

She took a few steps backward, wishing she could disappear into a telephone booth or behind a potted palm or anywhere Whit would not see her, see her as she saw herself, a lonely middle-aged woman watching her former lover with a beautiful young girl. She need not have worried. Whit and the girl, his hand proprietary on her arm, crossed the lobby to the cocktail lounge at the far end. They passed only a few feet from Clemmie, but Whit did not even notice her.

She returned to the ugly little room. A while ago she'd thought she'd go mad staying there alone. Now she knew she didn't have the courage to go out alone.

Clemmie switched on the light beside the mirror, removed her hat, and faced herself squarely. She was still attractive, as attractive as the girl with the blond pageboy, she told herself, though not in the same way, not in a youthful way. But she was still desirable. Then why did he leave, she taunted her reflection. She realized with a start she meant Tom rather than Whit. Tom was the one she was angry at. Tom was the one who'd hurt her.

She walked to the small end table where a tray with a bottle of whiskey and two glasses had been left from the previous night. The service in wartime Washington matched the accommodations. There was no ice, but she poured whiskey into the unused glass and took a long swallow. The undiluted taste made her grimace, but it did not make her forget what was bothering her. She was angry at Tom, hurt by Tom, but then what about Whit? She'd felt humiliated seeing him with that girl—more humiliated by his failure even to notice her —but humiliation had to do with her pride, not her heart. Was it possible, after all these years, that she actually cared less for Whit than she'd imagined? The idea made her feel foolish and at the same time exhilarated.

Clemmie tested herself. She pictured Whit making love to the girl, pictured the elegant body she'd once known so intimately tangled with the young woman's. She found no pain in the images she conjured. She thought back to the weekend in Virginia and that afternoon in the borrowed apartment after they'd returned. They were dim memories, without the power to wound or arouse. She thought of his talk of marriage that day. Was she sorry she hadn't married Whit? No, not sorry, merely curious what would have happened if she had. She wondered if he'd meant it, if he would have gone through with it, if he would have been a better husband to her than to Alison. He'd said he wanted to marry her, said he'd had enough of cheap affairs, but married to her, he might have discovered he hadn't had enough after all. Would she have been able to hold Whit, or would she have become another Alison, sitting alone in New York while Whit went off to Virginia or Washington or wherever his instincts and his women led him? Would she have sat home alone, hating his infidelities and pretending they didn't exist. No, she wouldn't have become another Alison. She was no mouse, no long-suffering and silent wife. She would not have accepted Whit's philandering, but she doubted she would have been able to stop it, either.

A moment ago she'd seen herself as a lonely old woman in a world obsessed by love and youth. Now she saw Whit as a foolish middle-aged man. No, not foolish, only self-indulgent and perhaps a little weak. Oh, he'd cared for her, all right. He might even have married her, but since he hadn't married her, since he hadn't won the one woman he professed to love, he'd gone on finding pleasure with women in general. Whit was a man of passions—her affair with him had taught her that—but he was not a man of passion. Tom was the man of passion. Perhaps that was why she'd sometimes been afraid of him, why she'd thought it so important to protect herself from him, because in his passion and strength he could have possessed her—and hurt her as well. Perhaps, too, that was why the affair with Vanessa Hodges so many years ago had hurt her so deeply, because she'd known Tom and the depth and strength of his passion. He was no Whit Morris, who could start an affair as easily and casually as he could buy a new horse or automobile.

Style was the word she'd always thought of in regard to Whit. He did things with style. Tom did them with determination and a kind of single-minded force. There'd been times, she knew, that for all his surface reserve, he'd loved her that way. Now he'd left her in the same way.

But he couldn't really have left her. She wouldn't let him. Somehow she'd find a way to make him come back.

For the next week Clemmie tried to reach Tom at his clubs, his office, anyplace he might light for a day or a night. No one had seen him, or at least no one was willing to admit as much to his wife. Finally she received a call from his attorney. Tom had left everything in order. He'd signed over the stocks and the house, taken care of all the legal details short of a divorce. Clemmie asked the lawyer where she could reach Tom.

"In care of me," he answered curtly.

For the rest of her years Clemmie would always remember the early months of 1942 as the worst she'd ever known. For the first time in her life she was entirely without buffers. She had neither husband nor lover, family nor child. For the first time in her life she was alone with herself. All around her people were caught up in the war and the intensity of their own lives, but she had nothing, only the aching emptiness within her. To be sure, she chipped in and did her part, as the radio and the magazines and posters urged her to, but raising money for British War Relief or the Free French or the

Red Cross required more effort than attention. It did not take her mind off herself. It did not consume her as the railroad once had.

The railroad was another lost cause. Adam, with the reins of power in his own hands, turned out to be less reasonable than she'd expected. She could not force her way into his office or badger him at home or cajole him into letting her have things her own way. He was running the railroad himself, keeping troops and material on the move and struggling to preserve regular service. All the extra-fare "limiteds" were having trouble keeping schedules these days when they'd be shunted onto sidings at the drop of a hat or, more to the point, the appearance of a train with a defense priority; but the Great American managed to maintain a better record than either The Twentieth Century or The Broadway. Adam was running the railroad himself and doing a bang-up job of it, but the fact offered little consolation to Clemmie. It only made her realize that all those years when she thought she'd been doing so much, when she'd been sure she was instrumental to the railroad's success, she'd been deluding herself. Oh, she'd had some good ideas, but they were nothing compared to the solid everyday work that maintained the railroad, or the vision that kept it in step and often ahead of the Central and the Pennsylvania. All the time she'd thought she was the one with imagination. Now she knew she'd been nothing more than a clever assistant to Tom—at best—and a meddling intruder at worst.

She had plenty of time to think about the railroad and everything else that winter and spring, too much time to think. Month after month as the war news grew grimmer—Manila fell, then Bataan, finally in May Corregidor; Rommel drove toward Alexandria; the Germans penetrated Stalingrad; and Hitler tightened his stranglehold on Western Europe—Clemmie replayed her life over and over like the newsreels that re-created the horrors of war, show after show, in the movie theaters. For the first time in her life, at a moment in history when nothing in the world made sense, Clemmie began to make sense of herself. She began to see herself clearly. At first, as on that night in Washington, she saw only flashes of truth as if someone had sent up a flare that illuminated the battlefield for a split second, then left it in darkness again, but gradually she began to retain the isolated moments of vision and the landscape started to fall into place.

In saving her own pride she had managed to destroy everything. She'd thrown away what she might have had with Whit, but that was nothing compared to what she'd thrown away with Tom. Years ago she'd told herself she'd married Tom for the railroad, and that was partly true, but once married to Tom, she'd found she'd got more than she'd bargained for. Only she was foolish enough not to accept what she had got, partly out of fear, partly because of her obsession with showing Whit, hurting Whit, loving Whit. But she couldn't have loved Whit as she'd thought or she would have left Tom when he'd asked her to. And yet she'd gone on hurting Tom until finally, with Adam's help, she had inflicted the last wound. And now Tom had done what she'd always been sure he would never do. Tom had left her and she was alone with nothing but the understanding of her own self-destruction.

At the end of January she received a letter from Lizzy. Porter was stationed in San Diego and they'd finally found a decent apartment, if you could call a living room, bedroom, and closet kitchen decent. Porter had wanted to get her a cook, Lizzy wrote, but everyone she'd interviewed had been too large for the small kitchen, so she settled for a girl who came in mornings to clean. She didn't sound in the least daunted by her new environment. Clemmie wondered what a girl who'd been waited on by a full staff all her life did in a closet kitchen.

Clemmie had reached the last paragraph of the letter before she found a word about Tom. She knew he'd enlisted; the attorney through whom he'd arranged everything had told her that, but he'd been willing to give no more information. Lizzy said she'd seen him the previous weekend on his way to New Guinea. Tom had gone Porter one better. He'd managed to get the navy to send him overseas. Apparently engineers were in even greater demand than doctors. The navy had given him a commission and sent him off to the South Pacific to build airstrips on one godforsaken island after another.

There was little news of Tom after that. Lizzy wrote that she received letters intermittently. They told of exotic scenery and strange peoples and the problems of making an airstrip out of a tropical field covered with sheets of corrugated steel and the difficulty of making an officer of himself after all these years. "He sounds sometimes," Lizzy wrote, "like an excited kid seeing the world for the first time." At other times he sounded, Lizzy said to Porter although she didn't write as much to her mother—like a tired and disillusioned old man.

In September Porter came East for some medical meetings. He didn't know if Clemmie would receive him, but he was determined to try to see her.

It wasn't exactly like old times there in the comfortable rear drawing room of the house on Fifth Avenue—Clemmie was too somber and distracted to seem like herself—but she was no longer angry at him. When he saw her face, pale above the dark dress and thinner than he remembered it, he thought for a moment that he would have preferred the old anger and impatience, the ability to blame everyone and everything in the world but herself.

She crossed the room and took his hand in hers. It was like ice.

"Lizzy sends her love. Obviously," he said. "She wanted to come East with me, but I wouldn't let her." He looked down at Clemmie, wondering how she was going to take it. "She's pregnant."

The pale face grew a shade whiter, then she smiled. "I think I can forgive you for everything, Porter, ex-

503

cept making me a grandmother." It wasn't much of a joke, but at least she'd made the effort. "When?"

"She's due in April. And she's fine."

"I don't have to ask how you are. I can see that for myself. You've never looked better."

They talked for a while about Lizzy and the baby, about the small apartment and the impossible housing shortage, about how hard Porter was working at the hospital.

"I saw Tom," he said finally.

Clemmie was sitting across from him and her face showed no emotion, but her eyes held his, begging him to go on. "He's in the hospital. In San Diego. He wasn't wounded or anything like that," Porter continued quickly. "It was sheer exhaustion. He drove himself too hard and then he came down with one of those damn jungle fevers. As far as I can tell, he's had it for months. Those things come and go, and I guess every time it went, he told himself he was over it. Only he wasn't, and he finally collapsed. I'm only surprised it didn't happen sooner. One of the men from his outfit told me Tom had been working an eighteen-hour day building those airstrips, driving himself harder than any of his men. Tom won't talk about it, of course. Won't even admit he's sick. All he keeps talking about is getting out there and back to work."

Clemmie stood and crossed the room to the window. The traffic on the side street was heavy but she did not notice it. "Why are you telling me this, Porter? Tom has nothing to do with me anymore. He's made it clear he wants nothing to do with me."

"That's only his pride, Clemmie. His pride's as strong as yours."

"I wasn't the one who walked out," she said without turning. At one time she would have shouted the words. Now she said them quietly.

"Look, Clemmie, I'm not here to discuss who's at fault. I don't know and, truthfully, I don't care. All I care about is the fact that you're both miserable."

"You said Tom was sick, you didn't say he was miserable."

"He made himself sick because he was miserable. Why do you think he was driving himself so hard out there in the Pacific? Why do you think he enlisted in the first place? To get away from you. To get over you."

"I know that," she said. "That's why I know he doesn't want to see me. He even instructed his lawyer not to tell me where he was."

"He may believe he doesn't want to see you, but he does, Clemmie. I'm sure of that."

"You've always been sure of so much," she answered, but there was no hostility in her voice.

"Certain things about you and Tom have been hard to miss over the years. One was that you were crazy about each other. Another was that both of you were determined not to show it. The two of you are more alike than you know, Clemmie. Maybe that's why you love each other so much. Maybe that's why you fought so much too." Porter crossed the room and turned Clemmie to face him. "Come back with me. Tom's waiting for you. He doesn't know it, but he is.

"No."

He started to speak, but she went on quickly, "I'm not saying I won't go, Porter, but I have to think about it first. And if I do go, I have to do it my own way, in my own time. I appreciate your concern, really I do, but this is between Tom and me. You can't help, though I thank you for trying."

He'd been foolish to think Clemmie had changed, Porter told himself as he left the house. She was chastened but not changed, and she'd sit alone in that mausoleum of a house, alone with her pride.

Clemmie gave little thought to Porter after he'd left, though she could not forget his words. Was it possible that Tom really did want to see her? Was it possible that he, like her, was simply too proud to show his need? Clemmie wasn't nearly as certain as Porter, but she knew she had to find out.

The trip West was the worst Clemmie had ever taken. The Great American, despite Adam's prodigious efforts, was five hours late. She missed her morning connection with the Chief and had the devil's own time getting a room on the Super Chief for that afternoon. It took every string the Chicago office of the A & W could pull. The Super Chief was late too, and she missed another connection. She arrived in San Diego exhausted, desperately in need of a bath, and trembling with anticipation.

Clemmie did not go to Lizzy's apartment, had not even told her she was coming. There would be plenty of time for that. Miraculously the hotel had not given away the closet of a room she had managed to book from New York at triple the rate the Office of Price Administration had decreed, although as she entered the lobby the desk was under attack by an assault wave of young men in stiff white uniforms.

It took her less than half an hour to bathe and change into a gray linen suit with one of the new shorter skirts —only a fraction of the time it had taken her two days ago to select what she would wear to see Tom. She was leaving nothing to chance, or at least she hoped she was leaving nothing to chance as she checked her reflection in the mirror. The jacket was tightly fitted above the gently flared skirt. The suit was flattering without being obvious. She was sure Tom would like it. He had to like it, she thought, and noticed that her hands were trembling as she pulled on her gloves.

At the hospital a nurse told Clemmie that Commander Hendreich was in the garden. Clemmie heard the title with a shock. Commander Hendreich. He was no longer simply Tom, her husband, but a strange naval officer who'd been through things of which she had no inkling, who'd grown away from her in ways she could only imagine.

The grounds were extensive, but she found him easily, as if instinct had led her to him. He was sitting in a wooden lawn chair under a palm tree, staring off into the distance at Coronado Bay. She stopped for a moment a little way off and looked at him. He'd lost a good deal of weight, but beneath the light hospital robe his body still looked powerful, like that of a man accustomed to physical labor. His face was thinner too, and deeply tanned, although when he turned, she saw there was a strange pallor beneath the color, as if even the sun could not banish the fever he'd carried for so many months. He sat there looking at her for a moment without expression. Clemmie could have sworn he didn't see her, but he had to see her. She was standing only a few feet away from him. Perhaps he was more seriously ill than Porter had said. Perhaps he didn't even know her. His face, even his eyes, gave no sign of recognition.

"Hello, Clemmie," he said finally. When he spoke she noticed two lines deeply etched on either side of his mouth. They had not been there when he'd left.

"How are you?" she asked.

"Fine," he said automatically.

"No, I mean how are you really. Porter said you were ill."

"Just a touch of fever. Everyone has it out there. I'm fine now." His voice was cool as he spoke, his eyes cold.

"Aren't you going to ask me to sit down?" She felt like an unpopular girl at a dance.

He moved the empty lawn chair beside him without drawing it closer to his own. "You'll have to excuse my manners. They got a little rusty out on those islands. Like a lot of other equipment I took along."

She sat beside him nervously. Things were not going as planned. "Porter said you were working much too hard out there."

"Everyone works too hard out there," he said without taking his eyes from the view of the bay sparkling in the distance. "That's one of the things about war."

"Well, I'm impressed all the same. He made you sound quite the hero."

Tom's head snapped around to face her. "I'm no hero, Clemmie. I was just doing a job. It wasn't particularly easy, but it wasn't particularly dangerous, either."

"You're not making this easy for me," she said.

He turned back to the bay. "Making what easy for you?"

"Surely you can guess why I'm here."

"As a matter of fact, I can't. I thought I'd left everything in order. I signed over the stocks, the house —everything, I thought. Did I forget something?"

"I didn't come about legal matters, Tom. I came about us."

He stood abruptly and took a few steps from her. When he turned, his face was taut with anger and the lines at the side of his mouth had deepened. "Whatever it is you want, Clemmie, I'd appreciate your simply coming out with it. You don't have to use your wiles on me anymore. In fact, you can't use your wiles on me anymore."

"You mean you're immune to me."

He ignored the comment. "What do you want? My signature on something?"

"Stop it, Tom." The words were almost a sob. "Please stop it."

He looked at her sharply, but said nothing.

"I didn't come here because I wanted something from you. At least not anything material. I came here to see you, to talk to you."

"I see. A convalescence call. Thank you." His voice was heavy with sarcasm.

She dropped her eyes as if she could not face him, and noticed that without realizing it she'd been twisting the gloves in her lap. She smoothed them out over the gray skirt. The irony of the gesture struck her. To think she'd worried about what to wear. To think she'd thought he would still care. It didn't matter how attractive she tried to make herself. Tom couldn't stand the sight of her.

"I guess I should have known," she said quietly. "I guess I shouldn't have listened to Porter. I should have remembered something I read years ago instead. Something I've been remembering ever since you left. Beerbohm, I think. 'Of all the objects of hatred, a woman once loved is the most hateful.' " She looked up at him and the gray eyes were as cold as his now. "That's assuming you ever did love me."

"Does it matter anymore?"

There was a catch in his voice, almost like a chink in the armor he'd been wearing.

"It does to me," she said quickly, rushing on as if she didn't dare give either of them a chance to think. "That's why I'm here—to make you understand. Because I finally understand, Tom. I've been over it again and again since you left and for the first time in my life I understand."

"There's nothing to understand."

"There's everything. About us. About me. About that business with Whit Morris."

"I don't want to hear about that," he snapped.

"But you have to, Tom. Because I finally understand it. And me. I didn't before. Years ago you gave me an ultimatum, and I accepted it. Afterward we both walked around pretending nothing had happened, but you never forgot what had happened and you never forgave me for it. Any more than I forgave you for Vanessa Hodges. But I know now that was as much my fault as yours.

"Adam said something to me once, during that summer you left me. He said he knew that I loved you but I couldn't admit it to myself. He was right, Tom, but I never knew it till this past year. I couldn't admit it, because of my pride and because if I had, it would have given you a terrible hold over me. The funny thing is that you had that hold over me anyway. I guess that's what love is about, at least partly, and I guess that's why I'm not very good at it."

He looked at her quickly, with interest. He'd never heard Clemmie admit she wasn't good at anything.

"When I first met you, Tom, I was frightened. I'd been in love with Whit Morris—I admit it—and I'd been hurt, though it wasn't entirely his fault. That's something else I realize now. But I came to love you too. I came to love you more. Until Vanessa Hodges." She saw the look that crossed his face and went on before he could say anything. "That was partly my fault too. Just as I couldn't admit that I loved you, I couldn't give in to you. On Max Clinton, on anything. It sounds silly and too simple, but I guess I was just rotten spoiled. Then after Vanessa I wanted to get back at you."

She looked down at her hands for a moment, debating whether to go on, but she'd sworn to herself that she was going to be honest. "And there was something else too. I wanted to get back at you, but I wanted Whit Morris. I wanted both of you—like a greedy child. And as things got worse, as you grew colder and more distant—and you did, Tom, whether you'll admit it or not—it seemed only *right* that I should have both of you."

"Is this the explanation that's supposed to make everything all right?"

"No, there's one more thing. I could have married Whit. After that weekend in . . . that time you gave me the ultimatum. Whit wanted me to divorce you and marry him. I wouldn't. I thought at the time it was because of the railroad. Maybe it was, partly, but it was because of you, too. I don't know if you believe me, Tom, but I wish you'd try to because it's true. I love you. I always have, but it took your leaving to make me realize it."

He was silent for a long time and when he finally spoke the words came slowly. "You say you want me to believe you, Clemmie. Well, trust is a funny thing.

That's one thing I learned out there in the Pacific. No, not learned, because I'd known it a long time ago, but on those islands with a handful of men, I remembered it because I had to. I had to know which men I could rely on and which I couldn't, and they had to learn the same thing about me. They were my men and I was their commander and we had to learn that about each other. And there were no second chances, Clemmie. For them or me. If I let them down—the way I did you with Vanessa Hodges—they weren't going to give me another crack at failing them. And if they betrayed me —the way you did me with Morris—I wasn't going to make the mistake of trusting them again. So maybe you do mean what you say now, but I just can't be sure."

He turned away from her again and stood staring out at the bay, his hands jammed deep in the pockets of the hospital robe, a dark silhouette against the sinking sun. She took the few steps to him quickly. He had not heard her move across the grass and he started at her touch. Her hand was light on his arm but she could feel the tension as well as the strength.

"If one of your men came to you, Tom, out there in the Pacific, where according to you everything is so clear, if one of your men came to you and said he'd let you down and he was sorry for it, sorrier than he'd ever been for anything in his life, and begged you to give him another chance, wouldn't you give it to him?"

"Clemmie," he said, and it was almost a plea. A plea to stop, she wondered, a plea to go and leave him in peace. She couldn't.

"Tom," she began, frightened to go on, frightened not to. There had been a certain logic to her argument and it had got through to him, but now she needed more than logic. "Do you remember that night at the lake? That night I rowed you out to the small beach where no one ever went?"

He kept his eyes averted and said nothing.

She reached up to touch his face, to force him to meet her eyes. "Do you?"

Amanda Russell

"Of course," he said as if he wished he didn't, then turned his back to her again.

She moved so that she was facing him again, and the gray eyes were soft, yet so intense he could not turn away from them. "Do you remember those moments on the beach?" she asked quietly. "They were singing 'Poor Butterfly.' And afterward? When we got home?"

"Everything."

She reached up and traced the line of his mouth with her finger. "I remember the way your mouth tasted on mine."

"Don't, Clemmie."

"And the feel of your skin. Your skin against mine and the cold water of the lake and then the warm shower. But that was only part of it, Tom. I remember the rest of the night too. You held me. All night. Even as you slept. I awakened several times during the night and you were still holding me. Even though you were asleep and didn't know you were."

"I knew."

"And everytime I awakened I thought how wonderful that you were holding me and that I was safe again. I felt so safe and so sure that night, sure that there'd never be a time when you didn't hold me or want me or love me."

"There never has been. Not even this last year. Especially not this last year. There wasn't a moment of it, Clemmie—not when I first left, not out there in the Pacific when I was tired or scared or sick, not even here at the hospital—when I didn't want you and love you. You were wrong about that. About the fact that I'd hate you now because I'd loved you once." This time it was he who reached out to touch her cheek. "I didn't love you once, Clemmie. I've loved you always."

"Always?" she repeated as if she didn't dare believe him.

"Always," he said, and his arms drawing her to him, folding her to him, turned the words into a tangible promise.